A
CURSE OF
CROWS

A
CURSE OF
CROWS

Lauren Dedroog

First published in Great Britain in 2024 by Gollancz
an imprint of The Orion Publishing Group Ltd
Carmelite House, 50 Victoria Embankment
London EC4Y 0DZ

An Hachette UK Company

1 3 5 7 9 10 8 6 4 2

A CIP catalogue record for this book is
available from the British Library.

ISBN (Mass Market Paperback) 978 1 399 61612 6
ISBN (eBook) 978 1 399 61613 3

Typeset by Input Data Services Ltd, Bridgwater, Somerset

Printed in Great Britain by Clays Ltd, Elcograf S.p.A

www.gollancz.co.uk

To the overwhelmed and stressed out girl who gradu-ated nursing school amid the greatest health crisis in years, who rushed home after her shifts to lose herself in a safer world to escape the absolute hell she left behind at work. Who learned to spot red flags and de-construct gaslighting like it was another language after her first kiss, and who grew and learned more about herself within the three years of writing and editing these pages than she did in the other twenty-five years of her life.

You knew nothing at twenty-two, but you know a little more at twenty-five, and you're having a hell of a lot more fun with life – and yourself.

In this world, it's almost rebellious to love yourself. But I promise you that there is so much to love.

Author's note

This is an adult novel with dark elements, containing the following content: explicit language, explicit but consensual on-page sex scenes in chapter 6 and 22, physical abuse (mentioned and shown once in a flashback scene), emotional abuse (mentioned and on-page), grooming (mentioned and on-page), history of an abusive relationship, blood, violence, torture, on-page death, punishment by whipping (mentioned and on-page), chronic illness due to magic suppression, mentions of grief, on-page panic attack, sexism (one character, to nymphs and female daemons), idolising captor, hinted at sexual relationship with captor while under their control.

Avalon
The Wastelands

Northern Sea

Achelois

Nordwell

Pennon

Brateton

Draven
High Court of
Clacaster

Melledyn

Apornia

Dyfeir

Vigdis

Peridan

Odalis
Royal House
of Aspia

Orna

Méraud

Aysel

Aletheia

Glossary

Celestials: Divinities and Greater Daemons
Divinities
Primordial Gods: the Primals

- Elyon Nathara (The Serpent): *Chaos, Mayhem, Trickery, Warping and Scheming*
- Eiran Néhaira (The First God, the Allfather): *Omniscient, Omnipotent and the Creator*
- Ellowyn Athelon (The Mother): *Light, Life, Abundance, Spirit and Creation*
- Dýs: *Death and Decay, Keeper of Souls, Ruler of the Afterworld*
- Zhella Néhaira (Daughter of Ellowyn and Eiran, and older sister of Antheia): *Sun, Day, Summer and Magic*
- Antheia Athelon (Daughter of Ellowyn and Eiran, and younger sister of Zhella): *Moon, Night, Stars, Winter and Darkness*

Major Gods: the Néhaian Gods

- Aestor Asvaldr (The Second God): *Healing and Mischief*
- Khalyna (The Third God): *War, Weaponry, Madness and Bloodshed*
- Lycrius (The Fourth God): *Nature, Animals and the Hunt*
- Melian (The Fifth God): *Oceans, Storms and Weather*
- Anaïs (The Sixth God): *Wisdom and Knowledge*
- Zielle (The Seventh God): *Love, Friendship, Vows and Loyalty*

- Keres (The Eighth God): *Malice and Revenge, Divine Punisher, Overseer of Dark Magic*

The Gods aren't blood-related to each other. Some were born from Ellowyn's power, others were crafted by the belief of mortals, like Keres. Since they all live under Eiran's rule, they all have his surname, except for Aestor. Should Aestor have to succeed Eiran, his reign will be known as the Asvaldrian reign. New gods forthcoming from his power would be known as Asvaldrian Gods.

Nymphs: Guardians of Nature

- Anthousaï: *flower nymphs*
- Auraes: *nymphs of breezes*
- Draiads: *forest and tree nymphs*
- Naiads: *nymphs of freshwater springs, rivers and lakes*
- Solerae: *nymphs of the day, created by Zhella*
- Vesperae: *nymphs of the night, created by Antheia*
- Vyrēnerae: *fire nymphs*

Minor Gods
There are many minor gods and goddesses in Néhaian mythology, ranging from spirits to diones (Lords and Ladies of certain aspects of life). Some have immortality, some only a prolonged life. Those who suffer from mortality often cling to certain Major Gods to win favour or try to find unorthodox methods to prolong their life.

Greater Daemons
Species

- Aepokrae: *immortal daemons with fangs that need to feed on blood to survive. Their venom is painful and renders* victims *paralysed. They have strict rules about what blood they're allowed to consume and carry a deep respect for all living things. Bloodletting and bloodsharing are sacred rituals within their clans, mostly executed according to the phases of the moon. They are a very disciplined, serious and intense people, and love fiercely.*

- Circederae: *immortal daemons with golden eyes, batlike wings and one pair of canines. Wings are a circedera's pride and joy, and they are very protective of their own wings as well as those of their loved ones. Their shadows function as an outlet for their intense emotions and also enable them to hear the thoughts of others, as well as feel their emotions. They require blood to heal quicker when sustaining an injury, though they don't need it to survive. They are loyal to a fault and share deep bonds with friends and family. Given that they can judge another's personality and intentions within a heartbeat, they tend to form strong relationships quicker than other species. Circederae mark their bodies with tattoos to honour important relationships and life-events. They are also minor skinshifters as they can hide away their wings and gild their skin with black circerian armour, which is impenetrable to most steel except for Erobian steel and Stygian iron.*

- Colchians: *immortal daemons with arched ears and delicate colourful wings, who worship life and nature similarly to nymphs. Like the circederae, they dearly love and are proud of their wings. They live and love very intensely and without holding back. They have many rituals to worship Ellowyn and the life she's granted, as well as to regulate their mental and emotional well-being. They can see auras, which enables them to feel emotions and even glimpse into the minds of others. Colchians are very mischievous and playful, and enjoy messing with other species. Though they worship life, they can* drain one's spirit or Lifefyre to strengthen themselves, leaving only an empty husk behind. Given their strong beliefs, this feat is illegal. Colchians who do use it without being provoked or who use it on innocents are to be severely punished and exiled. This will inevitably lead to suppression of their nature since they cannot regulate themselves, which will lead to severe blight of the soul, illness and eventually death.

- Sirens: *immortal daemons who mostly dwell in the Aenean Ocean in Hell and have fishlike tails to swim with. When they're out of the water, the iridescent scales still decorate their bodies in patches. Their gorgeous voices are used to lure mortal sailors to their death. They respect the King of Hell, and in case of war they join in to help protect their realm, but sirens keep mostly to their own region. Not much is known about their culture and powers.*
- Vampyrs: *these were once nymphs, minor gods or mortals who were assaulted by an aepokra, drugged with their venom, drained of their blood and then fed aepokran blood, whether deliberately or accidentally. This created a rift in their nature, making them half aepokran and half what they originally were. Divinities describe them as abominations and heavily look down on them, exiling any divinity who shifts. Aepokrae welcome them with open arms, teach them how to control their thirst and how to feed.*

Lords and Ladies of Hell

- Aloïs Márzenas: *Lord of Shadows, Daemons and Precious Stones. King of Hell, Ruler of Anthens*
- Bastian Alásdair: *Lord of the Circederae. Exiled and shunned by the circederae.*
- Dáneiris Eléazar: *Lady of the Colchians, Ruler of Osirion*

- Faolán Llyr: *Lord of the Aepokra and Vampyrs, Ruler of Persephian*
- Scylla: *Lady of the Sirens, Ruler of Aderyn*

Rulers of Aeria (mortal realm)
The Countries, their High Courts and Rulers

- Clacaster (Draven): *ruled by High Lord Sorin Cathános*
- Orthalla (Katrones): *ruled by High Lord Zale Losaño*
- Egoron (Václav): *ruled by High Lord Zale Losaño*
- Veshos (Ellosyr): *ruled by High Lady Meira De Mesogna*
- Aspia (Odalis): *ruled by King Lorcán Andulet*

The Aerelian Language

Aediore: *Aelerian for 'little one' or 'child'*

Æther: *The 'Æther' is the fabric of this universe, the matter that all things are made up of, the energy that weaves through everything and connects all. The very basis of life and magic. The 'Æther' is a semi-sentient essence that guides this universe and stirs it, that whispers into the ears of the Celestials. It is unable to take matters into its own hands or change things itself but its Chosen work hard to achieve the balance, chaos or goals that the Æther desires*

Ascension: *a ritual demiagi (magic wielders) go through to finalise their education in all magical arts provided to them by their mentor as well as other Aureales. This education lasts around seven years and in this final year, students are to convince the High Coven of their worth by inventing new kinds of magic, finessing a certain branch of magic, etc. The Ascension is a rare blessing given by Zhella, which renders them immune to aging. They're immortal unless they're lethally struck in battle by any sort of weapon or magic. Once this ritual is finalised, the student is considered a minor god and accepted into the High Coven, if they so desire*

Aura: *energy that surrounds someone, the shadow of the soul. Visible to Colchians*

Aurealis: *a magic wielder who succeeded in their Ascension, granting them a blessing by Zhella to become immortal*

Corusiar: *wing guardian and bodyguard for a member of the royal family in Hell. They share a special bond with the one they're supposed to protect. Both parties are extremely loyal to the other*

Damast: *steel forged in the waters of Ascredia. Lethal to deities and daemons*

Demenir: *mortals who do not possess magical abilities*

Demiagi: *mortals who possess magical abilities*

Dyad: *soulmates or heartmates whose life energy matches perfectly. They complement and strengthen each other, and can hear each other's thoughts as well as feel each other's emotions. These bonds are as unique as the people they connect*

Erobian steel: *steel forged in the Darkness of Erebus. Lethal to all deities and daemons, and sharper and deadlier than Damast steel*

Ichor: *golden blood of gods*

Inkor: *black blood of daemons*

Kalotra: *blood magic, a dark kind of magic used to bind someone to exploit them*

Ná'dýra: *Aelerian for 'my love'*

Ná'iaso: *Aelerian for 'my soul'*

Ná'laine: *Aelerian for 'my sun'*

Ná'nyl: *Aelerian for 'my moon'*

Netha: *a river in Aerelia on which one can place a binding oath. Breaking such an oath will result in a cursed existence*

Nyará: *Aelerian for 'home'*

Nyghtrá: *Aelerian for 'nightwalker', those who have visions while sleeping*

Nymph: *can be used to refer to a lifeform or as a synonym for courtesan/whore*

Stygian iron: *iron forged in the Styx that is lethal to daemons and induces agonising pain. The scars of this metal cannot be fully removed. It was often used by gods to torture daemons*

Varkradas: *darkness that functions as (semi-sentient) shadows and an outlet for circederae*

Várna: *a mark as unique as a fingerprint that circederae gift their children to showcase the bond between them*

Venatrix (Vena): *Aelerian for 'huntress'*

Viatra: *Aelerian for 'little bat'*

Výsa: *thread of Fate*

Výssar: *a hybrid, the child of two divinities from either the same or different species*

Prologue

On the dawn of what would become the longest-lasting Divine War yet, Elyon watched the mortals and divinities prepare for battle. His all-seeing gaze swept over every piece of the grand puzzle that would soon fall into place. Pieces that would control the prophecy that had followed the Primal into this realm. A truth he'd buried beneath willow roots and dust and death, and the secrets he kept like a grudge.

He had figured out most of the players of this divine game and how to make every little card fall into a pattern of his choosing. The Emperor carried no memory of his true identity or the schemes that had granted Elyon this much power. The Fool wouldn't be born for another fifty years and when he would finally come into this world, Elyon had plenty of ideas on how to manipulate him to spite Fate.

His Huntress would soon rise again, and this time, Elyon planned on claiming her first.

He had watched Lorcán Andulet, the crown prince of Aspia, sneak into the Institute of Vadones to kill the High Coven that once taught him the secrets of magic. The Andulet's open renunciation of the gods before they unleashed their war upon them. Elyon's voice had crept into Lorcán's mind then with an ease that had assured the crown prince these were his own thoughts. He had no idea that this plan was actually Elyon's, that the Serpent needed Ellowyn's chosen Acolyte dead.

Ellowyn, with her fondness for Life and Creation, would certainly loathe him for sabotaging her once more, but all that was on his endless ancient mind was the promise Laoise had left behind on a breeze, between the trees of Naether, where her footsteps still led to creeks and fields of wild-flowers: where Chaos was, she would loyally follow. Even in her death.

This war would lead to the rebirth of his dyad.

And it would stall *her* once more.

The Serpent felt the strings attached to his fingers tug and knew his puppets had started to play, flawlessly executing the script he'd written for them.

Chapter 1

Aedlynn

Aspia, the Royal House of Odalis
1762, 22 years after the War of Ichor

After six years, Aedlynn Eidothéan had grown accustomed to the wariness and vigilance of her masters. She'd also grown accustomed to the tormented screams of her victims and the eerie silence with which they fell. Some were to face a quick death, others had to be dragged out for amusement. She did so without hesitation or mercy. Once, she'd possessed such noble values, but there was no room for morality in the existence she'd been thrown into. That realisation had only helped her reach the top of her profession, as had the merciless training she'd started at only sixteen years old.

Lorcán had found her as a newborn during a hunting trip, abandoned in a forest in Peridan. He'd been captivated by the strangeness of her eyes; the left one a warm amber colour, the right one sky blue and broken up with hints of gold. The King had taken her into his household, where his servants had raised her to become a fine lady until she'd reached her sixteenth year. As repayment for the care he'd provided, she was to be useful to him, so he'd released her into the care of Aviod Nérdulet – Aspia's most renowned assassin. Though her childishness once tried to stop her, she'd soon learned that she was exceptionally good at what she did. Her skills with weaponry were supernatural, bordering on divine, with many rumours rising that perhaps the girl with the strange eyes was a halfgod.

No mortal could summon weapons out of thin air.

Top of the Academy and quicker than her masters, she'd grown used to the glares that followed her from within the shadows, the accusations that were meant to tarnish her reputation and other assassins who tried to sabotage her or made attempts on her life. She'd cleaned up a fair amount of them before any of those silly rumours could reach her beloved king.

The only thing she hadn't been able to fully control was the raw magic that simmered beneath her tan skin. Only last week had she set up two men in the corridors. A short fight had ended with one of them dead. Then last night, she'd taken care of two girls she'd shared a bedroom with who'd tried to poison her. Aedlynn had taken her time with them, and only when she'd been satisfied with her work, had she allowed the masters to find her. Covered in their blood, wearing the most radiant smile while they'd chained her.

She'd laughed at them, knowing damn well that the shackles would be useless if she truly wanted to escape – unless they were dipped in moonsbane. Only that sacrilegious poison could counter divine power and magic. It was even strong enough to incapacitate a god. But Aedlynn had a plan and the masters that now dragged her along to face her judgement had no idea that that very goal awaited her on the other side of the grand oak doors.

The hallway seemed to stretch for miles as Aedlynn was guided down the burgundy carpet and led to the throne room. To her left and right, masterfully created paintings of the Andulet bloodline decorated the black walls. Aleksander Andulet – Lorcán's grandfather, his wife Meryn and their three children. Rumour had it that Meryn, a halfgod, killed two of them when she'd lost herself to her divine power before Eiran – the Divine King – killed her.

She admired them – their typical violet gaze, black hair and sharp features that rivalled those of the forsaken gods – even though her heart thundered in her chest. If he wasn't behind those doors, her fate could take a turn for the worst.

Fate already hated her – a lot. And the feeling was very mutual.

Aedlynn glanced at the two assassins who flanked her. They paid no attention to her, though she saw Tertius' jaw clench and noticed how Caleb's hand kept stroking the woven hilt of the longsword at his side. They were alert enough, she knew.

Aviod walked behind her. His blue eyes burned in the back of her head as if her master was straining to find her plans. He moved to walk in front of the company, leading the way to the double doors to the throne room, decorated with magnolias and jasmine. Between the many flowers lay the Andulet crest, two slithering serpents devouring a full moon. An ancient family that had tried to destroy the gods when they'd turned against Meryn.

Aviod pushed the doors open, proceeding them further into the room, and for the first time in a year, Aedlynn stood face to face with the king who'd been her saviour. Her breathing became uneven when her eyes fell on the dangerous male who sat proudly on his black throne. Like the rest of his family, he was blessed with violet eyes. A golden crown adorned his long sleek raven hair.

Physically, the king still appeared to be around twenty-six years old, though he'd been born forty-seven years ago. He'd received a blessing from the Night Goddess, Antheia, that had rendered him immortal, even after the goddess had been slain at the end of the War.

His gaze didn't leave hers as she was ushered before him.

Aviod turned to order her to pay the king respect but didn't have to; Aedlynn had already dipped her head low. She knew of his divine might and dark power. She'd witnessed it herself plenty of times. Though she'd been taught to bow to nobles, she didn't respect them. They were weak, easily taken out of this life and thrown into the next. Yet her king was powerful, a god himself. He couldn't be taken so easily from this life. It was *he* who took.

His gaze swept over the iron bands around her wrists, the chains that were supposed to hold her, the three well-trained assassins that surrounded her. He knew his guards had their eyes on the woman, that they noticed her every breath, any small movement those wonderful eyes made while she appeared to casually study the room.

She smiled at him, a lovely smile that had sent many to an early grave. 'Your Highness, it has been a while.' Her voice was smooth and soft as velvet.

The assassin on her left curled his scarred fingers around the hilt of his sword. In a room with their king, no one was supposed to speak before Lorcán did. She'd been taught those principles, yet Aedlynn had always thought etiquette to be rather stiff and boring – and utterly useless. In a battle between life and death, silly titles and table manners wouldn't save one's life.

'It's good to see you again, little viper,' the king spoke with a sensual voice.

Her smile became even more charming as she held up her shackles to him, rattling the chains. 'Do you like my bracelets?'

His lips curled in response. She cared nothing about the lives she'd taken and the lives she'd continue to take. He'd heard much about her skills, witnessed them himself when he'd sent her on assignments under the guise of other nobles. 'I do not,' Lorcán said, nodding once to Aviod. 'Remove them.'

'Your Highness—'

Lorcán held up a hand to silence him. 'My viper won't harm me, Aviod.'

Hesitantly, the assassin unlocked the clasps of the wristbands and removed them. Aedlynn wrinkled her nose at Aviod and rubbed her nimble fingers over the tender spots on her wrists. She studied her nails. Though Aviod had ordered some servants to quickly clean her up to be presentable to their king, dried blood still stained them.

Lorcán leaned back. 'I understand that you killed two apprentices last night, is that correct?' Aedlynn nodded once. 'Apparently, there wasn't much left of them.'

Her smile didn't reach the frigid look in her eyes. 'There was plenty left, just not much attached.'

Aviod muttered a curse under his breath. He'd once seen much potential in the girl, potential that had been long fulfilled, but he feared he'd created a monster. Underneath that flawless skin crawled a ruthless and feral beast that devoured and destroyed, one that could smile with the light of a thousand suns while her eyes remained devoid of any emotion.

'Explain to me why you did it,' the king said.

Aedlynn tilted her head. 'They tried to poison me and

I'm bored of others plotting my death. I have been testing my food and drinks for poison for three years now. I barely sleep, as plenty have tried to kill me during the night. The stupid rumours, the accusations.' Her hard gaze swept from one assassin to the other, until they rested back on her king. 'It was a message.'

Aviod raised a brow. 'Well, you can sleep in peace from the safety of a prison cell from now on.'

She smiled at her master, sweet as sugar. 'I will not wither in a prison cell.'

'You killed two innocents.'

Aedlynn laughed humourlessly. 'I've killed countless innocents. The only difference with last night was that I received no payment.'

Aviod stared at the king. He couldn't fathom how the king appeared so . . . casual around her. She reeked of death, carried the sentence at her fingertips to bestow it upon anyone she deemed worthy. Her blades hid somewhere only the forsaken gods might see them and judging by how deeply the whole of Aspia had disrespected the gods, he very much doubted they would stop her from ruining them all.

Aedlynn turned her attention to Lorcán. 'My skills are too great to waste them on silly mercenary gigs,' she said plainly. 'You are an immortal king, one on bad terms with the other countries and the divine forces of this realm. I doubt your guards were trained to face off divinities, nor that they have what it takes to send them back to the Æther.'

Lorcán nodded once, his only signal for her to go on. She stepped closer to him, ignoring how the other three assassins took hold of their swords. 'Either you throw me into a dungeon – but it won't hold me for long – or you hire me to properly serve you.'

Lorcán's full lips curled into a cold grin.

Yes, he decided. She was ready – his first weapon. He would hone this blade until it shone silver underneath the *ichor* of the gods. Until it carried the spilt blood of Eiran and he'd have an open field to defeat him.

Lorcán leaned forward, resting his elbows on his knees as he looked at the woman in front of him. He was close now. He could nearly taste the sweetness of the *ichor* on his tongue. One weapon was ready for use. Now he just had to wait until Diana fell for his schemes as well.

Aedlynn came close to regretting her decision to join Lorcán's Cadre when the servant opened the heavy wooden door to reveal that once again, she was to share a bedroom. Even more so when the pretty girl looked up from her neatly made bed in surprise. Something tugged at Aedlynn's heart, though she kept staring her down with an intensity that made the servant next to her nervous.

Surprisingly, the girl didn't flinch away. Instead, she gracefully stood from the bed. The maroon dress she wore draped over her curves, nicely complementing the different brown shades of her hair, though the deep neckline and high slits left little to the imagination.

Her full, red-painted lips parted into a sweet smile. 'You must be new,' she said while extending a graceful hand. Aedlynn glanced at it before returning the cold look to the girl's face.

She raised a dark brow at Aedlynn while lowering her hand. Her almond eyes were a lovely light brown, nearly honey golden when the rays of warm daylight fell on her face through the large windows to their left.

The servant kept glancing back and forth between them like

she expected them to start slitting each other's throats. Unfortunately for Aedlynn, she doubted Lorcán would appreciate it. She wondered why this girl was here and how she served him, as this wing was reserved for Lorcán's inner circle.

She appeared to be around the same age as Aedlynn – twenty-two, but judging by the showy dress . . . she was probably nothing but eye candy for the men who walked around here. Someone to keep them happy and satisfied, to help them relax after a long day of dutifully serving their king. Aedlynn doubted the girl had much of a spine. At least she wouldn't have to worry about being killed in her sleep.

'I'm Kaelena Athelon.'

Aedlynn gave her a curt nod, then further ignored her while she lowered her bags onto her assigned bed. Kaelena seemed to enjoy decorating the room, as she'd planted colourful vases with wildflowers in any corner she could find. Little trinkets and pieces of silver jewellery lay scattered on the shelves of a dark wooden bookcase, on the mantle of the lit fireplace to their right and on a desk. There was also a pile of well-loved books and a bunch of gemstones Aedlynn recognised as moonstones.

Behind her, Kaelena politely dismissed the servant and closed the door behind them. 'First rule of being my roommate,' Kaelena started, 'be nice to the servants.'

Aedlynn turned to look at Kaelena, who scowled at her with an intensity that almost made Aedlynn like her. 'I said nothing wrong.'

Kaelena snorted. 'You said nothing at all, poor thing was terrified of you.'

She shrugged.

The girl cocked her head and crossed her arms. 'Aren't you going to introduce yourself?'

'Aedlynn,' she said flatly. 'Eidothéan.'

Those pretty brown eyes widened for the smallest moment. 'You're Aviod's protégée?'

Aedlynn wasn't surprised that the girl knew him. Given the fact that the assassin personally served Lorcán, she figured that Kaelena had warmed his bed plenty of times already. 'Yes.'

Kaelena leaned against the desk. 'You've quite the reputation.'

Aedlynn was beginning to tire of Kaelena's attempts at socialising. She'd already been tolerable to the rest of the Cadre when she'd been introduced to them by Lorcán. Her little jar of pretend-to-care was quickly running out. Besides, she was much better off on her own, without pretty girls faking interest in being her friend – only to stab her in the back. 'Doesn't explain why you're still wasting my time.'

Kaelena scoffed. 'Shove the god complex up your ass.' Something hardened in her eyes, an edge that warned Aedlynn not to push too far. It was also one of the first times in many, *many* years that someone dared talk back to her, which she found quite thrilling. Even Aviod had grown wary.

Kaelena sighed and remained quiet while Aedlynn unpacked, minding her own business. Aedlynn had just decided that she could bear being inside this room as long as her roommate remained quiet, when Kaelena tempted fate again. 'Are you always this pleasant or are you just secretly very shy?'

'Fuck's sake,' Aedlynn muttered. 'Mind your own business.'

Kaelena smiled at her. A mischievous smile, laced with sweet venom. 'Aspia's famous killer, just a shy little thing with sharp knives.'

9

Aedlynn nearly growled at her. 'Keep talking and I'll show you just how sharp those knives are when I cut out your tongue.'

Kaelena grinned. 'I think I hit a nerve.'

Aedlynn gritted her teeth, but Kaelena noticed her vexation and decided to let it go, lying back on her bed to read something. It took a while before her jaw relaxed again as she continued unpacking.

Perhaps she was a little shy. Maybe even somewhat self-conscious. Killing came to her easily enough, conversing not so.

She'd just finished hanging her casual clothes and dresses when Kaelena spoke again. 'That light blue one is really pretty.'

Aedlynn glanced at her, sensing the white flag the girl was waving. 'Thank you.'

Kaelena smiled at her. 'Gift from Lorcán?'

Aedlynn blinked. 'Ehm . . . Yes.'

Kaelena nodded her head towards the wardrobe. 'That silk was crafted in Averly, I have a dress of the same fabric. It's entirely lovely. For a man, Lorcán has surprisingly good taste in dresses. He's never given me one I don't like.'

Of course she received dresses from him, given her . . . *occupation.*

Kaelena wrinkled her nose. 'He seems to know I much prefer colourful dresses to bleak ones like Isolde wears. I often wonder if the queen even knows that colours exist, as she only ever wears black or grey or white.'

Was she . . . going to keep talking?

'Perhaps she has some strange phobia of colourful things. I hear that her wedding bouquet consisted solely of black roses and lilies. One might think she's not shallow enough to care about her appearance, but the amount of *jewellery* she wears . . . by the Mother, I do not envy her poor neck and shoulders. Horrible taste that woman has and the way she *flaunts* her wealth to all those around her – simply disgusting,' she exclaimed, throwing her hands up before letting them fall back on her lap.

Despite herself, Aedlynn smiled slightly. Seeing Kaelena like this tugged at something in her that was still human. Something warm and fuzzy.

'Like, there are poor families out there. Starving and struggling and then there's the she-daemon with her jewellery that weighs as much as a small child. But the only thing *she* cares about is *my* relationship with Lorcán.' Kaelena rolled her eyes and deeply sighed, focusing her attention back on Aedlynn, who couldn't help but be impressed. She doubted Kaelena had paused to catch her breath in between sentences. 'Sorry, got a little carried away.'

Aedlynn chuckled, running a light hand over the soft fabric of the dresses. 'Can't really blame her for not liking her husband's courtesan.'

Kaelena frowned, then sat up straighter. 'I'm not his courtesan.'

Was she truly not? Or was she just some foolish girl who believed that just because Lorcán bought her dresses and maybe promised her the world, that she was somehow different than the many whores he'd gone through before her? 'Then why are you here?'

Kaelena scrambled up from her bed, smoothing out the chiffon before she straightened her spine. Forsaken gods, Aedlynn had to admit the girl was utterly gorgeous. With a grace that left Aedlynn breathless, Kaelena walked over and leaned against the wardrobe.

'I grew up in Méraud, under the care of Madame Val-endair after I was orphaned near the end of the War, and when I came of age, she had me trained as a courtesan. But when I was about nineteen, I ehm . . .' Her cheeks flushed and mischief sparkled in those pretty brown eyes. 'I started showing some skills with breaking and entering. I was pretty good at sneaking around unnoticed, heard a lot of things – information people hoped to keep hidden in the darkness of the night hours. And then I overheard some lords planning to assassinate Lorcán the night after. So, I stole a horse and made for Odalis, slipped in without any of the guards noticing and then just kind of . . . showed up in his throne room with the message that those lords were planning on poisoning him.'

Aedlynn stared at her in disbelief. She was pretty good at sneaking around but *no one* managed to sneak into Lorcán's throne room without being apprehended. No one was *that* good.

Kaelena smiled. 'You should've seen Lorcán's face. He wasn't even angry, wholly impressed that a nineteen-year-old girl slipped through his every defence; skipping along his halls in a pretty dress. Those lords were apprehended, questioned and admitted their plans. Lorcán then bought me from Valendair, offered me a home here and a job.'

'I take it that job has a lot to do with you sneaking around unnoticed?'

'I'm his spy, but Isolde and many other nobles do believe that I'm his favourite courtesan, only his Cadre knows the truth. We keep it as a ruse so others don't hesitate to talk around me – a pretty thing to decorate his lap with.' Kaelena whistled. 'Isolde can be fucking vicious, though. Lorcán once threw a masterful insult her way to silence her and I couldn't wipe the grin off my face. She then said something along the lines of 'I'm not the one trained like a racehorse to be ridden for enjoyment' – still stings. She followed up with that, unlike me, she didn't need Lorcán's cock to decide whether she was useful or not.' Kaelena sighed, then her lips curled into a self-satisfied smirk while she crossed her arms. 'I then sweetly informed her that as long as she couldn't bear him an heir, she was disposable as well. That seemed to silence her just fine.'

Perhaps Aedlynn wouldn't sleep so soundly tonight after all. 'You're awfully talkative for a spy. Do you always ramble this much?'

Kaelena raised an amused brow. 'Only when I'm the one carrying the conversation.'

Aedlynn frowned. 'How the fuck am I supposed to say anything when you make as much noise as a small army?'

Kaelena wrinkled her nose, which made her look fairly adorable in Aedlynn's humble opinion. 'Secret? I was never good at those games adults make you play to get you to shut up.' Kaelena grinned. 'I think my record was a minute.'

Aedlynn chuckled.

'Sorry for getting under your skin,' Kaelena said.

Aedlynn glanced up at her, now realising she was slightly taller. 'It's fine.'

Kaelena stuck up her pinkie. 'Promise that you won't kill me in my sleep?'

She gave Kaelena a small smile.

Kaelena wiggled her pinkie.

Aedlynn's smile grew as she hooked her pinkie around the spy's. 'Fine, I won't kill you in your sleep.'

'Good.' Kaelena let go of her and walked towards the door. Before she left the room, she shot Aedlynn a sly smile. 'I'll let you know if I'll promise you the same thing.'

Chapter 2

Diana

Katrones, the High Court of Orthalla
1766, 26 years after the War of Ichor

Present day

I stared at the wall from the comfort of the cognac leather chaise with an intensity that could've burned a hole in the intricate light wallpaper that decorated our private living chambers. I'd grown endlessly bored, cooped up inside Zale's castle while incessant heat raged over the southern hemisphere. The heat and humidity didn't bother me for the same reason that it bothered others; my breathing and activity weren't affected by it. Even now, I still slept with my many, many covers; cosily tucked in and rolled up in them. I also still woke in the middle of the night, freezing and gasping for air whenever my nightmares returned and bled into the surrounding darkness. Even the ever-present headaches weren't worsened by the weather.

But I had grown so utterly bored and restless, and dying to just do *anything*.

Everyone stayed inside the castle as much as they could and kept the doors shut for as long as possible. The billowy curtains were drawn to keep the heat out and the servants had even boarded up some of the bigger windows and stuffed any crevices they could find. They treated the sun like it would come and visit on horseback, scanning the building for any opening it could use to infiltrate and suffocate us with its unforgiving warmth.

It reminded me of those myths about Keres, the God of Malice. There were enough stories about him visiting mortal villages like a servant of Death, cursing them with plagues and calamities while they hid inside their houses and prayed to other gods to save them from his wrath. I doubted the deities dared to question his judgement.

I felt like a trapped animal in here, surrounded by servants and highborn who said nothing to me unless absolutely necessary. I would spar with my guardian, Zale, but given the insane temperatures and the fact that any sane person *did* mind the heat, I couldn't exactly ask him to train my magic with me. Besides that, Zale had been pretty busy as High Lord of Orthalla and Egoron. I could visit Sorin in Clacaster, but my godfather was rather occupied as well with ruling his country and some family drama he was dealing with, so I didn't want to bother him.

Yet the longer I went without losing this pent-up energy, the more agitated I became. My nightmares worsened, my visions of *him* became more frequent and intense – even during the day. And as always, any strong emotions made me sick to my stomach. I hadn't shared that fun information with Zale yet. He'd send me straight to a physician for another sleeping draught or healing potion, but those only worsened things. They made me more vulnerable and susceptible to whatever connection I still shared with Lorcán.

No one knew why Lorcán had wanted me. How he'd found me as a baby, then studied and experimented on me until Sorin had intercepted a spy infiltrating Clacaster, and he and Zale had saved me from his clutches. It was strange to know he'd done that, to see it happening in my nightmares. Because I bore no scars – thanks to the king, at least. The only scars on my back were those of an . . . *incident* with Lord Rhosyn. Punishment for killing his son, Kallias.

One skill Lorcán excelled at was *kalotra* – bloodmagic, one of the darkest kinds of magic known to mortals, used to exploit and control another person. It'd been taught to him by Aeneas Losaño, who'd been his mentor at Vadones. Lorcán had taken his time with me. He'd marked me, claimed me, carved his name into my very soul. Even now, I often woke with his name on my lips and whenever I was alone, I heard him whisper the name *he* had given me.

Needless to say, Orthalla wasn't exactly fond of me. Aspia was a feared country and Lorcán was the main character in most horror stories. Parents had scolded their children for playing with me, scolded me for coming near their children. They'd warned me to stay away from them or to return to my master since they all believed Lorcán still owned and controlled me. And though I was technically Zale's heir and thus had official duties similar to a Princess, I carried little weight or influence here at Court.

Apparently being experimented on as a child by an immortal king was somehow *my* fault.

Sitting cross-legged on the chaise in our living quarters, I kept wiggling and tapping my foot. And in an attempt to distract myself, I viewed the paintings I'd made, which Zale had proudly hung up on the walls. Though I kept a whole bunch of them hidden away in my bedroom and study, I hadn't looked at them in years.

I tried to focus on those paintings, the serene images of

vineyards and beaches, to calm down, but it was no good. My heart raged in my throat, I couldn't keep my legs still and I'd been subconsciously tapping my fingers on my arms while I'd been staring at the painting of a lake.

I still felt like my soul was vibrating in my bones.

'You look . . . intense.'

My head whipped towards the sound of Zale's voice, to see his dark brows furrowed with worry. The casual linen shirt he wore today really contrasted his olive skin. It had tanned even more since the beginning of summer, yet my skin remained devoid of any colour, save for the dark circles that decorated my grey eyes.

'Yeah,' I breathed, still tapping my foot.

Zale sat down on the chaise next to me, resting his elbows on his knees while he studied me. A slight grin appeared, lighting up his dark eyes. 'You're bored to death, aren't you?'

I groaned and rested the back of my head against the chaise. 'I honestly believe not even Dýs himself can be *this* bored.'

'Have you tried painting?'

With my head still leaning back, I raised a brow at him. 'My attention span hasn't been too great.'

'Small paintings then?'

'I want to punch the sun,' I muttered with closed eyes, more to myself than to Zale.

He laughed softly. 'I doubt Zhella will appreciate that.'

I didn't quite care whether the Sun Goddess would take offence. If anything, I wanted to drag Zhella out of Aerelia and scold her, wag my finger at her and tell her that burning mortals isn't very nice.

'You could go take a swim, the pool's been refilled after last night's downpour,' he offered.

I pursed my lips and fondled a loose thread of my short pastel blue linen dress. I'd already tried that. The scars on my back were very noticeable and the stares from the nobles hadn't been subtle. 'Doesn't help.'

Zale nodded once, noting the sad look and immediately putting two and two together. He often knew me better than I knew myself. His last name had been mine from the moment he'd taken me over from Sorin and adopted me, and the soft hand that had held mine ever since had been my rock in any wild current.

'I just . . .' I murmured, still fidgeting with my dress. 'I feel like I'm losing my mind.' Especially since my nightmares and sleepwalking had been growing worse these past weeks. I smiled sheepishly. 'Maybe I should just pray to Lord Keres for entertainment, I'm sure he'd love a fight.'

Zale quickly shook his head. 'Absolutely not, you don't pray to Keres.'

'I know.' *Especially not after nightfall*, that'd been drilled into me.

To this day, Zale had no idea that I often offered to Keres to show my gratitude. I took respecting the gods earnestly, even the vilest of them. Keres had a reputation for loathing and tricking mortals. He made deals that always ended up devastating the receiver of his service. Enough to humble them, to remind other mortals to leave him the Hell alone or he'd show them his wrath. But when I'd begged him for help three years ago, he'd aided me without binding me to a bargain with him.

I'd only ever seen one god in person and it'd been him, though I didn't remember much about him. I'd been a little too preoccupied with the body of my dead fiancé and the fact that a fucking *god* stood in front of me. There was a difference between worshipping a god from afar and seeing them in person, to feel their raw power vibrate in the air. The pulse of it echoing in my bones. To know it was *Keres* standing in front of me, a wicked god who could've very well condoned or encouraged Kallias' actions. He could've lashed out at me for his own twisted amusement.

But he'd *calmed* me, pried my dagger from my trembling hands, had held me until my hysterical crying had ebbed away and then he'd cleaned up my mess. The blood and the body, no traces left of the bastard. That blessing . . . coming from the God of Malice, who normally never answered any prayers or offerings, had felt more like a blessing than if Eiran himself had come down from Aerelia to tell me I'd won a lifetime amount of my favourite fruit.

I'd never shared that little encounter with anyone but Sorin. I'd certainly not shared it with Zale, who'd have a meltdown if he ever found out. To this day, no one but my guardians knew where Kallias had disappeared to. His father had put some pieces together but I'd taken care of him as well. Though *that* incident had resulted in the scars on my back, one burned down wing in our Court, eight dead and me being hated and shunned by the entirety of the Court.

The final blow to my reputation.

The sound of Zale's deep sigh pulled me back from my chaotic thoughts. 'How about we go visit Clacaster?' he said. 'It's winter there, we could spar. Have a little vacation.'

'Really?'

'Pack your things, *Vaelip*.' He winked at me and started to get up. I smiled at the nickname – *little fox*. 'I'll take us to Clacaster. We'll go annoy Sorin until he takes some time off as well.'

'Should we warn him?' I asked, amused by a memory. 'Last time we surprised him . . .' I wiggled my brows at him. Zale had tried to explain to me what I'd seen happening between Sorin and Gabriel, but I'd been seventeen then. I'd known exactly what we'd walked in on. I'd received that talk years ago. In hindsight, I was extremely grateful that Sorin had explained sex to me – with biology and consent – because Zale had gone with the *special hug* approach.

Zale's face flushed a deep red. 'We should definitely warn Sorin.'

'Yeah, in case he's with a *special friend* again.'

Zale groaned. 'It's been years, Diana, let it go.'

I held up my hands in defence. 'I'm just saying, we should be careful. It's mid-winter there. What if their heating is broken? Or their hearths don't work?' I frowned in mock worry. 'They'll have to warm up somehow, maybe with that special hug you mentioned.'

He shot me a look that said *really?* 'A hearth only stops working if you run out of wood.' With mischief gleaming in my eyes, Zale must've realised I was about to make a dirty joke. 'Gods, Diana. *Don't*. I don't need a joke about Sorin's wood.'

I threw my head back and cackled.

Zale gave me a funny look. 'You two are so much alike, it's almost scary.'

'Oh, don't be jealous. I've been told that I have the same brooding look on my face as you do.'

He snorted and crossed his arms. 'You? Brooding? With that permanent half-smile of yours?' Playfully, he rolled his eyes. 'I raise you to be a fine lady and that's all you take from me?'

I crossed my arms as well and shot him a feline grin.

'Apparently, my demeanour is quite similar.'

A sly smile crept on to his lips. 'You don't say.' He leaned back slightly. 'It's a good thing that we're going to visit Sorin. There's something we wish to discuss with you.' That piqued my curiosity, but before I could ask him any questions, Zale held up a hand. 'Patience, little one.'

'We are literally the same height.'

'But I'm technically fifty-one years old, so I win.'

I raised a single brow. 'And yet you don't look a day over seventy.'

Leaning forward, Zale flicked my nose. 'Get your things, *Vaelip*, and get back here. I'm going to kick your ass the moment we get there.'

Gently, I rested the back of my hand against his forehead. 'I think the heat is messing with you. You elderly are so terribly susceptible to that.'

His grin grew wide. 'Maybe you do have some of my humour.'

Barely an hour later, we made our way through the hallways of Clacaster's High Court. Eiran's blessing made it possible for the High Lords to travel around by æriating; disappearing into thin air and then appearing wherever they desired.

The Court of Clacaster and the colourful neighbouring village Draven were lovely to walk around, especially during winter since the villagers decorated their homes with fairy lights and garlands of greenery. The palace itself was built hundreds of years ago, a collaboration of architects and artists that created one of the most stunning places I'd ever laid my eyes on. The interior was made of the finest white marble, and the black and white marble floor spread throughout the entire building like a grand chess board.

Golden details adorned the many columns, archways and tall rounded windows.

Sorin once told me it was a true ode to Eiran's home. He would know, as he often went there, which made me feel giddy. I'd grown up worshipping the gods and was taught by the Priestesses in Orthalla. I spent hours every day offering to every major god of our pantheon and I prided myself on the fact that most of them had answered my offerings and prayers at least once. Lycrius once sent me a bouquet of never-withering wildflowers I still kept on my nightstand and Aestor sent me a duck carved out of wood for some inexplicable reason. I'd still not forgiven Zielle for sending Kallias my way, despite my devotion, but I still offered to her in hopes of banishing the loneliness. And even Melian had answered me last night, when I'd kindly requested that downpour Zale mentioned so I could relish in the soft embrace of the lukewarm rain.

Maybe that was the reason why I adored coming here. The high ceilings were painted with myths of our gods and goddesses, and different kinds of nymphs. The deep colours had faded over the years but I still loved gazing up and taking it all in.

Most renditions were of Eiran and Zhella, father and daughter hunting or fighting together. There were multiple of Aestor, showcasing his mercy, grace and mischief. Khalyna in full armour, wreaking havoc. There was one of Ellowyn as well, who'd been killed by Elyon in order to drown this universe in his Chaos.

Somewhere in a corner, Antheia's stars shimmered. She was painted there as well, the Goddess of the Night and Hatred. *Once.* The only spot in the entire Court. Sorin once explained that the artists had hesitated to paint her but not painting her would've set her fury loose on them. So they'd compromised and painted her once, which I found very understandable and smart. Had she still been alive, I would've never dared to offer to her. Even years after her demise, the stories about her wicked deeds left me terrified. Most were scared of Keres but Antheia had corrupted him to become as twisted and mad as she'd been.

She was as magnificent as her stars. Her sleek dark hair covered her arched ears and flowed on a breeze, and her midnight-coloured eyes burned into mine. They were cold, piercing. A sculpted beauty that rivalled Zielle's and Zhella's, and had brought many mortal royals to their knees. She'd created kingdoms and built empires like it'd been a game and then watched, laughed, and hummed her haunting melodies while they'd burned down into black nothingness.

Zale followed my gaze towards the image of the goddess. The look on his face darkened and I knew he must be thinking about the War they'd fought in; when the Andulets turned against the gods. Both Zale and Sorin had lost family in those battles, and not just the ones by blood. All because Antheia had been bored and goaded the Andulets into taking revenge for Eiran killing one of their own.

'Those memories must be awful,' I whispered, reaching out to take his hand in mine.

Absent-mindedly, he nodded, still glaring at the painting. 'Even more so since I'm immortal, it keeps all memories vibrant and fresh like they're brand new.' He chuckled humourlessly. 'Time heals all wounds, they say. But it only deepens the ache and makes them fester.' There was a bitterness in his voice that I'd never heard before, one that made the hairs on the nape of my neck stand upright.

And there was an ache in those dark eyes that I knew would never truly leave his soul.

Sorin sat on one of the brown leather armchairs, already drinking the wine he'd readied for us. His usually short blond hair now fell to just below his ears, which made him look rather handsome. Anyone else would've been intimidated by the broad shoulders and air of power surrounding him, but he possessed a kindness many could learn from. The black tattoo that decorated the right of his chest and neck also helped to intimidate others. Not many people walked around with the sacred Ascension markings granted by an *Aurealis* of Vadones, certainly not ones drawn by *the* Yael Eléazar. She'd given him a grand sun and solar flames that covered half of his throat.

Sorin's boyish grin immediately made me feel at ease, soothing some of the bubbling tension in my body. He lifted his glass towards us in greeting. 'Evening.' His amber-coloured eyes shot to mine. 'I heard that a certain someone was bored.'

'You should shave.' I pointed at his face, at the blond stubble that surrounded his mouth. Though I had to admit that it did look handsome. Sorin only stuck his tongue out in reply.

'She kept staring at my paintings, looking like she wanted to burn every single one of them.' Zale shrugged innocently. 'It's already hot enough in Orthalla without her starting a fire.'

Sorin jumped up from the chair and pulled me into a tight hug. Feeling his warmth always made me feel at ease and the regular rhythm of his heartbeat could lull even my most dedicated nerves to sleep. That effect had become my lifeline after Kallias had broken me.

'She's always been a little chaotic,' he said as he planted a kiss on my hair, rubbing my arm. 'It's lovely to see you again.'

I pulled back from him. 'Try sitting in that heat for three weeks with nothing to do, then we'll talk about how bored you are.'

Sorin shrugged. 'I don't mind heat that much.'

'There's not minding heat that much and then there's wearing a leather jacket in a heatwave like you did last summer.' To this day, I frequently questioned Sorin's often peculiar clothing style.

'Isn't it well past your bedtime?' Sorin crossed his arms, a grin on his full lips. I scoffed and showed him a vulgar gesture. His amused glance turned to Zale. 'I truly believed you'd raised her well.'

'I tried, but there was this blond asshole who taught her cuss words when she was still a fucking child. It only went downhill after that.'

Sorin clutched at his chest. 'Language, High Lord,' he purred.

'Oh fuck off, I was fourteen,' I said at the same time, rolling my eyes.

Zale gestured at me in mock exasperation. 'Do you see what I have to put up with?'

Pretending to be some wise old sage, Sorin stuck up a finger. 'What Egoron will have to put up with.'

Zale's comment from before crept into my mind. 'You can't mean—' I started.

'Mean what?' Zale leaned against the armrest of one of the leather chairs. He tried hard to feign innocence, but I'd known him my whole life. He could try to hide his excitement all he wanted, it still sparked in his dark eyes. I glanced at Sorin, who'd pursed his lips in an effort to hide his smile. Zale clasped his hands together. 'Why don't we go outside for a bit? Train a little, the three of us.'

My brows shot up. 'Are you trying to distract me?'

'Yes.'

'It's working.' I grinned.

'I can join you for a couple of hours but I promised Marianne that I'd visit her. I haven't seen her since last week, things have been a bit busy.' Sorin rubbed the back of his neck. 'I want to check up on her.'

Zale looked like a tiny child in a sweet shop. 'You mean that girl you fancy?'

Curiously, I looked from Zale to Sorin. I'd seen Marianne around Clacaster a couple of times when I'd been there in the last year, but hadn't really spoken to her. I hadn't dared to, given my past experiences, and I highly doubted anyone was dying to befriend me.

'She's my *friend*.' Sorin crossed his arms. 'I haven't tried flirting with her.'

'Why not? Is she immune to your lovely charms?' Zale wiggled his brows.

Sorin stared at the wall behind Zale, the look in his eyes growing absent. 'She has very different things on her mind. Besides, every male that approaches her receives a death glare that makes me look around to see where Dýs is hiding.'

I'd seen those glares for myself. Antheia's cold and menacing gaze had nothing on hers. Antheia would've probably fled from Marianne. Another reason why I hadn't quite dared to meet her eyes.

'Maybe she's dating someone?' Zale offered.

I rolled my eyes at him. 'Or maybe not every woman is

waiting for some knight in shining armour to come and try to entertain her.'

'What?' Sorin stared at me with wide eyes and mock shock. 'You mean to tell me that not everyone in this castle wants to fuck me?'

Zale snorted loudly. 'It's a tough one to swallow, I know.'

The corner of Sorin's mouth curled in a feline grin. 'Oh, I can swa—'

'Do *not*,' Zale covered his ears, 'finish that sentence. Gods, you two are unbelievable.'

I threw my head back and cackled, doubling over from laughter.

Chapter 3

Lorcán

Aspia, the Royal House of Odalis
1762, 22 years after the War of Ichor

In the dungeon, Lorcán handed Aedlynn a towel to wipe the blood off her hands and daggers. On the cold ground behind her lay a Clastrian spy, whom Aedlynn had quickly motivated to spill his secrets.

Now, the king watched as she cleaned her blades in silence. She hadn't flinched once. Even when the spy had begged for mercy, she'd only looked at him with cold and empty eyes. The grip of Lorcán's magic on her was strong – flawless. She'd been fully his and his only for months now, his eager and devoted guard and assassin, and had yet to let him down. Though she refused to harm children and truly innocents, he was sure he could mould her to do so as well.

Besides, gods were no innocents.

'You did well, little viper.'

Aedlynn looked up from her blades and smiled at him. Her loyalty shone through his magic; she lived for his praise and compliments. 'Thank you.'

Lorcán nodded once and gestured for two guards to clean up the maimed body. 'How are things with the Cadre? How have you been settling in?'

28

'Fine,' she muttered, focusing her attention on a stubborn stain.

'And your roommate?' he prodded. He'd heard from Kaelena that their relationship was tense at best. Both had come close to throttling the other plenty of times. Kaelena was like a mountain cat, playing with prey to see what might set it off. Whether out of innocent curiosity or vicious intent, that depended on the receiver of said attention. He also knew Aedlynn's temper closely resembled her mother's, so she didn't need much provocation to explode.

Aedlynn glanced up at him. 'Can I speak plainly?'

'Always, my sweet.' He stroked a thumb over her cheek. 'You know that.'

'I despise her,' she nearly spat out the words. 'That nose of hers is always stuck in my business! She refuses to leave me alone and when I threaten her, she just laughs like it's the most amusing thing in the world! She can't shut up for dear life, always rambling on and on, and I'm honestly surprised that she shuts up when she sleeps.'

Lorcán tried hard not to grin. Though he could understand Aedlynn's dislike, he'd grown quite fond of his nymph – despite his common sense warning him not to. Those he chose to care for often decided to betray him. The last one who'd ripped his heart out had cost him the War – because he hadn't been strong enough to kill her when he'd had the chance. He'd loved her, but love had never done anything useful for him. 'I sense some frustrations,' Lorcán said dryly.

Aedlynn groaned. 'I'd rather sleep in the stables with your mares than share a room with her.'

'I'll admit that Kaelena has a talent for rambling but she's just trying to befriend you.'

Aedlynn pursed her lips. 'I have no need of friends.

Friendship is only a weapon others use to get something they need and I have no desire to find a blade in my back again because of stupid naivety.' She threw the bloodstained towel on the wooden table.

'At least promise me you'll refrain from killing her. I'm quite fond of her.'

Aedlynn frowned at him. 'Æther knows why you like her.'

'She carries a deep-rooted light inside of her that isn't easily dimmed and a kindness that has withstood many trials already.'

Lorcán didn't easily trust, especially after Sorin had betrayed him to aid the gods. Even more so when his then wife had betrayed him. He suspected Antheia's ego had been damaged one too many times when he'd killed more of her nymphs, and that she'd taken revenge on him by ruining his wife.

Aedlynn said nothing, though Lorcán knew a storm was passing through her mind. He knew what it was like to be powerful and the loneliness that came with it. Plenty of other assassins had attempted to kill her and she'd spent these past years on her own to protect her life, so he understood her wariness to trust Kaelena. Lorcán decided to change the subject, 'I don't think I've told you about your lineage yet, have I? What I've found out.'

She looked up at him, taken by surprise. 'No.'

Lorcán nodded once. 'Do you wish to know?'

'Obviously,' she said a bit dryly, which put a smile on his face.

'Your mother is Khalyna. Goddess of War, Weaponry and Bloodshed.'

Aedlynn blinked, letting the information sink in. 'So . . .

I *am* a halfgod?' She frowned at him. 'So the whole . . . summoning weapons thing, that's my power? The fighting skills?'

'Yes, I believe so.'

'But halfgods go insane when they use their power.' She worried on her lip. 'They lose their minds, their bodies can't handle all that divine power. It caused Meryn's downfall.'

Lorcán nodded again. His grandmother, Meryn, had been a halfgod child of Melian, and when her power had irreparably broken her mind, Eiran had brutally killed her instead of helping her. It'd been the start of what would later become their war against the gods. 'Khalyna is the Third God, created right after Aestor, so I believe that you lean further to the divine than a child of Melian for example. It seems to stabilise you enough for now.'

'Does she know about me?'

'What?' Lorcán frowned.

'Does she even know I exist?'

His frown deepened while he leaned against the table. 'Aedlynn . . . She gave birth to you.'

She blinked, then flushed bright red. 'I mean . . . ehm . . . I know that. I've just never seen her.'

'Of course not, Khalyna is Eiran's lap dog. Why would she visit you with the risk of Eiran finding out she broke his most sacred rule: no halfgods and no hybrids?'

Aedlynn shrugged. 'Must've been a pretty male then – my father, to risk Eiran's wrath.'

Lorcán's lips twisted into a crooked grin as he leaned forward. 'Would you like to know who your father is?' Aedlynn stared at him, appearing as if she couldn't care less, but he saw the curiosity burning in her eyes. The innocent need to know her roots. 'Aviod is.'

Aedlynn blinked. 'What? Really?'

He nodded. 'Khalyna had a bit of a crush on the Master of Assassins.'

'Does he know?'

'Yes, I told him some days ago.'

Aedlynn cocked her head. 'Why am I only hearing this now? And how do *you* know?'

'So many questions, little viper.' Lorcán grinned. 'You were quite occupied before you fully came into my service. Any time I wished to visit, you were gone on a mission.' The king shrugged. 'I've seen it in visions, during night-walking.'

She pursed her lips as she thought it over, while they walked out of the basement, up the stairs and through the many hallways. After they reached Lorcán's office, Aedlynn finally spoke again, 'Will you out me to Eiran?'

Lorcán stopped walking, turning to face her. 'No,' he said firmly. There was an uncertainty in her eyes as she looked at him. They even appeared wet, as if she were fighting back tears. Her hands hung balled at her sides. Lorcán realised she was scared.

His merciless viper. *Frightened.*

'If Eiran . . . If he finds me, he will kill me. He won't hesitate. He'll . . . Like he did with Meryn and I . . . I don't want to die.'

He walked over to her, resting his hands on her shoulders. Gently, he tightened his grip. 'I won't sell you out to my greatest nemesis, my sweet. And should he find out, if he dares to strike, I will protect you.' Her bottom lip quivered. Lorcán cupped her face with both hands. 'You are safe here, Aedlynn. You know I protect my family with any means necessary.'

She swallowed hard but nodded while he wiped some escaping tears away. He knew that divine body of hers had always felt restless, aching to be somewhere closer to her kin. Even though she was relatively happy here in Aspia, he knew she ached for a home – a family. These past weeks, he'd often caught her staring at fathers or mothers with their children. The girl ached to find a home and take root there, and as much as she claimed to have no need of friends, Lorcán sensed that underneath his dark magic, that big heart of hers yearned to love and be loved.

Oh, he could use this.

'As long as you serve me and prove your loyalty to me, my Cadre will protect you. They won't stab you in your back. Kaelena won't either. You don't have to like her but trust her,' he said. 'And if you truly loathe her, I will ask the servants to find you another room.'

She worried on her lip, appearing shy. It was a look he'd never seen on her before. Softly, she said, 'That . . . That's not necessary.'

He found it interesting to see a blush appear on her cheeks. Aviod had informed him some weeks ago that Aedlynn preferred female company. Perhaps she didn't dislike his nymph as much as she tried to let on. Now that he thought about it, he'd noticed plenty of times that Aedlynn's attention was solely focused on the pretty nymph in the room. He'd blamed it on the rivalry then but perhaps his little viper had an infatuation – the one person who didn't shy back and instead challenged her.

Within seconds, the king had formed his plan. Given how enticing the nymph could be, those dainty claws would dig deeply into Aedlynn's heart.

Kaelena would keep his honed blade sharp and ready for his use.

Aedlynn

Aedlynn stared at her bedroom wall. She should've told Lorcán to find her another room but something in her had stopped her. As annoying as Kaelena's rambling was . . . A room of her own would perhaps be too quiet and she'd got quite used to Kaelena's perfume, even on her bedsheets – since that insufferable twig aimed at anything and everything whenever she put it on. Cherry blossoms and blackberries. The lovely scent lingered on her pillow and clothes, on her cloak. Even on missions, she still smelled Kaelena.

It was annoying.

The door opened and Kaelena walked in, softly humming to herself while she carried a small pile of old books in her arms. The smooth way her silk dress moved and rippled reminded Aedlynn of water.

These past weeks, she'd learned for herself that Kaelena was indeed a master of sneaking around. It didn't matter how hard she tried, Aedlynn never heard her footsteps. But as soft as Kaelena's steps were, her laughter could bellow through the thickest of walls. And whenever she hummed like this . . .

Aedlynn stared at Kaelena, at the casual beauty and grace she radiated from deep within.

'Evening.' Kaelena dropped the dust-covered books on her bed, tilted her head and smiled sweetly at Aedlynn, who quickly returned her attention to the history book in front of her. She hoped that her loose tresses hid the pink shade of her cheeks.

Deep in her stomach, frustration boiled. Why was it that she couldn't stand the girl, yet every time Kaelena shot her one of those charming smiles, Aedlynn felt like she might melt? At the same time that she loathed her, Aedlynn yearned to be around her. While Aedlynn pushed her away, she secretly wanted nothing more than to hold Kaelena close. And even though Aedlynn was certain that Kaelena wouldn't hesitate to stab her in her back . . . Aedlynn would die to protect her. It was utterly pathetic and confusing.

'Still polite as always, I see.' Kaelena sighed and sat down on the lower end of Aedlynn's bed.

'Still annoying, I see,' Aedlynn shot back. 'You complain about Isolde's vanity, but you flaunt yourself everywhere you go. You may have left that brothel but you can't fool anyone about what you still are,' she spat at her. 'Some whore desperate for attention.'

Kaelena's face crumbled. That sweet smile withered and Aedlynn watched the corners tug downwards, how her eyes reddened and watered. Kaelena's throat bobbed as she looked away, hiding her burning shame behind her brown tresses while she balled her fists on her lap.

Gods . . . Aedlynn couldn't stand seeing her like that, hated herself for what she'd said – for hurting her. She wanted to reach out to her and brush those tears away. 'I . . . I'm—' she started, but Kaelena shot up and left the room, slamming the door shut behind her.

Fuck, why was she such an idiot?

Aedlynn rubbed her face, her cheeks heating horribly under the weight of her embarrassment.

Forsaken gods, she'd been so mean.

She's just trying to befriend you.

Truth be told, Aedlynn would like a friend. Someone

to laugh with, to tell those stupid jokes to that she was secretly fond of. But she'd spent so many years wrapping herself up in barbed wire to keep others out that she wasn't quite sure if she could be anyone's friend without hurting them. She knew she was quick to lash out, that her temper was horrible and that she was far too reckless. How could anyone want a friend like that?

And yet, she'd also been like that when she'd walked into the room four months ago and still Kaelena had tried. For weeks she'd attempted to shave off some of her thorns. Sometimes Aedlynn had allowed her to see the roses beneath them but every time Kaelena had come close to touch them, she'd panicked and pricked those nimble fingers, shutting her out completely until Aedlynn's defences started to melt again.

But now she'd really hurt her. She'd somehow felt the ache the spy had felt. Aedlynn's stomach twisted itself into a knot as the mental image of Kaelena's hurt haunted her. She hadn't registered that she'd left the bedroom until she nearly walked into a servant.

Aedlynn checked the library but she wasn't there. She wasn't in the kitchens either, though she knew Kaelena was often in there. She enjoyed baking little cakes and decorating them with colourful icing and silver stars. She wasn't great at it but she just liked doing it. She'd brought Aedlynn some *moelleux* a few weeks back, somehow knowing that she was quite fond of chocolate.

More heat crept into her cheeks. She hadn't even thanked Kaelena.

She slammed her back against a wall in a corridor, slapped her burning cheeks and viciously shook her head. She'd been sweet once, she knew she was capable of it. She'd been soft and tender and trusting and vulnerable. But the callouses and blood on her hands had removed all tenderness, no matter how often she scrubbed her skin and nails. The scars on her heart had extinguished any vulnerability.

But underneath those thorns, parts of her soul still bloomed. Yet what use was a soft assassin to her king? There was no room for vulnerability in her work.

Aedlynn decided to continue her search before she'd fully lost her mind with her many thoughts and feelings. They'd been quiet for so long, locked away, but now they came knocking at the walls of her mind. Demanding to be heard, to be felt.

Eventually, she pushed open the doors of a small library, housed in a tower in the west wing, where Antheia's silvery stars were painted on the dark blue ceiling. Those had once decorated their night sky until the goddess had been betrayed one time too many by the mortals and decided to remove them. They'd been gone for centuries now, leaving the evening sky black, but she'd always wished to see them in person. Aedlynn once sent a prayer to the dead goddess when she'd been a small child, with the humble request to see even just one star.

She swallowed hard when she found Kaelena sitting in the small, dark room. Her knees were pulled up, her arms hugging them to her chest. Her shoulders slightly shook and she'd buried her face in the small space between her chest and knees.

Relief flooded her that she'd found Kaelena but she was terrified to approach. Aedlynn closed the heavy door behind her and leaned against it, her hands still resting on the cold iron knob behind her. 'I'm such an idiot,' she said softly.

Kaelena looked up at her with puffy and wet cheeks, stifling the next sob when she realised who was in the room with her. Aedlynn fought hard not to flinch away from the glare, to run and hide behind a bookcase. She'd faced plenty of threats, had fought for her life on many occasions. Yet somehow, this was more challenging. 'We finally agree on something,' Kaelena's quivering voice sounded.

Aedlynn gave her a small smile but it quickly disappeared. 'I'm sorry for what I said. It was unnecessarily cruel, I didn't mean it.'

Kaelena warily regarded her. 'I don't get you. One moment you're sweet and you smile at me and I think you might actually like me, and then the next you act like a spiteful bitch. At least Isolde consistently reminds me that she hates me.'

'I don't hate you.' The words were nothing but a whisper.

Kaelena raised a brow at her. 'You called me a whore. Doesn't exactly scream *I like you*.'

Aedlynn shrugged and looked at the floor. 'I really am sorry.'

Kaelena wiped away the tears and mascara that had gathered underneath her eyes. Then she glared at the black stains on her fingers. 'Great, you've turned me into a raccoon.'

'I quite like raccoons, they're very cute. Those beady eyes, and those little hands and feet are adorable, and the way they—'

Kaelena shot her a look that made Aedlynn close her mouth again. But her lip quirked up. 'Now who's rambling?'

Aedlynn let go of a shuddering exhale as some tension left the room. She looked at her feet, playing with the tip of her black leather boot as she scraped it over the wooden flooring. 'I'm sorry. You didn't deserve that.'

'You're right, I didn't.'

Aedlynn glanced at her. 'I don't think you're a whore or desperate for attention. I don't think low of you at all.'

Those dainty lips curled into the mischievous grin Aedlynn had come to like. 'How could you think low of me when you're absolutely teeny tiny?'

Aedlynn scoffed at her but felt her lips break apart in a smile. 'I'm not that small.'

'Pocket-sized.'

'Am not.' Aedlynn stuck out her tongue, which made Kaelena laugh. She loved the sound, and liked that she'd been the one to draw it out.

'There you go again,' Kaelena said, rubbing her hands together. 'Now you're joking with me and smiling and being sweet, but—'

'I know,' Aedlynn whispered, looking back down at her boots.

'Why do you do that?'

Aedlynn swallowed. Perhaps it was time to let one of those walls down a little. 'I've kind of . . . closed myself off.' She nudged the tip of her boot into a crevice between two boards. 'Last time I . . . that I let someone in, they tried to kill me.'

'Oh.' Kaelena drew her brows together, though she didn't look at her with pity, which Aedlynn appreciated.

Aedlynn nodded slowly. 'So, yeah . . .'

'I'm sorry that happened to you.'

'Thank you.'

Kaelena sighed deeply and leaned back against the bookcase behind her. 'Fine, I'll forgive you for being a mean little bitch to me.'

Aedlynn snorted, the sound not at all elegant. 'Must you call me little?'

'Must you call me an attention-seeking whore?' Kaelena wiggled her dark brows.

'That's not fair!' Her cheeks flushed. 'I apologised.'

Kaelena cackled, her head tipping back. It was that laugh that broke through walls and carried golden daylight with it. 'I'm only teasing you,' she said, scrunching her nose.

Aedlynn blushed at the sight, shyly averting her eyes back to her boots.

Kaelena scrambled up from the floor and made her way over, soundless even though the boards underneath their feet were ancient and groaned with every breath Aedlynn took. She stared at Kaelena in disbelief. 'How do you do that?' Aedlynn gestured at the floor. 'Move without a sound.'

Kaelena smiled. 'My mother was a vespera.'

She blinked. 'Really?'

'No, I'm making that up.' Kaelena rolled her eyes. 'Yes, really.'

'You're half vespera?' They were Antheia's nymphs, had been her devoted handmaidens for aeons. They were spirits of the night and everything it encompassed; peaceful nights, hidden intentions, haunted dreams, the brightness of the stars, the softness of the moon and everything in between.

Kaelena nodded. 'Lorcán saw in a vision that my mother was Nyra Athelon, Antheia's first vespera. She gave birth to me months before the War started, but she was killed by Tarniq. Apparently, the previous king went a little . . . insane during the War. He was convinced that all nymphs were as wicked as the gods and went out of his way to murder them. Especially my mother since she served Antheia, who had been working hard to get rid of Lorcán.'

She pursed her lips. 'Lorcán doesn't know my father's name but he did say that they loved each other deeply. That they fought to keep me safe and that Lady Antheia wept when they were killed, that she avenged them.'

Aedlynn hadn't realised that she'd taken Kaelena's hand in hers, that she'd been running her calloused thumb over the soft palm. 'I'm sorry that you lost them,' she said quietly as she wiped away some of Kaelena's tears with her other hand.

Kaelena nodded and leaned into her hand, closing her eyes for a moment as if savouring the little touch. 'So, yeah . . .' She showed Aedlynn a brave smile. '*Quiet like the night*, I guess.'

Aedlynn blushed, torn between pulling her hand back or sweetly stroking her jawline. Flustered by the latter desire, she pulled her hand back. 'I'm a halfgod,' she blurted out, then blinked in surprise. Why did she say that? Sharing that information was extremely dangerous. If word got to the wrong people . . .

'Oh, who is it?' Excitement shone in her eyes while Kaelena took her hands and tightly squeezed them.

'Ehm . . . Khalyna.'

Kaelena blinked, then tipped her head back and laughed. 'Of course she is! But alas, that means we're destined to be enemies.' Kaelena elegantly rested the back of her hand against her forehead, dramatically sighing. 'With your mother being my mother's sworn enemy.' Aedlynn snorted and rolled her eyes. 'You dare mock the ancient vendetta between our families?'

'Khalyna might've hated Antheia and Keres, but that's none of my business. I've not even spoken to her, why should I share her silly grudge?'

Kaelena grinned. 'Careful, halfling. One might start to believe you're getting fond of me – enough so to talk poorly about a major goddess.'

Aedlynn blushed and rolled her eyes, tipping her nose into the air. 'Insufferable twig,' she muttered.

Kaelena planted a kiss on her cheek. 'Love you too, half-ling.'

Butterflies exploded in her stomach when Kaelena's soft lips brushed her cheek. She wondered what it would feel like to kiss her, what her lips would taste like.

But why would Kaelena even want her? There were plenty of nobles that could give her a title, wealth and a place in the upper echelons of this country. All Aedlynn could ever offer her was her heart, though it swelled with every smile Kaelena gave her.

Chapter 4

Diana

Draven, the High Court of Clacaster
Present day

I'd barely sunk one boot in the snow-covered grass in Clacaster's courtyard when Sorin used his magic to crash a heap of snow over me, covering me in pure white fluffiness. The ice immediately started melting and leaked into my hair and thick black coat, trailing down my neck. I shivered and my teeth started chattering. My heartbeat shot up. Though I didn't like heatwaves, I *despised* the cold. It always made me feel highly anxious and uncomfortable.

I scowled at the laughing High Lords, at Sorin who stood in only a dark tunic as if the cold didn't bother him at all. Without touching the snow, I moulded it into balls and sent a fair amount launching straight at their faces. Zale gasped when three hit his face. Sorin yelped and ended up catching snow in his mouth.

I kept more snowballs floating in the air. One corner of my lip curled up. 'Still hungry?'

Sorin intertwined his fingers and cracked them, his amber eyes glinting with mischief. 'If I win this fight, you're cooking tonight.' That might've been the worst threat I'd ever received in my life. Since my senses of smell and taste were awful, I struggled with properly seasoning my dishes.

With a flick of my hand, I'd dried up my clothes, but still shivered from the lingering cold that had infiltrated my body. Admitting that my joints and bones ached because of the weather made me feel like some dangerously suppressed elderly person.

'If I win, you'll have to introduce me to your girlfriend.' I shot another snowball at Sorin, straight at his nose. Zale made the wise decision to hide in the doorway while the two of us slowly backed into the courtyard, eyeing each other up.

We sparred for a good half hour.

I'd been trained by both of them and my magic skills were decent, but Sorin and Zale? They had been taught by the *Aureales* in Vadones, along with Lorcán and his paladin, Evalynn; a blood sworn, bonded guard. The latter had been killed by the King of Hell, Aloïs. Another figure I didn't dare mention out loud.

Getting into Vadones was no easy task. Only the truly gifted entered the Institute and only a select few graduated with honours and received a blessing of immortality – the coveted Ascension ritual – from Zhella, Patroness of Magic. I would've loved to go there, but alas . . . Another historical monument destroyed because an Andulet decided to throw a temper tantrum. Why the gods ever favoured that family was beyond my understanding.

I blocked every single one of Sorin's attacks, waiting for an opening so I could strike. It was no use to lash out at him with fire, though I preferred to fight with it. It'd always come easiest to me. But fighting Sorin with fire was like giving Keres a knife to stab me with.

Lorcán's speciality was darkness, which probably

explained why I saw flashes of him during the night – and why he'd been so fond of his paladin. She'd been his polar opposite, able to summon fire and light from the sun itself, to draw her power from the ferociousness of solar flares. It'd taken the King of Hell himself to vanquish Evalynn Denesta.

I shifted my weight to my right leg as I threw up another shield to protect myself from Sorin's roaring flames. The slippery ice cracked underneath my weight but I stood my ground while the snow around me melted. I decided to use that to my advantage and sent all the water crashing over his head like a tidal wave. And for good measure, with a sprinkle of revenge, I closed my right hand into a tight fist and froze the water in his hair.

'*Son of a bitch!*' he yelped in Clastrian. His flames instantly dimmed.

'Language, High Lord,' Zale purred with a self-satisfied smirk, leaning against a tree with crossed arms as he watched.

Sorin ran a hand through his hair to break up the ice and I used that opening to slam him against the stone wall of his castle. He grunted when his back impacted, sliding down behind some neatly trimmed bushes. I smirked at him and made a lazy knocking motion with my right hand, so the snow from the roof above him crashed down. I may have added some more flair to it by shaping the snow that encased him like a snowman.

'You're cooking,' I said, crossing my arms.

The heap of snow imploded, like there was nothing inside of it anymore. The scent of orange and cedarwood hit my nostrils and I somehow sensed him behind me, how his hand moved to reach for my braid. Like some hidden instinct had woken up. I'd never experienced that before.

I ducked and whipped around to plant my elbow in his side with my full force behind it, which was suddenly a lot. So much more than what my frail body could normally manage. Sorin stood exactly where I'd envisioned him to be. He stumbled and fell, staring up at me in as much surprise as I felt. 'Damn, *Vaelip*.' I stared from him to the snowman, trying to make sense of what had just happened. 'Since when do you have eyes on your back?'

'I saw you,' I muttered. 'In my mind. I saw you reaching for my braid.' I looked back to see his smile ebb away and his brows knitting together. 'And I *smelt* you – before I saw you.'

Zale watched us curiously. 'You did?'

I nodded, feeling a bit dazed as I stared at the spot Sorin had stood. 'Yeah.'

Another scent hit me. Clean linen with a hint of something citrusy – Zale. My mind envisioned him moving his arm to wrap it around my throat. My body reacted for me, lurching to the side while I turned.

Pure and wild instinct roared in my ears, bellowed at me to do something. My hands shook, my knees wobbled while an ancient intuition begged me to use it, and it took everything in me to shut it down.

But I couldn't.

Doing so sent wave after wave of nausea crashing over me, making my ever-present headache thunder in my temples and split my vision. It raised the tension in my body and the restlessness to an all-time high. I clenched my jaw while I faced the pain, and beads of sweat trailed down my forehead.

Breathe, Avaleen. I hated how wonderfully familiar and

soothing it felt to hear *him* in my mind. *Let go of those ridiculous fears. Use them.*

Though it felt like years passed before my mind lost the battle against my body, barely a second had passed before I threw out an arm and sent pure darkness to push Zale against the grass. Like I'd done when Rhosyn's men had forced me on my knees and tore open the back of my dress to humiliate me. When that lord had lifted his belt again and again.

When that darkness had danced with them until they could no longer keep up.

Sorin scrambled up next to me, wrapping a hand around my wrist to grab my attention. I couldn't tear my eyes away from the darkness that restlessly crawled around and seemed to connect with me. Time slowed as my eyes remained glued to it and I became aware of the strangest sensation. I could feel what that darkness felt, how sensitive it was and it . . . it tried to communicate with me.

Something still shielded me from it.

But it was mine. It belonged to me, it was *mine*.

I pulled my arm loose from Sorin's tight grip, not registering any of the words they said to me. There was only that darkness in front of me and the decreasing distance between us as I moved towards it in a daze. More scents hit me. Crisp air, wet grass, cedarwood, citrus. I tasted each scent on my tongue like a fine wine. They grew stronger the closer I came to that darkness, and I realised that it was made up of shadows that danced around, desperate to get to me.

Sorin tried to grab me around my waist but was met by another tendril that slammed him against an old oak tree. My shadows wanted me to come closer, wanted them to stay back. Though I sensed that they meant my guardians no harm.

I sank to my knees, reaching out a hand to touch and caress them. There was truth in that darkness, truth I was ready to face.

Come to me, Avaleen. Nothing more than a seductive whisper.

I wanted to. Gods, I wanted to.

My entire being focused on the shadows, which allowed Zale to finally grab me around my waist and pull me away. I screamed like someone had just torn off one of my limbs and then thrown me into hellfire. Zale pulled me further away, saying nothing of importance in a voice one would use to soothe a child. My soul was being torn out. Yet it lay there on the cold, wet grass.

Sorin stepped into my vision and cupped my face. His lips moved but I didn't register the words, they didn't hold any meaning while I screamed out in agony.

My shadows remained still – trapped. They wanted to come to me, longed to come to me with the same vigour I felt. But Zale's arms trapped me, held me back from re-uniting with them. Sorin moved and blocked my vision.

Come to me, Avaleen. If you wish to know your truth, you need only come.

I sagged through my knees while Zale held me, whimpering like a wounded animal. I was freezing, my bones were nothing but shards of ice. I despised the cold, the pain that always came with it. That no one had heard me, that they hadn't come to me when I'd called for them over and over. I'd needed protection from *him*, from the torture he'd given me. I'd yearned to look up at warm golden eyes, to feel the soft touch of my mother's hand. But I had never felt it.

I needed them, by the gods, I *needed* them. I'd missed them my whole life, had spent entire nights wondering about them and what might've happened to them, if I had siblings and what had happened to them. I'd prayed and offered and wished on every eyelash, clover and dandelion I'd got my hands on that I'd *find* them. I loved Sorin and Zale with my whole heart but I *needed* my family like my lungs needed air.

I sobbed, said words in a language I'd never spoken before, rambling on about my shadows, the stars and my parents. A language I'd heard Zale and Sorin speak, a language as old as our gods.

Because it was their language.

'What the fuck?' So near to my shadows, I felt Sorin's terror because I spoke Aelerian and what that meant. No one could be taught Aelerian. The gods were born speaking it. The High Lords were only able to speak it the moment Eiran's blessing had touched their very being.

Zale pulled me against him and æriated us inside, where he planted me in front of the hearth.

I forced my chest to move to draw in more air. My fingers and lips tingled, my chest became too tight for my raging heartbeat. I was *dying*. And my soul – my shadow was outside in the snow.

Zale wrapped his warm coat around me and rocked me back and forth, rubbing his hands over my back. Sorin draped blankets over me. 'Breathe, Diana.' Didn't he see that I was trying to?

'*Please*,' I managed to push out. Sorin entered my blurry vision, lined with tears and sweat. 'Help them. They're . . . still outside.' His throat bobbed. 'Please,' I whispered as I balled his shirt in my hands, eyes filled with desperation.

Sorin pulled me out of Zale's embrace and tucked me against his chest, using his magic to warm me. All the while, he caressed my hair and soothed me through my sobs and panic like he'd done three years ago.

I will wait for you. Your varkradas will wait for you. They are patient, as am I.

'I hear him,' I sobbed against Sorin's shoulder. His whole body tensed while he exchanged a panicked look with Zale. 'Lorcán.'

'Diana—' Zale started.

'Should we bring her to Eiran?'

'*No.*'

'She's speaking Aelerian, Zale! How much more proof do we need?'

Another vision flashed through my mind of fierce golden eyes, framed by laughing lines as he snickered at a joke while clutching his wounded side. Somehow, I knew it was a memory my mother had been fond of.

'Lorcán still has Antheia's blessing! Diana still carries his magic in her blood!' Zale feverishly gesticulated. 'What the Hell do you think Eiran will do if he thinks she's a halfgod? That she carries Lorcán's power? He won't hesitate to kill her.'

'She's hurting,' Sorin said. 'She needs help.'

Zale said wryly, 'Explain to me why a halfgod would hear Lorcán. It's his *kalotra*.'

Grey eyes flashed through my mind. *Please, let me hold her.* That pleading voice. My mother.

Another sob came from me. By the gods, I needed her warm embrace. I wanted to feel safe again, but most of all I wanted *her* to be safe, to stop hurting, because . . . because something had happened and I'd felt it. I'd felt her hurt and heard her scream and it'd frightened me.

My sense of smell withered until I didn't smell anything anymore. Something in me knew the shadows had disappeared again. I no longer felt Sorin and Zale's concern and worry like they were my own. I felt nothing but the pounding headache in my temples and how my stomach twisted into a tight knot. I gagged and let go of Sorin, whirling around to grab the nearest thing that I could throw up in. Cold sweat trickled down my forehead and back while I hurtled my guts out in an empty fruit bowl and Zale held my hair back.

'Should I get Aestor?' Sorin offered.

The thought of facing a god right now made me throw up again.

'I think that's a no,' Zale said.

I drew in a shuddering breath as the last overwhelming waves of nausea ebbed away. 'I think I just died a little,' I whispered, rubbing my eyes. My skin was drenched and heated like I was running a fever. Coldness stuck to the sweat, which I didn't welcome at all.

Zale rubbed my back. 'At least your panic attack is over.'

I nodded absentmindedly, staring down at the Orthallian carpet. I'd spent many nights glued next to the toilet. My headaches never left, and at least once a month, I'd get violently ill. But I had never . . . never felt like *that* before. Only Kallias had got me to feel something remotely similar.

Sorin gently took the bowl from me and left to empty it.

'What did he say to you?' Zale crouched down in front of me.

I blinked several times while I tried to remember; the memory was already blurring. 'He ehm . . . He wants me to come to him.' I looked up from the carpet to Zale, wrapping the blankets tighter around my body. 'He wants to tell me . . . my truth, he called it. Said that he was patient.'

He nodded, glancing up at Sorin. 'Lorcán told her to come to him.'

'I'm going to kill him,' he growled while handing me a glass of water, which I gladly downed. 'The fucking nerve of him.' I rubbed my face again and looked down at the carpet, feeling utterly drained. 'You look exhausted,' Sorin noted.

I glanced up. 'I genuinely feel like I lost one of my lives, you know? Like a cat.'

Sorin nodded. Do you want me to ask Aestor to check on you?'

I shook my head, which made the headache viciously throb again. 'I can't handle a god right now.' I'd rather not have a god's first impression of me be that of a sickly, pale woman drenched in her own sweat and tears. Seeing me like that was an honour reserved for my family. 'I'm just . . . exhausted.'

'You don't hear him anymore?' Zale asked me.

I shook my head, slower this time. 'I think he closed everything off again.'

'The pain?' Sorin brushed a hand through my hair.

'Gone back to the usual headache.' I didn't have the heart to tell them I still felt restless and tense, that I still yearned for those shadows.

Sorin sighed. 'I thought your headaches had got better?'

'Might've been a lie,' I muttered. 'Didn't want you to worry.'

'It's our job to worry about you, *aediore.*' Sorin kissed my hair and then looked at Zale. 'We really have to find something for those headaches.'

Zale rubbed his face and nodded. 'I'll contact Aestor tomorrow.' He eyed me like he was deciding whether I truly felt better. 'I'll draw you a bath. Give you a moment to relax.'

'Thank you.' I showed him a small smile. He walked out of Sorin's room, closing the door behind him. Meanwhile, Sorin still held me. 'I'm sorry for scaring you,' I muttered, my head leaning against his shoulder.

'You have nothing to be sorry about, *vyráso,*' he said firmly. I always adored it when he called me *fyrebird*. It'd been a nickname Yael had given Sorin when he studied at Vadones, because of his affinity for pyromagic. One he'd shared with Evalynn, whom he'd been friends with until she'd decided to follow her husband. He'd tried to convince her to leave Lorcán but she'd refused to listen to reason. In his frustration, he'd said things he later regretted. But he'd never had the chance to make it up to her.

'You really don't have to stay up with me. You can go visit your friend.'

'I'll pay her a quick visit while you take your bath.' I nodded. 'If anything feels wrong, you tell Zale. Don't hesitate.'

I snorted. 'I'm not a child, you know.'

He sighed and rested his chin on my head. 'I know. I just worry about you. I want Lorcán nowhere near you. He did enough already.'

I nodded and stared at the dancing flames in the hearth. 'I'm sorry about your fruit bowl.'

Sorin laughed. 'Didn't like it anyway.'

Zale had made sure the water was hot enough, that my favourite honey and lemon soap stood on the little table next to the bath. He'd even filled a glass of red wine for me.

Given how attentive he was, I found myself surprised again that he had no lover. Sorin liked to mess around but had never found *the one*. He'd sworn to never marry or start a family because their blessing didn't extend to family. Zale had never mentioned his concern about that but I'd never known him to date anyone. Though I had seen him kiss a pretty blonde lady in the gallery on her forehead once, when I'd skipped a lesson and had been playing on my own. In my childish imagination, she'd appeared to radiate a warm glow. But I'd never seen her since and when I'd asked Zale about her, the sad smile he'd shown me had been enough to make me shut up.

My head still pounded and the water in my stomach felt like lead. I held up my hands after removing my clothes, which trembled like I was going through a withdrawal of some sort, and when I touched my forehead, I didn't need a thermometer to know I was running a high fever. Maybe it wasn't the wisest decision to relax in hot water while my body was boiling on the inside but I didn't care. I simply climbed into the soapy water, fully submerging so my hair was wet as well.

I closed my eyes and focused on steadying my breathing, yet the tension and restlessness didn't agree with sitting still, it made me feel like my bones were vibrating. The longer I stayed still, the worse it got. Maybe it would be wiser to run around the castle to lose some of that pent up energy, but my muscles ached and my eyes were heavy.

Another ten minutes passed while I tried my hardest to find some control over my body, to no avail.

As I dried off, my thoughts went back to those shadows. I knew they were the answer to all my questions. Questions

I'd been asking myself for years. Questions Lorcán could answer.

There was power in me, a power that Lorcán had hidden away. There was a way for me to be pain-free, to be comfortable, and I couldn't let that go. I wanted that freedom. I wanted that power – because some instinct deep within me told me that it didn't belong to Lorcán. He'd locked it away and for some reason, today he'd decided to let go of the reins a little. Like he'd wanted to dangle it in front of me as bait to lure me.

I knew the stories about him. Blessed by Antheia with some of her darkness and immortality because Lorcán turned against Eiran, and Antheia and Eiran had an endless rivalry. He'd locked his country off, even from the gods. They knew it was a matter of time before Lorcán would strike again and only the Æther might know what insane powers or weapons he'd bring along.

And then there was *my* history with him, how he'd tortured me. Since I was only a baby then, I didn't remember specific things, but my nightmares were filled with violet eyes, cold hands, intense pain in my shoulders and soul, and pure desperation. I'd hear myself cry out to my parents, begging them to help me. And yet, here I was in this damp bathing room, wondering if maybe, just maybe, he wasn't that bad. Which was bullshit. I knew he was *that* bad.

Once I'd put my nightgown on, I started the task of combing my blonde hair, ignoring the pale, frail and thin reflection that haunted my mirror. The many knots were a great distraction, forcing my tongue to stick out a little while I tried to detangle the lifeless thin strands. I'd almost reached some semblance of inner peace.

'How did it feel, Avaleen?'

My body froze, the hairbrush hung forgotten mid-air. Through the mirror, I met those violet eyes. I whipped around, hoping this was just my imagination. I was probably exhausted and just needed a good nap. There was no way in Hell that Lorcán could actually be here. But he stood there, leaning in the doorway to my bedroom like he owned the damn place. Clad in dark trousers and a tunic, intricately embroidered with golden thread.

It took me a moment to compose myself. My pride didn't want the prick to know how terrified I was, though it was hard to keep my hands and knees from trembling. 'Get . . . Get out,' I stammered.

Lorcán held my gaze, slowly and elegantly moving towards me.

'This isn't real, you're not here,' I breathed, taking a step back. My hips hit the marble basin.

'You're right, I'm not really here but that doesn't mean this isn't real.' His accent sprung out, lilting the words. It sounded like poetry. Smirking, he stopped in front of me. 'But I believe it feels very real to you.'

The realisation that he was amused because I was scared turned a switch and the next second all my fear was gone. I glared at him with nothing but coldness in my eyes, turning them a freezing silver. I even bared my teeth at him, more out of instinct than anything else. Before I could think better of it, I swung my wooden brush at him. Right in his face. *'Fucking bastard,'* I spat at him in that ancient language I'd slipped into before in the courtyard.

For one heartbeat Lorcán just stared at me in shock, rubbing his sore nose. Then he started smiling. A disarming smile. I'd just smacked him in his face and he seemed to not care about it.

'That instinct really is something, huh?' He cocked his head. 'I've suppressed it for twenty-four years now, yet I allow you to use only the slightest sliver and here you are,' Lorcán gestured at me, 'burning to release it.'

I was about to try and hit him again but he caught my wrist. I'd expected his hands to be ice cold, like they'd been in my nightmares, but they were warm. Gentle even. Mine weren't, especially when I tried to slam my knuckles against his throat. Lorcán blocked the attack right before I hit him. He grabbed me and pushed me back to pin me between the wall and his muscular body. Despite only using one hand, his grip around my thin wrists was unrelenting as he forced them above my head, while that dark magic of his pooled at his feet and curled around my waist.

He chuckled softly as he took in my piercing glare. 'Come now, I'm not the one trying to hit you with a hairbrush, darling.'

I scoffed and balled my hands into tight fists. 'Of course not. You only tortured me.' The corner of my lips tugged up into a vicious smile. 'But if the brush isn't to your taste, I could tear you apart with my daggers.'

I'd expected him to become angry or irritated. What I didn't expect was for him to brush my cheek with his thumb, or to feel his magic caress my bare thighs. His scent tickled my nose – jasmine. I'd faintly smelt it before in visions but it really hit me this time, creeping into my every sense. It created a fog in my mind, one that pushed away those silly hostile thoughts of mine. There was no reason to fight him. I quite liked being this close to him.

'I could remove my *kalotra*, you know,' he mused, thumb gliding over the smooth skin of my cheek. His violet eyes never left mine. A prison of neatly fabricated lies. 'I truly regret what I did to you so many years ago but it was necessary. Know that suppressing your powers . . .' He sighed. 'I did it to protect you. That bastard King would've murdered you. It would've started a new war, and if by some strange twist of fate, he'd decided to spare you, those *mattas* would've reduced you to nothing but a breeding mare. You are far too powerful for such a tragic fate.'

I stared at him in stunned silence.

He smiled when he noticed the puzzled look. 'You will understand if you decide to trust me.'

'You would . . . You would give me my power back?' Warning bells should've gone off in my head but I could only think of the darkness that had beckoned and how I longed to reunite with it.

'I would give you *everything*,' he said, tenderly cupping my chin to make me look up at him. My gaze grew more and more dazed as his magic crawled along my skin, infiltrating and finding a tight control over my mind. I ached to belong somewhere and he . . . Maybe I could belong with him. 'You and I are connected by more than our history, Avaleen. Come to me and I will remove the *kalotra*, I cannot do it like this.'

I should've known I was in trouble by the fact that I didn't care he was using the name that haunted my nightmares and forced me into submission. I only stared at him, mesmerised as that jasmine scent lulled my common sense to sleep. My sluggish mind sparked alive and my head tilted to the side while he still held my chin. 'What do you mean "connected"?'

Lorcán leaned in, his face only inches away from mine. His warm breath played along my lips. 'You're my dyad.'

I blinked. Once. Twice. Dyads were two people whose

souls and energies connected on a level only few experienced. The rare bond made it possible to feel each other's emotions and hear the most intimate of thoughts, though the bonds were as unique as the people they connected. That binding love was pure and coveted; not two halves forming a whole but two wholes forming something beyond extraordinary.

They were destined to be together, by decree of the Æther.

You're my dyad.

I might not have had any good experience with romantic love but I sure as Hell knew that if I had a dyad, they wouldn't have spent a full year torturing me as a child. 'Why would I believe anything that comes out of your mouth?' I was startled by the viciousness that hid like a serpent underneath those words.

'Because you know the stories and what I've done to defend my family and kingdom. How far I'm willing to go to keep the gods from destroying both and yet . . .' His eyes darted to my lips and I hated that my stomach fluttered in reply. 'You want me – and know I will protect you with as much devotion.'

'I want my power,' I hissed. 'I want what rightfully belongs to me and was taken by you.'

'I didn't *take* anything, darling. I suppressed it.'

'I suggest you un-suppress it,' I bit out, 'before I pull your balls out through your throat.'

'So violent,' he purred. 'Come to Odalis and I will.'

I roughly pulled my arms loose from the tight grip his other hand still had on me, and took a step closer to him, closing that distance between us. 'I suggest you find a way to release your *kalotra* from the comfort of your throne because I'm not taking a trip to Aspia. I've no desire to find myself locked up in your dungeon again.'

'I wouldn't do that to you—'

'Yet you've done it before,' I hissed, dismissing him with the wave of my hand. 'Release your *kalotra* and then I'll consider listening to you.' I shoved him aside with my shoulder and made to walk past him.

'You are *so* much like her.' He sounded astonished, enough to pique my curiosity and make me turn around.

'Like who?' I asked after a long moment of silence where he just . . . studied me.

His dark brows were drawn together as he seemed to decide whether to tell me or not.

'Your mother,' he finally said.

I stared at him, feeling like someone had just dumped a bucket of icy water over me and filled my stomach with hundreds of sharp, tiny pebbles. *Your mother*, the words echoed through my mind.

He'd known her.

Anger coursed through my veins, threatening to set me on fire. I stomped over to him, hands balled into tight fists. 'What the Hell did you do to her?' I spat when we were face-to-face.

Lorcán eyed me levelly. 'What do you think, Avaleen?'

'Stop calling me that. That's not my name.'

'Neither is Diana, is it now?' His lip curled up. 'I could tell you your real name. The name your loving parents wished for you to have.'

'What did you do to them?!' I balled his tunic in my fists, stared up at him with hatred in my eyes.

'Your mother bled out mere minutes after she gave birth to you.' There was a dangerous, wicked gleam in his eyes.

'Birthing you resulted in cuts and lashes she bled out from – though slitting her throat definitely didn't help.' I fought off a sob, refusing to allow him to see me so vulnerable. What did he mean that *I* had wounded my mother? 'Your father was nothing but a beast that forced himself on a poor mortal woman. He took his pleasure from her and then left her alone with the consequences – a destroyed life and tainted honour.'

This time, I did sob. Lorcán cupped my face and forced me to look at him through the blur of tears. 'Stop wishing for them to love you, darling. Your mother is gone and your father would reduce you to nothing but a whore. There is no love there, no home.' He wiped the tears away. 'But I can give you what you want. I will give you that home you so deeply desire, we will bond and I will love you and keep you safe.'

'You're sick.' Again, I slipped back into that ancient language. 'Only seconds ago, you boasted about murdering my mother and you have the audacity to claim you're my dyad, that you'll *love* me, that I should trust you,' I spat every word at him like I was attacking him with a whip.

He took it, kept his eyes neatly planted on the burning silver flames in mine. 'I told you I regret harming you and I meant every word. I won't pretend that I didn't enjoy killing her, that hearing her scream and beg for mercy – for *you* – didn't settle our score.'

My rage vibrated in my bones and woke every ounce of magic in my system. Sparks of lightning travelled along my arms, to my wrists. Lorcán noticed the outpour of magic, the pure hatred on my face for him. He opened his mouth to say something else but I shut him up by violently shoving him against the wall, my fists balling the fabric of his tunic.

I growled at him, actually *growled* – like a beast. The sound was low and powerful. I'd never made a noise like that before but the slight discomfort that nagged at me because of it quickly withered when I saw the look on Lorcán's face. There was fear in his eyes, because my raging emotions were getting the better of me, intertwining with his *kalotra* in an effort to break his hold on me.

Fear because that leash had slipped for only the slightest second.

'A pity I have no *Damast* on me right now, or I would've carved that pretty face of yours clean off of your thick skull.' My voice didn't quite sound like mine. This voice sounded sweetly vicious and dark. Sugar to help the poison go down. But I liked the anger behind the words, the purring beast that stirred within my chest and lazily ruffled its feathers. It tethered me. Like it had done three years ago. 'Next time I see you, it better be to tell me you've removed your *kalotra*.' I planted a sweet kiss on his cheek. 'And if you disappoint me, I'll show you a fury to rival Antheia's. I'll drag you down to Hell myself – what remains of you, that is.'

Lorcán stayed perfectly still against the wall even though I'd released him. 'How about we make a little deal, Avaleen?' I wanted to laugh at the ridiculousness of this. I doubted Lorcán's deals were any better than Keres'. 'I'll find a way to remove my *kalotra* and when I do, you'll come to me to willingly bind yourself by blood.'

I shoved him back against the wall. 'How about this deal: get out of my face and stop pretending like it's a task *figuring out* how to remove it. You know damn well how to do it.

That's it. You receive nothing in return. You don't deserve anything in return.'

He let go of a breathy chuckle. 'Oh, I have great patience.' His gaze burned into mine. 'We'll see what *you* will do when your time finally runs out. One can only survive suppression for so long.'

I wanted to scold him some more, but he disappeared, leaving me glaring at the bare wall.

The idea was insane. Truly, this was the worst idea I'd ever had and I had quite a nice collection of those. But right now, my emotions were burning and eating away at me. The havoc from my suppressed powers raged through me, probably clouding my judgement.

Yet, it could work. If he wouldn't ignore me, that was.

I paced around the room, rubbing my face to wipe away the tears that kept escaping. I was running out of time, though I didn't know what was going on. I only knew that everything in me ached and throbbed and my magic was pouring out, leaving me utterly drained. Lightning crackled around my arms, silver flames burned at my fingertips, the air thickened around me enough to labour my breathing.

My body felt like a burning candle and my wick – my soul – was almost burned up, wax was spilling everywhere.

Praying to Zhella would probably be wiser. She wouldn't kill me on sight and might even want to help me since she was acquainted with my guardians, but *kalotra* was dark and nasty magic and fell under Keres' domain like everything foul and wicked did. So I fell onto the hardwood floor in front of the burning hearth in my bedroom, bruising my knees.

What was I even supposed to say? That I needed his help?

That I felt like I was losing my mind? That I honest to the gods felt like I was dying? Knowing the stories about him, he'd laugh at me.

Should I grovel? Should I insult him to get his attention? He'd drag me to Hell himself if I did and I knew for a fact that Keres and Aloïs were *not* people one would want to meet in a dark alley in the middle of the night. He'd been merciful last time and hadn't asked anything in return, but perhaps he wouldn't like my asking for help a second time.

With a frustrated groan, I slammed my fists against the floor and prayed to him.

Minutes passed where that raging storm inside of me swirled around and refused to settle down.

Lord Keres, please, I wouldn't ask for help if this wasn't import-ant.

Five more minutes passed.

He would ignore me.

Lorcán would win.

In an effort to soothe myself, I quietly kept repeating my favourite prayer. The one that had become my mantra, that filled me with hope and normally calmed me down. But when I got to *for Love surrounds her like effervescent Stars*, I broke.

He'd killed my mother, torn apart my family. The pain of that realisation was unbearable, resulting in more tears. There was too much pressure in my body, too much strain on my organs. The space between my shoulder blades burned and throbbed. A strange ache crawled over my chest and jaw like I desperately needed . . . *something*. A craving I couldn't place.

I was bursting at my seams and I wanted to make Lorcán pay for it – for all of it.

I was desperate to do so, desperate enough to offer Keres a deal myself. 'Help me and I'll serve you like a devoted nymph. I'll do anything you want, fulfil your every wish. I'll devote my entire self to you – worship you, be your Priestess. Anything. I don't care. Just help me, *please*.' I didn't care that I was begging, that I sounded desperate. 'Let me get my revenge on him, let me avenge my family. I'll give you anything. *Please*, Lord Keres.'

The fire went dead, leaving nothing but ashes in its wake and coldness seeping into my skin. And when I looked up from my submissive position, I stared into the eyes of myth's wickedest predator.

Chapter 5

Aedlynn

Aspia, the Royal House of Odalis
1763, 23 years after the War of Ichor

Even though Aedlynn had washed her hands over and over, she still felt the stickiness of the blood. The iron scent lingered on her skin and she still saw those bright eyes of the spy, filled with terror. The pleas for mercy still haunted her. Lorcán had watched from the side. He'd given her orders to execute, ways in which he wanted Aedlynn to hurt the woman. Hours later, when the spy had at last gone silent and Aedlynn looked up at Lorcán with the silent question of what he wanted now, he'd simply smiled and ordered Aedlynn to kill her. She had, though it'd all felt so horribly wrong.

And now she stood with Kaelena underneath the gentle autumn sun, staring at her while Kaelena placed a hand-made flower crown on her hair. Daisies and buttercups, flowers that'd bloomed in her presence despite the season. More precious than any gold crown could ever be. Kaelena's wonderful smile could've lit up Antheia's darkest nights.

An ache spread through her chest as she saw Kaelena like this – light and gentle. Everything that Aedlynn wasn't. And there was soul-crushing guilt. She'd done horrible things and now she had the audacity to stand here, wearing a flower crown like she hadn't just maimed and killed someone.

She was disgusted with herself. With Lorcán, for making her do it. With Aviod, for teaching her how to excel at killing when all she'd ever wanted as a child was to learn how to heal others.

Aedlynn must've been staring at her for too long because Kaelena's smile faded. 'Aedlynn?'

She swallowed. Her hands hung clenched at her sides. Kaelena brushed her thumbs over her cheeks, wiping away something wet. 'Hey, it's okay.' Her arms banded around Aedlynn to draw her closer. 'It's okay, Aedlynn.'

No, it wasn't.

Aedlynn couldn't stifle the tidal wave of self-loathing that washed over her, couldn't stop herself from crumbling apart. 'I killed her. He made me kill her,' she sobbed.

Aedlynn expected Kaelena to back away, to leave her behind on her own, but Kaelena pulled her closer, shifting her so that her face lay buried against her chest. Shielded from the world. 'I'm sorry he made you do that,' she whispered against Aedlynn's hair.

Aedlynn clutched the fabric of Kaelena's soft sweater, desperate to hold onto her.

'Breathe, Aedlynn.' Kaelena's hands rubbed Aedlynn's back while she gently rocked her from side to side. She'd sunk to her knees, sobbing in her embrace.

Kaelena was the first one to treat her like a person. She'd worshipped Lorcán for years, had put him on a pedestal like he was a god, but he only saw her as a weapon. Aviod too. But even though they all pushed her into that black cloak to kill, hidden within the night, Aedlynn felt the barest traces of sunlight wash over her soul during the darkest hours.

Because of Kaelena.

When Aedlynn had returned from another training session with Lorcán, Kaelena had pulled her into the bathroom to help her wash away the blood. She'd been too shocked by what had happened. The image of blood kept flashing through her mind. The innocent young woman at her feet. How Lorcán had violently killed her himself and dragged it out in front of her — all because Aedlynn had refused to touch her.

When she'd finally settled, Lena had left the room because she had an assignment of her own. If Aedlynn hadn't known any better, she would've believed Kaelena had felt ashamed for what she had to do.

She could relate to that.

Her thoughts raged while she sat cross-legged on her bed, cuddling her pillow to her chest and staring into nothing. She relished in the soft embrace of Lena's perfume, how it helped her remain calm. Nightmares would come and the only person she felt safe talking to about all of this was Lena. So she stayed up, tightly clutching that pillow while she sat there in the lonely half-dark.

Another hour passed before Aedlynn was stirred by the creaking of the door opening, which covered her in the warm light of the hallway. She looked up to see Lena walk in, rubbing her face. Looking exhausted and somewhat irritated. Aedlynn immediately jumped up, leaving the pillow on the bed. 'Are you okay?'

Kaelena blinked. 'Oh . . . You're still awake?'

She nodded. 'Couldn't sleep.'

Her light brown eyes travelled over Aedlynn's casual

clothes, which weren't her pyjamas. Aedlynn smoothed her hands over Kaelena's upper arms, revealed by her wine-red chiffon dress with so many intricate cuts and slits that Aedlynn was surprised it could hide any part of her body. Even just walking could reveal too much. 'You okay?' Aedlynn asked again with a soft voice filled with worry.

Kaelena nodded absent-mindedly, then slid her arms around Aedlynn's waist and rested her head on her shoulder. A silent request to hold her, which Aedlynn did. 'Just had a shit night.' She sighed deeply. 'Lorcán needed me to spy on some of his lords, so he organised some . . . private entertainment in his quarters for them.'

'Let me guess, they couldn't stop talking about themselves?'

Kaelena was silent for a long while. 'I wasn't there to talk to them.'

'Oh? Did he make you hide to spy on them?'

Kaelena snorted. 'By the gods, you can be so oblivious. It's almost endearing.' She pulled away to meet her gaze. 'Lorcán made *me* entertain them.'

Aedlynn tilted her head. 'Did he make you play the pianoforte?'

Lena blinked, then threw her head back and laughed. 'Scratch that. It's entirely endearing.'

It took her a moment to put two and two together. 'Oh. But I thought you weren't a courtesan.' Aedlynn frowned. 'You're his spy.'

Lena nodded again. 'I like to tell myself I'm so much more than that but I'm his spy *and* his courtesan. He summons me whenever he tires of Isolde, which is *often*,' she said with an awkward chuckle. 'Sometimes he allows other lords to spend a night with me, his . . . *favourite*.' She shrugged. 'So, yeah . . . those lords were more than happy to try his nymph for themselves and when they were finally gone, Lorcán made me stay to take his time with me. Like the old times, before Isolde had me whipped for seducing her husband – for being his mistress.' The look on Lena's face grew absent – sad. Lost in memories.

Aedlynn brushed some of Kaelena's caramel tresses behind her ears, feeling awful that she'd sat in their room worrying about her own troubles. 'Are you . . . fond of Lorcán?'

A sad smile crept on her lips. 'I used to be in love with him. I lived to warm his bed, yearned to feel his touches and he had a way of making me feel like I was so special and meant more to him than some courtesan – that he loved and craved me. I liked how the nobles whispered about us and how jealous Isolde was whenever I sat on his lap during meetings and parties, or she found us tangled up in their bed. I flirted with and touched him in front of her, simply to show her he was mine.'

Lena's cheeks heated with embarrassment. 'I know it's stupid but I was only nineteen when he bought me and I'd been invisible my whole life. Lorcán made me feel like the most precious stone in existence – rare, beautiful and wanted. And I latched onto that. I was nothing but his and I wanted to be nothing but his, but when Isolde finally snapped . . .' Lena crossed her arms and rubbed them. 'She said a lot of nasty and degrading things and claimed that I only lived to be fucked by him. She had her guard teach me a lesson by whipping me and I broke, and since I'd barely ever left Lorcán's chambers, I had no one to go to. Lorcán punished her for it by whipping her himself and she's stayed away since, so that's a good thing. I managed to pick myself up again and make some friends, and Aviod agreed to teach me self-defence – just in case, though Lorcán nearly killed him when he found the bruises from training.'

Lena hesitated to go on, worried that she was rambling again, but when she glanced at Aedlynn, she saw nothing but genuine interest on her friend's face. Attentively listening. 'I'm in a good place now but nights like these are rough. They all see me as a willing toy to pass around, a circus act to see for themselves since my skin sometimes glitters like the night sky, and I *despise* the voyeurism.' Lena shuddered at the memory of how those lords laughed and stared as they drank their wine and watched a noble touch or take her. How Lorcán's hungry gaze stayed on her, as if silently threatening her not to moan too loudly or he would have to remind her to whom she belonged.

Like tonight.

Aedlynn pulled her closer and Lena nearly melted against her, taking in Aedlynn's dewy perfume she'd come to like. 'I'm sorry about that,' Aedlynn whispered.

'It's fine, it's only certain nights.' She sighed. 'Are you okay, Aedlynn? I worried about you.'

'Yeah, just didn't want to fall asleep while I was alone.'

'You must be exhausted.' Judging by her weary voice, Aedlynn wasn't the only one beyond tired.

Aedlynn pulled away. 'Why don't you get changed? I'll light the hearth to warm the room for you and then you can tell me all the juicy kitchen staff gossip.' She wiggled her brows.

Lena's smile was tired but genuine. 'I should shower first.'

A sweet smile crept on Aedlynn's lips. 'I'll draw you a bath so you can relax. Put in some of those pretty flowers and oil that you like.'

Kaelena's cheeks flushed and shyly, she averted her gaze to the hearth. 'That's very sweet of you.'

'I have my moments.' Aedlynn's finger softly brushed over Lena's hand, her own cheeks blushing. She had no doubt that those lords believed they'd greatly entertained Lena, that they'd left her breathless and satiated, burning with an afterglow. Yet she knew Lena had faked every sigh and moan and Aedlynn . . . She'd treat her so much better, she'd be so wickedly good to her.

Aedlynn imagined she'd look so damn pretty sprawled out on her bed, begging for her, writhing in the sheets while Aedlynn showed her things no man ever had. She'd make damn sure Lena would never be able to lie with anyone else without wishing it was Aedlynn between her thighs. Sure, those nobles could give her titles and lands, but Aedlynn would gild the sweetest sins for her, gift her every raw patch of her soul and worship her as she deserved.

And yet . . . Lena deserved better. Someone not tainted by blood.

Aedlynn glanced at their hands, her heart free-falling in her chest when Kaelena intertwined their fingers and she silently scolded herself for thinking she could ever be worthy of her. 'Would . . . would you like some wine as well?'

Kaelena stared at her. It pained her greatly, but seeing Aedlynn like this – the blushing and stolen glances – reminded her of what Lorcán had ordered. Lena might've managed to tear her roots away from his bedroom but she was still loyal to him. He'd still elevated her position and given her resources she could've only dreamed of had she still been stuck in Méraud.

She didn't have the energy to lure Aedlynn into her bed tonight but she could definitely sow some seeds to reap another time. So Lena bent forward, placing a sweet kiss on Aedlynn's cheek. A little too close to the corner of her mouth. Aedlynn stiffened and Kaelena pulled away a little, her face only inches away from Aedlynn's. 'I'll only take a shower now, I'm too exhausted.' Her warm breath tickled Aedlynn's lips. 'But thank you.'

Lena slowly grazed Aedlynn's throat, who stared up at her with quiet longing like this close proximity was torture – the sweetest kind of torture. Like a yearnful moth drawn to a dancing flame. Her heartbeat pounded against Lena's fingertips. 'Though I'll definitely hold you to that offer,' Lena whispered. Her lips parted into a sweet smile and her thumb slowly circled the skin of Aedlynn's cheek. 'I've been growing quite fond of you, you know.'

Aedlynn couldn't look away, couldn't ignore the way her heartbeat reverberated through her entire body. How her heart fluttered through her chest, desperate to get closer. But there was no way that the wonderful girl in front of her felt the same. There was nothing special about Aedlynn. She didn't possess the same ease with which Kaelena befriended everyone around her or the natural grace that made the others look after her. That made Aedlynn pine after her if only to brush hands and taste her perfume on her tongue.

Because Aedlynn saw *her*, the witty, kind and bright woman in that revealing dress. The friend who held her through nightmares, who made her feel normal and human. The friend who gossiped to her about the servants, who tucked her in whenever she fell asleep reading or patiently helped her decipher a text because her mind always struggled with the ever moving letters.

Aedlynn opened her mouth. *I've grown quite fond of you* didn't even begin to cover what she felt.

In the warm lighting of the room, Lena's eyes twinkled with specks of gold. 'So . . . does that . . . Does that mean you can finally promise me you won't kill me in my sleep?'

Kaelena laughed. 'Oh! I completely forgot about that.'

A smile tugged at Aedlynn's lips, even more so when Kaelena hooked her pinkie around hers. 'I solemnly promise I won't kill you in your sleep, halfling.'

'Now I can finally sleep well.'

Lena snorted. 'Your adorable snoring suggests you've been sleeping just fine.'

'I don't snore!'

'Like a wyvern,' Kaelena purred.

Chapter 6
Aedlynn

Kaelena pulled Aedlynn into an empty entertainment room where she'd pushed the velvet couches aside to create some space. Aedlynn had mentioned that though she enjoyed balls, she was an awful dancer and since tonight was Yule, there was no way Kaelena would allow her to stay off the dance floor. So she pulled Aedlynn along until they stood in the middle of the empty room, before the tall windows with their half-drawn curtains, surrounded by the many candles she'd lit.

Aedlynn looked around to take it all in and then back at her, furrowing her brows. Kaelena curtsied and then took her hand. The callouses on Aedlynn's fingers that brushed over her smooth skin sent a shiver down her spine.

'I'm going to teach you to dance.' Kaelena watched how Aedlynn's cheeks flushed, how even the tips of her ears pinked. Part of Kaelena hated herself for tricking her, but the other half reminded her that her loyalty should be with Lorcán. Though that voice kept growing quieter and quieter.

'I'll ruin your shoes,' Aedlynn said.

Kaelena chuckled. 'If you do that, I'll throw you off of the highest tower.'

'So violent,' Aedlynn purred and Kaelena's heart nearly leapt out of her chest. She worked hard to compose herself and laid her right hand on Aedlynn's waist, assuming a starting position. Aedlynn timidly looked up at her and the moment their eyes met, she subtly dipped her face to hide her coloured cheeks.

By the Goddess, could she be any more adorable? 'So . . . ehm . . . I'm going to lead.'

Aedlynn nodded. 'Smart, I'd probably lead us straight to the infirmary.'

Kaelena laughed. 'Come now, you're not that horrible. Besides, you move very gracefully already, you just need to learn some steps and you'll be fine.' Kaelena took a step forward with her left foot, walking right into Aedlynn.

'Sorry.' She grinned sheepishly. 'Am I supposed to move?'

'Dancing could be defined as a sequence of movements, so . . . yes.'

Aedlynn huffed an awkward little laugh. 'Silly me.'

Kaelena smiled, softly shaking her head. She grew warm seeing Aedlynn so flustered simply learning how to dance. The girl could fight like a war god and yet dancing intimidated her. 'Think of it as a fight – self-defence. I step forward and you step back, I set my left foot forward and you take your right foot back.'

Those beautiful eyes brightened when Aedlynn understood what she meant. 'Oh! Okay.'

Kaelena assumed their starting position again. 'So, I'm going to lead and you're going to follow—'

'Yes, Ma'am,' Aedlynn said solemnly. 'I'll follow you to the end of the world.'

Kaelena grinned. 'As long as you're following me in a waltz, I'll allow it.'

Aedlynn wrinkled her nose. 'I'll try.'

Forsaken gods . . . Right . . . Dancing. Kaelena cleared her throat and set a step forward again. Aedlynn followed this time, her eyes glued on Kaelena's.

'Like this?' Aedlynn asked softly. Kaelena nodded, moving to her right to swiftly pull Aedlynn with her, then she took a step back and Aedlynn gracefully followed. They continued those simple steps, over and over. All while holding each other's gaze, dancing to soundless music.

'You're doing really well,' Kaelena whispered. She wasn't sure why she was so quiet but it felt right. Aedlynn smiled in reply, though the smile quickly fell. 'What?'

Aedlynn worried on her bottom lip. 'I've only been told that I'm doing well when I . . . whenever I was violent enough for Lorcán or deadly enough for Aviod.'

It broke Kaelena's heart to hear that. Lorcán expected her to trick Aedlynn and betray her, but Kaelena's own heart secretly wondered about the stunning girl in front of her. This girl who dropped everything to take care of her, who was so good to her.

She didn't deserve Aedlynn.

Kaelena cupped her cheeks. 'You're so much more than just his weapon, you know that, right?'

Her throat bobbed. 'I've been . . . I've been beginning to realise that, yes.'

'Good.' Kaelena drank in her pretty face. Those wonderfully peculiar eyes she loved staring into. The full lips, the soft glow of her tan skin. She imagined Zielle herself would envy Aedlynn's natural beauty and that Aestor would envy

77

her casual kindness. 'Don't ever allow them to make you forget yourself.'

Aedlynn nodded, her eyes lining with tears. 'I didn't quite know who I was anymore, but you've been showing me and I . . . I cannot thank you enough for that.'

Kaelena stilled, still holding Aedlynn's face. Perhaps Aedlynn had been showing her who she was underneath these dresses as well, underneath Lorcán's approval. Was it truly seducing and tricking if Kaelena's heart fluttered with Aedlynn's every smile and touch?

She'd always meekly reported everything back to Lorcán. Never had she betrayed that trust. Yet every time Lorcán had asked her if Aedlynn had complained or shown signs of defiance . . . She'd lied.

'You . . . you don't have to thank me,' Kaelena stammered.

Aedlynn cocked her head. 'Something on my face?'

Kaelena's cheeks flushed as she let go of Aedlynn. 'You'll be fine tonight.'

Aedlynn grinned and jabbed her side. 'Perhaps I'll steal some of your lovesick suitors.'

Delight filled her at the quiet confidence that hid behind the words. She knew Aedlynn didn't think too highly of herself – unless in a fight. Then she could get *utterly* cocky and arrogant, which Lena secretly found very enticing. She liked watching Aedlynn train, stealing glances at how her muscled shoulders gleamed in the sun and the tight fabric clung to her tan skin. Aedlynn had enough reasons to like herself. Kaelena could list them by heart.

'Oh, they'll *fight* over you.' Kaelena batted her thick lashes at Aedlynn. 'They'll beg you for dance after dance and when they have you in their arms, they'll find any good excuse to stay with you and touch you.' Kaelena traced a light finger over Aedlynn's side, who shivered beneath the touch. 'Your waist, your side, your back — even that cute butt of yours, if they're brave enough.' In an attempt to shake off the sudden desire Kaelena had to do exactly those things, she shrugged lightly. 'That's what they often do.'

'Do they . . . touch *you* like that during dancing?' Aedlynn cocked her head.

Kaelena nodded. 'Sometimes.'

Something close to jealousy crept over Aedlynn's face, though it disappeared as quickly as it came. Gods, Kaelena would give everything to know if Aedlynn actually liked *her*. Not the pretty exterior all those lords swooned over. The *alluring nymph* Lorcán had turned her into.

Though plenty of lords had attempted to court her, she'd rejected them all. The only thing they cared about was to boast that they'd captured *Lorcán's nymph*. She'd received the prettiest and most bedazzled jewellery and the most expensive silk Aspia offered. Yet she cared more about the lilies Aedlynn handpicked weekly for her in the gardens. The knitted sweater with silver stars and constellations embroidered on it that Aedlynn had handmade for her and smelled of her dewy perfume. The little bracelet she'd braided out of the leather of a dagger when the blade had broken. She'd even added a little silver crescent moon pendant.

Aedlynn saw her in a way that convinced Lena no one had ever bothered to truly look at her.

Lorcán

Lorcán watched his guests from the throne on the dais, with Isolde seated next to him, clad in a delicate icy blue evening gown, her brown hair gathered in a neat updo. He'd shared four dances with his wife, which was enough feigned affection to last the coming six months. Her dark blue eyes pierced into him like she was digging her claws into his soul.

He was watching Kaelena.

His nymph wore her smile like it was her most valuable piece of jewellery, all while dancing with noble after noble. The fabric of her chiffon dress mimicked the dawn. Shades of orange, pink and yellow with golden shimmers. He'd noticed plenty of lords showering her with attention, asking for a dance, offering her wine. Presenting her with useless Yule gifts.

His eyes scanned the crowd until he found Aedlynn standing awkwardly by herself, away from the exuberant crowd. It had been a while since he'd seen her in anything but the leathers the assassins lived in, so seeing her in her gold silk dress felt like a fever dream. Her shoulder-length sleek hair had been gathered into a simple half-updo, no doubt done by Kaelena.

He kept a close watch on them, wondering when Kaelena would finally capture Aedlynn in her web. She'd taken her time with his assassin, neatly moulding her and, judging by the violent yearning he sensed in Aedlynn, his nymph had worked wonders.

Aedlynn

Aedlynn was done watching Kaelena be swept up in dance after dance with the many Lords of Aspia. Four lords stood near her, waiting for their turn. Aedlynn decided they'd have to wait a bit longer.

Kaelena immediately let go of the lord, curtsied and politely thanked him. The other lords started to shuffle towards her but Aedlynn shot them a warning glare, though the frown immediately made room for a sweet smile as she offered Kaelena her hand. 'May I?'

Kaelena glanced at the startled lords with a hint of amusement in her eyes before she returned her attention to Aedlynn. 'If you hadn't come to ask me, I would've dragged you along.'

She smiled. 'I wouldn't have minded it.'

Kaelena smoothly pulled her along.

They danced and danced while the music swelled and slowed, moving in perfect harmony while nothing and no one existed but each other. Even though they were surrounded by plenty of other couples who were dancing, they hardly noticed how song after song passed while they remained paired.

Aedlynn noted the lingering nobles. 'I fear those poor idiots only came here to dance with you. They must be having a miserable Yule.'

Kaelena shrugged. 'Sounds like their problem.' A little twinkle entered her eyes. 'Besides, they aren't the only person wanting to dance with a certain someone.'

Aedlynn's stomach dropped. 'Oh.'

Kaelena nodded. 'Someone I'd love to spend the entire evening dancing with.'

Aedlynn should've known Kaelena had a crush on someone.

Kaelena tilted her head. 'Someone who I think is really pretty and sweet and funny. Arguably the best-dressed person in this room tonight.'

Aedlynn glanced around, wondering whom she could

be talking about. Probably someone who could give her so much more than Aedlynn ever could. Though Aedlynn would give her anything. Her books, her sweaters, her heart, her sword and her life. She'd never worshipped the gods but she'd fall on her knees for the girl in front of her, whose laugh sounded like summer and whose hugs felt like the first spring breeze after a long winter. The girl who defied autumn and instead demanded life.

Kaelena's lips curled into a mischievous smile. 'Perhaps it's someone I've adored for a while now. Someone who has completely enchanted me.' Aedlynn clenched her jaw. The disappointment that hit her was overwhelming and the jealousy . . . gods, it was violent and vicious. 'Someone with really pretty eyes, normally very clever and bright. She's beyond beautiful.'

Aedlynn worked hard to put a leash on her jealousy. It was obvious that Lena loved this person. She'd be a horrible friend if she'd let her own feelings get in the way. Though a small speck of hope sparked alive when she realised Lena was talking about a *woman*. 'What lady are you talking about?'

Kaelena raised a brow in amusement. 'Seriously?'

Aedlynn shrugged. 'I have no idea who you're talking about.'

Her other brow joined as Kaelena started grinning at her. 'What?'

'Nothing.'

'Who is it?'

'Sleep on it.'

Aedlynn groaned. 'Fine, keep your secrets then.'

She hoped Kaelena couldn't sense the frustration she felt and how hard she tried to appear like she wasn't utterly restless. Kaelena had mentioned before how she sometimes sensed her, the same way that Aedlynn often felt her. If she could feel her jealousy . . . that would be a bit embarrassing.

Absent-mindedly, she smoothed her hand over Kaelena's lower back. Aedlynn couldn't stand the thought of Kaelena loving someone — someone else. Not when Kaelena had become her home.

Kaelena's fingers grazed the skin of Aedlynn's bare back. Aedlynn shivered and found herself staring up at Kaelena, unable to look away. Unable to feel anything but her hand. The tender way with which Kaelena looked at her was a caress over her very soul.

When had the music stopped playing? Aedlynn heard nothing but her own thundering heartbeat as her heart crept into her throat. It stopped completely when Kaelena leaned in, her pretty face only inches away from hers, dousing Aedlynn with that wonderful perfume.

'Have you figured it out yet?' Lena whispered while her gaze dropped to Aedlynn's lips. Aedlynn blinked — slowly. Spellbound. 'Or do you need me to spell it out?'

'I'm not sure . . .' she breathed. 'Could be wrong.'

Kaelena brushed her lips over the corner of her mouth, sending another shiver along Aedlynn's spine. Electricity coated her every nerve.

'Maybe there was only one person that I . . . that I wanted to dance with tonight as well,' Aedlynn said ever so softly, her face growing tender as she looked back up at Kaelena. At this girl who'd welcomed Aedlynn into her light and then taught her how to grow in it.

Kaelena nodded solemnly. 'Isolde. I knew it.'

Aedlynn snorted, then giggled. Kaelena glanced around them, and swiftly pulled her along. She zig-zagged through the crowd of nobles while Aedlynn held onto her hand like a lifeline. Finally, they made it out of the ballroom and into the quiet hallway, which seemed too silent now that they'd grown used to the loud chatter and laughter and music.

Kaelena pushed open the double doors down the hall that led into a grand library, but Aedlynn barely had the time to admire the astonishing amount of books and enormous space because Kaelena pushed her against one of the tall, dark-wooden bookshelves, wove her fingers through Aedlynn's hair and kissed her.

Aedlynn sighed against her lips, all tension leaving her body. A string seemed to connect their hearts, dangling between them. It tugged every now and then as if urging them to come together. Aedlynn gratefully obliged and returned every single kiss Kaelena gave her, burying her fingers in her loose curls and enjoying how Lena's lips tasted of pomegranates.

Aedlynn turned them around so Kaelena's back rested against the wall and kissed her deeply, her tongue caressing hers. The sweet and somehow familiar taste of her was enough to undo her.

With one hand cupping Kaelena's face, she dipped the other beneath the fabric to brush it over one of her breasts, running her thumb over the stiff nipple that peaked against the chiffon.

'This okay?' she breathed against Lena's lips.

Lena answered by nodding and pulling her closer to kiss her again, only breaking apart to tell her, 'Goddess, I need you.'

Aedlynn æriated them back to their bedroom before she pulled the straps of Lena's dress down to expose her breasts.

Lena's back arched and she sighed as she rested her head against the wall behind her, her fingers curling in Aedlynn's now loose hair. Aedlynn leaned in, taking her time to kiss every revealed inch of Lena's chest. Her collarbones, the curve of her delicate throat. A soft moan bubbled up as Aedlynn teased the sensitive spot beneath her ear.

By the gods, Aedlynn would worship her as she deserved.

Aedlynn's voice became husky. 'I want to feel how wet I can make you.'

Kaelena panted, looking at her with nothing but lust in her eyes. She liked seeing Aedlynn like this. Confident, in control. The way she had Kaelena pinned to the wall with one leg between hers, to force her legs to spread . . . Lena wasn't the one seducing right now. She liked that. And by the Goddess, seeing Aedlynn like this was so fucking enticing she feared she'd melt.

Feeling Kaelena's strong desire, Aedlynn softly brushed her lips over hers. 'You'd like that, wouldn't you?' she breathed, softly biting down on Kaelena's bottom lip to tease her, drawing out another moan. 'I'll please you so well, you'll see stars,' she whispered against Lena's parted lips. 'I'm going to make you come until you're moaning my name.' She swallowed up another moan. 'Until I have you begging me for more and more and *more*.' She kissed her deeply. 'And then, when I have you writhing and senseless and dripping with desire, I'll well and truly start to fuck you, *ná'dýra*.'

Kaelena nearly melted when Aedlynn called her *my love*. The sinful way she spoke to her . . . the wicked confidence behind the words that she could deliver on those promises . . . If anyone else had said those things to her, she wouldn't have believed them. She would've prepared herself for five minutes of faking it. But by the Goddess, she knew Aedlynn would make good on those promises.

'*Please*,' she moaned softly. 'Gods, Aedlynn, I need you to touch me.'

Aedlynn slipped her hand through a slit of her skirts, teasing a finger over the damp fabric of her laces. 'Here?' Kaelena's breath hitched in her throat when Aedlynn kissed her neck and dug her fingers in ever so slightly, the barrier of the fabric still between them. 'Divine Hells,' Aedlynn whispered against her lips. She pushed in as deeply as the drenched fabric would let her, earning her a little mewl. 'You're so wet for me.'

Kaelena panted, moving her hips to enjoy some friction but Aedlynn firmly pinned her against the wall to keep her absolutely still, giving her a teasing smile while she rested one arm on the wall behind Kaelena, her other fingers twirling the fabric of her lingerie around them.

'And so fucking gorgeous,' Aedlynn breathed against her lips as she pulled at the panties to tease her. Lena sucked in a breath, her fingers desperately digging into Aedlynn's back. 'I bet you'll look even more pretty coming with my name on your lips.'

'Goddess have mercy,' Lena muttered to herself with closed eyes.

Aedlynn chuckled softly. 'I've spent many nights imagining how I'd please you if I'd ever have you.' She pecked her lips, the corner of her mouth. 'How I'd touch you.' She kissed her jawline and at the same time, let her fingers slip into her panties, running them through the thick heat, teasing that swollen bundle of nerves.

Lena moved her hips, silently urging her to move her fingers faster. Feeling how violently Kaelena yearned for her undid any common sense. If the world had started to fall apart around them, she wouldn't have even noticed it.

She held Lena's lust-hazed eyes while she worked her. 'I imagined you'd tell me no man ever made you moan like that, never made you feel any of the things *I* make you feel. That no one compares. I imagined how *you* would touch me, how good you'd make me feel because damn me if I'm not helplessly and shamelessly in love with you.' Kaelena's eyes half-closed as she clung to her, moaning while Aedlynn rubbed that nub just right. Overcome with the things Aedlynn was saying – admitting.

By the Goddess, Kaelena couldn't get enough of her. She loved her. Shit, she *adored* her.

'I'm yours,' Kaelena whispered against Aedlynn's lips. She didn't have the words to describe what Aedlynn meant to her, yet Aedlynn felt it – everything. 'I'm yours, Aedlynn, all yours.'

She didn't want to own Kaelena, didn't see her as some object to conquer, but hearing her dyad accept her – their bond . . . Mother, she wanted to hear those words over and over. She wasn't quite sure how she knew. She just did – like she knew spring would continue to come and the sun would continue to rise, she was certain that Lena was a part of her soul.

Kaelena curled against her, arching her back while Aedlynn worked her. Slow, inching in deeper and deeper with every thrust of her two fingers. Putting pressure on a sensitive spot in the walls of her core. Lena's head tilted back against the wall, her lips parted while blissful pleasure passed over her features. 'By the fucking Goddess,' she heaved. '*Oh*, don't stop.'

Aedlynn kept up that pace and pressure, and watched

how Lena's dark brows knitted together, how she panted and moaned — louder and louder — and clenched around her fingers as if to draw her in deeper. Aedlynn gratefully obliged, watching with great satisfaction how Lena's head rolled from side to side as she mumbled through her pleasure. Sweet nothings that left Aedlynn rubbing her thighs together in an effort to ease the aching emptiness there.

Lena's fingers dug into the skin of Aedlynn's back and shoulders, wove through her loose hair. Aedlynn swallowed up moan after moan by deeply kissing her and felt Kaelena clench hard around her fingers. And then her lover melted against that wall, her moan piercing through Aedlynn's very soul as she came.

Lena looked at her with the lovely haze of her afterglow on her features, softly illuminating her freckles. 'Take off your dress,' she whispered with a thick voice. 'I want to see you.'

Slowly, Aedlynn did. She took her time to let the silk straps glide down her shoulders and upper arms. All while holding Lena's gaze. The golden silk pooled on the floor and Aedlynn stepped out of it, her skin heating while Kaelena greedily took in the curves and dips of her body. Her breasts, the dampness between her thighs. Hungry, like she'd been starving for Aedlynn since the dawning of this universe.

That string between their hearts and souls tugged again.

Restless. Ancient. Powerful.

Unyielding and unbreakable.

'Mother, you're *stunning*,' Kaelena breathed as she lazily circled her. Like they had all the time in this life and the next to explore each other.

Aedlynn shivered, unable to look away. She needed her.

She'd needed her from the beginning and would need her long after the end. Aedlynn would use her name to pray, her hips as an altar to worship her.

Lena stepped back and in a few elegant movements, her dress joined Aedlynn's on the floor. Subtly shimmering freckles that connected like constellations decorated her body as she stepped towards Aedlynn, her eyes holding her captive in a way that felt like pure freedom. When she felt Aedlynn's growing need through their bond, her lips quirked into a feline smirk. 'Need something, sweet Aedlynn?' she breathed against her neck, pushing her backwards until her thighs hit her bed.

'*You*,' Aedlynn breathed. 'Make me yours. Carve your name into my heart, my love. It only started beating again for *you*, so claim it.'

Lena pushed her onto the bedsheets, driving her further down until Aedlynn had to lean on her elbows for support. Kaelena closed her lips around her nipple, sucking on it while her eyes still held Aedlynn's. She whimpered, overcome with relentless need as Kaelena's hand trailed up her thigh. Higher and more inward with every little nip and tease on her sensitive nipples. Any sensible language left her when Aedlynn saw Kaelena perched between her legs like that, when her fingers neared that slick heat. Her tongue swept over the stiff peak again and pleasure bloomed deep in her core.

'*Gods*,' she rasped, arching her back.

'My, my,' Lena mused. 'Look at my girl reverting back to heeding the gods because of me.' Aedlynn's entire body wanted to go limp and she could scarcely hold back from her lover but Lena noticed her struggle and gave her that teasing smile again. She pushed Aedlynn down fully, dipping her head to kiss her sternum. One breast and then the other while her curls caressed Aedlynn's skin. Lower and lower. She kissed her hip bones, her strong thighs. Working her way inward.

Her tongue pushed Aedlynn's folds apart to tease that bud, and Aedlynn tilted her head back and gasped. Her back arched off the mattress and her fingers gripped the bedsheets when Lena's tongue dipped in, though Lena firmly pressed her hips back down. She licked and teased until lightning coated every nerve in Aedlynn's body. Then she slipped two fingers inside, curling them to press against the inside of her core, still kissing and licking that nub. Drawing out moan after moan while Aedlynn's fingers wove through Lena's hair. Lena's other hand curled around her thigh to keep her legs still as Aedlynn rocked her hips against her mouth.

Kaelena worked her slowly, taking her time to get familiar with what Aedlynn liked. Panting, Aedlynn lost herself to the blissful feeling and when Kaelena found the perfect pace, the perfect way to stroke that bud with her tongue and her core with her fingers, Aedlynn writhed underneath her. Moaning her name, crying out from pleasure. She spoke half in Aspian, half in Aelerian. Too senseless to realise what exactly she was saying but it sounded like one love confession after the other.

Kaelena felt her pleasure through their bond, the glowing happiness in her chest that they were finally together. That Lena loved her. It was too much and not enough at the same time.

Aedlynn came with her dyad's name on her lips, uttering it over and over like a prayer. When Kaelena climbed up to kiss her lips, Aedlynn buried her hands in her hair and savoured the taste.

She looked at her, those honey eyes with golden specks, filled with a yearning Lena could no longer hide. Kaelena's soul fluttered in her body while they made love to each other, far away from what they were supposed to be – a mindless killer and a meek courtesan. Enjoying this little cocoon of light they'd created in the ever-looming darkness.

Kaelena had never been looked at like this before – with reverence, as if Aedlynn had forsaken all gods but her. Kaelena wasn't much of a warrior but for her lover, she would raise the Hells and burn down the world.

Even doom it.

Kaelena sweetly caressed her hair while they enjoyed each other's presence in the tranquillity of the crackling fireplace. 'I still have to give you your present.'

Aedlynn looked up at her, a lazy and content smile adorning her lips. Never in her life had she felt this relaxed or snug as she did in the arms of her dyad. 'I have one for you as well.'

'Is it a muzzle?'

Aedlynn scrunched her nose. 'I quite enjoy listening to you.'

Kaelena shifted underneath her, climbing out of the bed to put on a silk robe and retrieve the gift out of the drawer of her nightstand. She handed Aedlynn one of her other robes and climbed back in. Aedlynn scooted closer, resting her shoulder against Kaelena's before she handed Lena her present.

Swiftly, Kaelena tore the silvery paper off to reveal a small light-wooden box and when she opened it, her brows rose as she took the necklace in. It was a dainty chain, carrying a silver circle engraved with the moon phases and constellations, the design eerily reminiscent of a compass. The centre carried a small circular moonstone.

Kaelena stared at it in utter shock. 'Where did you find this?'

'I saw it in an antique shop when I was on a mission and thought you'd like it. I did some research, I think it's an amulet.'

'It is, and not one made by mortals,' Kaelena said with quiet reverence while she inspected every little detail of the necklace.

Aedlynn blinked. 'Really? How can you tell?'

'Because no mortal knows that moonstones were Lady Antheia's sacred symbol,' Kaelena said. 'No mortal knows that Lady Antheia created the moon phases and was severely punished by Eiran because it frightened the mortals.'

'I didn't know that either,' she said. 'How do you know that?'

Kaelena ruefully smiled at her. 'I guess it's the vespera blood. I often dream of the stars and aurora, how she once decorated our skies with the prettiest patterns – gifts to those she loved. She made aurora for Keres, simply because her dyad made her so irrevocably happy. She dedicated the entire east of the night sky to her son when he was killed.' She grew silent for a moment, caressing the smooth metal between her fingers. 'If she'd still been alive, she would've been my Lady. I would have served her.'

'Would you have wanted that?'

Kaelena nodded. 'I would've been honoured to serve her. She wasn't wicked, but the mortals and Eiran . . .' Her throat bobbed. 'One can only take so many beatings before breaking.'

Aedlynn nodded slowly, caressing her thumb over Kaelena's hand.

'Thank you, it's really pretty.' She kissed Aedlynn's brow and let Aedlynn help her put it on.

'I thought it fitting to gift you something night-related.'

Kaelena smiled at her. 'I appreciate that. I've been . . . training a little. I found out that I'm not just good at sneaking around. I can manipulate darkness a bit as well – like liquid night. I can slip through it, hide in it. It's not much, I'm not really great at it, but—' She blinked. 'I'm rambling again.'

The smile Aedlynn gave her made her melt a little. 'You know I like listening to you.'

Kaelena blushed, shyly stroking her fingers over the moonstone and then handed Aedlynn her present. She tore the paper apart to reveal a thick, leather-bound tome written in a language she'd never been taught but still understood. Aedlynn flipped through the pages, finding intricately detailed paintings of their gods, daemons and other creatures. Her eyes rested on a page depicting something known as a circedera, describing their *varkradas* as life-essential. Without those shadows intact, the daemon could die an excruciating death.

Aedlynn gasped when she flipped to another chapter and found it entirely dedicated to wyverns. Kaelena grinned at her. 'Thought you'd like it, as you always go on about them.'

'Look at those scales! They're bigger than my hands!'

'Your hands are tiny.'

'Fuck off.'

Kaelena giggled and took the book from her. 'As far as I can tell, these myths are surprisingly truthful. A stark contrast with the ones Eiran allowed to reach the mortals – the lies and such. The chapter on Antheia is entirely true. They don't depict Zielle here as some lovesick puppy either. It even mentions Kaltain, who was Antheia and Keres' adopted son. But then again, I'm not surprised, as it was written by Yael Eléazar and rumour had it that that *Aurealis* was close with the gods.'

Aedlynn nodded with every bit of information Kaelena gave her, drinking it all in. 'Thank you.'

She smiled at her. 'I figured you'd like to learn about your roots.' Aedlynn kissed her forehead, overcome by how thoughtful she'd been.

They stopped to view a painting of Khalyna.

'Shit,' Aedlynn murmured. The goddess had the same sleek, dark hair as her. The same cheekbones but her eyes were a pale and icy blue. Her skin was fair and the look in her eyes was a proud, disdainful one, as if she were looking down at Aedlynn from within the book.

'Intimidating, huh?' Kaelena murmured. 'If you think Khalyna looks like she might skin you alive and then wear your hide as a coat, you should see their illustration of Keres.'

Kaelena flipped the page while she said it, showing her the portrait of Eiran's Left Hand.

Chapter 7

Diana

Draven, the High Court of Clacaster
Present day

Mother above, he was *magnificent*.

His face seemed to have been sculpted by the artists I looked up to, crafted with love and attention to detail. Beautiful wavy honey-coloured hair framed his face, half of it bundled together at the back of his head. The rest fell to his shoulders. His dark green eyes held me willingly captive.

The outline of his muscles was visible through his black silk shirt, sleeves rolled up to reveal his decorated left arm, which covered him from his thumb up to his left shoulder and the left side of his throat, marking him as Eiran's Left Hand – his Punisher.

Black whorls and swirls, thorns and crow's feathers.

Laughter bubbled up in my throat, which made it clear that I was losing my mind.

I was ogling the God of Malevolence.

And I wanted to paint him.

Keres

The mortal sat on her knees, staring in awe. My gaze didn't leave her while I slowly sauntered over. The few mortals who dared request my presence always cowered before me but *she* didn't. Neither had she last time. There were but few mortals who could wield wrath the same way Antheia could; honed to perfection, merciless and violent, and capable of bringing even Eiran to his knees.

Yet this one could.

I studied the lines of her face with curiosity. Despite being sickly pale and thin, there was a delicate beauty to her features that longed to come out – and something disturbingly familiar, though I couldn't quite put my finger on it.

Quickly, she lowered her head with respect. 'Lord Keres.'

'You wish to devote yourself to me?' I noted how she shivered when she heard my voice. 'In exchange for my blessing your vow of revenge?'

'Yes,' she breathed, her brows furrowing while she tried to focus to keep her magic tethered. She'd balled her hands into fists to hide the flames.

I crossed my arms and those pretty grey eyes followed the movement. 'And what exactly would you do for me, little mortal?'

She dipped her head low. 'Anything.'

'I have quite enough servants.'

She seemed to bite her tongue but the words still tumbled out, 'Or your whore, I don't care. Whatever you want.'

I scoffed. 'You truly think I'd let some little mortal woman warm my bed?' Her posture stiffened. 'Are you truly so desperate that you risk insulting me like this?'

Like a tense string, her patience snapped and her head whipped up to glare at me. 'Stick the attitude up your ass and decide whether you want to help me or not.'

Wicked delight filled me. I was curious to see just how many times she could be pushed before saying something truly provocative – and I could remind the mortal of her place. I'd heeded her prayer last time – because she'd reminded me of Antheia, but calling on me *twice?* I was not a charity. Not for any mortal.

I also had no doubt that this lovely attitude wouldn't wither in front of other gods, which would be highly entertaining to watch given their frail egos. I knew exactly what I wanted to do with her.

Something else piqued my interest, a jasmine scent that embalmed her. 'You reek of *kalotra.*'

'Maybe it's the bloodmagic,' Diana said wryly.

I raised a brow and Diana braced herself for death, but I remained silent.

Why were Lorcán's fingerprints all over her? What was so interesting about her that he'd put such a dark claim on her? And why hadn't I noticed this last time?

Without moving, I mentally pulled at the threads of Lorcán's magic. It was complex and deep-rooted, an accumulation of dark magic that suppressed nearly everything in her body. I hated to admit it but Lorcán's mastery of *kalotra* rivalled only my own skills. Lorcán had been trained well by Aeneas Losaño – too well, unfortunately. The bloodmagic revealed no secrets of its master and I knew that if I continued prodding, Lorcán would sense it.

It was obvious Lorcán wanted her, so I decided I'd steal his toy and use her against him.

Like old times.

'Such a faithful little mortal,' I purred with a cruel smile. 'Praying to the gods like a good girl – all of us, even the most wicked of us. But I think I'll keep you all to myself for now.' It'd been so long since anyone had prayed to me, and though I had no desire to coddle a mortal, I wanted her piety aimed at me and my marking claiming her skin. Frail she may appear, but I'd seen her true nature crawl out when she'd killed her fiancé. I'd seen it again when she'd murdered a lord and his lackeys for humiliating her. She could be pure wrath, and I wanted another taste of it.

I flicked my right hand in her direction. 'You will devote yourself to me and worship me above all other gods. You will serve me like a nymph whenever I see fit, and every full and new moon, you will be by my side – to do whatever I desire. In exchange, I'll cleanse you and bless your vow of revenge against Lorcán Andulet.'

Ink crawled over her left underarm, covering her from thumb to elbow. Feathers and swirls that matched my own. The binding opened up a small connection between us and I found myself able to peer into her mind to gauge her thoughts and emotions. After admiring the marking, she looked back up at me – at her god. Maybe she would come to regret this but until then, she would live and destroy Lorcán, and when the Fates came to condemn her, she would drag that king down with her.

And I would be there to enjoy the show.

'Speak,' I ordered, once again crossing my arms while I leaned against the stone of the burning hearth.

'I feel like I'm losing my mind and could combust any moment now and Lorcán wants me to come to him, says he'll remove the *kalotra* if I do.'

I pushed away to crouch in front of her and studied her. Instead of flinching away like I'd expected, she held my gaze. 'I'll take you to Ascredia.' Diana frowned in confusion. 'It's an ancient cavern, created by Ellowyn, where her moonlight flows freely. It's the perfect place to cleanse someone of dark magic.'

Her breathing hitched as another bolt of pain shot through her chest. I noticed her struggle and wrapped my arm around her waist to pull her up, then wrapped my other arm underneath her knees to carry her. If she'd felt better, I'm certain she would've protested.

In the middle of the cavern, the floor split apart to create a pond of silvery water. A grand ancient willow tree humming with endless power resided in the middle of the pond, its roots slithering over the bottom. Thick and strong, they broke apart the surrounding stones. A wide hole in the cavern ceiling let the moonlight rush in, which bathed all in a serene glow.

Once again, that voice echoed through her mind, *You have made your decision despite knowing the consequences. Should you change your mind, I'd be most happy to retrieve you.*

Diana's eyes rolled back while she heaved and fought his grip, but with her withering body, she stood no chance. I tried to block Lorcán's control but my magic had nothing to latch onto. Like that damned Veil he'd thrown over his country, he'd thrown something similar over her. A strange sort of magic I was unfamiliar with.

I æriated, pulling her into the cleansing water in an attempt to weaken Lorcán's hold. The webs of Lorcán's magic seethed in reaction, a good sign, but her heart rate became irregular, slowing down even more. I let go of her knees and pulled her against me to hold her up. The moment the water touched her skin, her deafening scream echoed through the cavern and rattled the walls as she tried to push me away.

My hand wove through her loose hair, planting her flush against my chest while she shivered in her nightgown. Her next scream quickly turned into a bone-chilling growl. One that sent the hairs on my body erect and my heart racing in my throat. An ancient presence surrounded her, power and might I'd felt only a handful of times before, and never in a mortal.

When I met her gaze, her eyes were rimmed with violet and filled with a feral loathing – a beast set loose. Lorcán was now in full control over whatever power he'd hidden from her. I muttered a curse under my breath and swiftly pulled her deeper. Diana gasped and heaved, trying to fight me off. I'd barely noticed Aestor's arrival in answer to my summons, only realising he was finally here when he æriated behind us in the water and grabbed her. Her head lolled back, resting against his shoulder while she stared up in dazed confusion, almost if she were mesmerised by whatever she saw in his face.

'She's crashing,' I said to him. 'Keep her alive so I can remove the *kalotra*.'

'Who is she?' Aestor covered Diana's chest with his hand while he strengthened her heartbeat. The Fates obviously weren't ready for her yet, or he wouldn't have been able to do that.

'I thought she was mortal at first but now I don't think so.' I started to work on the *kalotra* but Diana let go of another blood-chilling scream, sending us back several steps before I regained my grip on the slippery floor. Aestor slipped in the pond, quickly crawling back up in an attempt to hold her back but Diana wasted no time and lunged for me, her nails now grown out into long black talons. Her lips curled to reveal two sharp fangs.

No fucking mortal had those.

She dragged her talons across my side before I could evade her, cutting open my divine skin so golden blood leaked out. I side-stepped, crashing my magic into her side to send her hard into the pond. The water didn't appear to bother her anymore, as she elegantly rose, bled into a shadow and then slipped out of another one near the willow tree. A cold grin adorned her lips. 'Didn't you wish for a chance to play with her, God of Malice?' She spread her hands as Lorcán used her voice. 'Now is your chance.'

Everything in me screamed that she was no mere mortal. No mortal carried such a suffocating presence with them, had claws and fangs or travelled through shadows. Yet she had no wings. Her eyes weren't gold. None of this made sense.

'Or perhaps I should make her kill herself if you're too frightened to fight a little girl,' she mused. 'Let some of that pent-up magic loose, huh?'

I opened my mouth to warn Lorcán off but Diana twitched and screamed again, sagging to her knees. Silver swirls of magic shot out, burning away everything in its path, scorching the roots of the willow tree and creating fractures in the cavern floor. Another wave of power escaped and silver flames shot out, slamming into us to force us back again, cracking the stones underneath our feet.

Shit.

This was too much like Antheia.

I pushed away the thick clump of grief that nestled in my

throat, the panic that swept over me at the memory of how my dyad had been poisoned and murdered, and how I'd been helpless to save her. Instead, I did what I did best and I drew upon the pure hatred I'd felt for Lorcán ever since that War and I promised myself his death would be slow and painful. He'd taken too much from me – from my family, both by blood and choice.

And I was God of Retribution.

Aestor made for Diana and grabbed her. She growled, using those claws of hers like knives to cut along his chest. But as much as Lorcán stimulated her fighting instinct, we were both well aware of her ever-paling skin. Of her stumbles. Of her struggling heartbeat.

Lorcán made her lash out against us, over and over. Forced her to bellow with feral rage to keep us away from her. All while her power slowly drained the life out of her.

Heaving, I watched her fall to her knees for maybe the hundredth time. I sensed how her spirit burned bright and furiously between the webs of Lorcán's magic, giving him the scolding of a lifetime as she fought back against his control. A taste of that wrath she hid away to protect her reputation.

She'd already sent us both crashing into the cavern walls more times than I was comfortable admitting. I'd considered using moonsbane but that would most likely be the final nail in her coffin. We needed a way to halt Lorcán's control before she dragged us all down in the inferno of her blazing power.

And given her fangs and shadows . . .

I called for another.

Aloïs

At Keres' summons, I abandoned the meeting I'd been attending and slipped out of the shadows and into the ethereal moonlight of Ascredia.

In other circumstances, I would keep my bat-like wings neatly tucked behind my back. Stretching them to their full wingspan was a showcase of might and in my case, my position as King of Hell, and thus Daemons. But I didn't like flaunting my power or barking orders at my subjects, as they'd have no choice but to obey me. Yet if I didn't do it now, that girl would die. So while I approached, my wings stretched wide. My blazing golden eyes didn't leave her while I studied her, sensing daemonic blood.

At a distance, I would've never felt her, Lorcán had somehow completely cut her off. But this close to her, I found weak spots in Lorcán's Veil where I could sense her bright spirit. I held that violet-rimmed gaze that gleamed with something malicious . . . like I had yet to understand the punchline of Lorcán's joke.

The girl fit the description of a suppressed daemon perfectly. Gaunt, sickly thin and pale. But there was something familiar about the sharp features of her face, about that relentless fire burning deep within. The sickly state that this poor girl was in made my *varkradas* restless, the shadows that loyally followed me everywhere.

I took another step and the girl roared at me, baring her fangs while she readied herself to strike, even though we all knew it would be the last thing she'd ever do. She reeked of death, and if I couldn't control her, she'd take us all out with her.

'Any moment now!' Keres urged me to do something. *Anything*.

I started to growl to silence her but Diana lunged for me. Before she could slam into me, I stretched my wings further, widened my stance and roared at her. She stopped short, eyes growing wide as she dropped to her knees. I held her gaze. '*Stand down.*'

Her throat bobbed. She was torn between Lorcán's control and my order that now tore at her very instinct. Keres didn't waste any time and grabbed her, dragging her back into the water. She screamed, scratching her talons over his chest and the sound tore at my very soul.

'Easy, love,' Keres said 'Let us help you.'

Aestor quickly followed to hold her in place while Keres tried again to remove the *kalotra*.

Lorcán stirred her and reluctantly, she tried to escape from Aestor's hold, still holding my gilded gaze like she was testing the waters to see how far she could go before I ordered her to stop. Only a soft growl sounded, yet her eyes grew wide in reply. She wanted to kneel for me, to show her respect and devotion.

Most of all, she wanted the pain to stop and to feel safe again. Still holding my gaze, she whimpered – a request for help. The desperate sound tore at my heart and soul until it felt like I was bleeding out. When our young were in danger, they whimpered like this. All circederae reacted to the sound, as they all looked out for each other's pups. But this . . .

Aestor worked hard to give Keres time, but we both felt her heartbeat wither away.

Diana sobbed, tears making their way down her cheeks, and I couldn't stand to hear that heartbreaking sound. Those walls Lorcán had put up started to crumble – because she was close to dying. Her magic started to pour out, thickening the air. She fought to breathe but failed.

She whimpered again and my *varkradas* shot out, no longer able to control themselves. They curled themselves around her limbs in an effort to soothe her, showing me her agony the moment they touched her pale skin. Refusing to leave her.

And I knew.

Gently, I pulled Aestor aside to wrap her up in my own arms. She latched onto me, tightly balling the fabric of my shirt in her hands while she whimpered and cried against my chest. Keres still cut and removed strands of *kalotra* but there was so much of it – too much. I held her close to me, caressing her hair and back. 'It's okay, I'm here, sweetheart.'

Aestor met my reddened eyes. 'Is it just me or do you react particularly strongly to her?'

I nodded once, carried her over to the edge of the pond, and lowered her to the ground so her legs were still in the water, then pulled her closer so she could rest her weary head against my chest. 'I'm here, sweetheart.' I caressed her face, noting how she leaned into the warmth of my hand to savour it. The little show of affection made my heart burn.

The colour of her eyes changed back to grey. A grey we all knew.

'Stay with me, pup,' I whispered. She nodded, holding onto me with both of her freezing hands. She was tired, so very tired. She wanted to curl up somewhere to sleep, somewhere warm, so she nestled against me – because I held her so gently. She understood nothing of what was going on and she was beyond terrified, but she was desperate to stay with me. She thought I smelled nice. Like soothing honey and lemon and a cosy campfire.

Like home.

I kissed her hair with tears filling my eyes, brushing it behind her ear. 'I'm here, sweetheart.'

Aestor could do nothing more, so Keres concentrated on those strands that had seamlessly merged with her lifeforce. Lorcán had made sure he'd have a way to get rid of her should his weapon go against him. The nerve. After *everything* that bastard had done.

Her drenched and torn nightgown clung to her violently shivering body and her skin was so pale it appeared almost translucent. I had seen her fangs but this delirious state wouldn't enable her to properly feed, so I moved her so her back rested against my chest, then tore my fangs over my wrist to let my black blood run free and brought it to her lips.

I sensed her exhaustion, how her resolve was slipping. '*Feed*,' I said, putting some authority behind the words. 'You'll feel better if you do.'

Slowly, she stirred. Her eyes fluttered when the first drops of blood dripped down her lips and into her mouth. She weakly wrapped her hands around my arm and started drinking.

'That's it, pup.' I kissed her hair. 'Take however much you need.'

'I still need to remove the *kalotra* on her wings and *varkra-das*,' Keres said. 'Would you turn her around for me?'

I gently did so, yet the moment Keres' magic connected with the *kalotra* that had clawed its way into her very soul, Diana convulsed and screamed in agony as all Hell broke loose inside of her.

Visions of the past took over.

Chapter 8

Evalynn

Nervously, the young grey-eyed girl stared up at Yael. She'd spent years hoping and dreaming that she'd one day find herself calling the Aurealis her mentor. 'My name is Evalynn Calliste Denesta, Heir to the Denesta bloodline and paladin to crown prince Lorcán Andulet.'

Yael nodded. 'And why do you wish to attend Vadones?'

Evalynn squared her shoulders and lifted her chin to look into her bright blue eyes. 'So I can learn to defend my future king.'

Yael seemed unimpressed. 'And why have you requested to be trained by me specifically?'

'Because if there is anyone who can teach me how to properly defend him, it is you.'

Yael leaned back in her chair, regarding the eager girl. She seemed to live and breathe his name and she had no doubt that the Denesta family had made being his paladin her whole personality. She knew Dusan and she'd seen enough of Madelynn to know all she cared about was status and appearances. It already showed in the girl's perfect posture and dancer-like physique. In the way that she spoke as if she were nothing but her last name.

Yael tucked a strand of white hair behind her ear and decided to try again, 'Who are you, Evalynn?'

The girl blinked in surprise. 'Heir to the Denesta bloodline and pal—'

'And who are you underneath all of that?'

Evalynn opened and closed her mouth. 'Ehm . . .'

'You are more than an heir to some family that will be easily forgotten by time, more than a paladin to a crown prince who can fall as easily as the autumn leaves,' Yael went on. 'Tell me who you are and will be when all of that has faded away. Tell me what is in your soul, bursting to break free.'

Minutes of silence passed while Evalynn struggled to find an answer. Though her pride reeled to show emotions, her eyes viciously burned. She wanted nothing more than to be trained by Yael, but she could feel the chance at an apprenticeship slipping through her fingers.

She'd been bred to serve the Andulets, to make sure Lorcán would spend years on the throne in Odalis. To serve and marry him one day. That was her duty, had been her duty since the moment she'd been born. But other than that . . .

Her bottom lip quivered. 'I do not know.'

Evalynn's fingers nervously tangled together, even though she could mentally hear her mother scold her for showcasing such unfitting behaviour. She was to be the perfect picture of quiet grace but the gods-awful crawling and sinking feeling in her stomach made her feel hollowed out.

One by one, the Aureales stood from their table to announce their new apprentices. Though there had been quiet chatter when all others had spoken, the room went quiet when Yael rose as she rarely took on apprentices.

'I will take on Sorin Cathános, who lives like wildfire and shines like the sun,' Yael said with a sweet smile. Then her eyes searched the crowd until they found Evalynn's. 'And I will take on Evalynn Denesta.' Yael held her gaze, those bright blue eyes piercing right into her soul like she could see the answer Evalynn had failed to *retrieve for her. 'Come out of your shadows to play, little one, and you will find an inferno at your disposal.'*

Evalynn stared at the empty reflection in her bedroom. At the expensive white dress, the pure white train. The veil her mother readied while a servant took her time with her blonde hair. Evalynn didn't recognise the woman in the mirror, the permanent mask she was forced to wear. The polite, proper and obedient girl that never made a fuss of anything. That always said exactly what her parents or her Royal Highnesses expected her to say.

These days, it was easier to hide behind that mask. To hide the mess she'd been ever since the Aureales had been killed. She'd come close to finding an answer to Yael's question but then her heart had been ripped apart by the sudden loss and now she had no idea what had been left of her. She feared her courage had been ripped out along with her heart. No, it was far easier to put on that mask than to face that numbness and dig deep enough to retrieve the endless grief and pain it hid.

Today, it was the mask of the giddy bride.

Despite the palpable tension in the room, the servant kept chattering. 'You must be so excited to finally wed Prince Lorcán, are you not, Lady Denesta?'

Evalynn tried to swallow but her throat had gone dry. Lorcán had been changing these past months.

'Yes,' she heard herself say. Though her voice sounded far away.

The door opened and Queen Morgane approached with a sweet smile. She looked at Madelynn, then at Evalynn. 'We are all so very excited to accept you into our family, puppet. You are truly everything our son would want in a woman. Especially since that foul witch is finally gone.'

Because Yael had come close to severing Evalynn's roots. Because for a while, Evalynn had dared rebel. Though her parents had *quickly taken care of her fiery words. Not a scar nor a marking was allowed to decorate her body and it had taken years to finally convince them to allow Yael to paint her upper back with phoenix wings. And though her father had wanted to physically remind Eva to keep in line, he'd used his magic to hurt her without leaving any proof behind. The shock of it had been enough to quench the fighting spirit that'd started to wake up.*

Evalynn inclined her head. 'Thank you, Your Highness.'

Morgane studied her. 'You don't appear excited. Is it not a great honour that I entrust him to you?'

'Yes, it is,' she muttered with a hoarse voice while averting her eyes.

Morgane took her chin to make her look up. 'Look me in my eyes when you tell me that.'

Evalynn obliged. 'I am beyond honoured,' she said quietly.

Madelynn brushed a hand over her daughter's soft, shiny hair. The girl was a project she was beyond proud of, a way to secure their status. 'She has been properly trained to take care of your son and his every need. We've also taken care of that foul witch's influence. There is no need to worry about that anymore. She will be a good wife to him.'

Morgane regarded Evalynn a moment longer. 'She looks like she's about to cry.'

'She's simply nervous. You don't marry a crown prince every day, especially one as powerful as your son.'

The answer seemed to soothe the queen as Morgane proudly smiled. 'Indeed.' Her attention returned to Evalynn. 'I expect you to be a good wife but remember the vows you took at sixteen. Above all else, you are his servant.' Morgane cupped Evalynn's chin again, gently brushing some stray hairs behind her ears. There was not a fault to be seen in her face – not a single flaw. 'I expect you to always put that above anything else. He will fight many battles during the coming war. He is to be king and you are only his consort.' A pang of hurt shot through Evalynn's chest. *'If the choice ever comes between saving my son and saving yourself, you will forsake your own life to protect him.'* Morgane kissed her forehead. *'Understood, puppet?'*

She nodded once, plastering the prettiest smile on her face that she could muster.

Evalynn stood with her sword drawn, the Andulet crest adorning the back of her armour as she looked down at her opponent with a cocky smirk. She'd fought him before, many times now. He seemed to call to her, demanding her presence in his vicinity. They'd been dancing like this for some months now.

The golden-eyed man stared up at her. Black smoke rose from his shoulders, from the dark waves that were gathered in a messy knot. From his bat-like wings. His darkness reacted to her light, to the halo that surrounded her. The more she challenged him, the more restless his shadows became. And the fact that he sat on his knees wasn't entirely because she'd won this round. With those piercing grey eyes and the intense halo of solar light that surrounded her, she looked every bit a war goddess herself.

'Get up, blackbone.' Evalynn rested the tip of her Damast sword against his throat. *'We both know you can do better than this.'* Her accent was music to his ears, a melody he could never grow tired of even if it carried the worst insults to his kind with it.

The man lazily pushed the tip of the sword aside and stood to fully face her. He was taller, forcing Evalynn to look up, which she certainly didn't like. *'You saved those nymphs from Tarniq's wrath, brought them to Aestor. Why?'*

She blinked, then narrowed her eyes, keeping her sword ready to strike again. *'They were innocent.'* She couldn't look away from those pretty golden eyes. They drew her in deeper than any jewellery *ever had. She couldn't help but secretly admire him, the rugged grace in his features and casual beauty that still shone through the grime and dirt. No one had ever had that effect on her and she hated how curious it made her.*

'Yes, they were.' *His head cocked and the daemon regarded her curiously.* 'It didn't stop Lorcán and Tarniq, but it did stop you. Why?'

'They were burning draiad's roots and tearing the nymphs apart!' *she snapped. Then her face fell and her throat bobbed.* 'I am not a monster,' *she whispered in defeat.* 'I don't condone such behaviour.'

He reached out to touch her cheek but thought better of it. He'd seen her temper, the feral rage that often escaped when she fought. He feared touching her would result in an amputation and his friends would never let him hear the end of that.

'You tore out your commander's heart,' *the male said softly.*

'He tried to assault a defenceless anthousai.' *Her voice filled with bitterness.* 'It was a message and a warning to the rest.'

He nodded once, curiously regarding her while he felt a different sort of war rage inside of her. It ached to feel her hurt, to know she was struggling and fighting with her own strong moral compass. She had lost her faith in the Andulets but believed she had no choice but to remain at Lorcán's side. If she would betray them, she'd lose everything, especially her father's approval, which meant the world to her.

Evalynn scanned the ruins of the forest, the grey ashes and smouldering trees. 'Meryn didn't deserve her fate, and neither did those nymphs,' *she said with a hollow voice.*

The man touched her chin to guide her gaze back to him, which caught her off guard enough that she allowed him to do so. 'You're fighting a war for a man you don't believe in while cleaning up his messes.'

'Lorcán is my husband,' Evalynn said, shame etching into the words. 'My paladin. I'm bound to him in ways not even the gods understand. I can't betray him.'

'You don't even love him,' he said.

She had loved him. Desperately. Childishly. And it had starved her.

'Love is useless – merely a distraction,' she spat. She thought she'd known love and that it had surrounded her since birth, but these past months had made it abundantly clear she was nothing but a naïve fool. 'It's just another weapon others use to get something they want.'

He regarded her, again feeling that ache in her. The hollow loneliness. And how she was slowly realising that they only cared because she was useful. A weapon. Something meek and obedient that Lorcán could parade with. They'd groomed her for years so that she firmly believed she was nothing without their approval. And yet . . . Yael had taught her that she was so much more than every name they'd ever given her. They'd stomped down her flowers but Evalynn's roots were stubborn.

Something old stirred within Aloïs, tugging at his chest and seething at the knowledge that she was deeply unhappy and trapped inside a gilded cage. It didn't matter how prettily they covered up the bars, it was still a prison.

He saw flashes of memories; how Lorcán abused their bond, draining her to strengthen himself with no regard for her safety. How he returned late at night smelling of other women yet seethed at Evalynn if she even looked another man's way. How she worked herself into the ground to appease her stern father and gain his approval.

How Lorcán locked her inside their private chambers – to keep her safe like some rare trinket. How she wept and begged them to let her out. How he simply ignored her and left whenever she

113

suffered another debilitating migraine and was bedbound. And how he forbade the healers from giving her anything strong enough to counter the pain in case she was with child.

There were many ways to kill someone. The slowest and most painful way was not loving them enough, and it appeared Lorcán was a seasoned killer in every sense of the word.

He wanted to tear him apart. No, he wanted to watch Eva tear him apart.

'If you keep this up, you'll help him kill thousands of innocents,' *he said.* 'And besides that . . . he killed Yael, Evalynn.'

She knew damn well Lorcán hadn't done that. He'd told her that it'd been Eiran. 'I don't know who you think you are, beast, but I—'

'Aloïs Márzenas.'

Her face paled, her eyes widened as she took him in. This male who'd captured her attention, whose darkness called to her light. Who'd challenged her to come out of her shadows any time they'd clashed. And he was . . .

'Yes, *the Aloïs of mortal nightmares. Ruler of Hell, Lord of Shadows and Daemons.' He smirked at her as he crossed his arms, raising a single dark brow at her in amusement.* 'But you, little sun, may simply call me Aloïs.'

Illuminated by faint candlelight, Eva relished in the soft rise and fall of Aloïs' chest as her head rested on it. His velvety soft wing draped over her naked body to keep her warm and his arm loosely curled around her, his hand resting on Yael's marking on her back.

Her fingers traced the black whorls and swirls her dyad carried on his tan skin, ones he shared with his close friends. And the sun with solar flames she'd painted on his right pec mere hours ago. She brushed her fingers over the marking he'd placed on her right collarbone. Swirls of darkness to mimic his shadows. A smile crept on her lips, feeling nothing but pure happiness. Like shyly blooming freedom.

Eva loved him. She loved the friends she'd made here. She loved his people, who weren't the monsters she'd been taught they were. Here, she was surrounded by people who genuinely cared, who didn't dress her up in pretty clothes and perfect make-up, who didn't dictate her diet, who didn't scold her for disagreeing on something. They didn't lock her up in her chambers for her own protection.

No, her friends pulled her right into the daylight where she could breathe and thrive again.

Aloïs had introduced her to Dáneiris, Yael's mother, and she'd helped Eva process her grief. She'd spent entire evenings chatting to her, learning about Yael's daemonic roots. Finally she was able to express how dearly she'd loved Yael without being silenced.

And Antheia . . . Eva still remembered how the goddess had soothed her as a little girl, when she'd been terrified of the dark but her parents refused to leave any lights on. And weeks ago, when she'd taken Eva's hand and helped her look in the mirror. Because she finally recognised her reflection.

She lifted her head and gently stroked Aloïs' cheek to wake him up. When her mate blinked the sleep from his eyes, she smiled at him. Tears lined her eyes, for with her decision came a feeling of pure elation. The weight of the world lifted off her shoulders and the shackles around her limbs seemed to finally disappear.

'I want to stay,' she whispered to him.

Lorcán was convinced that Antheia had broken Eva to get revenge on him and when she'd used that twisted obsession to return to spy on them, Lorcán had been eager enough to believe her pretty smiles and empty promises of love and devotion.

They believed they'd let in a meek little dove but the roaring lion that had torn their camp apart from the inside out, burning with *wildfire, wasn't something they'd expected.*

Lorcán had spent weeks searching for his docile wife but brought home a rabid banshee instead.

Gods and daemons had always walked a fine line between allies and enemies. To appease Aloïs and to reward Eva for her grand role in helping to defeat the Andulets, as well as protect and avenge all sorts of nymphs, Eiran took her to Ascredia to bless her with true immortality.

When Eva emerged anew from the silver waters in Ascredia with her skin and blonde hair aflame, she emerged as a *vyrenera* – a fire nymph. The first of her kind.

The flames died down until Aloïs could behold his dyad. The arched ears. The aura of orange feathers that spread out behind her like a *fyrebird's*. The flames that intertwined with the branches of her silver crown. The embers that smouldered in her wake as she stepped out of the glowing pond.

Though Eiran had aimed to only make her a dainty flower nymph, Eva had demanded her due and Ascredia had gladly given it.

Queen of Hell.

Queen of Nymphs.

And with Eva's rebirth, her paladin bond with Lorcán broke.

'What the Hell do you want?' Eva spat at him, rattling the iron chains he'd fastened her with. Cursing the moonsbane he'd forced into her system when he'd tricked her and the power she'd lost because of it. She knew Aloïs was desperate to find a way towards them but Lorcán had found a way to close off Aspia. He'd forsaken all gods, only allowing Dýs to receive his dead.

Lorcán's grin promised nothing good. 'There is a lot I want, my darling Evalynn.'

'I don't have the patience to deal with your games.'

'I suggest you calm down.' Slowly, he walked over to her. 'Because I don't have the patience to deal with your horrible temper and lack of manners. It's obvious you've been frolicking around with beasts.'

Eva glared at him but kept her mouth closed. Lorcán knew she was holding back, and the reason why. He reached her, crouching down next to her to rest his hand on her belly. She tried hard not to flinch, though she sensed Faelyn didn't like him so close. She'd been scared these past weeks – and worried about her mother. Eva continuously tried to soothe the little thing by sending images of the plushies from home and memories of a smiling Aloïs down that little bond they shared but it no longer calmed her down.

'You were mine – supposed to carry my child, not that beast's.' She didn't trust herself to speak. 'You were my family.'

He'd been her family as well, someone she'd believed to have loved her. But that obsession he had with her wasn't love. It was just that need of his to own anything and everything he wanted and if he couldn't have it, then no one could. She'd loved Lorcán once but that felt like another lifetime now. Too much had happened between them to ever go back to the close friends they'd once been.

'You were the love of my life,' he muttered.

'Do you usually chain the love of your life to a wall in your dungeon?' Eva spat at him. 'That's not love, Lorcán.'

Lorcán only stared at her, his hand on her abdomen closing into a tight fist. 'You destroyed my family with those beasts. You killed my mother.' Because when Morgane had come close to killing Aloïs, Eva had ripped her heart out and burned her to ashes.

'You took everything from me.' There was a hollowness to him, like Eiran's Divine Punishment at the end of the War had broken whatever had been left of his soul. 'Allow me to return that favour.'

The midwife stared in fear at the little babe. Tiny, almost black wings were attached to her back. She was smaller than a mortal babe, with soft blonde hair growing from her little head. Her equally tiny shadows were wrapped around her little legs to stay with her. They would tether in the days to come, but right now they were too small to do anything meaningful.

She didn't like being held by the midwife, calling out for her mother. Desperate to feel her gentle touch. Hearing her child call out for her had the same effect on her as it would've had on her dyad. Eva was desperate to get to Faelyn, to keep her safe and sound. To soothe her panic.

'Please.' Eva's voice was weak, coming from the bed they'd fastened her to. She'd lost too much blood and was still losing blood. 'Please, let me hold her.'

Lorcán studied the child with a strange gleam in his eyes. A výssar, so rare and yet so powerful. And this one would carry power unlike anyone had ever seen before. Perhaps he could tame that power and use it. She could serve Her.

Eva sobbed. 'Please, Lorcán.' Her child. He would hurt her helpless child.

He walked over to the midwife, taking the pup over before dismissing her. 'I heard a rumour,' Lorcán started, rocking the pup up and down. 'That their wings are extremely sensitive.' Eva said nothing, couldn't tear her eyes away from her daughter. 'I wonder if it's true,' he mused. 'Maybe I should test it for myself.'

The sound of the wing tearing made her nauseous. In his arms, the pup cried out in pain, whimpering and trying her hardest to get away from him. He only chuckled.

'You fucking bastard!' Eva cried, desperately fighting the shackles around her limbs.

'Sensitive indeed.' His eyes shot to her as he did the same to the other wing. Lorcán wanted to see the pain in her eyes, the

desperation on her face. She'd betrayed him, had taken his family from him and he would take hers. He would make her watch how he hurt her child.

The pup wailed, little arms flailing around in an attempt to protect herself.

'Such a little fighter. Feisty like her mother.'

'Lorcán!' Eva sobbed. 'Please, let her go. She doesn't deserve this, she doesn't have anything to do with this!' Her vision darkened. She was still losing too much blood, even with Eiran's blessing.

Lorcán smirked at her, still rocking the pup like he cared.

'He'll find her,' she warned him. 'He'll make you pay.'

'And I'll gladly greet that blackbone with Stygian iron for forcing himself on my wife. I'll make him beg for death.' Lorcán sneered at her. 'I have nothing to lose here, yet he's losing everything.'

'He loves me!' she bit out. By the Mother, she loathed him.

Lorcán snorted. 'Of course he does, darling.' He summoned a dagger out of thin air, never taking his eyes off her child.

Eva's blood froze over. 'Please,' she whispered. 'Please, don't hurt her.'

'You don't want me to hurt her like you hurt me?'

Eva's gaze slipped to the scars on his arms she'd left behind during their last fight. She tried to bite back her tears, hated how pathetic she sounded and felt. 'Please.'

'Okay, I won't.' He tilted his head, frowning at her. 'I'm not a monster.'

Drawing in a shuddering breath, some relief soothed her. Maybe there was still a hint of light in him – that boy from her childhood. The boy who'd convinced her parents to let her attend Vadones with him because he'd miss her, who'd made her smile whenever she'd felt sad by making a fool of himself. The bright and charismatic boy he'd been before the Andulets had corrupted him.

Yet all that hope bled out of her the same way the life bled out of her daughter as Lorcán made Eva watch over and over again how he hurt her child. Until Eva's voice went hoarse from screaming and begging. Until that fragile bond with her daughter broke.

Lorcán threw the dagger aside on the table, finally looking at Eva with empty eyes. He paid no attention to the silent and motionless babe on the table, even though Eva's eyes couldn't leave it.

There were no words. She couldn't breathe, couldn't think. The pain was unbearable, couldn't be real. She'd been so small, so godsdamned small and he . . . without a hesitation . . . he'd . . .

He picked up the dagger, wiping the black blood off of his shirt as he made his way over to Eva. 'I told you I would return the favour.'

Her vision had already gone black before his dagger slit her throat.

Chapter 9

Lorcán

Aspia, the Royal House of Odalis
1764, 24 years after the War of Ichor

Lorcán looked out of the stained-glass windows of his office, his arms crossed while he studied the two figures playing in the courtyard. These past weeks, his weapon had been refusing to cooperate and execute his orders and the root of all those problems fluttered through the garden along with her, hurling snowballs at her lover. His weapon was slipping away between his clenched fingers, yet any time he asked Kaelena about his weapon's troubles, she assured him that Aedlynn showed no disloyalty.

Lorcán gritted his teeth. He'd convinced himself that he didn't blindly trust Kaelena, that he'd gone through enough betrayals to know better, but feeling Aedlynn slipping back into the light and knowing that it was *Kaelena's* doing, that his nymph lied to his face . . . The pain was almost as unbearable as it had been when Sorin and Evalynn had betrayed him.

Yet he'd been here before, and as much as it hurt, he'd long decided love was only a weakness. Sorin had cast him away the moment Lorcán had started to speak up and the woman he'd loved had become a willing whore for a beast.

They'd reduced her to some eager nymph for that King and Antheia had apparently gone as far as making her *look* like a nymph as well with those ridiculous arched ears. A stamp and claim, a final blow that his once proud wife had become nothing more than a beast's plaything. And she'd carried its *child* – had been proud of it. She'd *loved* it and begged for its life with no regard for her own.

And she'd helped bring down his family and nearly half of his army.

His lip quirked up. If there really was an Afterworld, he hoped the bitch had watched him torture that little beast of hers. How she'd cried and tried to protect herself with those pathetic little shadows, how she still called out to Evalynn months after her death.

There had been moments where even Lorcán had felt sorry for the little thing, though those moments had been rare. He'd poisoned her, torn the dark membrane of her wings to shreds, broken every single bone in those delicate wings. He wondered how he could heal them when the time finally came to lure Avaleen to his side. He'd quickly sealed the still-bleeding wings away when Zale had arrived.

Lorcán focused his attention back on the girls outside, where Kaelena had pushed Aedlynn into a heap of fluffy snow. Aedlynn quickly pulled her down with her, grinning with mischief before she kissed her.

The time neared to do some damage control, to regain the tight hold he'd once had.

Lorcán walked into the living quarters of the wing where those of his Cadre resided. Aedlynn had been sitting upside down on the couch while reading – like she often did – but scrambled up when she noticed the intense gaze, quickly realising something was wrong.

'Kaelena is in the infirmary. She's alive but our healers will need time to fully heal her wounds.'

Her face paled. She'd never allowed anyone to see her emotions – only Lena – but she couldn't hide the panic in her eyes. Aedlynn was already trying to get past him to make her way over there, to tend to her, but Lorcán pushed her back, one hand tightly wrapped around her arm.

'What happened?' Her voice quivered. 'Who hurt her?'

'Isolde.' Cold fury spread over her features; she was ready to tear that bitch apart. 'You are to come with me.'

'But—' Aedlynn started to pull her arm free.

'Aedlynn.' He narrowed his eyes, regaining his grip on the *kalotra* he'd used on her. *'Behave.'*

Aedlynn

Lorcán took his place in the leather chair behind the desk, intertwining his fingers while he rested his elbows on the dark wooden desk. His violet eyes burned into Aedlynn, making her feel as if his study was much smaller than it really was. The intensity burned up all the oxygen in the room, suffocating her.

'What I'm about to discuss with you will stay between us. If I find out that you shared this sensitive information with anyone, I'll have you whipped until you forget your own name.'

Aedlynn stared at him, completely caught off guard by the threat. 'Okay,' she said quietly, hoping that her voice sounded more stable to him than it did to her own ears.

Gods, she wanted nothing more than to run to Lena, to see her and to take care of her. She wanted to tear Isolde apart for hurting her.

'Swear it to me,' he said, holding her gaze. 'On the Netha, if you will.'

She swallowed. Vows on the renowned river in Aerelia were serious business. Breaking such a vow led to a cursed existence. But Aedlynn trusted him enough to take the risk, knowing that whatever he wished to discuss deserved the secrecy surrounding it.

So Aedlynn vowed it.

Lorcán nodded once, and the thunder rumbled in the grey clouds that had been hovering over the castle for a week already. It'd barely stopped raining these past days. He gestured at the chair in front of the mahogany desk and she plopped down onto the upholstered chair, impatiently drumming her fingers on her knees.

Lorcán deeply sighed and dropped his gaze to the pen he was fumbling with. 'I'm certain Kaelena has told you plenty about Isolde's fickle temper. Not many dare stand up to their queen, fearing the repercussions for doing so. There is but one who never bent under Isolde's threats, who remains loyal and continues to serve me with rare devotion.

'Isolde frequently comments on my nymph's presence, even when her attention isn't directed at me. I always brushed it off as envy or insecurity but she has become paranoid and refuses to see rhyme nor reason.' Lorcán rubbed his eyes with his hand. 'And now she's taken it upon herself to send Kaelena another warning.'

Aedlynn knew the moment Lorcán was done, she'd find the nearest entrance to Hell to hand Isolde off to Aloïs. Tied together with a neat little bow. 'Kaelena is family to me. If

I continue to allow Isolde to do as she pleases, I'll fail her both as her king and her friend.'

Aedlynn cocked her head. It was strange to see for herself just how fixated Lorcán was on her dyad. Given Lena's stories about his jealousy, she wondered if the king was still in love with her, though the thought made her feel icky. Not because of jealousy – she knew Lena adored her – but because she didn't like how Lorcán had taken his time to groom a young impressionable girl into worshipping him and craving his approval. It nauseated her.

Something in his eyes hardened while he watched her, though it disappeared so quickly that Aedlynn convinced herself she'd imagined it. 'My queen was supposed to be someone who would help return glory to our country after the War. Someone who could show our people that there is still light and life ahead of them. Isolde doesn't do that. She bullies our people. Gets rid of servants when they cannot afford to lose their income and then prances around with jewellery,' he said. 'I could forgive her for being barren were it not for the fact that she knew she was infertile before we agreed on the marriage, before she had it written down that she would rule in my stead should I perish before her without any heirs to take my place.' His lip curled down in disdain. 'I consider myself cunning and ambitious but that woman didn't ask to share the crown. She made sure she could take it for herself.'

Aedlynn gaped at him. Isolde would be no consort but a true queen if he died.

Lorcán nodded when he noticed her shock. 'I was ill last week, was I not?'

She nodded. He'd retreated to his private chambers, claiming to have caught a seasonal flu. Given the weather and that Lorcán still tended to his mares with great care even in the rain, no one had questioned it.

'I was poisoned,' he said matter-of-factly.

Fucking Fates. 'She . . . she tried to kill you?'

He nodded again. 'Had my healer not made the antidote for me, she would've succeeded.' Lorcán rested his chin on his clasped hands. 'My wife turned against me as if it were nothing, and given the threat of Kaelena – of her *fertility* . . . I fear it will only be a matter of time before she makes another attempt on her life.'

The thought of losing Lena made Aedlynn feel like someone was tearing at her very soul, removing a part of it with a rusty serrated knife. Lorcán spoke so quietly that she barely heard him. 'I want Isolde removed.'

Aedlynn stared at him while the pieces started to fall into place. If she'd been a better person, she might've refused to kill a queen, but not when she'd hurt and still threatened her dyad. She had a feeling Lorcán knew that. Lena could calm her raging storms with a kiss or a hug, but the very idea of her getting hurt was enough to set Aedlynn's blood on fire. Enough to tear at that golden thread that connected them.

She'd begun to see more of those threads, floating around and encircling the people they belonged to. Some were thick or thin, and silver, and she suspected them to be *Výsae* – lifelines. Those were spun by the Æther at the beginning of one's life. Some were golden and connected two people by wrapping around their ring fingers, though she'd seen those only once before when Aedonis had visited Lorcán with his dyad. She'd thought that maybe they connected lovers, but there were plenty of those within the House and none had golden ribbons. Only Aedonis and Nascha did, and Lena and Aedlynn.

'You want me to kill her?'

'Yes,' he said.

'They will ask questions—'

'You'll make sure that they won't.' Lorcán opened the top drawer of his desk and took out a thick, dark green, leather-bound tome decorated with swirling silver vines. He laid it open, tapping the drawing at the top, a transfiguration circle made of thorns and serpents, and written instructions. Aedlynn leaned forward and tried to read it but had a horrible time deciphering the text. She loved reading but always had a hard time doing so because the letters kept moving. Reading in a rush never made it easier and her anxiety made the letters swim right now. The calligraphy seemed to hate her as well, since all the b's and p's were far too similar. So she glanced back up at Lorcán in silent question.

'Yael Eléazar was best known for devoting her time to studying alchemy. She's the one who figured out how to do it without lethal repercussions, but Yael did far more than just that.' He tapped the circle on the yellowed page. 'Yael studied the Æther and Primals; Ellowyn, Eiran and Elyon.'

She blinked, scratching her temple. She'd never heard of Primals, though she knew about Ellowyn, Eiran and Elyon. Everyone did. 'Everyone needs a hobby, I guess.'

He smiled thinly. 'The Primals made our universe, the realms and creatures that roam those very realms. For now, you need only remember that Elyon is the Primal of Chaos – hell-bent on toppling the universe into chaos and destroying Eiran. He's subdued for now but . . .' He tapped the circle again. 'Yael attempted to stir him from that slumber.'

She cocked her head. 'Sounds like a bad idea.'

'It was – nearly killed her.' He closed the book. 'The

demiagi in my Cadre will recognise her symbols – her work, when they find Isolde.'

'You want to make it look like Isolde attempted to awaken Elyon?'

'Yes, it will brand her as a madwoman. I will draw the symbols in the library in the tower to make sure they're right. You will do the rest.' His smile grew cruel. 'Do not hold back, little viper. Make it look like magic gone wrong.'

There was no bone or muscle in Isolde that knew any self-defence. She'd made her guards do all the work when it came to Kaelena, so when Aedlynn æriated to Isolde's room that night and grabbed her loose dark tresses, pulling her firmly backwards, she easily fell. Before she could sound the alarm, Aedlynn had already pulled them to the small and dusty library.

'You little bitch!' Isolde spat, her dark eyes blazing with hatred as she tried to grab Aedlynn behind her. But Aedlynn tied her arms to her back with the silver ribbon of her own *Výsa*.

Almost in a daze, Aedlynn reached for that ribbon, enjoying how familiar and powerful that felt. Her free fingers moved as if she were gathering threads of wool to knit with. Instinct overtook and when she found a grip on Isolde's *Výsa*, she wrapped it around Isolde's throat to choke her with it. Isolde's fingers clutched at her throat but she couldn't feel the lifeline, only her nearing death.

When she started to sag to her knees, Aedlynn was overtaken by a strange haze filled with infinitely echoing and coaxing whispers, and she made a cutting motion with her pointer and middle finger over the ribbon. A loud *snip* echoed through the deserted room.

She blinked rapidly as the daze ebbed away again.

Make it look like magic gone wrong.

So Aedlynn set to work.

'Wake up!'

Aedlynn shot upright, her hands instinctively smoothing over Lena's arms and back. 'Are you okay?'

'Isolde is dead,' Kaelena said, eyes wide with disbelief. 'I overheard the healers. Something about her trying to resurrect an ancient evil – some ritual that killed her.' Kaelena tightened the blanket around her. The bruises and cuts on her face had disappeared. Even the wounds and bruises on her back were gone. 'I mean, I never liked the bitch, but this? Forsaken gods, I knew she'd gone to Vadones and knew some magic but I never knew she was *that* powerful. She could've destroyed the entire world!'

Subtly, Aedlynn exhaled. Then she pulled Lena closer and rubbed her back. Aedlynn rested her cheek on Lena's hair while she held her, until Lena grew calmer.

Lena glanced up to study her through her lashes. 'You're awfully quiet.'

Aedlynn shrugged. She felt absolutely horrible for keeping this from her – for lying. Lena knew what she was, what Lorcán often made her do, but this was different. She'd killed a queen, and as much as Aedlynn kept telling herself she'd done it on Lorcán's orders, she'd done it to protect Lena. Because as time went on . . . Lorcán's orders didn't mean as much as they once did. But Lena's regard of her meant the world. She was a weapon to Lorcán, but she was simply Aedlynn to Lena.

There was also the little detail of her vow on the Netha.

'I was always taught that if I have nothing nice to say, I should keep silent.'

Kaelena grinned. 'I think even you would feel bad for her if you'd seen the carnage. It wasn't pretty.'

Aedlynn chewed on her lip. 'You . . . you saw her?'

Kaelena nodded. 'I sneaked in, wanted to see for myself what was going on because Nadir wouldn't tell me anything. Those *demiagi* sure love their secrets.'

Aedlynn brushed some hair behind Kaelena's ear. 'Are you okay?'

She shrugged and averted her eyes, and Aedlynn's heart dropped in her chest. 'She had cuts all over her body, her blood was quite literally everywhere. Her limbs just lay in such unnatural angles, as if that . . . *thing* had broken every single bone in her body.' She shuddered. 'And her heart had been torn out.'

Aedlynn stared at her. 'Her . . . heart?'

Kaelena nodded. 'It lay in the middle of whatever that circle was, like charcoal. Still smoking when I came to look. It was strange to see her like that . . .' Kaelena brushed a strand of loose hair behind her ear. 'It was like only . . . the shell . . . of her body had been left. I barely recognised her.'

Aedlynn hadn't touched Isolde's heart.

A horrible, horrible feeling swept over her.

Hell-bent on toppling the universe into chaos and destroying Eiran.

Was he not an *Aurealis* himself? He'd been trained by Aeneas, Yael's husband. Perhaps they'd been close enough to have her personal notes on transfiguration and rituals. He also had a vendetta against Eiran.

Magic gone wrong.

Maybe it hadn't gone wrong but exactly as planned.

Servants had cleaned the room, though the circle seemed hard to wipe off the dark wooden flooring. In the middle of the thorned circle there was a burnt mark of a slithering serpent flanked by two horns.

Aedlynn didn't like being in the room. The air was thick with something and a sickly-sweet perfume she couldn't place washed over her – as if to hide a rotten smell. Whatever magic had been used here would've been dark and twisted enough to corrupt even the purest heart or soul.

She wasn't keen on getting any closer. Her entire instinct roared in her ears to get out of that room.

'Good morning, Aedlynn.'

She turned to see Lorcán leaning in the doorway with his arms crossed. She grabbed a thick book from the nearest shelf and threw it at him. 'You tricked me!'

He caught the book. 'Calm yourself, Aedlynn.'

'What did you do?!' She pointed at the circle. 'I didn't touch her heart.'

'I will tell you if you tell me how you killed her without touching her.'

Aedlynn blinked. She'd forgotten all about that but she really didn't want to tell him about the *Výsae*. He'd only find another way to use it to his advantage. To make her even more of a weapon.

He simply held her gaze while a jasmine perfume crawled into her nose, loosening up her tongue until she couldn't stop herself from spilling, 'I see *Výsae*.'

Lorcán nodded. His eyes glinted with excitement. 'Tell me more, viper.'

Aedlynn opened and closed her mouth in an attempt to keep the words from tumbling out, but the stronger that scent grew, the more she reeled at the thought of keeping secrets from her king. 'I see them like threads that surround people or connect them to others. Mostly silver, though I've also seen golden ones. I've only ever seen those golden *Výsae* between Aedonis and Nascha, and—' Aedlynn bit her tongue before she could tell him about Lena.

Lorcán's grin grew. 'Thank you for telling me, my sweet.'

Aedlynn stared at him in stunned silence while her heartbeat thundered in her throat and ears, wondering how she'd suddenly been so quick and eager to share that information with him. Something seemed to have clouded her judgement. Was he using compulsion on her? Had he done that before?

'How did you kill Isolde? Did you use her *Výsa* to do so?'

She chewed on her lip and nodded. 'I . . . I cut it.'

His eyes gleamed dangerously. 'You *cut* her *Výsa*?'

'Yes,' Aedlynn breathed.

Lorcán's lips parted in a wicked grin. 'We will train this new skill of yours, starting today. Tomorrow, we leave for Aysel. I will continue your training there in private.'

She swallowed, then glanced at the circle. 'So . . . nothing happened?'

'Nothing happened, my darling.' Lorcán approached her. 'But you did *wonderfully*,' he said while he cupped her face and kissed her forehead.

Aedlynn's head rested on Kaelena's chest while she caressed Aedlynn's hair. The sweet and sultry smell of the wildflowers around them helped her forget what she'd done the night before. It helped her forget about the things Lorcán would continue to ask of her, certainly now that he knew about her ability to see *Výsae*. The wildflowers and tall grass tickled their arms and legs, while the night sky encompassed them. Dark as ever, only broken up by the little lanterns they'd taken with them.

'I have a present for you.'

Aedlynn lifted her head and softly smiled at her. 'You do?'

Kaelena nodded and Aedlynn's heart skipped a beat when her cheeks flushed. 'I have been training my magic for some months now and I've . . .' She smiled sweetly. 'I made something for you.'

Aedlynn sat up, figuring she'd made another flower crown or necklace, since Lena had been training the curious effects she had on the nature around her. Instead, she kissed her brow and pointed up.

When Aedlynn looked up, a sob tore through her.

A star. Bright and grand.

Kaelena chuckled and started wiping the tears away. 'I wanted to gift you an entire sky full of them but I could only manage one.'

'You gave me a *star?*' Aedlynn sobbed. 'A *star?!*'

Lena laughed softly and nestled her head in the hollow of Aedlynn's shoulder, wrapping both of her arms around her. 'Yes, *ná'dýra*. It's all yours.'

'A fucking *star,*' she whispered in disbelief, unable to tear her eyes away from the night sky.

'Only Lord Keres can say he received entire constellations and the aurora from his dyad. But now you can go and brag that your dyad gave you a star as well.'

'I can't even begin to tell you how much I love it.' Aedlynn took her hand in hers and planted a kiss on the back of it, then trailed kisses from her hand up her wrist and arm until eventually, their lips found each other. 'Gods, I love you.'

Aedlynn kissed the corner of her mouth. 'I found something out.'

'Hmmm?' Kaelena mused with her eyes closed while Aedlynn softly pecked her lips, which were curled into a content smile. It might've been night around them, but the warmth she felt blooming inside of her chest felt like the sun shone within her heart.

'I can see *Výsae*, and apparently, I can also see dyad bonds.'

The expression on Kaelena's face grew sad as she averted her eyes and looked down at their linked hands. 'Lorcán found out, didn't he?' she whispered. 'That's why he's taking you away.'

'Yes.'

Lena let go of her hands and instead cupped her face, resting her forehead against hers. 'You are no weapon and you are no monster. You have such a light in you, Aedlynn, that it often blinds me,' she said softly. 'You carry such love and loyalty with you, such a tenderness that I often fear I will melt when you look at me and I am honoured – *honoured* – to be your dyad.'

Aedlynn's bottom lip quivered, and as Kaelena pulled away to look at her, she couldn't stop herself from crying. Lena continued to wipe her tears away and kiss her nose and forehead. 'I thank the Mother every day for you.'

Aedlynn sobbed, uncertain what to do with herself. She loved her. She knew she could never love anyone else. They'd been together for a year, yet every day with Kaelena felt like a gift. So while she slowly managed to compose herself, Aedlynn whispered against her shoulder, 'Gods, I want to marry you.'

'I'd marry you right now.' That playful grin curled her lips. 'But I want you to properly ask me.'

Aedlynn smiled at Lena through her tears while she pulled some little flowers free from the dirt and wove them around Lena's ring finger. 'Would you marry me, *ná'dýra?* Right this moment? You are my light in the darkness, the first place and person that's ever felt like home. Even if you wouldn't marry me, I'd spend the rest of my life worshipping you, with your name etched into my soul.'

Lena's features grew soft. 'That might be the sweetest and most romantic thing anyone has ever said to me. That actually came dangerously close to poetry.'

Aedlynn tossed her hair behind her shoulder, spilling daisies and buttercups everywhere, and shot Kaelena her most radiant smile. 'I still have hidden talents, even from you.'

Kaelena chuckled, then kissed her nose. 'I adore you, *Nyará.*' *Nyará* – home.

Aedlynn's soul grew quiet when she looked at her then. 'Even if all the stars would return to the sky,' Aedlynn said to her, 'they could never shine as bright as my love for you.'

Aedlynn still felt the silk ribbon around her right hand, even hours later when they lay in bed. The lovely weight of the vows they'd spoken while the priestess in Aletheia had hand-fastened them still warmed her chest.

Kaelena had gifted Aedlynn her favourite golden ring; intertwining flowers that matched the crowns and bracelets she'd woven for her, the centres made up of colourful gemstones. Aedlynn had given her a silver moonstone ring.

Aedlynn glanced down at her dyad – her wife, curled up to her while she soundly slept. Kaelena's heartbeat echoed her own, her laughter reverberated through Aedlynn's soul. And as wicked as it'd once been . . . it now shone with warm daylight, the promise of more – of a different life. One where Aedlynn was no weapon, where Lena didn't have to uphold her image of being Lorcán's courtesan.

She decided that whatever Lorcán would make her do in Aysel, Aedlynn would bear it. And when Aedlynn returned, they would leave. She would get Kaelena far away from here, far removed from Lorcán's clutches. She was good and kind, a star in a sky full of darkness. A daisy in an ash-ridden field. And Aedlynn would plant her somewhere where she could bathe in the sunlight and grow, wherever that may be.

Chapter 10

Diana

Ascredia, East of Aerelia
Present day

Every single ache in my body had disappeared.

I felt light, so light I could float.

A lovely scent made itself known to me, grabbing my attention and anchoring me to the present. It reminded me of a meadow in full bloom, the scent travelling on a warm breeze. It was soothing; the first warmth after a harsh winter. Keres' scent.

I was surrounded by my shadows. They'd draped themselves over the stone and roots, still dazed from their captivity. They were content being out, gliding across the water. Some curled around my waist and fingers, trying to comfort me.

'Are you okay, *aediore?*' Aestor asked me.

'I remember,' I whispered, my head resting against his shoulder. Too emotional to realise I was holding onto the Second God of my myths. 'Eva and Aloïs – my parents. Lorcán, what he did. He . . . he just . . . *killed* her,' I sobbed.

Carefully, Aestor rubbed my back and hair. It took me a moment to realise why.

I had wings.

They were similar to my father's, although they were horribly broken, still carrying tears in the membrane that had never healed. Jagged silver scars ran along them, proof of the torture Lorcán had put me through. They hung crooked, one dipped in the cold water of the pond and I couldn't lift them, couldn't neatly tuck them behind me like I'd seen my father do.

I had *wings*.

Aestor hated seeing the damage Lorcán had done to them. His power meant that when he viewed wounds, he knew exactly what had happened for them to come to exist, so he saw what Lorcán had done, over and over. His heart strained for me, for what I'd been through. *Aestor* was my *godfather*.

He brushed my hair. 'Lorcán didn't know about Eiran's blessing, that she became a nymph. He truly must've thought the arched ears were Antheia's doing. Whatever weapon he used wounded her but didn't kill her.' Tears welled up and blurred my vision. It was an effort not to sag to my knees, both from the overwhelming emotions and my exhaustion – and the realisation of what he was implying. 'Aloïs left for her – to prepare her.'

I whimpered. 'She . . . she survived?'

Aestor nodded, smiling at me, though there was a hint of sadness. 'We all believed you to be gone.'

Keres rested his hand on my shoulder. 'Pups are terribly fragile. They can be killed by any sort of weapon.' He chuckled softly. 'I want to see the look on her face when she sees you.'

The noise that came from me was a mix of a sob and a laugh.

She was *alive*.

'I'll look at your wings when you're home, though I've removed the ache from the broken bones for now.' Aestor tore his gaze from the scars back to me. 'One thing at a time. Let's get you home first.'

Although my heart had been fluttering around in my chest like a frightened bird when Aestor had taken my hand to æriate us, that nervousness instantly melted away when we appeared in the grand hall and I found myself face-to-face with my parents standing some feet away. My father's arm was still around Eva to steady her, black streaks of mascara tainted her cheeks as she stared at me in a way that made my heart ache.

She feared that this was a cruel joke and that I would slip through her fingers again. That this would turn out to be just another dream she'd lost herself in, and she'd inevitably wake up with that gaping wound in her soul cracked wide open and bleeding all over again.

I opened and closed my mouth, uncertain of what to say and struggling to compose myself.

Aloïs' hand moved from her shoulder to her lower back, as if softly urging her to step forward, but she remained paralysed in place. Something about the fragility of the scene made *me* move.

Slowly, I reached out a hand, as if to make sure they were real as well. My shadows curled around my calves, but also restlessly slithered over the floor. Too shy to approach them yet.

'Mom?' I whispered, blinking back the burning of my eyes.

Her eyes widened. Grey eyes so similar to mine.

She took one step. Then another, and then ran to close

the distance between us, to wrap me up in her arms, that little bond between us snapping back into place now that Lorcán's magic was finally gone.

I startled when Aloïs appeared right next to us, stepping out of my shadows. He communicated with my *varkradas*, and they showed him some of my memories, told him most of what had happened to me. Silent tears streamed down his face while he cupped mine. 'My sweet little Faelyn,' he whispered, resting his forehead against mine. 'You're alive.'

Eva sobbed, 'My baby.' The fragile sound was enough to annihilate any composure I'd managed until now and I broke down crying. Aloïs pulled us close to him.

'You're safe now,' he whispered through thick tears, kissing my hair. 'We're here.'

'You're *alive*.' Eva's voice broke more and more with every word she spoke. 'By the Mother, look at *you*,' she sobbed while she brushed some of my tears away, her smile coming out like the sun might break up a storm. 'You've grown a little.'

I chuckled through a sob, leaning my cheek against her warm hand. 'Only a little.'

Drawing in a shuddering breath, I tried to calm myself by glancing around the magnificent grand room of black marble and midnight blue walls, accented with silver details. Richly coloured chiffon curtains decorated the many windows and arches of the throne room. Beautiful crystals that were fastened to the windows with silk ribbons reflected the moonlight and showered the room in a kaleidoscope of colours.

The entire place seemed to be a romantic dedication to the night sky, with the dark blue hues and shimmering silver that reminded me of stars. Or what they might've looked like. Though two years ago, one single star had entered our night sky.

'If I had known . . .' The look on my father's face was one of pain. 'If we'd had even the smallest hope that you . . . I would've . . . We would've come for you.'

'I know,' I whispered.

His *varkradas* settled around me, curled around my legs the same way mine had wrapped themselves around my parents'. They were excited to meet each other.

My mother gently pulled me out of his embrace and into hers, tightly wrapping her arms around me while she wove her fingers through my hair. Her scent reminded me of a summer evening; of the festival in Orthalla where we worshipped Zhella on Summer Solstice. I nestled my head in the hollow of her shoulder, enjoying the warmth she provided. That glowing aura I'd seen in my vision still subtly surrounded her.

Eva whispered, 'I've missed you every day since I lost you.'

I clutched the fabric of her simple silk blouse while my tears soaked into it. 'I missed you,' I sobbed. 'Even if I didn't know who you were − I missed you both *so* much. And I was so . . . so *worried* about you.'

'I know,' she whispered against my hair. 'You've been so brave and strong, sweetheart.'

I stifled another sob when I registered her words. I felt like a fraud; I had not been brave nor strong. I'd been a cowering, naïve and stupid girl, especially with Kallias. I didn't deserve such recognition.

'I kept wondering if I had any siblings, if Lorcán had got his hands on them as well.' I swallowed hard, still holding onto her. 'I didn't know what he'd done to my family.'

Eva gently brushed a hand through my hair. 'He dumped my presumed-dead body just over the border for your father to find. It took me weeks to physically heal but I couldn't . . .' Her voice broke again. 'I couldn't let you go, honey. I couldn't try again. It felt like . . . like I was somehow trying to replace you, yet you were in every single one of my dreams. I watched you grow up in them, held you close and dreaded waking up.' She sobbed, though my father was there to steady her.

My father rubbed the back of my neck with his thumb. 'That beast will come to regret what he did to my family.' He didn't raise his quiet voice, didn't need to. Even though his voice was soft and gentle as a summer night, there was a lethal edge to it.

My family. A cosy warmth spread through my chest at the words. I sensed that bond we shared, though it wasn't as strong and intimate as a dyad bond. They could simply sense my emotions.

Eva brushed some of my hair behind my ear and kissed my forehead. 'What happened to you, honey? Why did you need Keres?'

I rubbed my upper arm. 'Do you want the long or the short version?'

Eva smiled, caressing my cheeks again. 'The longest version you have.'

So I told them how Sorin and Zale had found out about Lorcán having me via a spy Sorin had caught, and how they'd tricked Lorcán and stolen me away into the night. How they had doted on me to the point where Zale had decided to keep me, made me his ward and raised me himself.

'The High Lords saved you?' Eva asked. 'Why didn't they tell Eiran?'

'They did but there was nothing special about me then.'

'Lorcán suppressed her entire nature – hid her wings and shadows, so she probably appeared to be utterly mundane,' Aloïs said to her. 'And Eiran didn't know we were expecting.'

'I grew up in Orthalla, almost always sick. No healing potion ever helped.' I took a deep breath. 'I've been incredibly sick before but it'd never been like it was recently. Zale and I went to Clacaster to visit Sorin, we went sparring outside. Sorin sneaked up on me and I somehow sent a shadow to push him onto the ground and I just . . . I felt drawn to it, longed to use it. Lorcán kept urging me to come to him, promising that he would give me my power back. He told me he would remove the *kalotra*, even claimed that he's my dyad.'

'Son of a bitch,' Eva spat. She cupped my face, studying every inch of it with worry. 'Did he touch you? Did he hurt you?'

I stared at her, furiously blinking to get rid of my tears. I wasn't used to motherly love and it was overwhelming to feel it through my shadows 'No,' I managed to bring out. I sensed her loathing, her fury that Lorcán had the audacity to trick her daughter like that. Like he hadn't done enough already. In an attempt to compose myself, I smiled sheepishly. 'I said I'd rip his balls out through his throat, carve his face off of his thick skull.'

Aestor grinned. 'She reminds me of a certain nymph.'

'Lorcán said that I was exactly like you,' I said to her. 'He seemed very caught off guard by that.'

'Good,' she said, pursing her lips and crossing her arms. 'Maybe that fucking asshole will think twice before bothering you next time, knowing you're too smart to fall for his manipulations.'

'I don't mean to insert my nose in someone else's business,' Aestor purred at Keres, 'but would you explain why my goddaughter carries your mark?'

'Ah, that.' Keres clicked his tongue and buried his hands in the pockets of his trousers. He'd cleaned up the *ichor* and dried his clothes. 'She wanted a little deal.'

'Elaborate,' Eva's voice was dangerously tight – like she was pulling the string back of a longbow.

Keres shrugged. 'She was a little desperate, offered to loyally serve me in return for my help, to devote herself to me. Like a nymph or a priestess.'

'And you *accepted* that?' Eva crossed her arms and shot him a stern look. Her grey eyes looked positively fierce and some stray flames woke up in her aura, dancing along her shoulders like those wings wanted to come out again.

'I didn't know who she was. I was convinced that she was mortal.'

'You made a deal with my daughter!'

Keres smiled apologetically. 'Oops.'

My mother looked like she wanted to tear him apart. 'Undo it. *Now.*'

Keres held her gaze evenly, all amusement gone. 'Eiran will wonder why I bothered to undo my deal with *your* daughter, when it's the perfect opportunity to gain some control in Hell. He'll already be interested because she's Aloïs' and because she's a *výssar*. Common sense will keep him away for now but if I remove that deal, he'll wonder why I made an exception for her – why she's so special.'

Aestor nodded absent-mindedly. 'Eiran will indeed wonder about her being a hybrid and the power that will come with it. The less concerned and threatened he is by her, the better.'

I looked from one to the other, curious about what their concern was for. This didn't sound like the chivalrous and kind Eiran I'd grown up worshipping. Aloïs met my gaze, sensing my confusion. 'We'll explain later, when you've had some rest.'

I nodded, sensing every single emotion, fragments of memories and thoughts through the shadows that slithered around me. They caressed my parents', Aestor's and Keres' shadows, communicating with them. Yet it didn't bother me, it felt more like I'd finally put on glasses after having a terrible vision all my life.

Eva glanced from me to Keres. 'What exactly is your deal?'

'She's to be my devoted priestess as well as serve me like a nymph during full and new moons. Basically, she's to be my ardent and zealous pet.'

Eva opened her mouth to protest but Keres cut in, meeting my gaze, 'I won't make you do anything you're uncomfortable with.'

Well, that was a nice change. An hour ago, I was certain he'd work me into the ground simply out of spite and for his own amusement. But he seemed to deeply respect my parents and that respect apparently extended to me.

I looked back at them. 'So . . . just so I'm up to speed, why is it a bad thing if Lord Eiran takes an interest in me?'

'Because Eiran has a habit of killing *výssars*, as he once killed his own halfgod son – the one Antheia adopted, and he despises daemons. Loathes me,' Aloïs told me. 'Eiran and Zhella don't encourage peace among our species. They forbid friendships and romantic relationships between gods and daemons – or nymphs and daemons. They're convinced we're impure, a blight on life. They like calling us "Ellowyn's mistakes".' Aloïs sighed. 'I've known Keres and Aestor for centuries, yet Eiran forbids them from being close with daemons. He claims it's an act of highest betrayal against their own kind. He even gave Keres Divine Punishments every time he sided with us during wars. Eiran finally believes that Keres is now his devoted puppy and has him spy on us for him. So if Keres lifts your deal, Eiran would know Keres lied to him.'

'If he believes you to be influential or dangerous, which you *are* simply because of your title and the small fact that you're a daemon *and* a nymph, Eiran will come for you,' Aestor said to me.

I nodded once. 'So I follow Lord Keres around like a puppy.'

Keres exchanged an amused look with Aestor, mouthing the word *lord* while he pointed his thumb at his chest. Aestor rolled his eyes in reply.

Aloïs scoffed. 'Eiran would adore it, seeing a daemon crawl for a god.'

Eva rubbed her face again. 'My pride doesn't agree with you having to lower yourself like that, but it would make sure that Eiran won't hurt either one of you. You wouldn't be a threat, just a silly nymph who knows her place.'

'Lord Eiran sounds like a true blessing to be around.'

Aloïs and Aestor snorted, both carrying a look as if to say *tell me about it.*

'If you're okay with it.' Keres pulled my attention back to him, his hands still buried in the pockets of his pants. 'A little ruse to fool Eiran.'

I shot him a feline grin. 'I'd love to fool the King of the Gods with you.'

Aestor's brows rose. 'By the Æther, chaotic tendencies really run in the family, huh?'

'You should've got used to that by now,' Aloïs drawled. 'Gods might think before they act, but we often think and act at the same time.' He jabbed Eva's side with his elbow. 'Right, *ná'laine?*'

Eva raised a brow at him and crossed her arms. 'Speak for yourself.'

Keres' grin grew wider. 'Elyon himself would be jealous of *your* chaotic tendencies, Eva. Don't even pretend otherwise.'

Aloïs wrapped his arm around my shoulders, keeping his golden gaze on Keres. 'I need to know how Lorcán managed to hide my child from me.'

'Aeneas taught him far too well. Not only did that bastard manage to hide a full-grown daemon and a *výssar*, he managed to hide his *kalotra* from me. I doubt even Eiran has any idea what he's up to.'

Keres casually calling me a 'full-grown daemon' hit me like a brick in the face.

'I'll leave you three, give you some time to catch up.' Keres looked at me. 'I'll update the High Lords as well.'

Oh, shit.

I'd completely forgotten about them with all the commotion. I had no doubt that Zale had come to check on me, only to find an empty bedroom. They were probably worried out of their minds. Maybe they thought I was on my way to Aspia. Also, the fact that Keres would go to them . . .

'Thank you, but . . . they don't exactly like you.'

'It's fine, I'll just let them know you're safe and sound in Hell.'

'I'm in Hell?' My voice sounded shrill.

'It's not that bad, honey.' My mother chuckled. 'Hell is not the torture empire from our mortal myths. It's a realm like any other. The only terrifying thing for miles around is the souvenir shop in the lower city.'

Aloïs shot her an amused look. 'Why is that shop scary?'

'Because it has that tiny clown in the corner that stares into my fucking soul.'

Aestor mentally wrote that down for future reference.

Keres said with a grin, 'I'll make sure your High Lords don't slip into a panic attack and I'll try my best not to kill them if they insult me.'

'If you harm them, I'll find my nicest *Damast* knife, hunt you down and feed you to some starving hell hounds.'

Aloïs shot him a sly grin at the threat.

'I'll go with him,' Aestor assured me. 'In case he accidentally makes another deal.'

'Oh, fuck off.' Keres rolled his eyes, the gesture so insanely human that it diminished the last of my wariness for him.

I tugged at the sleeves of the coat Keres had draped over my shoulders to cover my hands and glanced from one god to the other, then deeply inclined my head. 'Thank you – for rescuing me.'

Aestor smiled at me. 'You're very welcome, *aediore*. I'll visit you tomorrow to heal your wings.'

Keres gave me a polite nod. 'Princess.'

And with that, they disappeared into thin air.

My bedroom was beyond magnificent. The overarching theme of dark blues and silver returned here, with furniture of finely crafted black wood. White chiffon curtains framed the tall windows, allowing the serene moonlight to bathe

the room. And above me, the ceiling was painted midnight blue with iridescent stars splattered across it.

I immediately walked over to the tall, arched windows on my left that led to a small balcony, overlooking the city with its vibrant lights, cosy music and the sound of laughter and conversation. The evening air was warm and welcoming. And filled with millions of little stars.

I'd never seen any view quite as breath-taking.

My mother joined me on my right, watching me take it all in with a smile on her lips. 'Welcome to Anthens.' She brushed my hair. 'Welcome home, sweetheart.'

Tears blurred my vision. 'Thank you,' I whispered to her.

Aloïs ruffled my hair while he joined us. He wanted to give me space but he also wanted to smother me with affection, struggling to decide how to go about this. And since my shadows were still gliding around in excitement, they didn't give him a straight answer as to what I could handle right now.

They were like small puppies discovering their surroundings, too busy to pay attention to our emotions. One tendril of darkness stroked a soft blanket on the bed, curious about the texture of the fabric. Which felt *nice*, like that blanket rubbed over my very soul. Another one kept knocking on a mirror on the wall, confused as to why the shadow on the opposite side kept knocking back. The coldness of the mirror sent a shiver down my spine.

It would've been funny if I hadn't known how terribly sad this was. They'd never seen the sun and I now knew how much they'd enjoy the sunlight. My wings as well.

'They will be fine, pup,' Aloïs said, following my gaze. 'Give them two weeks and they'll be calmer. Leave them out as much as you can, they'll be thankful for it.'

I nodded, slipping my hand in his. They were warm, calloused from years of fighting, but painstakingly gentle as he squeezed mine. 'And my wings?' My heart dropped when I noted the sad look on his face.

'Do they hurt?'

'A little.'

His golden gaze travelled along every inch of them, took in how bent and crooked they were and how my left wing drooped down. He let go of my hand to stroke the bony part. Careful and light, like a breeze. I shuddered underneath the touch. It felt surprisingly nice, though they were insanely sensitive. 'Can you move them?'

'No, they're very stiff.' I tried again but only managed to rustle them like before.

'He locked them away, no doubt when they were still badly injured. I fear that they healed badly.' He stepped behind me and the warmth of his hands crept into the base, already loosening some of the tension there as he gently massaged them.

'I hope Aestor can heal them,' Eva said.

'He can probably heal the fractures but the scars . . .' He sighed. 'I'm not sure about those.'

I turned my head. 'Why can't Lord Aestor fully heal them? He's the God of Healing, after all.'

'Wings are terribly fragile. They heal on their own, like skin or bones would, but much more slowly. It could take days or even weeks before a wound stops bleeding, months before it closes. Healed membranes easily tear again. Aestor has studied wings for centuries, yet he struggles with healing even freshly wounded wings. We're not certain why.'

My mother brushed my hair behind both ears. 'You look exhausted.'

I wanted to protest but she didn't give me a chance to. Instead, she swiftly guided me to the comfortable bed, where she pulled me closer to cuddle up to her. With her magic, she'd dried, cleaned and even mended my torn nightgown and I let her drape a soft blanket over my lap, allowed myself to completely melt into that warm embrace. My shadows cuddled up to me as well.

I was already starting to doze off when I became aware of someone carefully touching my wings. My father sat on the bed while he gently massaged them. The scent of chamomile, honey and willow extract filled the air along with other herbs – a healing ointment. It helped with the ache, creating a welcome numbness, and when he was done, he stayed. My wings lay draped over his lap, along with another soft blanket on them, while he gently stroked my hair with one hand and the membrane with the other.

I started dozing off again, my shadows contentedly purring in their presence, though eventually their hushed conversation roused me from the best sleep I'd had in years. I couldn't even remember the last time I'd not been nauseous or hadn't felt a headache thundering against my temples.

'Poor thing,' Eva whispered while still brushing my hair.

'Given how she didn't hesitate to strike a deal with Keres to get revenge, I rather pity Lorcán. If she's anything like us, she doesn't know how to let go of a grudge.'

'Good,' she said softly.

A minute of silence passed before she asked, 'You were nervous the whole time, why?'

Aloïs was silent for a moment. 'You know the stories the mortals share about me – a beast that hides in the dark to feast on innocents.' He hesitated. 'She's grown up worshipping the gods, so she's grown up on those exact stories.

Why would she be happy that *I'm* her father?'

My throat closed up and behind my closed eyelids, tears threatened to come out.

'Because, *ná'nyl*, you are no beast,' Eva lovingly whispered his way. 'Because you fiercely loved her from the moment you felt her grow in my womb. And she likes you just fine. I watched her calm down when you held her – both of you.'

More silence, for such a long while, that I finally fell asleep.

Safe and sound in the arms of two people who would stop at nothing to protect me.

Chapter 11

Diana

While I enjoyed my first meal with my sense of taste and smell wide awake, Aloïs explained our realm to me, 'Hell exists outside of the mortal world, though the north of Persephian connects with Aurnea in Orthalla like a hidden portal. The Gates of Hell are located there to keep daemons from wrongfully entering Aeria – on Eiran's orders. To create a safer environment for the mortals.'

He showed me places on a map, tapping the different parts while he recounted what species lived there. His dark shoulder-length hair framed his face like a curtain. 'The further west you go, the closer you get to Erebus.' His tanned finger moved towards the left, tapping on a completely blacked-out spot. A river started into it but stopped some centimetres in, with a handful of smaller rivers flowing right back into the Aenean ocean. Even the river was wary of entering that place.

'Wouldn't recommend that,' I said before finishing my coffee.

Aloïs smiled. 'Asphiodel lies right next to Erebus and is what your myths describe as Hell. Since the Afterworld focuses on good people, I take in some of the most wicked souls in Asphiodel. I decide whether they'll burn in hell-fire for eternity or if I assign an erinyes – a malicious spirit – to torture them.' He shrugged. 'The punishment is more than deserved.'

I wondered if Kallias had ended up there, if my father knew . . . if he knew what he'd done. For a moment I hesitated, but I managed to find some spare courage. It'd been three years since his death and yet . . . I drew in a deep breath. 'You know everyone that goes there? And what they've done?'

He nodded while he drank from a fresh cup of coffee.

I wondered how best to ask the question without sounding pathetic. I smoothed over the fabric of the soft sweater I'd borrowed from my mother. 'Does the name Kallias Rhosyn ring a bell?'

Aloïs' brows furrowed. 'It does.'

My heart skipped a beat, though I tried to appear calm and disinterested while I stroked my shadows on my lap beneath the table. Pretending to be fine was a little use-less, given how he could perfectly read me. 'Any idea what happened to him?'

Aloïs smoothed a hand over his dark stubble. 'What-ever sanity he had when he entered was beaten out of him within days by Keres. He received special treatment on his orders, was sentenced with a Divine Punishment until his soul burned out.'

I forgot to breathe.

Keres.

Keres had . . . Kallias had received *Punishment*, even in his death. *Keres* had sentenced him.

A Divine Punishment. By *Keres*.

So much for making fun of my religiousness. It'd come back to bite him in his ass with vicious venom. Laughter bubbled in my throat and I buried my face in my hands, not caring that I looked a tad insane. Kallias, who'd used me for his twisted games, who'd held me under his thumb with threats and made me question my own mind. Every time he'd shown me glimpses of that beast underneath his skin, he'd claimed he simply loved me so deeply that sometimes he lost control and that he never meant to hurt me. That those bruises and broken bones were only proof of how deeply he cared.

Or that I was helplessly clumsy and had simply tripped and hurt myself.

Again and again, I'd believed him.

But the moment those cracks had widened enough to show his true colours . . . By the gods, I'd *loathed* him. It'd been overwhelming, enough to make me lash out.

Kallias' body had been found somewhere in the south of Orthalla, whatever had been left of it by Keres. He'd spun the story in the mortals' minds that we'd gone out on a stroll in the forest during our vacation and that we'd been attacked by wolves. That Kallias had been torn apart while protecting me and that I'd barely escaped with my life. Mortals loved a good tragedy, so they gladly ate up that story.

I couldn't turn to Zale, who'd been grieving the loss of his dear nephew. It was why I'd found excuse after excuse to flee to Clacaster; to Sorin's drama-free family. If it hadn't been for Sorin, I would've never been able to crawl out of that pit Kallias had buried me in. Sorin had helped me pick up the pieces of myself, glueing them together rather than taping them. And I had healed, though it would be a very long while before I'd trust anyone with my heart again.

Keres had sentenced Kallias with a *Divine Punishment*.

For hurting me.

Even when he'd still believed me to be some mortal girl.

I managed to compose myself again, appearing back from behind my hands while I wiped some tears away. They looked at me in concern, their expressions perfectly mimicking each other.

'Are you okay, pup?' Eva asked me, reaching out a hand to caress my arm.

'You know him,' Aloïs said. Not a question but an observation.

'He was ehm . . . my fiancé . . . He courted me for a year and we were to marry. Zale and his father agreed to the union, since we were both heirs of royal Orthallian bloodlines.'

My mother closed her eyes, hating this. She knew why he was in there, Aloïs had told her then.

On the table, Aloïs stretched and clenched his fist. I didn't like the change in the atmosphere, how his quiet fury charged the air with electricity. 'When I asked Keres why he'd done it, he said that the bastard broke his fiancée to the point where she'd been desperate enough to kill him – and then pray to Keres for help.'

It was an effort to remind myself that I didn't actually feel blood on my hands, that it was only my imagination. It was even harder to remind myself that it wasn't very nice to *like* how Kallias' warm blood had felt on my hands. But I had liked it. I'd relished in it. Sometimes I dreamed that I took my time hurting him like he'd hurt me, that I'd savoured the taste of his blood on my tongue. But proper ladies shouldn't think like that, right?

His voice grew quiet, barely audible. 'That was *you?* He hurt *you?*'

I nodded once, forcing myself to hold his gaze. I wasn't sure what he searched for in my eyes. Eva took my hand in hers, tightly holding on. Her own eyes were wet with tears. She'd promised herself that her child would never suffer like that, but she hadn't had the chance to protect me from him.

I swallowed. 'There was barely anything left of me when I finally . . . when I finally snapped.'

Aloïs nodded, clenching his fist again. Even if I didn't feel like sharing details, my *varkradas* were gossiping once again and it hadn't been pretty. Given how charming he'd been, Kallias had been great at convincing servants to give us privacy, and so no one had ever heard me cry or beg him to stop hurting me. No healer had ever wondered why it was always Kallias bringing me in with injuries. They'd gladly assumed it was simply my strange illness that made me clumsy and susceptible to breaking bones, that made me frail and barely able to keep food inside of me.

'If anyone ever attempts to hurt you again, Diana, know that they'll wind up in Asphiodel before they can even touch you – and that I'll personally see to their punishment.'

I gave him a grateful smile, glanced down at the marking that now decorated my left arm, noting the detailed crow's feathers. 'I'm . . . I'm quite surprised Lord Keres did that. I thought he didn't care much about mortals – at all, really.'

Eva sighed and rubbed her face. 'He's not unnecessarily cruel, not when it comes to innocents.'

Absent-mindedly, I nodded again while I studied the map, tilting my head when my eyes fell on the black paint that marked Erebus. My curiosity woke again. 'All I know about Erebus is that it's a place of pure darkness and that daemons spawn there. Is that true?'

'Erebus is primordial Darkness,' Aloïs explained. 'Greater Daemons don't spawn there, though it's rumoured that Ellowyn harvested darkness from Erebus to create us – our wings and shadows.'

I nodded, attentively listening.

'Many monstrous creatures are indeed born within that darkness and haunt both deities and mortals, though the Gates of Hell keep them mostly locked away here,' he said. 'It's a wasteland of ruins and darkness and chaos, and there are plenty of rumours that the Serpent spawned there as well.'

My eyes widened. '*The* Serpent? As in the monster that tried to kill Eiran and killed Ellowyn?'

Aloïs nodded. 'It's a place built upon utter carnage and dead lands, I've seen it for myself. And I've seen the feral creatures that bleed out of its Darkness and what they can do, so I believe that Elyon was indeed born from that wicked place.'

'Chaos Incarnate, indeed,' I said quietly while studying the map. 'If Elyon was truly born from the Chaos there.'

'Yes,' Aloïs said. 'Primordial power lingers in the darkness there and both Eiran and I agree that we know only the slightest sliver of the truths hidden within its walls. Eiran cannot come near Erebus as it might awaken Elyon from his slumber, so I keep an eye on it.'

'Why?'

His lips pursed. 'It's a place of both darkness and carnage; of dualism. We already saw it give birth to Chaos Incarnate, and we fear that maybe one day it will create Elyon's counterpart: Darkness Incarnate.'

'Oh, shit,' I whispered. Aloïs nodded when he saw understanding dawn on my face.

'Elyon wouldn't just rise again then, but have an ally as well. Someone who could drown the realms in darkness and so much worse,' he said. 'The truth is that we have barely any idea of what they might be capable of. Luckily, Erebus has been calmer and quieter since the War, which is a good sign. I'm not sure we could handle another deity on the same level as Elyon, given how even Ellowyn herself wasn't strong enough to survive him.'

'I know that that's bad and all but I'm also really morbidly curious now,' I admitted. 'I kind of want to know what it looks like . . . You know, in-person.'

'All daemons feel drawn to it to a certain degree, as we were all born from its Darkness. So it's normal that you're curious,' he said. 'Just promise me that you won't ever go in there, Diana.' He held my gaze, and for the first time since arriving here, there was something stern in his face. 'Nothing survives in there, not even the light, and certainly not your sanity. The deeper you venture into it—'

'How do you know that?'

He blinked. 'Because I go in from time to time. There's a small path leading into it.'

Now I was the one staring at him in surprise. 'And why would you do that?'

'To make Erobian steel.'

I raised a brow at him. 'So I'm to stay away but you can go in to forge some knives?'

His lips tipped up in a playful grin. 'I told you not to go *in*, but you're free to study it from the outside.' He grew serious again. 'I only enter it rarely – and for a *very* short time – after thoroughly preparing myself, and still I struggle.'

'Then why bother? What is so special about that steel that you'd risk your life like that?'

'Given how Erebus has some connection to Death, steel forged in that darkness contains traces of that power, making it highly effective against immortals. Even more so than *Damast*. Erobian weapons never miss their target. The cut is deeper and more painful, and the blood loss is more severe. Wounds don't properly close nor heal. Even Aestor has trouble healing wounds made by Erobian blades.'

'There's no steel that's as effective nor as lethal as Erobian.' My mother sat down her cup and handed me her dagger, a black leather hilt with pitch black steel that seemed to suck in the light around it. The coolness of the steel against my fingertips was welcoming. I studied it and I could've sworn whispers surrounded it, like it called to me.

'Very few own Erobian weapons,' Aloïs explained. 'Only my family, inner circle, Keres and Aestor do. Antheia owned a pretty dagger as well, though it was lost after her death.'

'And Lord Eiran?'

'Eiran thinks he's too *pure* for it,' Aloïs said with a hint of disdain. 'Claims it's a blight on the steel, a cursed weapon. He forbids Zhella from wielding it as well.'

'It's beautiful,' I said, caressing the steel with a finger. Reluctantly, I handed it back to my mother.

'You like it?'

'I do, it feels alive,' I said. I might've been fond of those pretty dresses in my closet back in Katrones, but I was also a sucker for a pretty weapon.

Aloïs summoned another pitch-black dagger from his shadows, which I found *really* impressive. I couldn't wait until he'd teach me how to do that. The handle was gorgeous, with black leather woven around it, embroidered with silver star flares.

He handed me the dagger with a sweet smile. 'This is *Aecéso*. Once my dagger, now it's yours.'

My throat tightened. 'Really?'

'Yes, really. It has been mine for many years, served me well during countless battles. It also saved me during my fights with your mother during the War whenever she used her sword to flirt with me.' He winked at her, then returned his gaze back to me. 'May it serve you with the same fortune.'

I fastened the dagger to my thigh, gently caressing the steel. 'Thank you.' I planted a kiss on his cheek, then thought of something else. 'You called me a circedera, but I don't know much about them. My teachers focused on the gods since daemon sightings are rare these days.'

'We're a species of Greater Daemons,' he explained. 'We can shift from a humanoid form to a full daemon form and anything in between. Inked skin that protects against Damast weapons, but not Stygian or Erobian. Wings and nails that grow into talons, and fangs so we can feed on blood.'

'Fangs?' I frowned. My father bared his teeth, revealing two delicate sharp fangs in the corners of his mouth. 'I have those as well?' I checked my own teeth but felt no fangs. Just regular, nice mortal teeth.

'Right now, you're still in a very human form and I'm not sure how much daemonic blood you've inherited, since Eva is a nymph.'

'So . . . we need blood?'

Aloïs nodded. 'To heal. Blood helps us heal quicker, especially *ichor* – divine blood. But we don't need it to survive like the aepokrae do. When we get injured, we crave blood until we've healed enough.'

'I had that craving yesterday, I think. The more I focused on it, the worse it got.'

'I'm not certain if you have fangs and can bite prey yourself, but when I gave you some of my blood yesterday, it seemed to work the same for you.'

I nodded, processing that for a moment – a *long* moment. I'd fed on blood, which strangely didn't upset me. 'What about my shadows? You have them as well, did I inherit them from you?'

Aloïs shook his head. 'Like I said: they stem from Erebus. No other daemons have them, only circederae do. We're a very . . . passionate people. Daemons feel emotions deeper and more intensely than gods and mortals do. Our wings are also terribly sensitive. Colchians can use their auras, many rituals and wings to destress, but circes mostly use their shadows as an outlet.'

'So Lorcán shutting them up . . . that put a cork in my outlet.'

'Which is why you grew so restless and were ill all the time,' Eva said. 'Daemons slowly burn out if they can't use their power or if something happens to their outlet. The more you let your nature out, the better you'll feel.'

I nodded, taking in all the information like a sponge. I had to admit that though I was fully interested, my mind was becoming quite fuzzy. 'I have another question, might be a bit weird.'

My father smiled. 'Yes?'

I pointed out the window, at the full moon that still decorated the morning sky. 'Why were there stars?'

'I was very close with Antheia. She was like a sister to

me. She removed them for the mortals and gods, but not for us. Their night sky is empty, with only the moon and that lone star to decorate it. We even used to have colourful aurora filling the sky.' Aloïs bit on the inside of his cheek. 'But those haven't appeared since she died.'

My father seemed gentle and his concern that I wouldn't like him because of our myths still tugged at my heart. Keres appeared different than he'd been proclaimed to be as well. 'What ehm . . . what was she like?' I asked. 'I only know the stuff from our myths.'

It was my mother who spoke. 'Antheia was a complicated soul, but still had a heart of pure gold for those she cared for. And though she'd been stabbed in the back over and over again, she always found some part of that fractured heart of hers to love someone new.'

That didn't sound like the vile goddess from my myths. It was strange knowing my parents were close with Keres and Antheia, knowing that Sorin and Zale despised them. Keres had attacked Nikos, who'd been their friend as well as the king of Veshos, after Nikos had murdered Antheia, leaving him behind to bleed out. If Aestor hadn't healed him then by Sorin's request, he would've died.

The fact that I couldn't find it in me to dislike Keres for what he'd done should've alarmed me. But she'd been his *dyad*. Her soul and heart and pulse had been his. I had no doubt that if Aloïs had truly lost Eva, he would've ravaged the mortal world.

If he'd gotten his hands on Lorcán . . . A better person would have felt pity for him.

In the middle of the lively garden was a large pond that housed an array of plants, colourful lily pads, pretty white fishes with swirling tails and a heap of white frogs that croaked like they were competing in a talent show. Needless to say, I adored the garden.

I ventured further into the water, scanning the lily pads and ferns to study the little frogs. They were cute enough with their beady black eyes and their bubbling throats. One of the fishes brushed against my leg as it swam past me, tickling my skin with its tail. The sensation of the warm rays of the sun on my crooked wings and shadows was wonderful, as was the sense of peace that blossomed within my soul. My shadows purred deep within my soul and every so often, they caressed my skin.

I'd learned that they were very affectionate.

I reached out a hand to caress the back of a tiny frog sitting on a lily pad, but startled when it combusted and exploded into hundreds of small white butterflies that scattered throughout the garden.

'They'll merge somewhere to take on another form,' Aloïs said behind me, sitting at the edge of the pond.

'What are they?'

'Kaboloses,' Eva said, sitting cross-legged next to him with a glass of wine in-hand. 'Small shapeshifters.'

I stared after the butterflies in awe. 'Do they always look like that?'

'No, they can take on any form, but they seem fondest of a form similar to a fox or a ferret – perfect for exploring.' Eva pointed at a small school of white fishes. 'Those are kaboloses as well.'

'When I was little, I often played in the forest with little white foxes.' I looked at them. 'Do you think they were kaboloses?'

Eva's face grew tender.

'Given their excellent noses, I'd say they were,' Aloïs said. 'They probably sought you out.'

I waded over towards the fishes and dipped a hand in to pet them, which they let me do. Some circled me and nuzzled their smooth heads against my legs. One changed from a fish into an otter and crawled up my legs and hips, inviting itself into my arms. It nestled itself against my stomach, contentedly purring while I petted its silky fur. I waded over with the little creature in my arms.

'They're adorable.' I sat down next to my mother and gently laid down the kabolos so it could sleep on my lap while I caressed its belly.

'They're fragile creatures, easily killed by mortals and other daemons – even with regular steel. So when they sense something that can offer them safety, they hide behind it. That also means we often find them hiding in our homes and other odd places. Sometimes they accidentally break things, which used to really annoy the mortals.' Aloïs looked down at the small creature. 'And who better to hide behind than the Lady of Daemons herself?'

I stared at him. 'What?'

Aloïs exchanged a look with Eva, silently discussing how much to share. Eva looked back at me and asked, 'Why do you think Eiran forbade *výssars*? Why he forbids gods from reproducing?'

'Because they're unstable?'

Aloïs shook his head. 'Children inherit power. Children of Melian can manipulate the weather, or cause the ocean to split and devour whole continents. Children of Zhella would be *demiagi* unlike ever seen before. Now imagine a combination of those gods. A child like that would be a new kind of god.'

'That does sound . . . like it could be a problem.'

'You're the only circes who can use magic, thanks to Eva.' He pointed at the kabolos in my lap. 'And it appears that you've inherited my title of Lady of Daemons.'

'You're Lady of Daemons?' I grinned at him.

'And my bad humour.' He pinched the bridge of his nose, though he was fully amused. He grinned at me. 'If you're done cuddling, I thought we might do some training.'

After donning some casual attire I'd borrowed from my mother, my father led me into the garden. I hadn't looked in a mirror yet, but I'd noticed that I'd put on some healthy weight overnight, like my body was regaining its strength. I wasn't as easily winded either. And again, I relished in the fact that I felt no aches or discomfort.

Aloïs clapped his hands together. 'First of all, your shadows are a part of you. They're an extension of yourself. In the first days after you're born, they tether and connect with your soul. They're a means of transportation, as all shadows connect with each other. They can be formed into a weapon or merge with our skin to form armour. They're also another sense, making it possible for us to develop another skill—'

'Read emotions and thoughts?'

He nodded. '*Varkradas* communicate with each other, which makes it possible to both read others and share thoughts with anyone we wish, even if they have regular shadows. Though we can also draw up walls to protect our privacy. So generally, our relationships run deeper and form more quickly than those of other deities.'

'But mortals and gods can't use their shadows as an outlet?'

Aloïs shook his head, finally stopping in the back of the garden where we were surrounded by thick oak trees and poplars. 'This might give you a headache, but there are different kinds of shadows and darkness. *Varkradas* stem from Erebus itself. Mortals and gods have regular shadows, because their bodies block the sun or any other light source.'

'So there are two kinds of shadows?' I asked. 'Ours and regular?'

'Yes.'

'You said that there were different kinds of darkness as well.'

He nodded. 'Darkness is all and nothing at once.'

I shot him a sly grin. 'How vague and poetic.'

Aloïs returned my grin. 'There is the darkness we fear; that hides monsters, schemes, secrets and ill intentions. Darkness that weaves itself between our stars and sows fear in the hearts of even the most seasoned warriors. There is darkness that soothes us and grants us rest. Darkness that cradles us through sleepless nights, that caresses lovers as they lie intertwined in linen. Darkness of the soil where the roots of Life grow, which nourishes and protects a sprouting sapling. Darkness from which we were born and to which we return when our time comes.'

He took his time explaining my abilities and giving me pointers on how to summon my instinct. I needed a good few hours before I managed to somewhat control my *varkradas*. But eventually, I travelled through a shadow. It was only a short distance, but when I saw the proud look on my father's face, I didn't quite care that it had taken me hours to get to this point.

'Well done.' He stepped out of the same shadow that I'd just appeared from. 'Shadowtravelling will get easier the more you train it, and when your *varkradas* have settled down, they'll inform you of any shadows in your vicinity – even hidden ones.'

I nodded and closed my eyes to concentrate on slipping into the shadow that I stood in. It took me a moment to feel that familiar darkness but when I opened my eyes, I stood about fifty yards away from my father. His brows rose and his mouth fell slightly open. He hadn't expected me to go so far so quickly.

'Again,' he called to me.

I did, stepping out of the shadow of the black marble fountain on the opposite side of the garden, surrounded by the colourful wildflowers that grew there. As I turned my head to look back at him, I saw that he'd disappeared. The next second, his honey-lemon scent came from my right.

'Try indoors now. Your room.'

Melting into the darkness started to feel like breathing and this time I was aware of all possible exits. I chose my bedroom and stepped out of the shadow next to the tall wardrobe.

Black smoke rose from my shoulders and wings like it did with my father; like darkness was evaporating from me. That deep instinct in me stirred and tugged and purred, grabbing my attention. It was ancient, palpable. Like I was staring into the deep end of a dark ocean.

And it whispered to me what else I could do.

This time, I didn't connect with the shadows around me. I connected with the ones I was made of and became pure darkness – a shadow myself. When I materialised again, I shot Aloïs, who'd followed me, a sly grin and crossed my arms, enjoying his bewilderment.

'It's starting to become easier.' I flicked my hand like I was about to grab something and at the same time, I closed my eyes and concentrated on a certain something I wanted, something guarded by the shadows I now connected to. The weight in my hand told me that I'd managed to do it and when I opened my eyes I found myself holding a gilded pear that I'd just stolen from the kitchens in Katrones – my favourite fruit.

I held it up, showing it off to my father. 'It's from Orthalla.'

A wicked and proud grin broke loose on his face, golden eyes so bright that they reminded me of the brutal sunlight during a heatwave. 'Now hide it,' was all he said. The fact that he didn't explain how to do it made it clear he was convinced I would know what to do.

I made the fruit disappear.

His grin widened even more. 'Don't let Aestor know that you can steal things with your *varkradas*. He'll make you tag along to mess with the mortals and pickpocket Eiran.'

I stared at my father in shock. 'He'd do that?'

'It's more like a regular Thursday for him, really. He actually spends a lot of time in the mortal world, likes messing with them. He's rather fond of Veshos, spends a lot of time there.'

I nodded, then thought of something I'd been wanting to ask. 'Do you think that he appreciates that I offer him our finest wine?'

Aloïs raised a brow at me. 'You offer him wine?'

I rubbed my arm, suddenly self-conscious. I really didn't want to dishonour or displease our gods. Nothing good ever came from that and my conscience didn't agree with it. 'Doesn't he like that?'

'Try honey apples next time. He'll fall on his knees for you.'

I smiled and nodded.

Aloïs eyed my shadows, which had gone back to exploring my room and hugging my calves, bumping against my hand to ask for pets, which I absent-mindedly gave them.

'Why does it suddenly come so naturally?' I asked him. 'I struggle to control them for hours and now . . .'

He eyed me for a moment. 'Remember what I said about being my heir?'

'Yes.'

'By Ellowyn's courtesy, I'm Lord of Wealth of the Earth and Fertile Soil, but I'm also Lord of Shadows. And those things you just did, other circes can't do them. They can't become pure shadows or control shadows that aren't their *varkradas*. You've inherited some of my titles. You're Lady of Shadows, as well as Lady of Daemons.'

I gaped at him. 'You mean . . . like how Keres is Lord of *Kalotra* and Zielle is Lady of Vows?'

He grinned. 'How's that fuzzy head of yours now?'

'Breaking,' I admitted.

He chuckled softly. 'Let's get some food in you before you melt into pure darkness again.'

'I'm actually a *deity?*' I gaped at him. 'An actual fucking deity? *What the Hell?*' I whispered that last part. For the first time, it truly hit me that I was no simple mortal anymore.

His brows furrowed in worry. 'You okay?'

'I'm sorry,' I said softly. 'I just . . . It's a lot.'

'Don't be. We've been feeding you information all day.'

'I do like it, though.' I gestured at my shadows. 'It feels good.'

'You just need some time.' Aloïs planted a kiss on my

hair, pulling me closer to hug me. 'How about you take a warm shower before dinner? The vesperae added some clothes to your wardrobe.'

'Clothes?' I tilted my head, looking up while he still had his arms around me.

'Pretty dresses and some casual attire, though you can ask the vesperae to fetch you anything you like. There's also leathers for when we start proper training.'

'You want me to stay?' A timid smile bloomed on my lips while my heart constricted in my chest.

'Of course we do, sweetheart,' he said. 'You're more than welcome here.'

Never in my life had I imagined I'd need a manual for showering or taking a bath, but trying to wash myself with my wings out was a true challenge. The warm water on them felt wonderful but touching them with a washing cloth had been a mistake, as the texture of the cloth didn't agree with their sensitivity. It felt like someone just tried to electrocute me. And the moment I started carefully patting them dry, I knew it'd be no use. The towel was unbeliev-ably soft but I feared my wings had experienced enough sensory overload for a day. They felt sunburned.

'Fuck it,' I muttered to myself, leaving them wet while I put on soft loose leggings and a simple ribbed shirt. The neckline at the back was cut low to accommodate my wings. My mother had explained that most shirts had small cut-outs and buttons in the back and that I could withdraw my wings before putting them on, and then summon them to let them glide through the holes. But it was risky doing that with wounded wings, so we'd settled on backless shirts for now.

The water droplets on my wings did feel nice, soothing the burning sensation while they trickled down the membrane. While I let my wings air-dry I loosely braided my hair, and as I looked in the mirror, I realised that I really did resemble my parents. I grinned when I noticed the arched ears. Given the stories I'd heard about daemons, I still felt some anxiety about being one. But knowing I was half nymph made me feel pretty giddy. Little me had grown up on stories about ethereal nymphs and their pretty dresses and how everything they touched became instantly more alive and brightly coloured. How their laughter was like music and their charm could make someone fall in love within the blink of an eye.

Though my mother certainly was not *that* type of nymph. She was a blazing inferno.

Staring into the mirror, there were two other things that caught my attention.

There was *colour* in my face, a healthy blush on my cheeks and no bags under my eyes. The hollows in my face had filled out as if my body had been strained for years by the suppression of my nature, slowly starving, and now with the *kalotra* gone, it'd regained its strength. My muscles had hardened and strengthened, though it was softened by my curves – I had *curves*.

I looked healthy and fresh. I looked like *me*, like my body had finally become mine; a welcoming and fitting home for my soul. Seeing myself like this in the mirror made my throat close up. I looked *alive*. And as I stared at my reflection, I even thought I looked rather pretty.

Something snapped in me, lining my eyes with tears.

I'd spent so many nights sick to my stomach, not able to keep any food in. Nights where Zale had stayed up with me, making me drink hot broths and water to keep me from dehydrating. Nights where he'd held my hair back while I'd hurled my guts out, where he'd stayed with me even when I'd finally fallen asleep. There'd been so many training sessions where we'd had to take a break because I was hyperventilating, because my body couldn't take the physical strain. Times where I'd passed out because my body had shut down, where I'd woken up many hours later feeling like a massive wreck. I'd never been able to properly train my magic due to my chronic exhaustion.

All because Lorcán had shut me down completely.

There was no way in Hell that I'd ever allow anyone to shut me down like that again.

Not Lorcán. Not those servants from Orthalla. Not even Sorin or Zale.

I would be me.

And I would be proud.

Chapter 12

Diana

Anthens, the Capital of Hell
Present day

I spent the rest of the afternoon roaming around the palace, slipping in and out of shadows at random to explore the many rooms. Some vesperae came to meet and get to know me. Their dark blue skin shimmered in the many lights, and iridescent freckles on their cheeks, shoulders and backs created the illusion of constellations on their skin. Sleek black hair cascaded over their shoulders and their silk dresses and shirts draped over their bodies like liquid silver, hugging their curves and muscles.

I wondered where I could find dresses like that because *damn*.

Eventually, I found myself in the grand library, surrounded by thousands of ancient leatherbound tomes with yellowed pages and age-old maps dating back centuries. There were maps depicting kingdoms often forgotten by mortal history, like the kingdom of Avalon, which had been annihilated by Antheia.

I found some thick novels with hand-painted images of our gods, written in Aspian and I melted away into the stories. These weren't the myths I'd been taught by the

Priestesses, the many tales of Eiran's chivalry and kindness, the ballads of Zhella's achievements and the horror stories of Antheia and Keres' deeds. Zale once told me history was written by those who won the wars and took the thrones. Those winners could've waged the bloodiest wars and yet history would favour them, since the narrative had been twisted to favour them. This tome had been written by the silent survivors who remembered what had happened from the other perspective.

Years after the King of the Gods created the mortals, he wished for his children to bless them with gifts.

Competitive in nature, the Goddess of Day, Sun and Summer immediately visited the first mortals and granted them the knowledge to create fire. Eiran commended Zhella for her gift, presenting her with his favourite Damast *sword as a reward.*

The Goddess of Night, Moon and Winter had noticed how mortals saw stories in everything. The mortal children were grateful for the stars in the night sky, as they lit up the darkness and drove away the preying monsters that hunted the humans.

She adjusted her stars for them, creating patterns in the skies that resembled animals and shapes. Both the youngest and eldest mortals now spent their nights gathered around campfires, pointing up at her night sky as they told each other stories inspired by her stars and constellations. The King wasn't impressed with the gift and there was no reward for Antheia, only scathing insults.

It didn't take long before the mortals used Zhella's gift against each other, burning down settlements and enemies, yet Antheia's stories lived on.

Many years later, the King ordered the same thing of both goddesses. This time, Zhella decided to grant the mortals the

ability to wield magic, creating the first demiagi. Antheia re-
membered what Zhella's gift had brought forth last time, the
misery that had come with it. She knew it would be no use to
try and impress her father, but she could take this opportunity
to protect the mortals – especially the young ones. So Antheia
spent the following day and night creating thousands of little
carved wooden figurines of different animals and instilled them
with her own gentle magic. They carried enchantments and
protective spells so that when Zhella's gift would backfire, those
little ones would remain unharmed.

When she was done, Antheia told her father that she had
gifted the children toys to make up stories, like she had done
with her stars. He paid no further attention to the toys, but
when the first mortals finally turned against each other with
magic, Antheia's enchantments ensured the safety of their chil-
dren without anyone realising.

I leaned against a desk and frowned. I'd been taught that
Antheia was the competitive one, that Zhella had guarded
the mortals and that Eiran had scolded Antheia for putting
them in harm's way.

Turning another page, I stumbled upon an image of
Keres, looking *exactly* like I remembered him from yesterday, but with longer hair. Next to the image was another
story that I'd been taught by the Priestesses; the story of
how Keres became Eiran's Left Hand. The competition
between him, Khalyna, Anaïs and Lycrius. I skipped some
pages and my eyes fell on several words that completely
caught me off guard. No Priestess had ever mentioned
it before. According to this book, Eiran had gifted him
Zhella's hand in marriage as a reward for his devotion
and loyalty.

Though strange, it explained some of the tension between the sisters.

I found no further stories regarding them in this first
instalment, so I closed the book and neatly put it back on
the shelf. My eyes then fell on a wooden box, illuminated
by a small light on a desk. There was a coat of arms burned
onto it; a crescent moon hidden inside a solar flare, flanked
by a pair of antlers, around which wildflowers crawled.

In a cursive handwriting, someone had written a quote.

*Blessed by the Moon with eternal love and nights that are
evermore triumphant,*
　　May this union bless you with happiness abundant.

I opened the wedding gift to find a great heap of things
inside. The first thing my eyes fell on was a hand-carved
wooden figurine, like the one I'd read about. It was a bear,
painted with vibrant colours. Next were the pictures of my
parents, both dressed in white. A golden ribbon tied around
their wrists, dancing at their wedding, drinking wine and
laughing.

There were pictures of Keres smearing wedding cake on
Aestor's face, a wicked grin on his lips. Another one where
my father carried Aestor in a bridal style, one where Keres
danced with my mother, as well as one where Eva danced
with a dark-haired man I hadn't seen before – a friend, I
guessed. And then there were pictures of my mother with
Antheia and a brown-haired woman whose brown eyes
were rimmed with wine-red, their arms wrapped around
each other's shoulders and waists, their cheeks a subtle pink
– courtesy of the wine. They seemed like close friends.

Antheia's sapphire blue eyes were decorated with laugh

lines, a wide smile on her delicate lips. There was another where Antheia kissed my mother's cheek. One of Keres and Antheia, looking at each other with such tenderness that I ached for Keres losing her. Keres didn't look like a malicious god here, like he hadn't yesterday. Antheia didn't look like evil incarnate.

And I was beginning to believe that I barely knew anything of our true history and mythology.

I didn't sense the man in my bedroom until he stood right behind me. One moment there'd been no one, the next there was. I yelped, years of self-defence kicking in, and before I even turned to look who it was or could listen to my overwhelmed *varkradas*, I'd grabbed his arm and locked it behind him, kicking his feet away. Though I nearly tripped myself with the foreign weight of my wings holding me back.

I shoved him down on the marble floor with my Erobian dagger resting against the back of his neck.

'Diana?' I looked up to see my father appear out of a shadow, amusement on his face as he took in the scene before him. Next to him, Eva doubled over giggling. Aestor's shoulders shook as he laughed underneath me.

'Oh my gods.' I scrambled up with burning cheeks, quickly hiding my dagger. 'I'm *so* sorry, My Lord.'

I truly hadn't paid him enough attention yesterday, which I couldn't exactly blame myself for as I'd been dying and overwhelmed. He was handsome, physically in his mid-thirties, with hazel eyes that sparkled with playfulness and carried hints of golden specks. With his lips permanently curled into a slight smile, he appeared like he was waiting to tell me a good joke – and would probably laugh about it the hardest. Today, the Second God wore official attire;

a black tunic, overlayed with black leather. And a golden circlet in his hair.

I dipped my head in a bow to him.

'Are you looking for something?'

I glanced up, uncertain what he meant. 'My Lord?'

He lazily pointed at the floor. 'Are you looking for something?'

I stared at him. Out of the corner of my eye, I spotted my parents exchanging an amused look. 'I'm . . . I'm bowing for you – to show respect.'

'Oh!' He clasped his hands together. 'I thought you were looking for the teeth you slammed out of my mouth.'

I snorted, not at all elegantly. 'I truly am sorry about that, Lord Aestor.' I flicked my hand like I'd done this afternoon and held out a honey apple to the god, bowing my head again. 'Forgive me.'

Aestor theatrically gasped, accepting the piece of fruit. 'Forget I said anything.'

I laughed, my eyes creasing at the corners as my sense of unease started to ebb away. The god winked, taking a bite from the apple while he made himself comfortable on an armchair near the fireplace. 'Well done, by the way. Now you can brag that you kicked my divine ass.'

'I *am* sorry, I didn't know who you were.'

'If she'd known, she would've kicked harder,' Aloïs purred.

'You wound me.' Aestor finished his apple, throwing the core to Aloïs' with an impish smile. 'Be a dear and clean that up.'

'I'll shove it up your ass.'

'Use some olive oil if you do.'

I cackled. My mother laughed next to me and Aloïs

rubbed his forehead in feigned exasperation, shoulders shaking from laughter as well; still holding that damn core.

Aestor's hazel eyes studied me, then moved on to my wings. 'Can I take a look at your wings?'

Drawing in a deep breath, I walked over. Aestor slowly circled me while he took them in. He ran a light hand along the thick bony part of my left wing, the touch barely more than a breeze.

My *varkradas* liked him, climbing up his leather boots. They were excited to meet him. Aestor didn't mind them and was careful not to step on them when he moved, which I appreciated. They were still very sensitive and being trampled on wasn't exactly a favoured hobby of theirs.

'Both of your wings carry so many fractures in so many different spots that I cannot even guess how many times that bastard broke the bones,' he said, then sighed. 'And the scar tissue . . . Even if I manage to heal the bones, there's still a chance your wings will forever be delicate and fragile.'

'So . . . No flying?' My heart sank down into my stomach.

'Not in this condition, no.' Gently, he rubbed the leathery membrane between his thumb and pointer finger. It tickled and made them twitch. 'They're extremely thin as well.'

'But you can heal the bones, right?' My mother walked over to stand next to him.

'Ehm . . .' Aestor shot her an apologetic smile. 'Technically, I can but . . .'

'You'd have to break them again.' My father leaned against the fireplace. He wasn't happy with that prospect and I wasn't too great a fan of it either. Yet there was something calming about the energy that surrounded Aestor. It was what made my shadows like and go to him.

'You wouldn't feel a thing, as I can take away the pain. You'll hear it, though. Won't be great for the stomach.'

'You can heal my stomach then, if I do decide to hurtle my guts out.'

Aestor snickered. 'I'll need another honey apple to do that.'

'You'll get two more, but if I do puke, I'll shove that core high up your ass.' I poked his chest. 'Without any olive oil.'

Aestor stared at me in horror. 'You wouldn't dare desecrate me like that.'

'Pray you won't find out.'

He said to Eva, 'She reminds me of the worst aspects of both of you.'

Aloïs grinned at him. 'Should you ever decide to have a child, Aestor, I pray that they won't have as bad a sense of humour as you have.'

'Oh, they'd no doubt have worse humour.' Aestor rubbed his hands together. 'You up for it?'

He looked at my parents. 'Perhaps wait outside.'

After they left, I plopped onto the soft bedding and kicked my shoes off.

'You look a thousand times better than yesterday.' His warm smile melted away some of the nervousness. 'Healthy, radiant. You looked more like a corpse yesterday.'

'Thanks, I felt like one as well.'

'And how do you feel now? With your nature free, being home.' He genuinely cared, truly wanted to know how I was feeling, that I was settling in well.

I smiled. 'I've never felt better, truly. I spent the day with them, hugged a very cute kabolos that kept following me around. I've learned to use my shadows.' I grew more and more excited as I told him. 'I can shadow travel like it's nothing.'

'You radiate with the same light your mother can summon,' he said. 'Happiness suits you, *Viatra*.'

I swallowed at the compliment, then chuckled at the nickname. *'Little bat?'*

'You look like a cute little bat.' He shrugged. 'You'd rather I call you *little circedera*? That doesn't roll off the tongue quite as nicely.'

'Fair point.' I smiled slyly. 'Little clown.'

Aestor wagged a finger. 'You're getting far too comfortable around me.'

I grinned and let myself fall onto the mattress. 'Normally I'd say "break a leg" but I guess I should say "break a wing".'

Aestor cursed quietly. 'I should remember that one, that was a good one.'

'Thanks.'

Aestor climbed on the bed as well, sitting cross-legged on my left. With a light touch, he draped my wing over his lap. 'You won't feel a thing, Diana.' He handed me a pillow so I could rest my head on it. 'Ready?'

I closed my eyes and nodded. It was strange to feel his magic gild my nerves, blocking out any pain. My heartbeat still rose in anticipation, yet, as quickly as that sense of panic came, it disappeared. Aestor slowed down my heartbeat, easing my breathing until my body calmed and a sense of peace washed over me. Only then did he set to work, his touches deliberate but light. The cracking sounds made my stomach twist and turn but he took care of that as well. I didn't dare open my eyes and look, so I kept them tightly closed and buried my face in the pillow.

Hours passed while he worked. He chatted with me about my life in Orthalla and how I'd been taught by the Priestesses, and he told me some about himself. He also mentioned that he'd recently discovered he had a dyad – though he didn't appear keen on sharing *who* it was. I wondered what kind of person she was, if she had the same sense of humour or if she was more of a serious type.

Finally, he patted my back. 'I suggest you summon your sense of vanity and peek in the mirror.' Aestor removed his magic, opening my senses again.

My wings felt lighter, like they could finally breathe. I scrambled up from the bed, immediately noticing the difference. There was no imbalance, I no longer leaned towards the left, but stood perfectly straight. My wings were neatly tucked behind my back.

I stretched them, actually stretched them instead of just rustling them. They spread out to their full wingspan, covering us both in their shadow. I walked over to the mirror to study them and covered my mouth with both of my hands while I took them in. They'd been more silver than black but there was a new contrast to them. There were still jagged silver scars and the membrane was still thin, but the difference was immense.

I couldn't stop staring at them while I spread them out, tucked them in and spread them out again. I was at a loss for words and quietly crying. The daemonic instinct that I would cut down anyone who ever tried to hurt my wings was overwhelming. I yearned to fly, to feel the sunlight on them. The wind caressing my body and the membrane. The wonderful feeling of free-falling through the summer air while I laughed with . . . with friends. Gods, I wanted that so badly.

Aestor leaned against the wardrobe, taking me in with reddened eyes.

'I am never retracting them again,' I whispered.

'As you should, they're beautiful.' His lips quirked. 'Also, you should show them your wingspan.'

'Why?'

His cocky smile reminded me of Keres. 'The greater the wingspan, the more powerful the circes.' I spread them out fully, which made Aestor's grin widen. 'Aloïs once mentioned he has a span of three-and-a-half metres ten feet.' His gaze slipped from one wing to the other. 'I may not be the God of Measuring, but I'd say yours is about the same.'

'Oh, I'm definitely showing them.' I tucked them in and turned, tightly hugging him. 'Thank you. Thank you *so* much, My Lord.'

'My pleasure, *aediore*. And please, just call me Aestor.' He pulled me closer. 'Go rattle the stars and dance with them.'

Chapter 13

Diana

I stepped out of the shadow that surrounded my father, who sat at the dining table. His dark hair was gathered in a low bun on the back of his head and his short beard was neatly trimmed. He wore a black button-up shirt, embroidered with silver on the cuffs and collar. On his dark hair rested a silver circlet. The crown Eva wore was identical, the meaning behind it clear as day. She wore a dark blue off-shoulder dress and the iridescent fabric reminded me of the stars I'd seen last night. My heart nearly leapt out of my chest when I realised I would see them again in a few hours, filling me with childlike excitement.

It *did* leap out when my eyes settled on the two guests who sat in front of my parents, who'd jumped up at the sight of me. Even now, visiting the King and Queen of Hell, that idiot wore a leather jacket. Sorin stared at me, his open mouth covered with his hands. His amber eyes glided over my face, body and wings while he drank me in and his eyes watered when he noted the positive change that had appeared overnight. 'You look . . . *healthy*,' he whispered, his voice uneven while he gathered me in a tight hug.

I beamed at him and nodded. Though I'd never really smelled his perfume, the cedarwood and blood orange was achingly familiar. 'Good air and the absence of *kalotra* will do that to you.'

Sorin chuckled while my eyes settled on Zale. His dark eyes didn't leave mine and I couldn't quite read his face, nor his emotions. Not because he was hiding them but because he was struggling with his many feelings himself. Zale opened his mouth but Sorin shot him a warning while he kept his hand on my back, '*Don't.*'

He ignored Sorin. 'Next time you decide to take a midnight stroll, *warn* me. I truly thought you'd left for Aspia when I couldn't find you. You were nowhere to be found and then *Keres* of all damned gods shows up in Clacaster.'

'He was a bit worried,' Sorin added, smoothing out the silver silk fabric at the back of my dress; one a sweet vespera had readied for me after I'd commented to her how pretty their dresses were.

Zale gritted his teeth, glaring at him. 'Was I not allowed to?'

Sorin sighed deeply. The exasperated look on his face told me they'd had this discussion before, and knowing how much of a worrier Zale was, I had a feeling they'd had this discussion several times.

'I'm sorry,' I said, feeling so sickeningly guilty that it erased my appetite. 'One thing led to another and . . . yeah . . . I'm sorry.' I knew he couldn't stand the thought of ever losing me. I could only imagine how frantic he'd been last night.

Zale pulled me into a tight hug, taking a long moment to relish in the fact that I was okay. 'I'm just glad you're feeling better,' he said softly. He let go to curiously view my wings, aching when he noticed the scars.

Sorin thought my wings were neat but seemed more surprised by my arched ears. 'So you became a nymph?' he asked Eva.

Eva nodded. 'Little present from Eiran.'

'I like your aura. Are those *actual* flames?' Sorin appeared half in awe and half envious that he didn't have flames licking his shoulders. 'You're permanently on fire?'

Eva's lips parted into a crooked grin. 'It's not really fire, it's my aura. But I can change into a fyrebird the same way a vespera can melt into the night.'

Sorin gaped at her. 'You can turn into a *fyrebird?*'

She grinned, nodded and around the neckline of her off-shoulder dress the orange glow of her aura took on the shape of feathers, as if it longed for her to take on that shape once more. Right now, she only let them grow out into her feathery wings. Next to her, Aloïs looked absolutely smitten.

I silently wondered if I'd ever find someone who'd love me like that – so fully.

Zale's brows rose while he leaned back in his chair, fully impressed.

Sorin still gaped at her. 'By the gods, Yael would've been so jealous.'

Zale tapped the corner of his mouth. 'You're drooling a little.'

Eva snorted while Sorin rolled his eyes. Like old times.

While they continued bantering, I watched my father circle the top of his wine glass with a light thumb as he studied them in silence. He didn't show it but there was an edge to him; as grateful as he was for them taking care of me, he didn't like them. Though he tolerated Sorin because of the genuine respect he showed Eva and because she wanted to rekindle their friendship.

'There was something else we wanted to discuss with you,' Zale said after we'd finished dessert, laying down his spoon on the now empty plate, still a smear of rich and decadent chocolate on it. He looked over at me, sitting at the head of the dining table.

If this was the same thing they'd wanted to discuss with me in Clacaster, I had a pretty good idea what it would be about. Zale had been alluding to it for years now, often joking that ruling two countries would make him go fully grey one day, even with Eiran's blessing.

'It's about Egoron, isn't it?'

'Yes,' Sorin said. 'We trained you for years. Politics, languages, anything to give you a head start.'

'And we think you're ready.' Zale smiled. 'If you want to, that is.'

'High Lady? Of Egoron?'

They nodded, almost in perfect unison. 'If you agree, we'll contact Eiran,' Zale said. 'He'll test you, to see if you're worthy. Like he did with us.'

I mulled it over like I was tasting a fine wine. 'I do want to,' I mused. 'But I want to learn more about Hell first – my parents, my people and our culture. I want to train my powers as well.' I looked at my parents. 'I mean . . . I can stay here right?'

'Of course, honey.' Eva, sitting to my left, sweetly smiled while taking my hand.

Sorin thought of something else, 'If you pass Eiran's test, he'll make you immortal.' He'd always ached whenever he'd noticed me growing up and he'd often struggled with the fear that he'd lose me one day.

'She already is.' Aloïs looked at me. 'You were conceived when Eva was already a vyrenera. There's nothing mortal about you.'

'But she ages,' Sorin countered.

'All deities do until they're somewhere between twenty-five and thirty-five. If Diana hasn't stopped ageing yet, she will soon.'

Zale spoke up. 'I mean no offence, but . . . I noticed some things during the War and how your . . . *kind* . . . often treats women. I won't have her become some breeding mare for those be—' He stopped himself before he could finish that word. *Beasts.* The word hung unspoken in the air between us all.

Aloïs leaned back in his chair, eyeing Zale in silence.

Eva's gaze pierced him into place. 'There was indeed a period of time where *mattas* viewed *matska* as nothing but something to carry their pups, to do their housework. That time is long gone.'

'Long gone?' Zale scoffed. 'That War was only twenty-six years ago. Wasn't there some Daemon Lord murdering innocents simply for the thrill of it?'

My father's eyes narrowed. 'Wasn't there some Orthallian crown prince murdering innocent pups?' My father's quiet voice was stone cold, sending shivers along my entire body.

'Fuck,' Sorin muttered, rubbing his face. He leaned back in his chair, knowing damn well what my father meant. Sorin didn't approve, not in the slightest.

'They were already dying,' Zale said in an attempt to defend himself.

'Didn't it occur to you that a certain god roamed that battlefield, scanning the carnage for the injured? That all you needed to do was pray and he would come?'

Zale said nothing.

'If those pups had been mortal, you would've cared. But they weren't mortal, were they, High Lord?' Aloïs eyed him with disdain, lip curling down in disgust. 'No, they were only *beasts*.'

'I don't agree with what Zale did then – with many things he did during the War,' Sorin calmly spoke up, still not looking at Zale. 'That War brought out the worst in everyone. We killed more than we saved and came to a point where we would've slain anything to finish that War, no matter how innocent.'

Aloïs' gaze slid to Sorin. 'If you all turned into stone-cold killers, explain to me why *you* stopped him and brought those pups to me.'

'Because like I said, I didn't agree with what he did. But he lost his entire family only days before. That tends to fuck someone up. He lashed out at something innocent and he shouldn't have.'

Ice cold pain radiated from Zale, piercing through my shadows like ice shards. It overwhelmed me; a pain that he normally managed to keep under control. But not now, not when my father had ripped the scars open to reveal the wounds that had never healed.

'Gods, Zale,' I whispered, my eyes watering in response to his emotions. He flinched when I said the words, convinced that I was disgusted with him for what he'd done. Because *he* was.

My father started to say something else but I cut him off, *'Don't.'* It was more vicious than I'd intended, and I did understand my father's anger but I also understood how broken Zale had been. How broken he still was. Zale didn't need salt in his wounds. 'Keres lost Antheia and ravaged the mortals on that battlefield, sparing no one in his way. He cursed an entire family when it was Nikos who killed Antheia. I see no judgement there,' I said with a surprisingly even voice.

I knew I'd stepped out of line. He was King of Hell, whether he was my father or not. If he'd been Eiran, I would've thought twice before openly challenging him, before shutting him up.

My mother was his dyad, his equal in every way.

I was not.

Would he punish me? To remind me of my place? But my mother would surely appear more worried if he was truly angry with me, right? Or maybe she thought I deserved it. Maybe she agreed.

And maybe they were right.

Aloïs rose to slowly walk over to me. My mother watched him with a slight frown but looked calm enough. He lowered next to me and touched my cheek with a gentle hand. 'You are my equal as well, Diana. You don't bite your tongue and hide your opinions. You don't swallow down your challenges.'

I swallowed hard, unable to look away from that intense gold – from the stray ache in them.

He was hurting, hurting because I believed he could hurt me.

Why would she be happy that I'm her father?

My eyes burned. 'I'm sorry,' I whispered.

He brushed some hair behind my arched ear with his other hand before taking my hand. 'There's no need to apologise, pup.' I let out a shaky exhale as the tension left me and nodded. When I glanced at my mother over his shoulder, I felt her tug at that little connection we shared as she softly smiled at me. Three times she tugged, to emphasise each word she sent over. *I. Love. You.* Something my parents did through their dyad bond, my *varkradas* informed me. Aloïs' hand was still wrapped around mine, and I felt him squeeze it. Three times.

My very soul calmed at that, like something fundamental had finally found even footing.

'I should apologise,' Zale's voice was uneven, his body tense. 'What I did was despicable.'

My mother spoke before Aloïs could. 'We all did things we're not proud of. I was his paladin for fuck's sake. I did things that still haunt my nightmares.' She looked at Zale with compassion. 'We all lost terribly, both on the battlefield and far away from it. I just hope you've managed to find some sense of peace.'

Zale met my gaze, a soft expression on his face as he took in my healthy appearance. Slowly, a smile formed on his lips. 'I have.'

Chapter 14

Aedlynn

Aspia, the Royal House of Odalis
1764, 24 years after the War of Ichor

Lorcán made them hike through the mountains in Aysel, throughout the day and far throughout the night. He didn't allow Aedlynn to stop walking to eat or drink, or even to catch her breath. He only stopped to allow her to sleep – and even then it was for no more than an hour.

Aedlynn didn't consider herself weak but she was growing exhausted. She had to actively remind herself to lift her feet, to take one step at a time. Her eyes were heavy and she could scarcely keep them open. The weather didn't help either, with the heavy snowfall. Aedlynn might not have been complaining yet but her freezing toes definitely were. Thankfully, the inside of her coat, one Kaelena had given her, was lined with thick and soft fur. Her perfume lingered in the coat as well, which softened Aedlynn's melancholy.

Aedlynn missed her. It'd been two weeks, yet it felt like a lifetime.

She glanced at Lorcán, who walked two steps in front of her since the path was so narrow. When she took another step, ice cracked underneath her boot and she nearly slipped over the edge of the path. Lorcán looked back just when she managed to regain her balance. 'Careful, it's slippery here,' he said dryly.

She glared so viciously that Lorcán grew uncomfortable. 'Why don't you slip and fall down the mountainside, at least I can take a nap then,' Aedlynn spat.

Lorcán raised an amused brow but remained silent. He turned around and continued walking.

'Where are we even going? You still haven't told me anything.' Aedlynn stared at his back, at his long and loose hair, wet from the snow that stuck to his long leather coat.

'We're training.'

'You said that yesterday already, yet I don't feel like I'm training anything but my patience.'

A snort sounded. 'Do you complain this much around Kaelena?'

Aedlynn bit on her bottom lip. Mother, she missed Lena so much that it ached to think of her.

'Continue walking.'

Aedlynn muttered an insult before she took another step.

They'd been training for three weeks now and Aedlynn was at her limit. She was exhausted and cold and she hadn't spoken a word to him in two days. Not because she was annoyed with him, though she was, but because she simply didn't have the energy.

Lorcán handed her another tea after dinner, while they sat in the snow next to a fire Lorcán had started for them. 'Drink up.'

Gratefully, Aedlynn wrapped her hands around the warm cup. The tea smelled a little strange – bitter, but she needed something warm in her body. So Aedlynn drank, welcoming the warmth it provided, and when Lorcán offered a second cup, she downed it as well.

'Good girl, Aedlynn,' he said, brushing a hand through her wet hair.

She shivered like a small fawn, already losing the warmth of the tea and desperate to scoot closer to the fire, yet Lorcán pulled her closer to him instead and wrapped an arm around her to give her some of his own body warmth. The tea spread through her body until it hazed her mind, until it went utterly blank.

She stared up at Lorcán, exhausted and empty-feeling, her gaze growing absent.

Her defences crumbled down around her.

'You're doing really well, darling,' he said with a low voice.

Was she? Because she felt vulnerable and Aedlynn didn't like feeling like that, she only did around . . . around someone.

Before long, her eyes closed.

Two days later, Aedlynn groaned when Lorcán woke her from her nap. Lorcán hoisted his bag on his shoulder and started walking. Her eyes were still lined with sleep but her pride made her get up and follow behind him, jogging until her legs caught up with him. While Aedlynn ran, an unfamiliar perfume crept into her nose, coming from the lining of the coat.

When she reached him, Lorcán smiled and Aedlynn stared at him, overcome with her heart skipping at the sight. He reached out a hand to tuck a damp string of hair behind her ear. 'Did you sleep well, darling?'

Aedlynn blinked, surprised at the affection. 'I'm still tired,' she managed to bring out. She had a feeling the only reason she hadn't collapsed yet was because of her stubborn divine blood.

He leaned forward and kissed her forehead. 'We'll arrive at a small cabin soon, we'll rest there.'

Aedlynn stared at him in stunned silence, forgetting to walk.

Lorcán stopped as well. 'Is something wrong?'

'You haven't done that before.' She pointed at her forehead.

His eyes held hers captive and something in her chest tightened at the affection she saw in them. 'Perhaps I'm growing tired of pretending.' Then his eyes trailed up and down her body. 'It was very nice of your roommate to lend you her coat.'

Aedlynn frowned. 'She did?'

Something close to triumph glinted in his eyes. 'Yes.'

'That explains the perfume.'

'You don't like it?' Aedlynn shrugged. He smiled thinly. 'Kaelena appears fond of you.'

Aedlynn snorted. 'She's a courtesan, she's fond of any sort of attention – even if it's insults.'

'That's not very nice, Aedlynn.'

She shrugged again. 'I wasn't bred to be nice, Your Highness.' Aedlynn continued their walk, unaware of the triumph that blazed in Lorcán's eyes.

Aedlynn took off her coat and hung it over one of the wooden chairs while Lorcán snapped his fingers to light up the hearth. Something about watching that fire filled Aedlynn with a sense of familiarity, like she'd watched it before. With someone she loved.

Lorcán walked up to her. 'Are you warm enough, darling?' The more he called her that, the more confused she grew. Aedlynn's brows drew together while she looked at him – the chiselled cheeks, full lips and tanned skin, too surprised to move when he started caressing her face – when he cupped it. 'Are you?' Lorcán whispered.

Aedlynn couldn't help but blush. She quickly nodded, then dived away and pulled up her sleeves to cool off while she walked over to the kitchen and stared out of the window. She looked back at her arms, only to find her skin painted with swirling black markings. She knew those markings. She knew what they meant and yet . . . she couldn't remember.

She noticed the ring on her finger and knew it belonged to Kaelena but why was it on *her* finger? Why had she lent Aedlynn her coat? They couldn't stand each other.

Lorcán's arms draped around her from behind and Aedlynn tried hard not to flinch, but almost immediately a wonderful cloud of jasmine swept over her and she relaxed in his embrace, letting herself melt against his warm, hard body. Though a part of her recognised that she was more used to a soft body, with curves.

Had she . . . Had she perhaps lain with Kaelena? The thought was ridiculous but . . .

Lorcán's lips brushed over the shell of her ear, the side of her throat and Aedlynn stilled when his lips started trailing. Placing kiss after kiss from her jawline to her collarbone. 'Forgive me for not being able to keep from you any longer,' he said with a low, husky voice. 'But now that Isolde is finally gone, I wish to be with my dyad.'

Her eyes, which had been half-closed as she'd enjoyed his advances, flew wide open.

Dyad.

Light brown eyes flashed in her mind, the sensation of Lena's lips on her skin and the faint sound of giggles as they play fought in the snow. Her gaze fell on that lone star shining brightly in the night sky, although the happiness she normally felt by viewing it was overshadowed by the guilt and shame she felt that now felt because she'd forgotten her dyad. The other half of her soul. Her *home*.

The things she'd thought and said about Lena these past weeks disgusted her, pulling her back to every moment she'd ever watched Lena crumble apart and how she'd held her crying dyad in her arms because Lena felt like she was *nothing*. Nothing but the names they all hurled her way. Nothing but a toy. Nothing of importance.

And *Lorcán* had made her speak like that about Lena. He'd made her forget her own dyad.

She tried to whirl around, ready to pounce on Lorcán for whatever he was trying but she felt a sharp pain in her left side. Lorcán withdrew the dagger, holding her firmly in place against that counter while blood seeped out and coated her shirt. Her *ichor* spilled onto the counter top, slowly dripping onto the old wooden flooring.

'Now, Aedlynn, *behave*,' he shushed. 'You were right before, you know, you weren't bred to be nice. You were bred to be a weapon. Perhaps I shouldn't have let you get so close to that nymph, though I must admit my surprise that you're even capable of loving anything – given what you are. You weren't bred to be loved and you certainly weren't made to worship anyone but me.'

Aedlynn clenched her jaw, tried hard to fight against his hold, but the dagger had been laced with moonsbane. His arms weren't the only thing keeping her in place as his dark magic coiled around her limbs. She'd been taught enough by Lorcán to know that he'd formed a *kaloptis* between them. A fake dyad bond, one used to fully control the other person. Though as far as she was aware, a *kaloptis* could be broken if the person had a true dyad.

'I find it rather funny that my hold broke the moment I called you my dyad. I find it even more curious that you thought of *her*,' he mused. 'Sweet little Kaelena.'

Aedlynn kept quiet, refused to admit what they were. He'd find a way to use it against them.

Lorcán sighed next to her ear. 'Very well, Aedlynn, allow me to explain to you how this is going to go. You won't fight me, you'll be a good girl and do exactly what I ask of you – or I'll whip Kaelena until her bones are visible and when I'm finally done, I'll burn her alive.'

Aedlynn couldn't hide her terror at the thought of him being so violent with her when she was nothing but kindness and light. Aedlynn should've left Odalis with her weeks ago.

'Do as I say and your dyad will live. She will remain unharmed and simply forget about you.'

Aedlynn stared at the star in front of her through thick tears. Kaelena's gift. The warmth of her wedding ring seemed to burn into her skin. 'Don't make me hurt her,' she whispered.

'Oh, viper, don't worry about that. You won't even care about her when I'm done with you.' His voice grew cruel. 'I will fix these faults of yours and bring you back to what you were meant to be.' Lorcán smoothed his hand over her bloodied leather armour, hovering over the wound to heal it until only a faint scar remained.

Aedlynn gritted her teeth. Perhaps years ago, she would've believed that she was nothing more than a killing machine but Kaelena had pulled her out of that belief. She'd dusted off Aedlynn's soul and heart and then decorated it with flowers and stars. 'I thought *you* cared about her,' she spat. 'You seemed awfully protective of her when it came to Isolde. Enough so to have her killed.'

Lorcán chuckled lightly. 'I did love her but I've been betrayed by plenty of people, so I wasn't simple enough to fully place my trust in some pretty nymph and it appears I had every reason not to. I ordered her to seduce you and to report back to me should you ever stray. Instead, she planted ridiculous ideas in your mind that you are capable of love.'

She already knew that; Lena had confessed it days after that first night together because she'd felt horribly guilty. She'd been terrified to admit it but was scared that Lorcán might tell Aedlynn himself and that she'd lose her; that she'd lose the one person who'd ever truly seen and loved her. So she'd wept and confessed what she'd done and how somewhere along the lines of pretending she'd found that there was too much fragile truth in her deliberate smiles and touches. And Aedlynn, although hurt to have been played with again, had cared more about making Lena smile than her scorned pride. Perhaps it had been a trick once upon a time, but their happily ever after had resulted because of it.

'If everyone you love at one point turned against you, perhaps that's *your* fault. And if the Fates gave your weapon a dyad, perhaps they're biding their time to cut you down – roots and all.'

'Fate is on *my* side, Aedlynn, and she guides me. How the Hell do you think I've got this far? I know the gods are biding their time and that Eiran quakes in his well-polished boots with the knowledge that I own most of Yael's work. She was the only one Eiran ever feared aside from Antheia – she made herself a god.'

Right now, Aedlynn truly couldn't care less about some *Aurealis* he'd killed. She tried to think of a way out of this mess but there was nothing she could do. The moons-bane blocked her magic. She couldn't æriate, couldn't do anything except fight with her hands because she'd been foolish enough not to have any weapons on her. They'd been too heavy to carry around. And even though she'd been trained well by Aviod, she knew Lorcán was too powerful to defeat without divine magic.

Lorcán turned her around and pushed her against the cabinets, placing both hands on the marble countertop behind her. His smirk infuriated her. She wanted to tear it off his face.

If she could even manage to make a run for it, she had no idea where they were. For all she knew, they weren't even in Aysel anymore – or Aspia. If she ran, he would hurt Kaelena.

She knew Lorcán. Mercy didn't exist in his dictionary.

'It's quite amusing to hear those raging thoughts of yours.'

She spat in his face. Lorcán clicked his tongue and used his sleeve to wipe away her spit, then his eyes rested back on hers and Aedlynn felt his *kalotra* pull at her. 'Keep disrespecting me and I'll bring Kaelena to her knees again.'

Isolde hadn't decided on her own to hurt Kaelena, she realised. Yes, Isolde could be vicious and merciless but not without reason and she certainly was no fool. Aedlynn had the sinking feeling Lorcán had given her enough reasons. All to use her as a pawn in that little game he was playing to gather and keep power.

She clenched her fists so tightly that her nails dug into her skin and the look on her face grew cold. 'Swallow me whole, Lorcán, while you have the chance,' she said in a low voice that didn't sound fully like it belonged to her but something older. Something angrier. Something not easily vanquished. 'Because if you leave anything behind, I will haunt you and not even your little Fate can protect you then.'

Lorcán took her chin in one hand and brushed his thumb over her lips. His *kalotra* crawled over her skin like thousands of spiders. 'Don't worry about Kaelena, little viper. I'm sure she'll soon find someone else to warm her bed; someone who *does* deserve her attention.'

Tears burned in her eyes. Aedlynn couldn't stand how lightly he dismissed what Lena felt for her. As if he truly couldn't understand anyone wanting her. She was about to make another retort, but as he lashed out with his dark magic, the breath slammed out of her chest. She slumped forward while every single sense of hers fought against him, but the jasmine scent grew stronger until her mind went blank.

Aedlynn sat in the large bathtub in Lorcán's private quarters, the hot water reached up to her chin while she relaxed. They'd returned only an hour ago after spending another month in Aysel. He'd continued training her, both her magic and using *Výsae* as a weapon. They'd also discovered a handful of tricks she could do and he'd helped her hone those skills, all while guarding her divine blood to keep her from crashing. Apparently, Aedlynn could scream and use it to kill anyone near her – like a banshee.

She'd just closed her eyes, enjoying the servant who was washing her bloodied hair from their last training session, when Aedlynn heard someone vigorously throw open the double doors that led into Lorcán's private wing.

Immediately, she sat up straight in the tub, closely listening to what was going on.

'Where is she?!'

Kaelena.

Aedlynn rolled her eyes and sank back against the back of the tub. Kaelena might be annoying, but she was no threat to Lorcán.

'Calm yourself, Kaelena.'

'Why the Hell are they removing her belongings from our room? Where is she?!' It almost sounded as if she was worried about Aedlynn.

'Aedlynn wishes to stay by my side.'

'What the Hell did you do, Lorcán?' The tone of her voice made Aedlynn sit up again. There was a seething anger in it that she'd never heard before. She didn't even address him properly.

'I did nothing, little dove,' he shushed her. 'I trained her skills and now Aedlynn wishes to remain by my side, where she can fulfil her duty.'

'*Bullshit!*' Kaelena yelled at him with a viciousness that rattled her, slipping right into Aerelian. Aedlynn quickly scrambled out of the tub, barely drying herself off before she hastily put on the silk robe the servant handed her. Weapons ready if necessary.

'Where is Aedlynn?!' Kaelena yelled, and as Aedlynn opened the heavy door, she saw the bitch had a dagger against Lorcán's throat. Kaelena soon found herself tackled and brought to her knees while Aedlynn's own blade rested against her throat. Lena's knees bruised from the impact on the hardwood floor.

'Here she is,' Lorcán said softly. The way he looked down at Kaelena and the cruel smile on his lips left the hairs on Aedlynn's arms erect. Kaelena's throat moved against the cold steel of her dagger when she swallowed. She trembled in Aedlynn's grip but it wasn't out of fear; she was boiling over with a loathing worthy of Antheia.

'It's quite all right, Aedlynn,' Lorcán said. 'My *loyal* nymph won't cross another line.'

Aedlynn let go and Kaelena immediately turned. Her hands landed on Aedlynn's cheeks to cup them while she desperately searched her face for something. Aedlynn stared at her with a risen brow and firmly pulled her hands away. 'Keep your hands to yourself, whore. I have no need of your services.'

Lena's eyes slipped to the black markings Aedlynn wore on her arms and chest, proof of her dedication to Lorcán. While Aedlynn watched her, the anger seemed to drain out of her face. Aedlynn wasn't sure what was going on in her mind but whatever Kaelena had decided seemed to give her peace.

Those red-stained lips parted into a sweet smile. 'All the stars in the sky.'

Aedlynn blinked at her. She'd heard that before some-where and somehow knew the continuation of it; *could never shine as bright as my love for you.* Jasmine clouded her senses again and the confused look on Aedlynn's face made room for a disinterested one. But there was a gleam in Kaelena's eyes, especially when she shifted her gaze to Lorcán with the same sickly sweet smile. 'Rest well, little king, attempting to conquer something always leaves you tired.' She didn't wait for Lorcán to say anything before she stormed out of his chambers.

Kaelena

The servants quickly fled from the Cadre's wing while Kaelena threw vase after vase at the wall. She should've got Aedlynn out when she'd had the chance. The devoted way she'd looked at him, how she'd lunged at Kaelena without hesitation . . . and those *markings*.

It made her sick to her stomach.

Aedlynn deserved so much better than this shit life Khalyna had thrown her into.

Kaelena reeled at the thought of Lorcán touching her, of having her wrapped around his fingers. She loathed him for what he'd done. She wanted to grab Keres by his collar and make him kill them all. She wished Antheia still lived so she could answer her prayer to haunt him. *Anyone.* She wished she held more power, enough to actually protect herself and her loved ones instead of being so damned vulnerable and dependent on others. But there were no gods here. There was only a playground for those who wished to strengthen their power and a dungeon for those who opposed them.

Kaelena curled her fingers around the amulet Aedlynn had gifted her, around the burning moonstone. In the days leading up to Winter Solstice, the stone had been growing warmer and seemed to subtly vibrate with power.

The longest night of the year. A day dedicated to Antheia, a day to worship her.

If there was anyone who was known for viciously protecting and avenging their dyad, it was her Lady. Perhaps it was time to remind Lorcán who'd created the vesperae and that her Lady's dainty nymphs could be just as cruel and violent as their Goddess.

Especially when provoked.

Chapter 15

Diana

Given that my father often had meetings with Hell's rulers, he'd asked a member of his Guard to help me train my wings for usage, as well as improve my physical condition. Castriel had been training me for two weeks now and I'd already noticed the difference this morning, as I no longer wobbled around like my wings were a foreign object attached to my back, but with a grace I hadn't expected of myself.

I'd learned a lot about him already. Some of it had come to me through his shadows. Most of it had come out of his own mouth because Cas had a habit of telling funny anecdotes about his brothers, his mate and even my parents. My parents had been teaching me a lot about Hell in general but these training sessions with Cas taught me a lot about Anthens and the circederae who lived here. How they lived, as well as the way Hell was ruled. There was a ruler for each region of Hell, and they were overseen by my father. Those rulers were also Lord or Lady of the respective Greater Daemons they governed.

Dáneiris was Lady of Colchians and thus ruled over Osirian. Scylla, Lady of Sirens ruled over Aderyn, and Faolán,

Lord of Aepokra and Vampyrs, ruled over Persephian. I hadn't met the Lord of Circederae yet, nor had anyone really mentioned him.

My curiosity got the better of me during another training session in a cobblestoned square near a creek when Cas fleetingly mentioned him, so I asked about it. 'I haven't seen Bastian yet, though I've seen the others a few times already. They came to introduce themselves to me.' I accepted the weight he handed me to exercise my shoulders. 'And nobody really talks about him. What's that about?'

'Knowing Aloïs, he'd dump Bastian's body in Erebus if he did decide to come visit you,' Cas said. His golden eyes were fixated on where my muscles were tightened, to see if I was doing the exercise correctly. The daylight reflected beautifully on his bronze skin and warmed his handsome features. He could give Zhella herself a run for her money as a sun deity.

'Ah, great friends?'

Cas snorted. 'Bastian is Lord of Circederae in name only. Aloïs rules over Anthens instead. We've all shunned him and he's exiled to the darkest pits of Hell.' He gave me a knowing look as he said, 'Even his sons rejected him.'

I blinked. 'You, Eos and Aiden?'

He nodded and gestured for me to continue because I'd paused. 'Before Aloïs became King, Hell was pretty much a dark playground for monsters to exert control. Circederae had clans, much like we still do, except then they were more like cults and, now, they refer to families. Some of those clans had very distinct beliefs on the hierarchy within our society, especially regarding *matska*.'

'They saw us as lesser than them?'

Again, he nodded and changed the weights, giving me an

approving nod when I did the exercise right. 'The Alásdair and Déyanira clans were very extreme in their opinions, with the Déyaniras blindly following Bastian's example. When *matska* first bled, their wings were clipped or torn off. They were servants – slaves to their forced mates,' he told me grimly. 'If they deemed a newborn pup to be weak, they were either thrown back into Erebus to die in the darkness or killed in front of the mother to warn her not to fuck up again.'

I stared at him in blatant disgust, holding the weight as I paused. 'And Bastian *condoned* that?'

'Encouraged it,' Cas said softly. 'Aloïs killed most of the Déyanira clan when he became King, sparing only the innocent. And as his Guard, we helped him do so. And of *our* clan, eventually, only Aiden and I survived. The rest swore allegiance to Bastian, so Aloïs had them executed.'

'And Eos?' He was my father's Right Hand.

'Eos was born later,' Cas said before taking a drink from his bottle of water. 'Bastian hid him and raised him to become his spitting image and when Vanora helped start a revolution against those old beliefs, those two clashed often.' He grinned thinly. 'Vanora can be *very* spiteful and aggressive when crossed and Eos liked lighting her fuse a little too much, but when Bastian captured her and tore off her wings as a lesson, it was Eos who saved her and brought her to us. He changed after that – became a better man. And given how he tended to Vanora's wounds without ever pitying her or making her feel like she'd become less of a circes due to the loss of her wings, they stuck together and eventually mated.'

Absent-mindedly, I nodded while I tried to process that story and continue my exercise. I'd met Vanora and genuinely liked her bubbly and dramatic personality, but the absence of her wings had been very obvious. I ached for her, for what she'd had to withstand. I couldn't imagine losing my wings, especially so violently. Those wounds healed *very* slowly, easily infected and the pain was pure torture. No one deserved that – except maybe Bastian.

Cas flicked his fingers against my exposed stomach. 'You're not using your core.'

I blew a stray strand of hair away from my face. Beads of sweat had gathered on my forehead. My hair was damp. But Cas had promised he'd take me flying later today if I did well, so I tightened my abdominal muscles and repeated the exercise.

'Better.'

'I want five gilded pears after this exercise,' I muttered, then yelped and almost dropped the weights when he moved to tickle my side again. 'Ten pears if you – KEEP TICKLING ME!'

I backed away until I hit something with my back – someone whose laugh sounded like music. A lovely mix of smouldering wood and a pine forest curled in my nose. I turned my head to look at the circes behind me and my breathing hitched in my throat. He was *gorgeous*, with the same bronzed skin as Cas had but unlike Cas, whose dark shoulder-length hair was gathered in a messy bun with a string of leather, this brother had short hair.

I stared at him with my mouth open. My mind went completely blank.

He smiled and extended his hand to me. 'You must be Diana. I'm Aiden.'

I looked down at his hand and it took me a good second before my brain restarted, before it reminded me that I was supposed to shake it. 'Thank you . . . I ehm . . . I'm Diana.' The words tripped over themselves in my mouth.

The corner of his mouth quirked up. 'I know.'

Divine shit, he's pretty.

I nodded while I tried to remember what I was doing before I'd backed into him. Luckily, Cas came to the rescue before I could further embarrass myself. 'You want to join? She could give you a run for your money.' Cas' eyes gleamed. 'She's a witch.'

'You can do magic?'

I nodded, mentally slapping my face to get rid of this stupid daze that had settled over me. 'Yes.'

'That's really neat.' He grew excited. 'Circes normally can't use it. Colchians can use a little depending on the moon phases but real magic is mostly for gods and mortals. Yael was a strange exception. Though I guess we shouldn't be too surprised given how strong Eva's magic is.'

He was genuinely impressed, which made me stare at him in quiet shock. I averted my eyes while I nodded again. 'Yeah, I guess that's the benefit of being a *výssar*.'

Aiden sensed my discomfort, though I'd pulled up my walls to keep my own secrets well hidden – some privacy my father had taught me.

'You're still coming for dinner, right?' Cas asked him, to which Aiden nodded, then he smiled at me. 'Would you like to come as well? Maeve will be there, you can meet her.'

I was honoured that he wanted me to meet his pregnant mate and that he wanted me there but that old self-consciousness nagged at me, one of the less visible scars Orthalla had gifted me. 'I'd love to,' I heard myself say, even though my nerves coiled in my abdomen.

'Perfect. Half seven, my place.'

I worried how long it would take before they'd turn on me. I knew it was stupid. They were in Aloïs' Guard, they'd be fools to go out of their way to hurt me. But then again, everyone who'd ever tried to get close to me had done just that.

Cas clasped Aiden's shoulder. 'Will you join training?'

The look Aiden gave me was a challenge. 'If Diana can handle me.'

Cocky bastard. Maybe it was a good thing that my competitiveness was sparked alive by the comment. It eased some of my anxiety. 'I'll kick your ass so violently that you'll be singing soprano for a week.'

I summoned a pear from my shadows to snack on.

His lips quirked up, revealing the dimples he had. 'Allow me to serenade you then, witch.'

I wrinkled my nose. 'If you bother me with your singing voice, I'll throw rotten tomatoes at your face.'

'I'll help you.' Cas dramatically sighed. 'Aiden sings like a siren with a fishing pole up their ass.'

I nearly choked on my pear.

'Fuck off, Cas. You sing like an aepokra with a blood allergy.'

'And what exactly do those sound like?' Cas asked him, fully amused as the warrior crossed his muscled arms.

'Dead.'

I cackled at the dry reply, then yelped when the pine scent hit me from behind and Aiden grabbed me around the waist to throw me over his shoulder. My pear fell. 'Put me – *down*!'

'I thought you wanted to spar.' Aiden teased me by shaking me up and down. 'Do you think if I shake her violently enough, more of those pears will fall out of her shadows?'

'You're a fucking prick, you know that?' His wings smelled nice, like he'd rolled around in the grass. I liked the scent.

'I do.'

I snickered, making another attempt at escaping. 'If you don't put me down this second, I'll lick your wings.'

'How scandalous,' he purred. 'Take me on a date first, *matska*, then I'll let you lick my wings to your heart's desire.'

Tension coiled in my lower abdomen at the comment, at the way he called me *matska*. I'd meant it in a teasing manner, like I would tease Sorin that I'd stick a wet finger in his ear. But wings were sensitive and circes didn't just use them to fly. They weren't ignored in the gentle darkness of lovers – not at all. And though I was beyond curious about that, I couldn't allow my thoughts to wander there.

'Do you flirt so desperately with every woman you meet?'

'Only with witches who blush when I smile at them.'

My pride reeled, couldn't handle the smug satisfaction I heard in his voice and felt in his shadows.

I kicked my knee into his stomach, which he blocked with a shadow. I tried to push myself away from him, to wiggle free. I felt stupid – because I *knew* I could fight better than this. It was just that he smelled very nice and I secretly liked how his body warmed mine.

Which was utter *bullshit*.

Frustration lit me up, creating an inferno that cleared my mind. I melted into darkness, slipped out of his arms, and when I materialised behind him, I kicked his legs away. My shadows wrapped themselves tightly around his limbs. Aiden readied himself to move through his shadows and I blocked those pathways while I summoned my dagger.

Slowly, I sank down to sit on his stomach with my legs cradling the sides of his chest. And I firmly planted *Aecéso* against his throat.

I smirked at him, tightly holding him down. His wings were tautly pressed between his back and the warm stones, and Aiden stared at me in a mix of awe and something I really didn't want to see in those beautiful honey eyes – desire. But my body reacted for me, made me lean forward so my braid slipped over my shoulder and caressed his cheek. So my breathing caressed his lips.

Even my shadows settled around us. Happy to watch.

'What's wrong, *mattas*?' My voice was nothing more than a careless whisper that filled the too-small space between our faces. 'Cat got your tongue?'

Aiden's eyes slid from mine to my lips, then travelled down further as he took me in. Something fluttered in my belly. *Get yourself together,* I silently scolded myself. He leaned towards me and those dimples made another appearance while his grin became utterly arrogant – and so godsdamned lovely. 'Don't worry, *matska*, I can still use my to—'

I rolled my eyes and loosened my grip to get up. 'You *fucking* men and your *fucking* hormones.'

Cas laughed behind us. I let go of Aiden, who teasingly tugged at my braid while I started to get up. 'All silliness aside, that was impressive,' he said.

I focused on my dagger, on the black smoke that rose from it and how it whispered to me.

'It must be nice to finally use your *varkradas*, huh?' Again, that genuine interest. I stared at the pitch-black blade in my hands. 'Diana?'

I conjured up a polite smile. 'Thank you.'

Aiden blinked, then drew his dark brows together. 'You okay?'

I kept that smile securely in place, working hard to make it reach my eyes. I'd worn that mask plenty of times in Orthalla. 'It does feel nice.'

Cas laid a hand on my shoulder. 'What's wrong?'

'Nothing but I should head back, clean up before dinner.' Was I a horrible person for thinking of different excuses so I wouldn't have to go? Ironically, I couldn't complain about being sick anymore.

Cas' eyes trailed over my face to find the truth there but there was no truth, only that mask. 'Are you uncomfortable because Aiden flirted with you?'

I blinked. I hadn't expected him to ask that – outright.

'If so, you can tell me.' Aiden crossed his arms. 'You might not be used to it but unlike mortals, we do talk to each other. Miscommunication isn't exactly in our dictionary given our *varkradas*.'

I snapped at him, 'I can handle some stupid flirting.'

Aiden eyed me curiously. He sensed the war inside of me, how I really couldn't handle it. Because of that bastard. But I didn't want to think about Kallias anymore, I just . . . I wanted peace. I had no desire to wonder whether the person I loved actually loved me or was playing some twisted game.

I glanced at Cas and when I felt his concern as well, I decided I'd had enough. I summoned my jacket from the side of the square and made to leave.

'You're really just going to run off?' I ignored Aiden as I put on the jacket. 'You call that training? You flaunt your shadows for a minute and then you run off?'

'I already told you,' I bit out. 'I'm going to take a shower before dinner.'

His gaze hardened. 'No, you're not. You already decided minutes ago that you're not coming.' He gestured at me. 'You're thinking up excuses as I'm talking to you.'

I blew some air through my nose and looked away. 'Your point?' I was fully aware of how conceited I appeared, like I couldn't care less. Though the very opposite was true.

'Something's bothering you. Spit it out.'

'Aiden, if she doesn't want to talk about it, let her go.'

Aiden walked over, though he didn't touch me. But his shadows were restless. 'Cas wouldn't invite you into his life if he wanted nothing to do with you.'

'Stop reading me!' I hissed at him.

'I wouldn't be arguing with you if I didn't want to get to know you.'

'Please, just *stop.*' My voice broke. My hands were balled into such tight fists that my nails dug little crescents in my skin. I wanted to run away. To flee like a coward before I'd find a dagger in my back again, gilded in the sweetest promises.

He opened his mouth but closed it again and simply nodded once. I crossed my arms over my chest, looking away while I fought off the tears. 'This isn't Orthalla, Diana.'

'Stop reading me!'

'He can't help it if your emotions are overflowing,' Cas pointed out.

I threw my hands up in frustration and turned around to leave but Aiden slipped his hand around my wrist to stop me. 'Come tonight, just humour me.'

'Why?' I croaked, not looking at him.

'Because I promise you won't regret it.'

215

Soft blonde waves cascaded down my shoulders and breasts to cover the light white dress I wore. It contrasted the stark black of my wings, which I quite liked.

While I put in my earrings, my thoughts ran. Would Maeve like me? Maybe Aiden only wanted me to come because he pitied me. I didn't need pity. I didn't need friends. I'd survived twenty-five years without any and the one year I'd decided to trust someone, they'd nearly had to bury me.

But maybe . . . maybe things could be different.

Truth be told, I'd like some friends. To not be so lonely anymore. To feel like I belonged.

I glanced down at Keres' marking, smoothing my fingers over the dark ink. What if Aiden thought I was just some easy *matska* to conquer? Some eager and desperate girl to get his pleasure from until he grew tired of me. Or what if Cas' sweetness would dissolve until he would sneer at me? What if Maeve would despise me like those noble ladies had for the stares their husbands had given me – even if I'd never wanted their attention? A mating bond was as intense as a dyad bond, though it was a chosen bond crafted of blood and shadows. Maeve would tear me apart.

My shadows lay nestled against me as I sat on the bed. They were trying to soothe me and I hugged them to my chest, enjoying the cosy sensation it brought forth.

A knock sounded on my bedroom door. 'Figured I'd accompany you.' Aiden's muffled voice sounded through the thick black wood.

'I don't need a chaperone, I'm not a child.'

He pushed the door open to come in and I stared him down, far too aware of my red eyes and puffed cheeks. He said nothing about it, simply sauntered over and perched on the midnight-coloured and gold embroidered duvet next to me.

'I understand that there are things you'd rather keep private.' His shadows circled mine. 'And I'm sorry for pushing you back there. But you were hurting – *are* hurting, Diana.'

I closed my eyes. His voice was so damn gentle, a weapon against that thick ice wall I'd built.

My mother had told me how she thanked herself every day for putting her trust in Aloïs and her friends; especially Eos, Antheia, Vaeric and Emeryn. And I remembered how I'd watched her heal in those visions, how she'd grown stronger with their help. The words felt like marbles in my mouth, foreign and strange. It was hard to let that wall down, but I wanted to. And I felt something like genuinity swirling in the darkness of Aiden's shadows, giving me that final push I needed.

'I might not . . . not be used to that,' I quietly admitted. 'Those nobles were . . . They were cruel.'

'You survived them.' Gently, he took my hand in his. I watched our hands, and this time, I didn't scold myself for liking his warmth against my skin. 'But you're no helpless mortal anymore, Diana. They'd be fools to cross you.'

I nodded absent-mindedly. 'I do like Cas.' I wiped away a stray tear. 'And you, even if you're a pain in the ass.'

He chuckled. 'A strange compliment but I'll take it.' I laughed softly and Aiden caressed the back of my hand with his thumb. 'You're no longer in Orthalla, Diana. Maybe it's time to leave surviving behind you and start living.'

There was an annoying lump in my throat, one that didn't leave no matter how hard I tried to swallow. 'I'm sorry that I behaved like an ass.'

'It's fine. I'm sorry I pushed you.'

'It's okay. A lifetime supply of gilded pears will help me forgive you.'

His shoulders shook as he laughed. 'A lifetime supply? You're immortal.'

'Better start collecting them then.'

The cosy house appeared small, but once inside, I quickly realised it wasn't small at all. It was lovely, with deep colours, wooden flooring and cosy beige sofas. Their open kitchen connected with the living room, which had glass doors that led into a deep garden with a little patio where the table was set for dinner. Maeve's auburn hair was gathered up while she stirred some of the pots and pans on the furnace. Her rounded belly was covered with an apron. Cas walked us over, happily chatting with Aiden.

Maeve inclined her head in a little bow. 'It's lovely to meet you, My Lady.'

'Please, just call me Diana.' I smiled and fidgeted with my fingers. 'Can I ehm . . . Can I help? Though I have to warn you that I'm a horrible cook.'

'You can serve the drinks if you want.' Aiden's hand moved towards the salad to steal a tomato but Maeve slapped it away with a shadow. 'And guard my tomatoes.'

She turned around to help Cas. Aiden shot me an impish grin and dived for a tomato, then threw it to me. I threw the tomato at his face but he caught it in his mouth. Glancing at Maeve's back, I stole three more tomatoes. Aiden gaped at me, drawing a thumb across his throat while he feverishly pointed at Maeve. I giggled – actually giggled. I couldn't even remember the last time that I'd made that sound.

Maeve turned around as I hid them in my *varkradas*. 'What's funny?'

I blinked. 'Ehm . . .'

'Mortal taxes,' Aiden said dryly. 'Those are pretty funny,

aren't they, Diana?' I threw my head back and laughed at the stupid comment. Something light sparked in Aiden's shadows as he watched me.

Maeve noted the salad bowl and scowled at Aiden. 'Where are my tomatoes?'

'Why are you so obsessed with your tomatoes?'

'Why are *you?*' she bit back, though her eyes shone playfully.

'Because they taste good!'

'Then buy them yourself.'

'Yeah, bring your own like I did.' I showed them a cherry tomato and nibbled on it.

Maeve started laughing. Aiden's eyes gleamed with amusement.

I frowned at him. 'What's that?'

'Huh?'

I pointed at his ear. 'That.' I stepped closer and brushed my hand behind his ear. My shadows opened up. When I pulled my hand back, it was filled with a healthy amount of mini tomatoes.

Aiden gasped. '*Witchcraft.*'

Maeve rolled her eyes to the ceiling. 'Dear Mother above.'

I laughed, the corners of my eyes creasing as I did, and helped them set the table.

After dinner, we gathered around a fire bowl to drink and share more stories while the day slipped away and the stars illuminated the sky above us. I'd spent a good hour chatting to Maeve about her job as Anthens' renowned healer – how Aestor himself had taught her, and curiously asking her about pups and the differences with human babies, as well as receiving her advice on how to take care of my wings with moisturising oils and how to groom them. Though she'd assured me I was welcome anytime to have her look at them and groom them for me, and teach me in the process, which I was endlessly grateful for. It was nice knowing I could ask a friend instead of bombarding my father with endless questions about the logistics of being a daemon.

I sat cross-legged on the chair, clasping my bottle with both hands as I smiled at Maeve and Cas, who'd snuggled against each other while Cas sweetly caressed her belly. Their shadows lay happily intertwined underneath their chairs. Aiden sat on the chair next to me.

'I've been to Aurnea,' Maeve said. 'Can't exactly say that I enjoy the people there.'

'I don't blame you.' I traced the opening of the small bottle with a finger. 'Why were you there?'

'Cas and I are in charge of aepokra-hunting,' she explained. 'Aloïs senses it if someone uses the Gates, so he warns us that there's probably an aepokra on the loose to feed on mortal blood, and if they don't return within hours, Cas hunts them and I drug them so we can drag them back to Persephian.'

I shivered involuntarily. Aepokrae survived on mortal blood, could drain mortals whole before they were satisfied. They were gorgeous and had mastered the art of compulsion, could seduce their victim by simply making eye contact and the only thing that warned one of their true nature was the red ring around their pupil.

Cas said, 'Mortals generally don't take notice, and if they do, Maeve wipes their memories with some potions. Which we ehm . . . *gently* force into their mouth.' He smiled mischievously. 'Side effects include thinking it's Wednesday instead of Saturday and some light bruising around the jaw.'

Fully amused, I shook my head. 'I couldn't care less if it's a light or intense bruising.'

'Damn, you really don't like them, huh?' Maeve raised her brows at me. 'How come?'

'They're excessively cruel. It got so bad that I prayed to Keres for help a few years ago.'

Cas' eyes widened as he sat up straighter. 'That was *you?*'

I nodded, surprised that he seemed to know. I glanced at Aiden, who looked at me in bewilderment, starting to put two and two together. Even Maeve had paled. I swallowed hard and played with the fabric of my dress. 'So ehm . . . yeah . . .'

'Keres was with us when he received that prayer,' Cas said. 'When he came back, he left straight for Asphiodel.'

I cleared my throat and looked at the bottle in my hands, rolling it between my hands. 'Yeah . . . I found out that ehm . . . the person – the reason I'd needed Keres, that he made sure they received the worst torture possible in Asphiodel.'

'What happened?' Aiden spoke this time.

I drew in a deep breath. 'In Orthalla, I'm nothing more than Lorcán's plaything. They only pretend to be polite when Zale is around, but behind his back, they're absolutely vicious. I once thought that their dismissal of my existence would be the worst of it but then I met Kallias,' I laughed humourlessly. 'A charming, promising noble heir convinced me that he was in love with me. He courted me for a couple of months, but soon proposed to me because he was so "enamoured" with me, and I gratefully accepted. Once we were officially engaged, he spent months breaking me down – gaslighting and manipulating me until I truly believed my memory was faulty, that my mind wasn't quite right. He ridiculed me for easily crying and claimed I always overreacted. He would hurt me, bruise me and then get angry saying that I was the one hurting *him* and when I . . . when I finally told him that I didn't want to marry him . . . Kallias lost his patience and he . . . he whipped me to . . . to teach me how to be a compliant wife.'

I swallowed. The memories kept flashing before my eyes but it was like I'd turned a faucet open. I couldn't stop talking. 'He said that if I wouldn't do what he wanted, he'd tell the nobles that he'd found me sacrificing some innocent girl to Elyon. That he'd make me regret my defiance and that I'd still beg for him,' I spat. 'And I just . . . I blacked out, and when my mind cleared, I was sitting on top of him, covered in his blood. I didn't know what to do or where to go. I knew I'd be completely ruined if anyone found us.'

My voice grew quiet. 'And I believed I deserved to be punished for what I'd done . . . So I prayed to Keres. He removed the body, the blood, left nothing behind. Keres calmed me down and returned me to Katrones and then convinced the villagers in Medos that we'd been attacked by wolves. I had to live with that guilt and it ate at me. I was convinced that I'd overreacted, that I'd gone mad and that Keres would show up again to demand payment or punishment. And when Kallias' father put two and two together and Zale was in Václav, Lord Rhosyn had me brought before him – forced on my knees. He had his guards humiliate me and tear my dress apart and then he had me whipped for killing his son. I snapped again, and when I came to, that lord was dead. His guards were dead, like I'd attacked them with claws. I was covered in blood, even my face and mouth. The entire wing of the castle around me was burning down to ashes. My reputation was completely ruined after that but funnily enough, those weeks after . . . I felt *good*. I wasn't as sickly. Dad thinks that I fed on those guards and that that's why I felt better.' A slight grin crept on my lips. 'I hope I did. I hope the last thing they saw was a beast tearing them apart. I hope they were terrified of me.'

Maeve made her way over, perched on the armrest and slid an arm around my shoulders, pulling me tightly against her while she hugged me. Cas joined and put his hand on my shoulder to squeeze it.

'I don't want pity,' I whispered.

'Pity is only aimed at those who cannot defend nor avenge themselves,' Aiden said as he crouched in front of me. 'You are perfectly capable of both or you wouldn't have shown that monster your wrath. You wouldn't have killed those bastards.'

I nodded once, elbows resting on my knees while I still held that bottle.

'You're a survivor and a warrior. Wear those scars on your wings with pride, they're proof of what you've withstood – survived. Laugh at those nobles in Orthalla when they dare insult you again and then show them just how monstrous you can be. Let them scatter before you like frightened little birds.'

Aiden's eyes seemed to burn into mine. I couldn't look away from him, from that intense gaze. 'And when you decide to ruin your enemies, *Princess*, let us be your sword and shield.'

I was overwhelmed by the support, the genuine care I felt through my *varkradas*.

And yet at the same time, I'd never felt steadier.

Aiden walked beside me over the cobblestone streets, illuminated by the pretty streetlights. The lovely scent of rain hung in the air, warning us that the clouds were preparing for a downpour. I glanced at him, gathering up the courage to ask him something I'd been wanting to ask him from the moment he'd said he'd walk me back home. I watched his lip curl up while he still looked in front of him. 'If you keep staring at me, witch, *I'll* start blushing.'

I snorted and stopped walking. 'I was just . . . I wanted to ask you something.'

Aiden gestured for me to go ahead, coming to stand in front of me. I bit my lip, worrying that maybe he'd think the question stupid. My cheeks heated horribly. 'It's just . . . ehm . . . I've been training with Cas these past weeks . . .'

'Uh-huh.'

'My wings are still rather thin, so he wanted to be extra careful but he promised to take me flying today and he didn't because I had a bit of a meltdown.'

Aiden gave me a sweet smile. 'I'd rather call it a break-through.'

I returned the smile, glanced down and then back up at him. 'I've wanted to go flying ever since I got my wings back and I ached to go flying when Aestor healed them. I have a feeling it'll be wonderful and—' I was rambling again, so I shut up.

Aiden's smile grew. 'Do you want me to take you flying?'

My heart skipped a beat. 'Would you?'

'I'd be honoured to.' He offered his hand, which I took. His shadows started curling around my legs and waist. 'Your wings are still terribly thin, so I fear it's not wise for you to rely on them just yet but I'll hold you.'

'Don't drop me,' I breathed. 'Please.'

Aiden smacked his forehead. 'My goodness, why hadn't I thought of that?'

I laughed, a loud sort of laughter that tugged at Aiden's own lips, and playfully slapped his arm. 'Prick.'

Aiden grabbed me, pulling me closer while his wings spread out, and before I'd had a chance to blink, he'd pushed off from the cobblestones. I yelped when gravity pulled at me, clutching onto him and burying my face against his chest while I tightly shut my eyes.

'I thought you wanted to fly?' Aiden laughed, his voice contorted by the wind around us.

'I did!' I complained. 'But you didn't warn me!'

'Yeah, because you called me a prick and my frail ego couldn't handle that.'

'Well, you're still a prick.'

Aiden pulled his hands back to tease me and I made a very unladylike sound while I tightly wrapped my arms around his waist and pushed myself against him. My heartbeat thundered in my chest and I feared I'd fall but his shadows never let go of me, keeping me securely in place and tied to his body.

'Open your eyes, Diana.'

'Fuck you.'

'Was that an insult or your to-do list?'

I snickered.

Aiden brushed a hand over my back. 'Open your eyes.'

Slowly, I did, pulling away to glance around, down at the city below. The colourful houses, the school Vanora taught at, Maeve's small hospital. The many lights that lit up the streets and parks. The cosy chatter that travelled along the wind from the nightlife in the city, as well as the sound of

Aiden's wings gently flapping to keep us up in the air. And I glanced up at the stars above.

Aiden's smile grew while he watched me take it all in. 'Move your wings,' he whispered. 'Stretch them first, give them some time to get used to the wind.'

I obliged, carefully stretching my wings to their full span. And I flapped them, once and then twice. Feeling the wind caress the membrane made my breath hitch in my throat and a strange sort of sound escaped from my lips. I'd never felt anything so freeing. The daemonic instinct within me stirred and purred in contentment and slowly, I kept flapping my wings.

'That's it, nice and slow.'

Aiden's arms moved to rest around my waist, his shadows still twined around my legs. But ever so slowly, he let go little by little. And I stayed in place, only dipping lower whenever the wind surprised me. But I was doing it, I was keeping myself in place.

I was *flying*.

I beamed at him, feeling something wet slither down my cheeks, but I didn't care. Aiden's face grew soft when he noticed my emotions. He heard my heartbeat, felt the ecstasy that coursed through my veins. Pure childlike elation blossomed in my chest.

After some more minutes, my wings started to ache from the exercise and I couldn't keep up that pace without straining them, so I closed my eyes and let myself melt against Aiden again, wrapping my arms around his waist while I stretched my wings for one long moment to relish in the sensation of the wind tickling the membrane.

'That happiness you feel right now,' his voice sounded raw, like Aiden himself was biting back his emotions, 'remember it – always. Because *this* is what you deserve to feel, every hour of every day. Don't ever let anyone pull you down again now that you know just how damned high you can rise despite the scars you bear.'

'Thank you,' I whispered against his shoulder. 'For tonight – for everything.'

I looked down at the sketch, my tongue stuck out a little as I worked on the colouring. I was so caught up in getting the shading right that I didn't notice my *varkradas* stirring to greet someone.

'Evening, love.'

I snapped the dark green pencil in two, my head whipping up. True horror spread through me when I found myself eye to eye with the face I'd been trying to get right for an hour now. The shit-eating grin he wore sent me blushing. 'Keres.'

He cocked his head and pointed at the drawing. 'Who's the handsome bastard?'

'A true prick, to be honest.' I wrinkled my nose. I'd got to a point where I felt rather comfortable around him. He'd visited a handful of times already while I'd been settling in.

'Just admit that I've captured you with my wicked charms.'

'Yet you're the one standing in *my* bedroom,' I shot back.

Keres chuckled, plopping down onto the carpet next to me. He pointed at my sketchbook. 'So when are you going to paint me naked?'

I scoffed. 'I'm not.'

His grin became boyish. 'Pity, I would've loved to model.'

I mean . . . I wouldn't mind studying him. Certain . . . *parts* of him.

'Are you truly *that* bored?'

'Eiran doesn't have any jobs for me right now. I'll take any entertainment I can get.'

I tried to stifle a yawn but Keres still noticed. 'I'll let you get some rest.' He took the blanket from the armchair, neatly draping it over my shoulders. 'Or I'll leave you with your wild fantasies.'

'You are *insufferable*.' I rolled my eyes at him, though I was grateful for the blanket – the sweet gesture. 'It's only a sketch of your face.'

'For now.' He wiggled his brows at me, which made me laugh. 'I'll make you paint smut for Eiran's tests. So explicit that it will send even Zhella blushing for the hills.'

I snorted. 'Maybe I'll paint *her*.'

His eyes gleamed with something I couldn't quite place. 'I don't really like sharing, love.'

'That sounds more like your problem than mine.' I shrugged.

Keres shot me a grin. 'Yet you're *my* Priestess. You vowed to worship me above all other gods.'

Growing serious again, I nodded slowly. 'And I do.' I said softly, 'You punished Kallias for me. Why? You didn't even know who I was. You thought I was mortal.'

'Because you always offered to me. You prayed and offered and you never asked for anything. You simply did so because you believed all gods deserved to be worshipped even though you were taught not to pray to me, and then when you did ask for help . . . I felt your desperation, your fear. I saw what he did – everything. How he broke you until you ran out of light. Mortal or not, no one deserves that. I tortured him myself until his mind broke, then I let the erinyes do their thing.'

'Thank you,' I said, leaning towards him to kiss his cheek, which seemed to surprise him. I knew the things Keres said right now . . . they should've nauseated me. I should've been horrified by the admission of his violence. Instead, I found myself feeling unendingly grateful – and safe.

I readjusted the blanket while Keres cleared his throat. 'Summer Solstice is in three weeks, a big festival where we're all supposed to worship Zhella.' The corner of his mouth curled up and something triumphant twinkled in his eyes. 'It'll also be a full moon.'

My heart skipped a beat. *Summer Solstice in Aerelia.* I'd always dreamed of knowing what these festivals would be like for the gods. 'Are you going to take me with you?'

Keres nodded. 'I'll come get you. I'll ask Asra to help you get ready.'

I tilted my head slightly. 'Asra?'

'One of my vesperae.'

I felt his sadness, the cold claws that dug deep into his heart. I'd felt that ache before when he'd visited me earlier this week, but this time it wasn't because of the loss of his dyad. Visions flashed through my shadows, snippets of his memories. Midnight blood, fallen vesperae and a goddess who laughed and ridiculed him when he went to Eiran to report her crimes. And how slowly, he helped most vesperae move to Hell to find safety with Eva; like many nymphs had done.

I stared at Keres with wide eyes. 'Why does Khalyna do that?'

Keres looked away from me for a moment, towards the burning fireplace. 'Jealousy. She wanted to become Eiran's

Left Hand but Eiran had already chosen me, even before our trials. Ever since then, she's hated me.'

'And Eiran doesn't do anything about it?' I frowned, my own anger bubbling up.

Keres turned his head to look at me. 'Khalyna may be a bloodthirsty mutt but she's not stupid. She never leaves tracks, always has a working excuse or alibi. I can never prove that it was her.'

I raised a brow at him. 'But you're his Left Hand. He should trust you over her.'

'If it'd been solerae and Zhella had gone to him, he would have, but they're Antheia's nymphs, so he doesn't care.'

I swallowed hard, not quite knowing what to say in response.

'The gods may feel grand and mighty but you'd be surprised at just how cruel they can be.' Keres sighed. 'At least with Bastian you know he wants to kill you – see it in his eyes. Eiran can smile at you, shake your hand and then get you to hold the lantern above him while he digs your grave.'

I raised both eyebrows. 'As lurid as that is, it's impressive.'

Keres shook his head, laughing. 'I'm trying to warn you about him.'

I tilted my head and gave him my sweetest smile. 'Maybe you should warn him about me too.'

The corner of Keres' mouth crept up again. 'Oh?'

I leaned back a little, causing the blanket to slip off of my shoulders, and looked at him with cruelly sparkling eyes. 'Orthalla is still restoring the wing I set ablaze when Rhosyn struck. One lord decided to defy me and nine men were buried the following day – what was left of them anyway.'

Something shone in those beautiful green eyes of his,

almost as if he were impressed. 'You say such wonderful things to me, love.'

I snorted. 'You're welcome.'

'So when are you taking that wrath to Lorcán?'

Pursing my lips, I glanced down at the sketchbook. 'I think it wouldn't be wise to go after him just yet. My wings are still healing and I'm learning new things about my magic everyday. Mom is thoroughly training me, but I'm not stable enough yet to face him.'

'I agree.'

I looked up at him. 'But once I've properly settled into my power . . .'

He grinned. 'We'll tear him apart.'

My own lips curved into a vicious smile. 'Until nothing remains of him – not even his soul.'

Keres leaned his back against the armchair next to him, studying me in silence for a moment. 'Do you mind playing my nymph – for our deal?'

I shook my head. 'As long as I can wear one of those pretty vespera dresses, I'm fine with anything.' Keres looked at me with raised brows. I shot him that sweet smile again and batted my long, thick lashes. 'I have a weakness for pretty dresses.'

'I'll remember it for when I need something from you.'

I wrinkled my nose at him and thought of something I'd been wondering. 'Have you actually ever removed a deal before?'

'No, but I did extend a favour to a friend like I did with you.' He smiled. 'Eiran didn't appreciate it then but that was because even Eiran was unnerved by her – terrified really.'

I was surprised to hear that Eiran could be scared of anyone, given the things I'd learned about him these past weeks. 'Who was she?'

'Yael.'

I gaped at him. 'You were *friends* with Yael Eléazar?!'

Yael was my idol. When I'd found the books she'd given my mom, I'd nearly cried from excitement and I'd spent entire evenings losing my mind while Eva taught me some of her teachings.

'I was; Antheia was her godmother, actually. When she was convicted for her crimes against the High Coven, she made a vow of revenge to burn them all until their screams were the only music in this world – and I blessed that vow. Antheia and I broke her out of her exile.' Keres grinned. 'Poor Eiran was terrified of her. Yael spit out rituals and ancient magic not even Zhella knew of, perfected alchemy and developed her own spells. Yael actually *taught* Zhella some things.'

I clapped my hands together, grinning like a child. 'She changed our entire society, the Institute of Vadones and the High Coven.' I sighed dreamily, then grew a little sad as I thought of her fate. 'Gods, I would've loved to meet her.'

Keres tapped the corner of my mouth. 'You're drooling and I think your fangs are showing because of your excitement.'

I rolled my eyes at him. 'Watch it or I'll bury my fangs in your neck.'

Keres showed me an arrogant grin. 'Look at you. Weeks ago, you were still trembling and hiding behind me when we brought you home and now you're threatening my delicate immortal skin, arrogance itself.' I couldn't help but laugh. He clicked his tongue. 'I'm starting to get quite fond of having my devious little nymph around. A shame that you've only given me your full moons.'

I leaned towards him, my own eyes bright with playfulness. 'Would you like my waxing crescents as well?'

'Maybe even waning,' he mused.

I chuckled. 'You don't need any deals to visit me, Lord Keres. You're welcome anytime.'

His cheeks turned a subtle shade of pink. 'You can just call me Keres, you know. You don't have to call me Lord. And . . . thank you.'

My own cheeks heated as well. It sent a little bolt of aching through my heart, to know that that meant so much to him. I truly did like him, even my shadows did. They'd settled down around us like sleeping puppies.

Keres gently took my left wrist, the movement slow, like he wanted to give me the chance to pull away, and his fingers traced the ink on my skin, which sent small jolts of lightning along my nerves. His eyes were still on mine. 'You belong to my household now and fall under my protection, even during our ruse. No one hurts you. If they do, I'll ruin them.' His thumb circled the crow in flight on my wrist. I watched how strands of silver *æther* circled my wrist – his magic. How the ink on my arm lit up with bright light. He met my eyes again. 'What you carry on your arm is the mark of our deal as well as a blessing. No one will ever be able to taint you with *kalotra* – ever again.'

I stared up at him in stunned silence. 'Thank you,' I whispered in awe.

'I do expect daily offerings from now on, since you're still my devoted pet,' he said while getting up to leave. 'And a grand mural dedicated to my divine cock.'

I threw my head back and laughed, then shot him a sly grin. 'Of course, *My Lord*.'

'I'll see you around, Diana.' He shot me a last grin. 'Don't bite the bedbugs.'

Chapter 16

Diana

Aerelia, Eiran's palace
Present day

I stared at my reflection in the tall mirror while Asra put my loose waves up in a braided half up-do for Summer Solstice. Today was the longest day of the year, a day to worship Zhella. Yet her sister's moon would shine at its brightest tonight.

I'd learned that Keres had indeed been married to Zhella for a short while before he'd left with Antheia, still bleeding from the lashes Eiran had put on her back. Yet Eiran hadn't been the only deity who'd been absolutely vicious. Khalyna had targeted her plenty as well.

'Ever since her death, Khalyna's made it a hobby to hunt vesperae down,' Asra told me while she wove a golden ribbon into my hair. 'She got me as well, though Aestor intervened before she could kill me.' I ached for her, for the horrors Khalyna had put those sweet nymphs through.

'Winter Solstice used to be a night where we celebrated our Lady but now Khalyna uses that night to haunt us. But we are rather stubborn.' Asra smiled at me through the reflection of the mirror. 'So Keres guards us every year. We are not to leave his side then, so he can watch over us while we honour our goddess.'

234

It was strange to hear someone speak about Antheia and Keres with such respect and reverence. Like Keres was a hero in their mind instead of the villain the mortals crafted him to be. Hearing a nymph speak about a god with such fondness was surprising as well. Gods often viewed nymphs as nothing but servants or courtesans and most used the words *nymph*, *servant* and *whore* interchangeably.

Eiran blessing my mother hadn't been out of the goodness of his heart. Turning his rival's dyad into a *pretty little nymph* had been a subtle way of ridiculing her. Though my mother had laughed the loudest when she'd ordered Ascredia to give her more. She'd scraped her nails over the swirling *æther* in that pond, digging in deep. She'd demanded her due and received it, and when she'd recounted the experience to me, she told me she could've sworn Ascredia had laughed at Eiran.

I met Asra's gaze through the mirror. 'It must hurt horribly to have lost her. To have lost so many.'

Asra's face grew sad while she nodded. 'Antheia couldn't bear a child because Eiran cursed her but she always considered us to be her children. I still hear her soft laughter in the night air. I feel her soothing presence whenever I grow scared or sad, as if she's still holding my hand. No one's sure what happens to a god when they die.' She finished braiding the ribbon and smoothed her hands over the golden silk of my dress. 'What we do know is that she entrusted us to Keres before she died. Eva looks after us as well, both because she's our Queen and to honour her friend. We still sense our Lady in each other and we like to believe that somehow, she still watches over us.'

Asra stepped in front of me, her brows drawn together. 'I understand that you want to wear your wings but be careful.

Not all gods respect your people the same way Keres and Aestor do.'

I sweetly smiled. 'Thank you for your concern, Asra, but I promised myself I wouldn't hide away any longer and I've decided that if anyone wishes to insult me, they'll have to deal with the repercussions.'

Her worry didn't leave. 'Be careful of Khalyna, my Lady. I don't want her to hurt you.'

'I'll be careful.' I smiled. 'Thank you for caring, it means a lot to me.'

'Of course.' Asra picked up a small glass jar with gold paint.

'Would you leave my *vārna* visible?' I pointed at the black swirls that adorned my right collarbone. Circederae were fond of marking each other. Our bodies were a canvas that carried every important event in our life, every high and low, every relationship that held meaning to us. A *vārna* was a marking circes gave their children, unique like a fingerprint. My parents had painted me the day after I'd come home.

She nodded and started to smear the paint on any skin the plunging neckline revealed. Her tongue stuck out slightly while she concentrated, which tugged at my lips.

When Asra was done creating patches of gold on my skin, she took a step back to take me in. Her smile grew wider as she did and she beamed at me with such sweetness and warmth that it nearly made my eyes water. 'You look lovely, My Lady.'

I dared a glance in the mirror to my right and let my eyes trail over the liquid silk of my dress. It had a deep cowl neckline and two high slits that rose up to my waist. My body was fully healed, which meant that my curves had finally come knocking on the door. With the special vespera-woven fabric and the gold ribbons that were braided into my half-loose hair, I was really channelling the nymph part of my blood.

'Can I hire you?' I grinned at her. 'For events and such. Or do you reckon Keres will haunt me for stealing you?' Asra's midnight cheeks flushed dark blue and the twinkle in her eyes reminded me of stars. Before she could answer, a knock sounded on the bathroom door, and when Asra told him to come in, Keres waltzed in.

He whistled while he looked me up and down. 'You are riveting.' My blush crept over my cheeks, the top of my arched ears and even hid underneath the body paint.

Did he really think I was pretty? Or was he just being polite?

'Lady Diana seems pleased with my services, as she wondered if you would haunt her for stealing me.' Asra smiled at him, her hands neatly clasped behind her back.

Keres ruefully smiled at her. 'You'd certainly enjoy tending to a Lady again, wouldn't you?'

Asra's cheeks flushed again and while she nodded, she shyly looked down at her light loafers. She'd adored dressing up Antheia, picking out pretty dresses and hanging out with her. Braiding her hair while Antheia sweetly hummed some melodies and Asra told her about her day.

Keres knew she missed it. It was why he'd asked her to take care of me tonight.

A villain, my ass.

I'd envisioned grand rooms made of finest marble and solerae to serve his every wish when I'd imagined Keres' private quarters in Eiran's palace. They were all that but they were also very, *very* empty. As pretty as the intricate black and gold wallpaper and furniture were, this place was as hollow as a rotten tree trunk. Only the living room had been decorated, filled with trinkets like moonstones, star maps and dried tuberoses to honour his late dyad.

While I curiously studied the room, Keres came to stand behind me. His fingers slowly traced the white streaks on my back, left visible by the silk. Aestor had removed Rhosyn's scars when he'd healed my wings, though the newly healed skin was paler than the rest of my back. The touch sent a shiver down my spine, following the path of his fingers. It felt strangely intimate and the quiet anger that simmered in his shadows caught me off guard – Keres knew how I'd got those.

I didn't need to turn around to know he was studying the scars on my wings. Aestor hadn't been able to remove those completely, the same way he couldn't heal scars left behind by Stygian iron.

'I know you're no damsel, Diana, but the next person who tries to lay a hand on you will lose more than just their hands.' His soft voice came from near my right ear.

Tries – as if Keres would personally make sure they would never get further than trying.

I wasn't quite sure how to reply to his protectiveness, but after opening and closing my mouth a couple of times, I eventually settled on softly saying, 'Thank you.'

It was still so strange to now be surrounded by people who cared about me and my well-being, who'd decided for themselves that they would guard my back and remain by my side. Sorin and Zale had been the only ones who'd done that for me for so long, so Keres promising me that he would make sure no one would ever hurt me again . . . It had me biting back tears and balling my fists, clutching the silk between my fingers.

Keres lowered a fine golden chain in front of my face. My eyes focused on the golden sun pendant that carried a pretty citrine in its centre. Both the stone and the gold had been polished with such care and attention to detail that the stone seemed to radiate like the sun itself. 'You like it?'

I nodded while I fondled the pendant with my fingers. 'It's gorgeous.'

His fingers brushed my skin while he took his time putting it on. I liked feeling the warmth of his hands, of his body close to mine and how it casually caressed against my wings.

Keres stepped into my view. 'It'll soothe Zhella's jealousy when she notices your lovely earrings.'

Crescent moons.

I snorted and my emotions settled again. 'Such a fragile ego. She reminds me of a certain green-eyed god.'

His lip quirked up. He made me look up at him by lazily taking my chin between his thumb and forefinger. 'Be a good nymph tonight and you can keep it.'

I clicked my tongue and batted my lashes, which made his lip curve even more. Gods, I loved seeing that smile of his. It was utterly cocky, dripped with arrogance and the dimple that came with it made my chest flutter. 'You say such wonderful things to me, love,' I teased him.

Keres chuckled, light and breezy, and I watched how his shoulders relaxed a little. Asra hadn't been lying when she'd mentioned his concern. I touched his hand and smiled. 'I'll be fine, Keres.'

He nodded while studying me. 'We should discuss what you're comfortable with doing.'

'How do you usually treat your nymphs?'

'It depends,' he said. 'Vesperae are like children to me. Eiran forced some solerae into my wing in an attempt to keep me . . .' Keres looked for the right word. 'Satisfied, I guess. But I do entertain them from time to time.' An uncertain look passed over his face, hesitant to admit it but it still slipped out, 'Since it . . . you know . . . can get lonely in here.'

My brows drew together and my heart fractured. I knew loneliness and how hollow it'd made me feel. As if all the cold rain in the world had gathered to soak my bones until I melted into the mud, merging with the fallen and forgotten autumn leaves. It wasn't something I wished upon anyone.

Keres cleared his throat, looked away and let go of my hand. 'Anyway—'

I slipped my arms around his waist and hugged him, letting myself melt against his body. Accidentally coating his clothes with gold body paint. Keres' arms banded around me. It felt wonderful to be held by him like this, to feel his calloused but gentle hands smooth over my back. His scent of springtime had quickly become one of my favourite scents in the world and I felt myself grow calm, like a sort of inner peace had started to manifest.

'I'm sorry about that.'

'How those bastards could ever bring themselves to shun and hurt you like that is beyond me.' His hand cupped the back of my head. 'There's such a lightness and softness to you.'

'Same goes for you,' I whispered. 'Do you think Eiran will expect you to treat me like a solera?'

'Knowing Eiran, he'll probably enjoy watching me drag you around like you're my meek and devoted pet. That one look at you would bring you to your knees, that I'll show off how you're neatly wrapped around my fingers.'

I pulled away and met his gaze. 'I'll do that, I'm rather good at acting. But don't be cruel – don't use nasty words. Don't call me a beast.'

He nodded gravely. 'Never.'

'And I don't mind you touching me, just don't go anywhere too intimate.' The solemness in his eyes when he nodded erased some of my nerves. I cocked my head. 'What about you?'

Keres blinked, surprised by the question. 'Me?'

'Is there anything you're not comfortable with? That you don't want me to do or say?'

Keres stared at me like he'd never expected me to ask that question. Eiran certainly didn't care whether Keres wanted something or not.

He considered it. 'I'm quite fine with anything, but . . .' He looked at the flames in the hearth. 'I'm only capable of being myself when I'm in Anthens or when I'm with Zielle, Aestor or Lycrius. When we get there, I'll be the God of Malice – the god your Priestesses warned you about.' Keres looked back at me. 'But remember that that's not all I am and that I will never be *that* god to *you*.'

I gave him a crooked grin. 'I'll remember that if you remember I'm not actually a meek little *matska* who'll let you rub her belly whenever you see fit.'

'Unless I dangle a pretty pear in front of her face.'

Eiran's palace was ethereal, like I'd become lost in a fever dream. The festival was held outside and I was eternally thankful for that. Magic flawlessly intertwined with the flowers, making them all appear richer and more alive. The colours were deeper than they were in Aeria and the lovely scents were more prominent as well.

Amused by the blatant awe on my face, Keres gave me a moment to drink it all in. The entire pantheon I'd worshipped since childhood surrounded me, unaware of how I was melting in their presence.

Keres' hand rested on the small of my bare back. 'I'll be over there with Jasán, Dharren and some of their acquaintances.' He nodded to a round table under a golden tent where a handful of men were sitting and drinking. 'Come to us when you've got the wine.'

'Friends of yours?' I asked with a low voice.

Keres snorted. 'By the Æther, no. They're minor gods of the seas. They always feel the need to overcompensate.' He flashed me a wicked grin. 'Which also means they try to bluff when gambling. I'm terrible at card games but their obvious bluffing actually gives me a chance to win.'

I consulted my *varkradas* to make sure no one was watching, then drawled at him. 'Really? I hadn't yet noticed how bad you are at those. I thought you meant to lose every game we played.'

'The only reason I lose to *you*, *matska*,' he purred, 'is because you cheat with your *varkradas*.'

Before I could even try to deny it, he turned around to join the group of minor gods. I stared after him, feeling rather . . . strange. I liked being teased by him. I liked taking his hand and hugging him. The one thing that really took me by surprise was the fact that I'd really, *really* liked the way he'd called me *matska*. How something had fluttered in my chest.

I wasn't quite sure what to do with that realisation.

While I made my way over to the white-clothed table

where the snacks and drinks stood, I let my eyes dart around the garden. A smile tugged at my lips while I watched a group of anthousaïi – flower nymphs – dance, laughing while holding each other's hands. There were also solerae, with their gilded skin and shimmering golden hair.

Then my eyes darted to the table Keres sat at and my lips curled into a grin. He sat on that damn chair like it was a throne he'd stolen from some coward king, one leg lazily crossed over the other. Leaning more towards one side of it, where he rested his chin on his hand.

A casual, very uninterested predator.

With the filled wineglass, I walked over. Two gods stared at me – at my wings. Disdain tainted their blue eyes while they trailed over the thick bone and the scarred membrane. These past weeks, that membrane had been growing thicker thanks to the special moisturising balm Maeve had crafted for me.

I sat the glass down in front of Keres and deeply inclined my head while keeping my *varkradas* on a tight leash. If the neckline of the dress had been any less decent, it would've given him a nice view. 'Your nectar, My Lord. Would you like anything else?'

One god snorted, though I sensed that he quite liked my floral perfume, my features, the way the dress clung to my curves.

'No, love. Come sit.'

'Aloïs must be seething at the knowledge that his bitch heir serves a god,' the one who was shuffling the cards said to Keres.

I remained silent and gracefully slipped onto his lap and, as he loosely draped his arm around my waist, another stray flutter wandered through my chest. Keres met the god's gaze, still resting his chin on his hand, appearing completely disinterested – bored even. 'Language, Dharren. No nymph of mine will be addressed like that.'

'She's no nymph,' said another one. 'Just a beast.'

I hated that word. It was dehumanising and so filled with vicious prejudice. They called *us* beasts, yet they were the ones who enjoyed scheming and back-stabbing and hunting us down. If I allowed myself a small moment to feel an arrogance worthy of Keres, I could remind the idiot that rank-wise, I exceeded him – by a lot. If anyone should kneel in this situation, it was those little minor gods.

Keres drank from his wine, letting his hand caress the skin revealed by the slit in my dress, resting it on the inside of my thigh. 'Do I look like I'm in the mood to deal with your sense of self-importance and arguments, Jasán?' he said in a low voice, charged with electricity.

'No, Lord.'

'Then perhaps think twice before opening your mouth around me. I've not cut anyone's tongue out yet, but the night is still young.' His lip curved into a vicious smile. 'And I don't want to stain her pretty dress before dawn, so do behave yourself.'

Dharren glanced back and forth between us. 'It's only a daemon, Lord Keres. Who cares?'

I shot the minor god my sweetest smile, though it didn't reach my eyes. 'And *you* are only a minor god, yet you keep yapping like my Lord has any interest in what you have to say.' Keres stiffened but I sensed no reprimand in his shadows – in the little connection I'd crafted between us so we could gauge if the other was still comfortable. If anything, he liked seeing me like this, the confidence I showed.

Jasán forgot about the wineglass he'd brought to his lips, staring at me in silent shock.

I fluttered my lashes. 'Yes, sweetheart, *it* talks.'

Dharren glanced at Keres like he expected him to reprimand me but Keres only took a slow swallow of his nectar, amusement twinkling in his eyes. 'She also bites,' he purred. 'And I quite enjoy watching when she does.'

When Dharren realised Keres wasn't planning on chiding me, he started handing out the cards. I made myself more comfortable on Keres' lap, crossing my legs so that one slipped through the high slit of my dress and elegantly draped my arm over his shoulders.

Keres took the cards and leaned back, the arm around my waist smoothly pulling me closer. Dharren laid down three cards on the table while the conversation picked up again. I glanced at the ones Keres had received, which were quite good ones. Those other three gods didn't have high enough cards but Jasán did, and I really didn't want Jasán to win, so I let my voice slip into that connection, *Bet one dionyris, keep your cards well hidden.*

I lightly caressed the skin of his throat, pretending to be preoccupied with admiring my god. Glaring at a solera who threw her golden gaze his way, waiting for her chance to occupy his lap. I wasn't completely sure if all of the hostility I decorated my eyes with was feigned. I didn't want their treacherous hands anywhere near the god who'd been my saviour and now my friend.

Jasán noticed – of course he did. The god grinned at Keres. 'Looks like you trained it well.'

Keres didn't look at him but did lay down one dionyris. His voice sounded so bored that I wanted to apologise in Jasán's stead for bothering him. 'I barely had to do anything.

She begged me to take her and make her mine, fearing her fate of becoming some breeding mare. And she knows damn well that her only place is with me now. Don't you, love?'

'Yes, My Lord,' I said with a breathy voice.

Dharren laid down the fourth card and smirked. 'You mean *underneath* you.'

'Mmm, that as well,' I softly said and trailed my fingers over the fabric of Keres' shirt while smiling up at him like a lovesick puppy.

Jasán let out a soft laugh when he saw me like that. 'If you wish to take a break to fuck her in a guest room, go right ahead, God of Malice. She certainly looks at you like she's drenched.'

I wanted to break his wineglass and then shove the shards up his ass. Without olive oil.

Keres' lip quirked up. 'I already had some fun with her before we came here. *Matska* certainly enjoy being dominated.' He tipped my head up. 'And I treated you very well, didn't I, *phádron?*'

Phádron – beauty. I made a show of leaning into his hand and timidly looking away, pretending to be too shy to say anything. Which wasn't all that hard. The thought of *Keres* finding me beautiful was enough to make me as much a flustered mess as I'd been when I'd met Aiden.

Jasán grinned. 'Maybe I should find myself a little beast to decorate my lap with as well. They seem awfully keen.'

I worked hard to stop myself from gritting my teeth and balling my fists. If that prick called me *beast* one more time . . .

Keres didn't even acknowledge him.

I threw myself into my acting, distracting them all – to

make sure Keres would win. I leaned into his body, trailing my lips down the side of his throat to kiss him there. Realising that I *liked* doing it heavily confused me. I hadn't laid with or touched anyone since Kallias. I hadn't really felt aroused even when Kallias had been sweet. I'd never understood why men were so focused on sex or why people even cared about it.

But I liked the sweet taste of his divine skin on my lips, how his grip on my waist tightened. His hand lowered to cup my rear and for the first time in my life, lightning shot down my belly. I tried to fight the blush that travelled along my cheeks but it was no use. I was just grateful no one could read my *varkradas* while I kissed his neck and jawline.

Jasán watched Keres become more interested in his nymph's seductions instead of winning the game and smugly placed a bet of three dionyris. Dharren revealed the final card and luckily for me, my crazy competitiveness cleared my raging thoughts when I realised I could make Keres win.

When Dharren asks if you want to add another bet, pretend to be preoccupied with me and pass.

Keres' amusement crept into my shadows – almost in my bones. *Are you cheating again, love?*

Your cards are higher and I refuse to let that asshole win. I'm going to pretend to be in desperate need of your attention and then you're going to crush their happiness so I can soundly sleep tonight without a cranked pride.

He definitely liked the idea of wiping that smug grin off of Jasán's face. *Do your worst, matska.*

While two other gods placed their bets, I turned to face Keres, cradling his lap between my thighs. The slits of my skirt rode up my thighs and Keres' hands smoothed over the sensitive skin there. My mind went blank, which was probably a good thing. I cupped one side of his face and kissed his jawline – near his ear. Slowly working my way down and down. Then I kissed the corner of his mouth.

I didn't dare kiss his lips yet.

'Keres? Do you want to place another bet or do you need a room?'

Keres chuckled softly, weaving his fingers through my hair. 'Pass.' His other hand came up to brush the side of my throat to hold me in place and before I had time to panic, his lips found mine.

My heart crept up my throat. I didn't even register Jasán adding another five dionyris to his betting pile. Keres' soft lips parted mine, tasting of the nectar he'd been drinking. Honey apples and cinnamon; such a warm and cosy taste. When his tongue caressed mine, my breathing hitched in my throat. His other hand cupped the back of my head while he deepened the kiss to keep me in place but in a gentle way I'd never experienced before. And he continued kissing me – softly.

The feeling his touches and kisses brought forth was foreign, so utterly foreign. It was a language I'd never been taught but longed to learn. One of tender hands that held no treachery, that knew how to give instead of only taking. That promised evergreen golden brilliance and little meadows blooming in my soul with the brightest of wildflowers.

My heart swelled up in my chest but unlike with my panic attacks, it didn't feel claustrophobic.

I kissed him back, hesitant at first, scared of what he might think of me. But I reminded myself that this was only a ruse. Did it really matter if Keres didn't like the way I kissed?

Keres leaned more towards me and softly bit down on my bottom lip. I couldn't help but sigh against his mouth, especially when I felt that he *enjoyed* kissing me. It lifted a burden from my shoulders that Kallias had left behind.

I met his every demanding kiss, relaxing against his muscled body while I smoothed my hands over his chest and throat, tangling my fingers in his hair. One hand rested on my waist to guide me closer, to guide the movements of my body. His other hand curled around my bare thigh and his fingers dug deep into my heated skin.

He liked it. I knew he liked it because he'd grown hard underneath me.

This meant nothing, I reminded myself. It was simply his body reacting for him. It was only natural. I was touching him in rather suggestive ways, it was only normal that his body woke up for me. There was no way that Keres . . . that this was because of *me*.

A deep blush coloured my cheeks as I was overcome with another alien feeling. A thick heat. A slickness that ached for him. And I wanted . . . I wanted his strong hands to explore my wings to make me moan. I wanted his lips to rove the curve of my wings, his teeth to scrape over the membrane.

This was becoming too much. I'd never felt any of this. Kallias' kisses had never come close to . . . to doing *this* to me. And I was terrified that I would only end up disappointing Keres and pushing him away and I couldn't stand the thought of losing his friendship.

Keres pulled away, lazily brushing my cheek with his thumb while I tried my hardest to hide the miserable truth. That I was terrified of what he could make me feel.

Luckily for me, Dharren ordered them all to show their

cards. The crestfallen look on Jasán's face when he saw Keres' was enough to pull me back into the present. 'And here you had us all fooled you were too busy frolicking with that beast of a whore!'

Blame it on my fried emotions.

He'd barely finished the sentence before I'd slipped out of his shadow and slammed his face hard into the table, which painted the white tablecloth with golden blood.

In my defence, the colour of tonight *was* gold.

I slammed *Aecéso* into the table, right next to his face, gashing his ear. 'Call me a beast again and I'll show you just how monstrous I can get,' I hissed, then roughly let my grip on his hair go and pulled my dagger out of the table.

Jasán shot up, clutching his broken and bleeding nose, with a fury that should've made me back away. He opened his mouth to further insult me but I brought my face closer to his, silver flames burning in my narrowed eyes. 'Insult me again and I'll neuter you.'

Jasán balled his fists and shot a furious look at Keres. 'Put your damn whore in her place.'

Keres merely raised a disinterested brow at the minor god, still leaning back in the chair like he couldn't care less. But he was ready to jump in between if that god decided to attack me.

Though he was really enjoying the show.

Keres clicked his tongue against his teeth. 'If you take such delight in fanning the flames, Jasán, you should be prepared to get burned.' Jasán's nostrils flared but he remained silent. He'd be a fool to cross Keres.

Keres' gaze was ice cold. 'Apologise to her. Or I'll order my nymph to make true on her threat.'

'I will not apologise to a be—' Jasán's hands shot to his

throat, to claw at it. It took me a heartbeat to realise he was choking. And that it was Keres who was doing this to him.

'Are you truly so braindead that I need to tell you I won't accept anyone insulting Diana *twice?*'

Holy shit. I thanked the Mother that Keres' frigid gaze wasn't directed at me.

'Fine!' the minor god spat my way. 'I'm sorry!'

'Do it again and I won't be as forgiving.' I batted my lashes at the flustered minor god.

Keres let go of his hold. 'Neither will I.' He rose from his chair and gestured for me to take his arm, starting to guide me away from the table. 'My nymph may still believe in mercy but I have long forsaken it. Be glad I'm sparing your tongue for now, but don't try me again.'

I followed Keres and ignored the existence of those minor gods, but through my *varkradas*, I saw Khalyna's piercing light blue eyes dart from Keres to me. To my wings. Despite myself, I met her gaze. I'd seen her face plenty of times in my textbooks, though none of those books had shown the scar on her face. A thin golden line crept from her temple, over the bridge of her nose, corner of her mouth and right down to her cheek. Her piercing eyes swept over my wings in a calculated way, like she was wondering how she could best break and dissect them.

Khalyna's gaze slipped to how I'd curled myself around his arm, then back to Keres. 'Did you decide to bring her instead of your lovely little vesperae? A new toy to play with?'

A new toy for him to play with, or a new toy for Khalyna to play with. It was rather obvious she meant both. My grip on his arm tightened, both to steady him and to remind myself not to snap at Khalyna. Swatting the Third God like a housefly might not exactly scream *meek matska*.

I blinked and Khalyna stood in front of me, her gaze lowered to my necklace and her eyes gleamed with something malicious.

'Very pretty.' She smiled at him. 'Enjoy her, Keres.'

While you still can. The unspoken threat echoed in her words.

Back in his private chambers, Keres plopped down next to me on the couch in his living room. I didn't exactly dare look at him, what with kissing him and the little stunt I'd pulled with Jasán.

'You okay?' he asked.

I nodded, fumbling with my mother's garnet ring on my finger. 'I just hit a limit on the number of times I could stand hearing the word "beast".'

'Yeah, I figured but that wasn't what I meant.'

I glanced at him, drawing my brows together. 'Then what did you mean?'

Keres rested his elbows on his knees, curiously studying me while he intertwined his fingers. 'You seemed more comfortable lashing out at Jasán than you were kissing me.'

I flinched and quickly looked away while my face heated. 'Because of Kallias?'

Timidly, I nodded. I couldn't bring myself to look at him.

Keres slowly took my hand in his and gently squeezed it. 'Do you want to talk about it?'

'No. Yes.' I shrugged. 'I don't even . . . I was just over-reacting – it's fine now.'

His thumb drew circles on the back of my hand and his voice was gentle like I hadn't heard it before. 'You weren't overreacting, Diana. If you don't want to talk about it, that's okay. I'll let it go,' he said quietly. 'But I'm here to listen and help you make sense of it if you do want to talk.'

'It's . . . ehm . . . just . . . don't laugh at me, please,' I whispered, glancing up at him.

'Never.' He brushed a strand of hair behind my ear. 'It's just us.'

I swallowed and drew in a deep breath. 'I . . . talked about it with Sorin a lot, but it . . . There are things Kallias said that I've realised . . . he only ever said those things to keep me close to him or to make me behave a certain way and I recognise a lot of it now – looking back at that year. Sorin helped me understand that and mostly . . . I *have* healed.'

Keres nodded.

'And a lot of that is because I proved to myself that he was wrong. Kallias said I wasn't bright, so I taught myself Aspian. He said I had a faulty memory, so I played memory games with Sorin to prove that I did remember things correctly.' I glanced at him. 'You know?'

'You taught yourself Aspian?' he asked with a sweet smile.

I nodded. 'I chose Aspian because I was sick of all those servants claiming I was Lorcán's bitch. Figured I'd terrify them next time they insulted me by spitting flawless Aspian.'

'That does sound very Diana-y.'

I couldn't help but smile a little. 'Yeah.' Glancing back down at our intertwined hands, I worried on my lip for a moment. 'So, yeah . . . I proved him wrong with a lot of things, but . . . not everything. Things I haven't been able to prove to myself.' I shrugged lightly in an effort to appear casual. 'He didn't like the way I kissed. He didn't like it when I touched him – the way I touched him. But he also didn't like it when I didn't touch him.' My cheeks flushed. 'He said I wasn't anything special, that I was lucky he'd somehow fallen in love with me. Part of me knows that he just tried to get under my skin, to keep control over me. But I can't shake the worry that he couldn't have lied about *everything*.'

Keres nodded again.

'And I . . . ehm . . . The thing that made me panic tonight wasn't only that you kissed me. When I laid with Kallias . . . Didn't matter how hard I tried, I always . . . *failed* at it. Didn't really matter what Kallias did, he never . . . ehm . . .' My cheeks were on fire. 'He never made me . . . I never . . . you know.'

I didn't dare look at Keres, awfully embarrassed admitting all that. I wasn't even sure why I kept talking. 'And it just makes me feel like I'm failing, especially because Maeve and Vanora mentioned how passionate circes are.' I dared a glance at him. 'And . . . it's embarrassing, but . . . When you were kissing and touching me . . . I ehm . . . I . . . you know.'

Keres squeezed my hand again. 'You became aroused?'

I managed to nod, even though I wanted to melt into the floor or hide behind the couch.

'Did you tell anyone about that? That you never felt anything?'

I shook my head. 'I'd already told them all about Orthalla. I didn't want to keep complaining.'

'It's not complaining, love,' he assured me. 'You have every right to speak up about things that bother and hurt you, every right to be listened to, no matter how soft your voice.' I nodded, still not meeting his gaze. 'As for the arousal thing, I have a feeling it had to do with the suppression.'

I stared up at him, caught off guard. 'Oh.'

It made perfect sense. Everything had been suppressed then, even my menstrual cycle, and it'd all only slowly unfurled and returned in those first weeks days back home.

'Your entire nature was repressed; your *varkradas*, your instinct, your powers. I wouldn't be surprised if that's why you never felt anything. I also doubt you ever felt safe enough with him to relax enough to enjoy yourself.'

I nodded absent-mindedly, a little lost in memories. 'You're right about that.'

Keres rested his arm on the back of the couch, right behind my head, and brushed his thumb over my shoulder. 'As for those other concerns.' His eyes trailed over my face. 'You are not "nothing special", love. Quite the contrary, you truly are riveting.'

I averted my eyes, not sure what to do with myself.

His lip quirked in amusement. 'If you'd flirted with Dharren, he would've let you drag him to a bedroom. Jasán might've insulted you the entire evening but he couldn't take his eyes off of you. Half of those minor gods despised you for being a daemon and, yet, all of them would've fallen on their knees to have a moment alone with you.'

'That's not true,' I muttered.

Keres' lip quirked up even more. 'It is.' He brushed my hair behind my ear again, which I quite liked. 'And your kissing was more than fine, I enjoyed it.'

'Your kissing was quite tolerable as well. Wouldn't have guessed it was your first time.'

His dimple appeared. 'There she is.'

I smiled and rested my head on his shoulder. 'Thank you – for being so patient with me.'

He ached at the choice of my words. 'Try to go easy on

yourself,' he said while wrapping an arm around me to pull me a little closer. 'And know that I'll be right there when you want to talk about something – *anything*. No matter what time of day – or night, no matter the subject.'

I wished I'd met him sooner, that younger me had had such a kind friend when she'd desperately needed one. But I had him now, as well as my other friends. I'd already spent so many days and evenings getting to know them; messing around with Cas and Aiden, having game nights with Vanora and Maeve where Eos had to intervene because Vanora and I were overly competitive – and Maeve was laughing her ass off. Evenings where Vanora told me about our revolution and customs, where Maeve taught me how to take care of my wings so they would grow strong again.

I wasn't that lonely girl anymore.

Closing my eyes, I melted into that warm embrace that smelled of springtime.

And I told him everything. From the day Kallias approached me during Summer Solstice three years ago, where I'd danced with him in the courtyard in Katrones. To the day I sat on his dead body and cried my heart out, my trembling hands covered in his blood.

Chapter 17

Aedlynn

Aspia, the Royal House of Odalis
1764, 24 years after the War of Ichor

Aedlynn glanced at the dainty ring on her finger, which was searing hot against her skin. Twirling it between her fingers, she studied the precious stones. Part of her wanted to throw it aside but then the servants would put it with the other jewellery and somehow this ring felt strangely important, so she put it back on, figuring that she was just imagining the heat.

Lorcán had left this morning to visit Aedonis in Aletheia and had given her permission to do whatever she wanted but to make sure to stay within the castle. She didn't feel like hanging out around the Cadre wing, though she was curious to see Kaelena again. Aedlynn couldn't help but wonder about the nymph. She was almost disappointed that the fiery girl hadn't approached her since their run-in yesterday. She was half-tempted to let Kaelena try to put her hands on her again.

Aedlynn took another turn. Though she'd lived here her whole life, she'd somehow managed to get lost. Just around the corner, Kaelena leaned against the wall and watched her. Subtle wafts of darkest blue smoke rose from the carpet underneath her feet, like she'd stepped out of the night and into the corridor.

Some string around Aedlynn's heart tugged like it wanted to pull her towards the nymph but a lovely haze settled over her mind – smelling of jasmine – and Aedlynn ignored her whilst moving past her. In her attempt to ignore Kaelena, she paid little attention to her hands.

Swift as night, Kaelena grabbed Aedlynn and pushed a poison dart into her upper arm.

'Son of a—' Aedlynn shoved Kaelena against the wall while she summoned a dagger. Only nothing happened. Aedlynn tried again. Nothing.

The bitch had poisoned her with moonsbane.

Kaelena shot her an apologetic smile. 'Sorry but I had to make sure you wouldn't murder me.'

Aedlynn wrapped her hand around her throat. 'I don't need any weapons to tear you apart, *whore.*'

Kaelena raised an amused brow, pretending to be un-bothered by the chokehold. 'Perhaps you should squeeze a little harder, *ná'dýra*, this feels more like our foreplay.'

Aedlynn was so caught off guard by the comment that her grip faltered, but she was even more shocked when Kaelena managed to slip behind her through that darkness and planted her foot against the back of Aedlynn's knee, forcing her down.

Fast as lightning, she pulled a dagger from the strap on her thigh, shot back up and whipped around with the weapon in-hand. Kaelena barely managed to dodge, scarcely escaping Aedlynn's aim at her heart.

She'd hoped the moonsbane would've been enough to give her an advantage over Aedlynn, as it should've suppressed her divine powers and her fighting prowess, but she still was a force of nature in battle. Seeing Aedlynn still being capable of defending herself this well, all while being magicless, felt like the Fates were laughing at her and taunting her, reminding her that she should've trained harder instead of allowing Lorcán to keep her flightless.

Given Aedlynn's elegant movements, their fight almost mimicked a dance and all Kaelena could think was that she'd trade the moon and sun to be back in that room where she'd taught Aedlynn how to dance. She hated the bruises they gave each other, the superficial cuts and how Aedlynn laughed at her in a voice that sounded eerily similar to Lorcán's.

Again, she dodged Aedlynn's attack with a dagger of her own as she aimed for the right side of Lena's chest – *scarcely*. Aedlynn whipped around, this time aiming at the left side of her throat.

The only reason Lena survived the onslaught was because she'd watched her dyad train so often that her movements were ingrained in her mind like a dancing pattern.

She ducked, and Aedlynn hadn't expected her to, shoving the blade into the wall behind Lena. The blade got stuck in the crevice and the split second where Aedlynn considered pulling it out or abandoning it and pulling a different dagger free from the strap on her thigh, gave Lena the opening she needed.

She called on her fragile magic, on the tendrils of pure night and made them latch onto Aedlynn to force her down on her knees and tie her down.

Aedlynn fought against her hold but the moonsbane blocked all her magic. She glared at Kaelena while she cupped Aedlynn's face. She couldn't stand those pretty brown eyes and the lovely curve of her full lips. Her perfume nauseated her, filled her with a sense of dread like

Aedlynn was betraying Lorcán simply by being near her. 'Perhaps you're a witch after all,' Aedlynn spat. It would explain the strange effect she had on her.

'Gods, I wish I was,' Kaelena murmured, caressing her hair back. Aedlynn grew more confused by the minute. 'I'm sorry about the moonsbane, *Nyará*, but you'd kill me and Lorcán would know what I'm doing. He probably knows already, so we have to go – *now*.'

Nyará. Aedlynn gasped for breath.

Kaelena spoke in a hurry, 'Lorcán painted you with *kalotra* to control you, to take away your mind.'

Faint memories of a cabin crept into her mind. He'd tricked her into his bed. All to increase his control over her, to strengthen that fake bond. Guilt ravaged her but Kaelena wasn't angry with *her*.

Kaelena wiped away her tears and kissed her brow to soothe her. '*You* have nothing to be sorry about, my love. Lorcán will pay,' she said softly before kissing her brows. 'But first, I'm getting you out of here.'

'Odalis? The House?' Aedlynn asked, feeling completely lost between the webs of his magic.

'No, I'm getting you out of Aspia,' Kaelena said firmly. 'And once we're over the border, I'll drag Keres down from Aerelia to remove those markings.'

'But Eiran—'

'Can go fuck himself.' Kaelena's eyes grew cold.

With their fingers intertwined, they paced along the magical border that distorted the meadows that lay ahead in Clacaster and searched for an opening.

'Enough spies managed to slip in, there must be weak spots,' Kaelena mused.

'Most stumbled upon them by accident,' Aedlynn said, looking over her shoulder to make sure they weren't being followed.

'Can't you sense anything with your magic?' Lena asked.

Aedlynn raised a brow, amused.

'What?'

'Moonsbane, remember?'

Kaelena's cheeks flushed. 'Sorry . . .'

'How much did you give me?'

'A vial. Those small ones I hid in my nightstand.'

She nodded. 'Okay, I'll be powerless for probably another hour or two.'

Kaelena sighed and kicked against a rock. 'Stupid idea, I'm sorry.'

Aedlynn kissed her nose. 'No, it was smart, really. I wouldn't have hesitated to gut you.'

'You say the sweetest things to me,' Lena purred. 'We just have to wait until Aviod shows up. He said he would bring help; a *demiagi* who could warp the Veil and make us an exit.'

While Aedlynn turned around to check their surroundings again, Kaelena took off the amulet and put it around Aedlynn's neck, who looked at her in surprise. 'Perhaps it's childish superstition but I sense her tonight. Perhaps whatever power of hers still lingers in the amulet can protect you.' Aedlynn curled her fingers around the amulet, then flinched when the moonstone actually burned against her fingers. 'See? I think some of her power still lingers in that necklace, maybe it's waking up since it's Solstice.'

'I doubt a dead goddess will be helpful but I appreciate the gesture.'

'Dead she may be but Lady Antheia is also the only deity

Lorcán didn't exile.' Kaelena grinned. 'I've spent these past years still worshipping her and then my dyad coincidentally gifts me an amulet crafted by the Goddess herself?'

Aedlynn found it adorable how devoted Lena was, though it saddened her to imagine how greatly the vesperae must hurt to have lost their goddess – because she knew how much Kaelena ached without even knowing her.

She took Lena's hand in hers and pulled her along to some trees that would hide them from sight. 'If we're to wait on Aviod, you could just as well take a moment to catch your breath.'

Lena winced, her cheeks burning with embarrassment. 'I'm sorry.'

She squeezed her hand. 'It's okay,' she assured her. 'When we're out of here, I'll train you some more.'

'I'd like that,' Lena admitted. 'I'm starting to become really sick and tired of being helpless.'

'You're not helpless. And please don't blame yourself. As long as someone holds his interest, I fear no one has any freedom of choice,' Aedlynn said as she pulled Lena down to sit with her against a thick oak. Despite the foliage, they still had a pretty view of Lena's star burning brightly in the sky above them.

Lena only shrugged, convinced that part of the blame *did* lie with her. She'd been too docile, too content with the bare minimum he'd given her and too scared of a life where she'd have to decide things for herself instead of looking to him for permission. It had almost cost her Aedlynn. She rested her head on Aedlynn's shoulder, still holding her hand. 'I think we should go to Draven.'

'Why?'

'In case Lorcán comes after us. He doesn't like admitting

it but he's intimidated by Sorin, the High Lord there.'

'Draven is also very popular with the gods,' Aedlynn reminded her. 'And I'd like to keep winning my hide and seek game with Eiran.'

'Maybe that High Lord would help.'

Absent-mindedly, Aedlynn nodded while brushing her fingers over Lena's arms. 'What do *you* want to do? I don't really care if that High Lord decides to use me as an assassin like Lorcán did if it means keeping you safe and Eiran away, but if he so much as looks at you with the intention of making you a courtesan for him as well, I will gladly face Eiran because I murdered his High Lord.'

Sweetly, she smiled at Aedlynn. 'Would you mind if I searched for Keres? I would . . . I would live with you in Clacaster, but I really . . . I want to learn more about my family.'

'Of course not,' she said. Aedlynn's eyes widened as she thought of something and she grinned at Lena. 'Or we could try and find a way into Hell instead of staying in Draven. We could watch the stars there.'

Lena's smile grew bright. 'I'd love that. Perhaps Aloïs would agree to hide you – given his relationship with Eiran.'

She nodded, then asked, 'Would you mind it terribly if I brought a pet wyvern as well?'

Lena blinked and then started to laugh. 'Fine, you can have *one* pet wyvern.'

Aedlynn chuckled and nestled closer against her, planting a kiss on their intertwined fingers. 'But what if they have a friend? It'd be cruel to separate them.'

'By the gods, Aedlynn.'

Innocently, she shrugged. 'And what if they have children? I can't separate them, Lena.'

'Perhaps you should try and leave some room in our house for *our* children.' Lena wiggled her brows at her.

With blushing cheeks, Aedlynn looked down at their intertwined hands, growing silent at the mention of such plans for the future. She'd never thought so far ahead before. 'You would want that? With me?'

'Perhaps not immediately, as I do want to explore the world more. There's a whole world out there – and many more.' Lena kissed her shoulder. 'But yes, one day.'

Aedlynn's smile grew soft as she looked at her dyad. 'I'd love that – with you. Everything with you.'

'And all the stars in the sky, Aedlynn. Whether here or in Hell or anywhere else,' Lena whispered lovingly as she caressed her face and turned Aedlynn to look at her. 'They will never shine as bright as my love for you.'

Aedlynn melted into Lena's embrace, into the soft kiss. Relished in her perfume and the taste of her lips. The softness of her skin and the fragile hope and elation she felt blooming within Lena's chest at the prospect of their new life.

Had the moonsbane not been in her system, Aedlynn would've felt them. But now, she was caught by surprise when someone grabbed her and roughly pulled her away from Lena.

Shit.

Kaelena whipped around but another man grabbed hold of her as well. Aedlynn hadn't seen him before in Lorcán's Cadre. His tanned skin was in stark contrast to Kaelena's pale skin.

Someone clicked their tongue and Lorcán's voice came from behind her. 'Kaelena, you devious little nymph. Must you defy me again and again?'

Kaelena glared at him with a fury worthy of her goddess. 'May you choke on your own blood by a hand that once cradled you.'

The thickness and weight of the curse clung to Lorcán, curling around his *Výsa*. The other man seemed almost impressed with her spitting rage. Lorcán didn't even acknowledge the curse. 'And *you*, Aedlynn.' He sighed deeply. 'Didn't I warn you of what would happen should you fight me?'

'I didn't fight.' Aedlynn shrugged, more worried about Kaelena in that man's arms than the *Damast* dagger Lorcán held against her throat. 'The poison weakened your *kalotra*.'

'And yet here you are, only a metre away from our Veil, ready to flee to my nemesis,' Lorcán said. 'I would've kept to our deal had you not broken it. Luckily Aviod warned me in time.'

Her heart groaned and a fracture shot through the delicate muscle. Her father had betrayed them. Aedlynn tried to fight him and stomped on his foot, but his magic had her in an iron grip. Kaelena didn't fare any better, subdued by the dark-eyed man's magic.

More poison slipped into her blood by Lorcán's hand, though this was no moonsbane. This was painful, weakening her muscles until she could no longer use them and sagged to her knees. She had no strength to fight while he chained her wrists and ankles. Iron chains dipped in moonsbane to subdue her. Aedlynn tried to pull free but she could scarcely move.

The man forced Kaelena on her knees some metres away from her. Her dyad fought him like a feral beast and if she'd had claws like one, she would've carved his face clean off. The man wrapped a fist in her hair and roughly forced her down, bound with ancient magic reminiscent of a *demiagi*.

He stepped back from her, smoothing a hand over the bleeding cuts Kaelena had made on his throat and cheeks to heal them. 'Perhaps we shouldn't have allowed the nymph as much freedom as we did,' he said to Lorcán. There was a subtle accent to his words she couldn't place but he didn't sound like he'd been born in Aspia.

Lorcán walked over to Kaelena, studying her with a curiosity Aedlynn didn't like. 'I figured the anthousai blood would temper the vespera blood.'

The *demiagi* chuckled. 'Apparently not. Antheia and the vesperae may be vicious but Lycrius and his nymphs aren't docile either when provoked. You saw that yourself during the War, *aediore.*'

Lorcán cupped Kaelena's face to make her look up at him. 'Indeed not.'

Kaelena glared at him. 'I wonder how you keep your secrets and lies so neatly organised that you don't lose track of them.' Her voice was cold, colder than Aedlynn had ever heard it. 'I'm a full nymph, aren't I?'

'You were always too smart for your own good.'

'For *your* good, Your Highness,' Lena purred. Her eyes gleamed with fury while visions of the truth washed over her in waves, courtesy of her potent vespera blood and the power of Antheia's Winter Solstice. Tarniq hadn't killed her parents. Lorcán had, slowly – to hurt Antheia. Antheia had guarded Lena and watched over her to protect her like she'd been her own but that protection fell away when she'd been killed. And Lorcán had been more than happy to have something else to study.

Kaelena decided she would leave nothing behind of him.

'You act all high and mighty – like you're some chosen

saviour. But the truth is that you're only some pathetic mortal clinging to any grain of power you can get your scarred hands on because no one gives a shit about you. Not even Elyon would want you,' she spat. 'You have the audacity to use my Lady's blessing, to claim she favoured you! She *despised* you – for killing my people! You killed my parents!' Tears burned in her eyes. 'You sent Isolde after me on purpose – let her hurt me! You manipulated and controlled me!' She stifled a sob. 'You hurt my dyad. All that and you dare wonder why no one loves you – why we all run from you. You don't know how to love anything!' she bit out with pure hatred burning in her eyes. 'You'll rot in Hell!'

Lorcán's eyes darkened to a shade that tightened Aedlynn's chest with panic. On the grass, she attempted to move but her sluggish mind was laced with fog and her muscles were far too liquid-like to use.

Kaelena's cry echoed through the forest, making birds scatter in a panic, when Lorcán's whip struck against her back. 'No!' Aedlynn writhed in the chains, her voice weak from the poison. He lashed out again and again while Aedlynn tried to beg for him to stop.

Lorcán struck against Kaelena with his magic, torturing her like he'd done with Evalynn so many years ago. She couldn't keep from screaming, nearly collapsing in the dark bindings he'd placed on her. Meanwhile, the *demiagi* gave Aedlynn the same treatment, though she cared nothing about her own pain. She couldn't stand seeing Kaelena in pain. She *needed* her safe.

'Stop! Please!' Aedlynn weakly screamed at Lorcán.

Every single frustration he'd felt, every piece of pent-up rage that was aimed at Evalynn, Aedonis and Sorin – he let it all out on Kaelena as he landed blow upon blow. *Ichor* ran out of her wounds, soaking her clothes. Aedlynn cried and fought but her muscles refused to oblige.

Didn't he have anyone he loved? Didn't he understand how excruciating this was?

That mortal only cared about his throne and removing Eiran and he was prepared to damn the realms to do so. He'd told Aedlynn his plans before leaving. He expected her to kill Eiran so he could set Elyon free, though he'd need a certain someone to help him. Someone from Orthalla to serve as a *Válar* – a vessel. He'd called them an Acolyte of Darkness.

She wasn't sure how much time passed while Lorcán threw everything he had at Kaelena, all while Aedlynn tried to scream and beg for him to stop. Even though the moonsbane was out of her system, she still couldn't do anything because of those damned restraints.

But her strength was returning, little by little.

Lorcán wiped his arm over his forehead to remove some of the sweat that coated his skin. On the cold forest floor, Kaelena groaned. His face remained insultingly neutral when he looked down at her battered body, the deep lacerations on her back.

The *demiagi* met his gaze and held up a dagger for him. 'When Evalynn betrayed you, you let her escape and it cost you everything. Do not make that same mistake now, not when we are so close. Not when that *výssar's* power is almost ready to be reaped.'

'No,' Aedlynn whispered. Tears stained her vision. 'Please, *stop.*'

Gods, that amulet burned.

Lorcán approached the *demiagi*, carrying cold loathing in

his eyes when he glanced at Kaelena. Something in Aedlynn snapped at the sight of her dyad laying broken on the ground, beneath that lonesome star whose light was dimming little by little, while Lorcán retrieved another thing to hurt her with. She managed to scoot closer, to reach Kaelena while she was still bound. Aedlynn just needed to be with her, even if it was the last thing she would do.

'Your halfblood is trying to escape,' the *demiagi* dryly observed.

Lorcán snickered. 'How heart-warming.'

Aedlynn carefully caressed her face, the chains rattling as she did. She was no healer but she wished she was; Kaelena was in such pain and she could do nothing. She wished she'd become a healer instead of an assassin. She wanted to take it all away, she wanted to hold her and tell her they would be all right.

'Go,' Kaelena croaked, her voice barely a whisper. '*Go.*'

Feverishly, Aedlynn shook her head, sobbing like a small child. She hated how both just watched them like this was a little show – like Aedlynn was no threat and she hated it even more that right now, she was indeed no threat. Aedlynn was powerless. Another wave of that strange poison had her so nauseous that her eyes burned and she didn't trust her muscles.

Aedlynn kissed Lena's brow, brushed her hair. She kept apologising to her but Kaelena somehow found the strength to cup her face with one hand. There was an urgency to her touch, a firmness with which her fingers dug into her skin to make Aedlynn look at her.

'You cannot stay here,' Kaelena whispered. 'You have to go.'

'No.'

Tears filled her eyes. 'He'll ruin you. You're too good for such a fate.'

Behind her, Aedlynn faintly heard them laugh. 'I'm not leaving you!' Aedlynn tried to gather Kaelena in her arms but she couldn't get close enough. Still, Lena leaned her head against Aedlynn's hand and still, Aedlynn held onto her other hand like a lifeline.

'How utterly touching,' Lorcán drawled behind her. 'And fucking pathetic.'

'He'll kill me.'

'I won't let him,' Aedlynn sobbed, though she was in no state to fight. Aedlynn was heavily bleeding herself, from the throbbing wounds on her back. Moving was nothing but pure agony. Golden blood steadily flowed from the stab wound Lorcán had given her and the wounds that *demiagi* had added.

'Go,' Kaelena whispered. Her fingers traced over Aedlynn's collarbone.

The *demiagi* grabbed hold of Aedlynn's hair to roughly pull her back and Aedlynn screamed out when he pinned her to the floor with a sword piercing her back, the blade laced with another dose of poison. The *demiagi* started adding new markings to her skin, new *kalotra* that clawed and stabbed a way into her soul. Somehow this magic felt more stable and mature than Lorcán's.

She met Lena's gaze, sobbing when she noted the sheer terror in her dyad's face as Kaelena realised what was happening. How again, someone was marking Aedlynn. Claiming her. Using her.

Taking away her choices.

Aedlynn sobbed, trembling and terrified and stared at Kaelena through her tears. For the first time in her life, she prayed to her mother for help.

No, not prayed. *Begged.*

Kaelena mouthed the word *go* while Lorcán grabbed a fistful of her hair to force Lena half upright. It was only then that Aedlynn saw the dagger in his hand. The wave pattern on the light steel. *Damast.*

There was heart-stopping pain in Kaelena's eyes but as she held Aedlynn's gaze, that pain made room for a final determination. A fire in her eyes. A promise.

'A shame that there will be no epic songs to recount your pathetic love for each other, one that was doomed from the start,' Lorcán taunted her. 'You were never meant to have love, little Aedlynn. You were only ever made to be conquered and used.' The world seemed to slow down around Aedlynn and hold its breath as Lorcán moved the dagger towards Kaelena's throat.

Lorcán rested the steel against Kaelena's pale skin. Tears cleared a path through the blood and dirt on her face. *I wish I could've held you under the stars there,* Lena's fragile voice whispered across their bond. *I will find you again in our next life, I promise you that.*

'All the stars in the sky, *Nyará,*' she whispered to Aedlynn with a mournful smile.

And then Lorcán slit her throat.

Aedlynn thought she'd known pain when he'd tortured Kaelena. But that was nothing – *nothing* compared to what she felt when the bond tore, when Lorcán dropped Kaelena's lifeless body in the dirt, illuminated by the watery light of her star.

Her mind went empty and filled with nothing but breath-taking pain.

If she'd been free from those shackles, perhaps she

could . . . her *Výsa*. Aedlynn could've saved her. It was beyond cruel, a twisted way for Lorcán to isolate and control her. To make her watch the death of her dyad, knowing damn well that if she'd just been *free*, she could've saved her.

None of this made sense. Kaelena's *Výsa* had been strong, glowing with a fierce warmth.

This had never been supposed to happen.

Aedlynn was so caught up in her grief that she didn't stop to wonder why no one spoke, why there were no movements. Even the wind didn't move. The grass and tree branches remained still.

Aedlynn, rise.

She couldn't. The poison still had her weak, she could scarcely lift her head.

Lorcán didn't move, neither did that man. Like they were frozen in time.

Aedlynn. She had never heard that clear voice before. *Go.*

She couldn't make herself move. Her body had hit a limit with her wounds and the poison in her system, and her mind was torn apart because . . . because Kaelena was gone.

Her dyad. Her *home*.

Do not let her sacrifice be in vain, aediore. *You do not have much time before the Veil returns.*

Without Kaelena, there was nothing. Aedlynn was terrified of the world, of life outside of Aspia. The gods who lingered there. The King who would smite her the moment he learned of her existence. She'd been ready to face that all with squared shoulders and lifted chin – with Kaelena at her side.

She was all alone now. Lorcán would win.

He'd already won.

Strange visions entered Aedlynn's mind of black and

white floors. Of amber eyes and the scent of lavender. Of bat-like wings and stars. *Call on Keres. He will come but you must go now.*

She couldn't tear her eyes away from Kaelena. How she just . . . lay there. Unmoving. Not breathing. Broken. Her blood still flowing out. Lorcán wouldn't bother to honour Kaelena, to show her any respect or even bury her.

But night caressed over Kaelena's body and around her, flowers sprouted and bloomed until her body melted into pure night and the tendrils sank deep into the earth. More flowers grew there; daisies and buttercups, lilies and wildflowers. Her favourites. Until nothing of Lena was left behind.

Then something wrapped around Aedlynn's waist and chest and pulled at her, though it didn't feel threatening. It reminded her of the night Kaelena had pulled her into only hours ago. When it let go, she sat in a meadow, still facing the Veil but not from Aspia's side.

Call on Keres. The voice had become barely audible. *Find Di—*

A breeze passed over her, much like a gentle caress. If Aedlynn hadn't imagined that voice, it meant Kaelena had sacrificed herself to save her. If that were the case, she couldn't give up. She couldn't dishonour her.

Even if it seemed impossible to go on.

Would he even answer her prayer? Aedlynn drew in a deep breath and prayed. She waited a minute, then another but he didn't show. The moonstone on her amulet remained scorching hot for a moment longer and then grew ice cold. A crack appeared in the stone. She was relieved that it didn't fully break, since Kaelena was fond of the necklace.

Thinking about her hurt so deeply that Aedlynn lost her-self in grief – not noticing the man in front of her. The god looked down at the sobbing girl, silently wondering what was going on. He'd sensed a vespera die. Minutes later, the small moonstone on his necklace had nearly burned a hole in his skin and when he'd received her prayer, the stone had cracked.

He crouched in front of Aedlynn. 'You're not from here, are you, *aediore?*'

Aedlynn was too tired to startle. To notice that he was speaking Aelerian. She stared at the green-eyed god through thick tears. 'Aspia,' she managed to bring out.

'A halfblood,' he said quietly while he broke the curse on her bindings, removing the shackles. Aedlynn's eyes grew wide. Panic tightened her chest until she couldn't breathe anymore.

He was Eiran's Left Hand. Maybe he'd bring her straight to him.

Keres took off his thick dark coat and draped it around her. 'It's okay, I won't drag you to Eiran.' Only when the warmth of his coat crept into her skin did she realise how badly she was shivering. The god remained silent for a moment, studying her. 'What happened to you?'

She opened her mouth, closed it and then started sobbing. Wailing like a wounded animal while the evening flashed before her eyes over and over.

She told Keres everything. She even told him how Kae-lena had gifted her a star, one that still shone brightly above them. She had the distinct feeling that it would always watch over her, though she'd trade all the stars in the sky and all the riches in the world to have her dyad back. She'd hand Elyon the divine throne if he'd promise to revive her. She'd spite the Fates and break into the Underworld to bring her back herself.

Keres set to work to remove the *kalotra* markings, only pausing when he saw the marking of wildflowers Kaelena had drawn on her collarbone. 'Your dyad wrote a request for me.' He smiled sadly. 'She requested a blessing, to protect you against *kalotra*.'

Aedlynn sobbed again, burying her face in her hands to hide from the world. She'd *known*. Had she known it all along? When she'd grabbed Aedlynn in Odalis? Or only at the very end?

Keres gave her a moment to gather herself, while he used a vial with silvery water to remove the *kalotra*. The only marking he left behind was Kaelena's. When she calmed down, he rested a hand on Aedlynn's shoulder and pressed the thumb of his other hand on her forehead. Blessing her.

'Are you not going to force me into a deal?' Aedlynn asked in a daze.

He shook his head. 'I only make deals with mortals and deities I loathe. And *you* have already been through enough.'

Her blood froze in her veins when she saw the outlines of people approaching the Veil. Keres turned to follow her gaze, making a sound that came damn close to a growl when he saw Lorcán.

Lorcán's eyes were on Aedlynn and there was nothing but pure loathing in them. Those violet eyes returned to Keres, who was ready to tear the king apart. Yet Keres couldn't destroy the Veil, only Zhella could. And Zhella had received orders from Eiran to leave it.

Aedlynn wanted to make him pay but she was exhausted, horribly wounded and bleeding. She felt like she would collapse any moment, and she was terrified of what Lorcán would do to her if he caught her in this vulnerable state.

So for the first time in her life, Aedlynn took the coward's route.

She decided to flee to somewhere – someone Lorcán wouldn't dare follow.

Lena's first suggestion.

She æriated to Draven, right in the middle of the throne room of the High Court of Clacaster, collapsing in front of a blonde man with amber eyes.

Chapter 18

Diana

Draven, the High Court of Clacaster
Present day

I'd been learning more about my shadows these past weeks, especially how much they liked exploring. So from time to time, I just went to places so my shadows could sniff around. They were excited to explore anything in their path but listened perfectly to my commands, only breaking away to greet family and friends whenever they crossed our path, to wrap themselves around their legs in a sign of affection or to play with them. They were rather fond of pickpocketing Sorin as well, who'd taken up the hobby of hiding shiny things in his pockets for them to find.

Whenever I had spare time, I just walked around to let them stretch out and explore. Today, I'd decided to visit Sorin's greenhouse in Draven. There was something wholesome about seeing my shadows interact with delicate flowers with great care. How they melted beneath the sunlight, practically purring in my soul.

I'd learned much about my nature, and thus my people. I'd also learned much more about the true myths. Especially the truth about Antheia rattled me. Finding out that many of her worst deeds had never even happened . . . How could history remember someone as a spiteful and wicked villain, forgetting all about the great and benevolent deeds they'd once done? Granted, Antheia hadn't been fully innocent but still . . . She'd fought for the mortals and they'd never once fought for her.

In the greenhouse, the noon sun burned on the glass dome above me and the damp heat in the room felt thick, like I was wading through it rather than walking. The flowers were absolutely beautiful, especially the wildflowers. I smiled as I watched different shades of pollen stain tendrils of pure darkness, reminiscent of the colourful powders colchians used during festivals to paint their loved ones with.

I took a turn and startled when I walked into a woman, making a very unladylike sound. My *varkradas* circled her and climbed up her stained slim trousers and a simple long-sleeved shirt. I tried to rein them back in but they wouldn't listen to me.

'Sorry, didn't mean to startle you.' She smiled sheepishly before looking down at the *varkradas* that were tugging at her sleeves like toddlers begging for attention. I couldn't help but admire her for a moment, now that I finally saw her face-to-face. Her sleek brown hair fell to her shoulders, perfectly complimenting the warm colour of her tan skin. She seemed to have been made by Zielle herself, with the way her muscles and curves perfectly balanced each other out. In my mind, I was already outlining a painting where I'd paint the rays of sunlight bathing her in their warmth, wearing a wine red dress to accentuate her skin tone. But what truly set her apart from any other woman I'd ever met were her unique eyes; one amber-coloured and the other sky blue, broken up with hints of golden specks.

'I'm *so* sorry, they don't normally do this,' I said while I used my hands to gently remove them from her arms and shoulders. In my mind, I could hear them protesting.

I'd tried to describe their language to Keres but it'd been rather hard for him to understand. Their language felt like whispers in the dark, echoes in the cavern of my mind.

She simply laughed and put down her iron bucket with gardening tools. 'It's fine, they're like puppies.' Her lilted accent decorated her words, making it sound like she spoke in cursives. Before I could pull more tendrils away from her, she crouched down and started petting them – actually *petting* them. My lips parted while she caressed them, her touch light and warm. They purred underneath her hands – wholly content, the sound reverberating in my soul. It felt like she ran her fingers over sensitive skin, and I had to admit I deeply enjoyed the sensation.

My shadows were still shy unless I was around people they trusted. They still startled when a kabolos leapt onto them, instantly shot back inside of my soul to hide. And here they were, letting a complete stranger pet them like a house cat. Not only that but whenever she pulled her hand back, they wrapped themselves around her wrist to pull her back to request more pets.

'I'm Marianne.' She looked back up and wiped some brown tresses away from her face. 'You must be Diana?'

I rapidly composed myself and nodded. 'How do you know?'

'Sorin speaks of you – often and highly.' Her lips quirked up. 'There are also not many people in this Court with wings.'

I raised an amused brow. 'How observant of you.'

She shrugged casually. 'Observing is what he hired me for, so I'll take that as a compliment.'

Right, she'd become one of his advisors.

'I'll rest easy knowing that he has such a spymaster at his side,' I quipped.

She smiled, but there was an ache in her soul, piercing and cold. Similar to the pain Keres still carried with him after losing Antheia. There was also deep-rooted loneliness and self-loathing. My *varkradas* had sensed it before I had. They'd reacted to it, smothering her with their affection the same way they'd always wanted to take care of me.

Marianne started to rise, careful not to step on my shadows but every time that she lifted her foot, my shadows tried to wrap themselves around it like they were desperate to hold onto her. 'I should go,' she said softly. 'You must be busy.'

The timidness in her features and the listless hopefulness I sensed in her gave me the impression that perhaps Marianne didn't want to leave, and something in me didn't want her to leave either. 'I've been a little bored, so I decided to take a stroll but it's quite boring to wander around by myself,' I said. 'I could . . . I could use some company – if you want.'

A shy smile bloomed on her lips. 'I would like that.'

Hours passed where we chatted and bantered and I came to learn a little more about her; that she'd come here from Aspia, though she didn't want to share yet how she'd got here. I followed her around the greenhouse and handed her tools or the watering can in an effort to make myself useful. I didn't exactly have a green thumb, yet Marianne seemed to possess two fully green hands.

'Sorin mentioned that you paint,' she said at some point. 'He showed me some portraits. They were very pretty.'

'Thank you.'

'He might be your greatest admirer, given how enthusiastic he was.'

'Actually, Zale is my biggest admirer.' I handed her a small shovel. 'He makes me show him every single drawing and painting I make.'

She grinned. 'Maybe you could repaint those stuffy ceilings in the throne room.'

Maybe I should. Clacaster had become what Aspia used to be to the gods so many years ago, a haven where they were worshipped and celebrated.

She glanced over at me and looked me up and down. Her gaze landed on the tips of my wings. 'Actually, you should add daemons to the ceiling.' She grinned. 'I'd kill for wings like that. Colchian wings are very pretty as well but I don't think they would suit me.'

I couldn't stop the smile that blossomed on my lips. Other mortals whispered behind my back, pointed at me and seemed generally confused or even disturbed, but Marianne spoke to me like this was something so utterly mundane. No panic, no wariness nor prejudice.

'I'm not sure Sorin would let me fingerpaint his ceiling.'

'*Please,*' she scoffed. 'He'd pay you to add something ridiculous to it as well.'

'You seem close,' I noted.

She shrugged, rose and wiped her dirty hands on her trousers. 'It was rather hard to make a living here when I was so obviously Aspian and didn't even speak Clastrian. Sorin helped me learn the language and helped me . . . process what happened back home. So now I repay his kindness with stupid jokes and random cacti I leave in his room.'

I snorted.

She smiled at me. 'I'm still healing but I've come far. If

Sorin hadn't fought for me like he had, I would've withered long ago.'

A lump formed in my throat. I could definitely relate to that.

We shared more stories and I even told her about my parents and friends in Anthens. Marianne told me a little about Aspia, keeping most of it to herself. She had thick walls and I had a feeling she protected herself with them so she wouldn't have to be vulnerable.

She reminded me a little of myself when I'd still lived in Orthalla – maybe a lot.

Some days later, I spent the evening with Marianne in her room. I'd spent my day training with Cas in Anthens. My muscles ached, my wings tingled and I was absolutely ex-hausted but I'd come to really enjoy Marianne's company and dry jokes, so I'd scared her half to death by slipping out of a shadow in her bedroom with a wine bottle and snacks.

I never knew Aspian held such colourful cuss words.

I'd draped myself over one of the armchairs while read-ing a mythology book I'd brought over from Keres' private quarters from the last time I'd been there. Though the true entertainment came from watching a tipsy Marianne lie on her bed with her head resting over the side of the mattress while she attempted to read a sappy romance book. I'd learned she was dyslexic but still loved reading. Though I think she loved commentating on the writing even more. Her dry remarks left me cackling.

I finished another chapter and took a page from her book. 'I've learned that Eiran has two hobbies: bothering Antheia – when she was still alive – and my father, and lying about it.'

Marianne glanced over. 'In his defence: my hobby is bothering Sorin – and you.'

I snorted and closed the book. 'I think Eiran did worse things than leaving random cacti in Antheia's bedroom.'

'I'm not even surprised anymore by the stories. He's an ass.'

'He ruined her reputation,' I said as I sat more upright. 'Hell, he blamed Avalon's destruction on her when it was he and Aestor who ruined it while warring.' Because shortly after she'd left with Keres, Eiran struck against her in an attempt to recapture her. Aestor had protected her, fought Eiran and nearly killed him. She'd stopped him from doing so, believing her father could be redeemed.

Marianne shrugged lightly. 'Aspia doesn't favour the gods anymore, so the stories I grew up on are filled with dirty laundry. They only tolerate Antheia and Dýs – Death. They view her as a martyr, a daughter who died for the sins of her father.'

She shot upright and gaped at me as if suddenly remembering something. 'You're from Hell.'

My brows rose. 'Yes, but—'

'*Oh my gods,*' she breathed while slamming her book shut. 'Do you have wyverns there?'

I blinked, caught off guard by the sudden change of subject. 'I haven't seen any yet but Hell's pretty big and some creatures only keep to certain regions.'

Her eyes widened. 'They *exist?!*'

'Yes.'

Her elbows rested on her crossed legs. She covered her mouth with both hands. '*I mwanna seem.*'

'What?'

She removed her hands and grinned like a child. 'I want to see them.'

I snorted. 'They'd eat you.'

'They won't,' she'd slipped right back into Aspian due to her excitement. 'It's common knowledge that anteaters do eat ants, so I hold to the fact that those creatures are not called people-eaters.'

I cackled.

She grinned. 'Just tell me I'm wrong, *Nychter.*'

'I wouldn't dare to,' I purred – in Aspian.

Marianne blinked, then started laughing. 'Gods, your accent is *horrible.*'

'Oh, fuck off.'

'It does make me feel better about mine.'

'My Vehonian is even worse. There are too many tongue-twisters.'

Marianne scoffed. 'I tried to learn it and I gave up after the first chapter of the textbook. There is no sensible reason why their words for cock and turtle should be the same.'

'They're not the same.'

Slowly, she grinned. '*One* accent, Diana. *One.*' She heavily gesticulated the word.

I giggled.

'Oh, you have such a cute pet cock,' she crooned. 'And is that a turtle in your pants or are you just happy to see me?'

I cackled and hid my face in my hands. 'Why was that in the first chapter?' I wheezed.

'I didn't necessarily mean the *first* chapter. I just opened it randomly and it was the first chapter I read.'

'And then you're frustrated that you don't understand any of it?' I shook my head, still laughing.

Marianne joined in my laughter. 'Ah, now I understand where I went wrong.' She slapped her forehead. 'I never understood biology. When I read about childbirth, I was just confused about how those gremlins got in there in the first place.'

'*Mother above,*' I wheezed.

'Must've been that damn turtle.'

I was so caught up in the drawing I was making with charcoal that I didn't notice Keres slipping in until my *varkradas* stirred from their nap to greet him. I looked up from my desk to see him perched on the windowsill next to my desk, curiously watching how I was drawing a herd of kaboloses disguised as foxes while he gently stroked the *varkradas* that'd nestled on his lap, which felt wonderful.

'I know I often tease you but you're really good at that.'

Something warm crept through me. 'Thank you.' I wiped some strands of loose hair behind my ears, which made Keres softly laugh. My fingers were still covered in charcoal, as were my cheeks now.

He watched me attempt to wipe some off with the back of my hand, but I was only making it worse, though I refused to admit that. 'If you keep rubbing your face like that, you'll end up looking like Aiden threw you into Erebus.'

Keres summoned a towel and handed it over. Muttering my thanks, I wiped off the charcoal from my cheeks but when I focused my attention on my hands, Keres took the cloth and my right hand, cleaning my fingers and the rings with meticulous care.

I stared at our hands, blushing like a lunatic. 'Didn't know you were God of Cleaning as well.'

Keres' gaze snapped to mine and I watched how the corner of his mouth quirked upwards until he showed me that wonderful smile that made his dimples come out. And once again, my heart fluttered around in my chest like it threatened to free-fall.

'I made a friend,' I said in an attempt to distract myself from my growing confusion. 'A mortal girl from Aspia.'

Keres' hand stilled. His walls were drawn up. 'From Aspia?'

I nodded. 'She knew what I was and wasn't intimidated. My *varkradas* liked her as well, I couldn't tear them away until I'd decided to hang out with her.' I hesitated a moment. 'She was lonely.'

Keres took my left hand and gave it the same treatment. 'You've experienced such deep loneliness yourself that you seem to have made it your personal mission to make sure those around you never feel it.' The soft smile he gave me tugged at my heartstrings.

Timidly, I looked away. 'I expected you to warn me against befriending a mortal, certainly one from Aspia.'

'I think you're more than capable of deciding for yourself who to place your trust in.'

My eyes snapped back to his. *Don't be ridiculous, Midór,* I heard that awful voice, with words that were such a stark contrast to those of Keres. And a nickname I hadn't heard since his death. *You wouldn't know how to make the right decision even if the answer stared you right in your face.*

'You okay, love?' Keres' brows drew together. 'You suddenly became awfully pale.'

My eyes burned. My hands trembled. Visions flashed through my mind of a mangled body, endless blood and sightless eyes staring up at a ceiling. My chest constricted and breathing started to become harder. I was losing my grip on reality.

It's not real, it's just a memory, I thought to myself. Over and over.

But the charcoal on my fingers felt too much like blood. I was so godsdamned cold and my hands wouldn't stop shaking. More visions crashed through me. I tried to tether myself like Sorin had taught me but couldn't focus on anything but the lifelike visions.

Keres dropped the towel and cupped my cheeks to make me look up at him. 'Bad memory?'

I managed to nod once.

'Focus on me,' he said. 'Breathe with me.'

I tried to focus on my breathing but couldn't stop hyperventilating.

The floor didn't feel like it was there anymore. I couldn't breathe and I'd drown in those visions and—

Keres cupped the back of my head and pulled me close. 'It's okay.'

I squeezed my eyes shut and tried to focus on the rise and fall of his chest and shoulders. How my head moved along at a slow and steady rhythm.

'You're safe. You're not in danger.' He held one hand on the base of my wings, lightly caressing it with his thumb to ground me. My *varkradas* climbed up my legs, gently caressing me and slowly, I felt that outlet do its work.

'You're not in danger,' he repeated, resting his chin on my hair. 'And I'll be damned if I let anyone hurt you.' I let myself melt against him, sobbing against his chest while he just . . . held me.

Gods, he probably thought I was pathetic. Like Kallias. That nickname had come into existence for a reason. *Midór* – someone dramatic and hysterical, who always overreacted.

'I'm sorry,' I blurted out, ashamed of the way I'd reacted.

'For what?'

'For overreacting.' I didn't want him to get angry with me for behaving like this. 'I'm trying, I really am but I can't . . . I can't help it. I'm sorry. I can't help the crying – I'm sorry, it just starts and it doesn't stop and I—'

Keres kissed my hair, somehow pulling me even tighter into his warmth. 'You're not overreacting, love, you're recovering. There's a difference – and you don't *ever* have to apologise to me for crying.'

Slowly, I started to be able to breathe normally. All the while, Keres held me. Breathed with me. Said soothing and sweet things to me.

I took another shuddering breath while I grew calmer, although I was a little embarrassed. I didn't want anyone to pity me or treat me like a fragile piece of glass. 'Bet you're no longer bored, huh?'

'How could I ever be bored around *you?* It's always a surprise whether you'll take the high road or castrate a minor god.'

I snorted. 'Don't blame me, it was a full moon. People do strange things during full moons.'

Keres chuckled and rested his chin on my hair.

'I'm still not going to draw you naked, you know.'

'There she is,' he muttered to himself. His relief that I'd calmed down could've lit up the whole room. 'Wise choice, actually. Your canvases don't seem big enough to accommodate me.'

I looked up at him and raised a brow. 'Someone is awfully full of himself.'

'Someone has to be.' He sighed with a dramatic flair that could've rivalled Marianne. 'All my vesperae are in Anthens and my most devoted servant decided to stick with you.

Though I've heard that Asra loves it in Anthens.'

'Poor you,' I purred. 'Maybe you should start answering prayers at the first call to pass your time.'

'No.' The look on his face hardened.

'Why do you hate mortals so much? Eiran, I understand, but not the mortals.'

Keres pursed his lips, still brushing my back with his knuckles. 'They blame *their* deeds on me, *their* murders, betrayals and wars. And yet, though they can't stand the truth they see in my mirror, they have the audacity to ask me for favours and blessings. None of them pray, none of them offer.'

The way he explained it, I understood his reasons for hating them. Though what he'd done to Nikos rung in my mind. The curse he'd left behind on that family was beyond violent and from what I'd managed to put together out of hushed late-night conversations between Sorin and Zale, Meira – Nikos' daughter and now High Lady of Veshos – had been severely struggling with her family's curse.

'For someone with a quick mind and loose tongue, you're surprisingly silent right now.'

I looked back up, worrying on my lip. 'I just . . . I can't forget about Nikos.'

I didn't really remember much about him but the times that I'd seen him, he'd been kind to me with jokes to rival Sorin and a warmth that made me forget the other children didn't want to play with me, especially since Meira *did* play with me until she stopped visiting due to her curse. The few times I had seen her since, Meira had always treated me with respect and been kind to me.

'You knew him.' It wasn't a question.

'Not very well but I saw him from time to time . . . until

I didn't anymore.' I'd been too young to understand what had happened.

A dyad for a dyad.

'He manipulated her,' he spoke softly. 'Flattered her, claimed that he knew the truth behind the mortal myths, that Antheia was another victim. She'd been starved of mortal affection for so long, had been on the receiving end of so much hatred in those two years where they blamed her for their suffering. We lost Yael. We lost vespera after vespera while they tried to defend mortals. Antheia felt them hurt and die. And it was never enough proof that she wasn't wicked. She'd been breaking for months, pulling herself together enough to function but I felt her wither more and more every day. And that bastard . . .'

Keres rubbed his face. 'That bastard gave her hope – because there was a chance the mortals might favour her again. Nikos never believed Antheia couldn't revoke her blessing and started accusing her of being exactly what those myths claimed she was. Said that he was disgusted with her. Antheia broke fully then.'

His voice quivered. 'She fell apart, screamed that she'd never had a choice, that this life had been forced onto her.' His throat bobbed. 'She claimed that if I hadn't taken her from Eiran, none of this would have happened. I knew she was lashing out at me out of pain, because I was the nearest thing to her. Hell, her brokenness cut my own skin apart. But I took it. Even though it tore me apart, I took it.'

His voice became utterly quiet. 'I let her go and she went straight to Nikos to beg for his forgiveness – as if he had any right to judge her. He tricked her into trusting him and poisoned her with something Lorcán had given him. It made her break under the weight of her divine power

– like a halfgod normally does.' Visions of that night flashed through my mind. A burning and screaming deity, swallowed up by divine fire, the agony Keres had felt as his own. The earthquakes, the fracturing plains caused by her unstable power. The entire world had been at the brink of destruction.

'Aestor couldn't heal her. Aloïs couldn't get to her. Zielle went to fetch Eiran, hoping he could somehow help her. Lycrius had his hands full with keeping *me* alive. Lorcán was there as well, ready to kill Antheia for murdering Tarniq.'

I heard her screams. His screams. How desperate he'd been to get to her.

'And that fucking mortal decided *he* had the right to decide her fate.' He closed his eyes. 'I felt her desperation, how she latched onto her life and it . . . it just didn't matter.'

He whispered, 'My dyad, who'd been broken over and over again and yet found it in herself to go on . . . Eiran once gave her such an intense Divine Punishment that her soul actually fractured. She barely survived it. Hell, she couldn't walk or use her legs for months after. She broke again after we lost Kaltain. Every time she found hope, it was taken from her in the cruellest way possible and yet she fought on.'

His voice broke. 'If we'd had more time . . . Fuck, even Eiran was beside himself. But some arrogant *mortal* thought himself important enough to kill her.'

Silent tears streamed down my cheeks in reaction to his strong emotions. My *varkradas* had climbed up my legs in an effort to soothe me. They'd done the same with Keres. It was hard to imagine Nikos so cold-blooded but I hadn't known him well. And Zale had done things he regretted . . .

'So, yes . . .' His voice felt empty. 'I lashed out and I don't regret it. All of his scheming to save and protect his little family, so I cursed them to be beyond miserable. His mock injuries while protecting her on that battlefield to prove his devotion, so I gave him true injuries. He took my dyad in cold blood without hesitation, so I made sure he felt the same certainty when he took his own dyad's life. Antheia didn't deserve her fate but that bastard most certainly did.'

I wasn't sure how to react, what I could possibly say. But there was nothing I could say that would take away his pain and anger — anger that I found justified.

Her bright smile was etched into the back of my mind.

Keres' memories snapped through my shadows; how Zhella had ridiculed her for believing Keres had any interest in her since she wasn't anything special or pretty; a little goddess who barely held any power in her hands — dangerous power Eiran had suppressed to keep her under control. And he'd flawlessly convinced the others that Antheia was some dark and wicked goddess, feasting on the blood of innocents. Addicted to taking lives and the dark power that came with it.

I slipped my hand out of the sleeve of my cardigan, took his hand in mine and squeezed it. 'I'm sorry that you lost her, that you lost her so violently.'

'She was good,' he whispered, fighting his emotions. 'But Eiran broke her — made her a mosaic of broken hearts and bones and then wondered why she grew claws and fangs to tear him apart.' Keres finally tore his eyes away from the wall in front of us, looking at our intertwined hands.

I rested my head on his shoulder. 'Every time you speak of him, it's plain you despise him. Why serve him? Why remain his Left Hand?'

'Because I don't have a choice.' He sounded dejected.

'Eiran is cruel but smart. When I came into this universe, I had no pantheon I belonged to. Eiran offered me a home in exchange for unwavering loyalty – a blood oath.'

My eyes widened. Those oaths were extremely rare. It was a willing submission, a show of purest devotion to the bestower. Eiran could order Keres to do anything and Keres would not be able to refuse.

Keres squeezed my hand. 'Never trust him, no matter how charming he appears. Never take his deals, never take his oaths. No matter how shiny and pretty his jewellery appears, it's laden with curses. Be polite but never give him anything of value. Be honest but never share your secrets.'

I nodded. 'Now I'm secretly hoping Zhella will give me a riddle if Eiran agrees to test me.'

Keres rose a brow. 'Why?'

'I'm shit at those,' I admitted.

Keres grinned, opening his mouth to say something but stilled and absent-mindedly rubbed his left arm. 'Looks like Eiran needs me for something.' He studied my face. 'Will you be okay?'

I nodded. 'I'm fine now.'

'Let me know if you need anything, okay?'

He squeezed my hand one last time and then disappeared. The soothing scent of his perfume wafted through the room. The calming fragrance clashed with the image the myths had crafted in my mind, all the past months clashed with it. I'd grown up fearing Antheia, even though she'd been long dead. The Priestesses had brainwashed me to be terrified of Keres, to never pray to him and here he'd been, pulling me out of a panic attack. I'd believed in Eiran's benevolence and goodness, in Zhella's kindness. That Eiran had fought to protect the mortals and to achieve divine peace.

All of them were nothing but lies and yet mortals fell to their knees for the King of the Gods.

I knew the images on the ceiling in the throne room like the back of my hand. Every single major god was woven into the imagery.

Except for Antheia.

Except for their son.

And I decided I would change that.

Chapter 19

Diana

Within an hour, the golden trail underneath Eiran's chariot disappeared and became replaced by the spilt blood of the many battles that had raged throughout our history. Mortal red, *ichor* and *inkor*. He hadn't come this far with his slate clean, and he could wipe his hands off all he wanted, the iron scent would still linger around him. Like it should.

And I painted her; Antheia.

I couldn't quite explain where the nightly visions had come from but they'd started the moment Keres had freed me from Lorcán's magic. I'd seen flashes of the past, lifelike visions of Yael and the changes she'd brought forth. How she and Aeneas had started a revolution, leaving the High Coven terrified of their combined might. Of Antheia – and what she'd been through.

I painted Antheia bathed in her own moonlight, her raven hair flowing on an invisible breeze. Her night-blue eyes weren't cold like they'd been in my books growing up. They were filled with the radiance I'd seen in the wedding pictures. I connected Keres' right hand with hers with a golden thread that twined around their ring finger. In the other hand, she wielded an Erobian dagger.

I painted Kaltain with his short raven hair and gold-specked pale green eyes. I let that golden thread flow through the halfgod's heart. Eiran might've been his birth father but Antheia had saved the little babe from being killed by the King – an effort to hide the boy before anyone found out about his mistake.

I was roused from my concentration by a slurping sound, which made me look around to see where the noise came from. A woman sat on Sorin's throne, her back resting against one side and her legs comfortably draped over the other armrest. She looked up at me, slurping from the drink in her hands. There were even ice cubes in it – in the middle of winter.

When she met my gaze, Mar waved and gave me a thumbs up.

'Isn't it well past your bedtime?' I called over.

She showed me her middle finger, continuing her slurping. I cackled, the shaking making it harder for my wings to keep me in place. 'I should fetch an exterminator, it appears we have a bat problem,' she called back. 'Do you sleep upside down as well?'

I cast my eyes to the ceiling but couldn't stop grinning. 'No, I was too busy feasting on the blood of my enemies.'

Mar chuckled. 'I see you took my suggestion.'

I slipped out of the shadow next to the throne and Mar pulled her legs up so I had room to sit. 'Keres visited, told me more about Antheia.'

She nodded. 'I like Keres.'

I blinked. 'You do?'

Her mask slipped while she decided what to share. She pulled up her sleeve, revealing the inside of her right wrist.

Crow's feathers. I stared at it with my mouth open. 'He helped me when I escaped from my country.'

He knew her? 'Ho . . . How?'

She bit the inside of her cheek. That mask kept flickering on and off. I sensed that she wanted to share her history with me, how she ached to talk about it – especially with me because of Lorcán. 'I had *kalotra* on me. Keres removed it and placed an enchantment on me so that the king wouldn't find me – not until I wanted to be found. I will remain hidden from him until I speak his name.'

Maybe that was why Keres had pulled up his walls – to protect her.

I took her hand in mine, running my fingers over the marking. She stilled underneath my touch but I didn't sense any discomfort. If anything, she seemed to relax. 'Did he make a deal with you?' I felt that same protectiveness my mother must've felt.

'No.' She looked at our hands. 'He told me he wanted to give me a fresh start, a choice.'

I found myself respecting Keres more and more every day. 'Why did Lorcán want you?'

'Why does he do anything?' She didn't plan on sharing the reason with me – not yet, anyway.

'Are you lonely here?' I asked her, still brushing the back of her hand with my thumb.

'Sometimes,' she admitted, though I had a feeling it wasn't *sometimes* but *often*. 'It's not home but . . .' She shrugged lightly, not sure what else to say.

'Orthalla never felt like home either, so I can imagine how that feels.'

She nodded once and I felt a hint of sadness coming from her, wistful like a longing for something. 'It's not the place but the people that make it a home, though I have little people around me and the person who made my flowers grow with her love . . . I lost her.' Mar swallowed hard. 'I love Sorin, I do. But he has so many other friends he visits and family that loves him.'

She looked up at me. 'He once told me that I should talk to you, that you would . . . that you could be a friend. But I didn't dare approach you, I didn't . . . it didn't feel right – after everything I did there . . . I didn't feel like I deserved to be your friend.'

'It's okay to admit that you're lonely here, even if you're grateful for Sorin's help. That doesn't make you a bad person.' I squeezed her hand. 'And I can only imagine how others might treat you when they find out you're Aspian.'

Mar drew in a deep breath. 'They avoid me like a plague. Even though I was born after the War, they still somehow treat me like I started the damn thing. My accent is as obvious as an elephant in a chicken house even though I try my hardest to hide it. Sorin doesn't tolerate anyone giving me shit and it's mostly whispers and glances I have to deal with now, but I had to reject everything Aspian just to find a semblance of acceptance here, but it was still my home for so long.' Her throat bobbed. 'I try so hard to fit into the crowd but I'm not really good at . . .' She blushed, averting her gaze to her pulled-up knees. 'I don't deserve . . .' Mar swallowed as tears filled her eyes. 'No one wants me but I can't help but long to be wanted.'

Tears burned in my eyes in response to her raging emotions. To that damn mirror she was holding up. 'I do,' I whispered. 'Sorin does.'

'Sorin is an exception. There aren't many men like Sorin.' She wiped away some tears. 'He could've sold me out or used me but he didn't and I'll never deserve his friendship,' she muttered. 'But if you knew . . .' Her voice quivered. 'You wouldn't want me either.'

'Why wouldn't you deserve him? Why wouldn't I want to be your friend?' I brushed some hair behind her ear. 'You deserve to be looked after, to be cared for.'

She shook her head.

Gods, I wanted to prove to her that she didn't have to be alone. I thought of Aiden and how he'd fought for me, how protective my friends were. I decided Mar deserved that as well and that Sorin wouldn't be the only one looking out for her. 'Yes, Mar. You do.'

She sobbed, still shaking her head. 'I'm not even supposed to exist. I'm on borrowed time anyway.'

To Hell with that, whatever it meant.

I pulled her close, wrapped my arms around her and caressed her hair, shielding her from the rest of the world with my wings. She sobbed against me. 'I still want so much and I shouldn't. It's greedy and selfish and yet if I don't live, I'm haunted by guilt because she sacrificed *everything* for me. Yet I deserve *nothing*.'

It broke my heart.

Some of my *varkradas* draped themselves over her like a blanket, intertwining with her fingers. Others tugged at me to grab my attention. They wanted me to stay with her, were begging me to. Not that my shadows needed to ask me to do so, I'd long decided to stick with her.

'I don't know why I keep coming back to you,' she said in between sobs. 'I feel like a fraud. After everything – everything *he* did, I shouldn't even hope for your friendship.'

I closed my eyes, resting my chin on her hair. She smelled like cherry blossoms and blackberries, and a dewy forest underneath that perfume. I could almost imagine the leaves crunching underneath my bare feet.

She'd said something similar before – to Sorin.

Sorin hadn't been spared by Lorcán's manipulation, he'd shared that with me during the evenings I'd told him about Kallias. How he'd been in love with Lorcán, watching from the sideline how Lorcán courted my mother. And how later, during the War, Lorcán had tried to use it to his advantage and manipulate Sorin into aiding him, even going as far as claiming he wasn't in love with his wife but had married out of duty. That it hurt to know Sorin had so easily given up on him, that he could be better if only Sorin stayed with him. The only thing stopping him from falling for Lorcán's slippery magic-stained lies had been Zale.

'You are not Lorcán and you are not his actions either,' I said firmly. 'You deserve love, no matter your past. Sorin cares deeply about you and I do want to be your friend.' I tightened my grip on her. 'If you can't find your home here, loosen your roots and venture to find it elsewhere. It's daunting, terrifying even. But you won't be alone.'

She sobbed again. 'I want to *live*. I've been doing nothing but surviving for years and I'm sick of it. I want to *live*. But I cannot live without her.'

I couldn't stifle my own sob, overwhelmed by her emotions. The desperation in her voice. The visions that tore at me of a young woman with light brown eyes and brown wavy hair, slipping her golden ring on Mar's finger. The ring she played with whenever she was nervous or scared. Visions of snowball fights and nights tangled up in linen or between blooming wildflowers, until they weren't sure where one of them started and the other ended, whispering sweet nothings to each other. Of late nights bundled up in blankets in front of the hearth, of Mar playing the piano-forte while her lover softly sang to her – utterly smitten. And how she hadn't touched a pianoforte since her death.

Her dyad. Lorcán had killed her dyad.

By the fucking Æther, I *loathed* him.

In an attempt to distract myself from the murderous rage that was settling in my bones, making me tremble, I asked, 'Why don't you come with me?'

'To where? Hell?'

'Yes, meet my family, my friends. I often visit Clacaster, so I'll bring you back any time you want to see Sorin.' I thought of something else. She'd need a place – something to do, though I'd have to discuss it with Sorin. 'Sorin wants to present me to Eiran as a potential High Lady for Egoron. Should he agree, you could come with me, be my advisor there – if you want that.'

She thought it over. 'You would have me?'

'I'd like it very much to have you around, the current one is rumoured to be a two-faced dick and you strike me as someone who'd speak her honest opinion – to my face. And I want to be your friend. I'm starting to sound rather desperate with how many times I've said that now.'

She chuckled through her tears, drawing in a shaking breath. 'I know that I am quite irresistible.'

'Speak of a one-eighty,' I teased her, glad to see her humour returning.

Mar nestled her head on my shoulder and closed her eyes, still shivering from her emotions. I bent one wing enough to cover her like a blanket. 'Do you think your parents would want me in your home?'

'Mom would be ecstatic to have another person around. She grew up in Aspia, so she knows where you're coming from. Dad would find your humour wholly amusing. I do have to warn you about my friends though, they do enjoy teasing.'

She nodded. 'I'll tickle their wings if they annoy me.'

I held her while I slowly – very slowly – felt her calm down.

Covered in paint smears from assisting me, Mar looked through one of the tall windows as dawn came knocking on the door, casting the room in a gentle and warm orange glow. It illuminated her, making her appear as if she'd been set on fire or made from flames. Like a phoenix rising from its ashes. Her eyes found mine and in the light of the rising sun, they appeared ethereal – glowing. Like she wasn't completely from this world. An ancient presence filled the room, pressing down on me like Aestor's power had. Yet this felt older. It was definitive, deciding, a choice, a shackle around my leg and freedom all at once. And it came from Marianne.

I stared at her with a brush in my hand, a bit dumbfounded. 'You don't have to answer if you don't want to.'

She tilted her head in curiosity. 'You're not mortal, are you?'

Her mask slipped on but it immediately disappeared again. Exhaustion tainted her face and it wasn't the result of lack of sleep. It was the look of someone who'd been on the run for too long, of someone tired of hiding. 'No, I'm not.'

Excitement crashed through me. Partly because I was really, *really* curious to know what she was. Mostly because I'd been worrying about being friends with a mortal. She would age, while I didn't.

Mar chuckled. 'Look at you getting all excited.'

'So you're immortal?'

'It appears so.' She shrugged, wary of how I would react. 'Enough have tried to kill me and severely wounded me. None have succeeded and most of those wielded mortal weapons.'

I practically squealed, 'You're *immortal?*'

Mar threw her head back and laughed. 'Yes, *Nychter.*'

'Oh, this is going to be such *fun.*' I clasped my hands together, grinning widely. 'I suggest you get used to my bad jokes and clinginess, Mar. You'll be stuck with it for a while.'

She softly laughed. 'I don't mind that.'

'Good.'

'And you'll have to accept my dryness and social awkwardness. I tend to just leave conversations I don't wish to partake in, which has caused some confusion among the other advisors here.'

I could very much imagine that. I leaned against the armrest of the throne, fidgeting with the brush in my hand. 'So what exactly are you?'

'My real name is Aedlynn. My father is Aspia's Master of Assassins, and my mother . . .' Aedlynn pointed up at the ceiling. My gaze landed on the goddess in the chariot right behind Eiran, his ever-loyal follower. ' . . . is Khalyna.' She glared at the image with such viciousness that I was almost scared for the goddess.

'Does anyone else know?'

'My dyad, that king. My father knew.' She sighed. 'Sorin, Keres, Aestor and now you.'

Keres really did know her. He'd helped her, even though she was Khalyna's daughter. Which I respected a damn lot because Khalyna hadn't helped Kaltain.

'Aestor healed me when I arrived in Clacaster, summoned

by Keres, who informed both Aestor and Sorin of what had happened and who I was. I've been taking moonsbane to subdue my power. I don't recommend that, it makes you feel awful. I feel like I am living a half-life, but at least it's a life.'

I took her hand in mine. 'They all know?'

She nodded. 'I expected Keres to despise me but he seemed more furious with the fact that Khalyna dumped me with the royalty in Odalis. I can't say I don't share that same anger.'

'Have you seen her since?'

'Once, in Clacaster. She couldn't care less about what had happened to me, how broken I was. She ordered me to stop behaving like a pubescent child, insulted my dyad, ordered me to return to that shit king and threatened to drag me to Eiran herself if I didn't comply.'

'*Bitch*,' I muttered.

Her eyes darkened. 'Should you ever meet her, ask her what happened to her face. I decorated it.'

My mouth fell open. This woman in front of me had maimed the *Third God* for threatening her. Aedlynn was many things but not fragile. She wasn't helpless, no damsel and she knew it.

Her gaze travelled back up, this time resting on Keres. 'I called to him for help and he came yet again. Not only did he scare her off, but he also lashed out at her for threatening me. For slapping my face.' Her lip quirked up as she showed me her sweetest smile. 'Divine Punishments, Diana, can be *lovely* to watch.'

Chapter 20

Diana

Anthens, the Capital of Hell
Two months later

Aedlynn shot me a sly smile when she walked into the living room to find Keres and I sitting there together with snacks and wine, having our own little feast. He'd also brought over a bottle of Lycrius' finest nectar – made of gilded pears because he knew how fond I was of those.

'Perhaps we should assign you a bedroom,' she said to Keres. 'Given that you practically live here.'

Keres chuckled and took another sip from his wine. His legs were comfortably spread and one arm hung over the back; casual and comfortable. The complete opposite image of the intense God of Malice I saw in Aerelia. 'I fear poor Eiran would miss me.'

'Has he said anything about our deal yet?' I asked him, curled up on the couch with my legs tucked underneath me and a blanket Keres had draped over my wings. 'He's been surprisingly quiet about it.'

Keres nodded. 'He asked how I had found you, how you had been hidden and ordered me to keep a close eye on you and report back if anything unusual happened,' he said. 'He didn't say much else about *you*, which doesn't sit very well with me. When Eiran goes silent, it usually means he's obsessing over something. Though he did mention that he found it interesting that I let you insult Jasán and that I shut up Náyel last full moon – when he called you a whore.'

'Uh-oh.' Aedlynn plopped down next to me and I rested my head against her shoulder. Physical touches helped me calm down, as well as talking, and Aedlynn was glad to be a human outlet. Any time I woke her up after having a nightmare or visions, she helped me de-stress, which I deeply appreciated.

'I told him that I found it hilarious to watch their frail egos crumble, which he seemed to believe. But he doesn't believe I'd do just anything with you; he fears that perhaps *you* are seducing *me*.'

'Oh?' My cheeks flushed.

'So now Eiran thinks that Aloïs is planning something and that he's using his pretty heir to stir the ol' cauldron of Chaos by seducing his Left Hand. He didn't say much after that.'

I playfully slapped his arm. 'Why are you only telling me this *now?*'

Keres mouthed *ow* while he rubbed the spot with his marked thumb, pretending to be greatly hurt. 'Because he told me tonight when he summoned me, and then I really just wanted to get drunk and forget all about that.'

I snorted. 'Such a healthy coping mechanism, love.'

Keres shot me an impish grin.

'So why not use that?' Aedlynn said. 'If Eiran is so concerned about Diana, make him believe that you're seducing Diana for him to control both her and Aloïs. Show him you have her wrapped around your finger and that you can do whatever you want with her – and that Aloïs can't do anything about it without risking divine wrath.'

Keres raised an amused brow. 'Your scheming Khalyna side is showing.'

She stuck her tongue out in reply. 'Just admit that it's a good idea.'

'It is,' I agreed. 'Though I'm not sure what else to do to convince Eiran. I already follow Keres around like a love-sick puppy, sit on his lap and glare at solerae when they try to approach him.'

Keres wiggled his brows. 'Even when we're not pretend-ing.'

My face flushed so horribly that my cheeks could've lit up the entire room and Aedlynn had to duck because I threw a pillow at his face. 'Arrogant prick,' I hissed.

Tucking the pillow on his lap, Keres threw his head back and cackled. 'I'm just teasing you.'

My lips curled into a playful smile. 'Fine, we'll just have to convince him some more.' I started rising from the couch. 'Now, I'd love to forget about Eiran and enjoy the rest of my night, so if both of you can handle my competitiveness again, how about we play another game?'

Keres raised his brows at me in indignation. 'You nearly killed me last time.'

'You cheated!' I gesticulated so vigorously that my wings shook, which made Aedlynn snort.

Keres laughed and shook his head. '*We* didn't cheat, love.' he Keres purred. 'But you certainly did.'

Aedlynn's head whipped around to look at Keres. 'What? Really?'

I shot him my most seductive smile. 'Keep that our little

secret and I'll paint you an entire mural. You know, to accommodate your assets,' I purred.

'Diana!' Aedlynn gaped at me. '*You* cheated?!'

I shrugged while I walked over to the shelf with fluid grace, searching for a game to play. 'Can't remember, who's to say?'

'There she is,' Keres muttered behind me, but there was an ardent softness to his voice that made my cheeks heat and my stomach dip.

I stood in the small doorway that led to the balcony adjoined to my bedroom, leaning against the frame while I took in the great view of Anthens underneath the waxing gibbous moon. Magic used to crawl throughout the mortal lands for aeons, much like veins in the earth, but mortals had done what mortals did best. Everything different from them had been destroyed until extinction came to claim its due and magic had gone back to its ancient slumber, only waking up in certain mortals.

Yet it was wide awake here. I felt it in the silver moon and the lunar magic used by the colchians. There were no veins here but arteries that carried the strong pulse of the *æther* within. It seemed to draw me in – to call to me and demand my attention.

A noise came from behind the bathroom door, like something was walking around there. My shadows peeked through the small gap but didn't see anything and I was too curious to converse with the shadows in the room, so I walked over and opened the door while I sent a silent prayer that nothing scary haunted my bathroom.

Soft chirps came from the marble bathtub, and when I peered in, the tension in my body immediately dissipated.

A kabolos lay in it, disguised as a white ferret. It looked at me with its beady black eyes, shifting at the bottom to reveal that it wasn't alone.

'Oh my gods,' I whispered, clasping a hand over my mouth while I sank to my knees to cuddle the newborn kaboloses. I knew how fragile they were, how they snuck into homes to hide from predators. And though they weren't dangerous in the slightest, mortals had traumatised them enough to make them wary of any contact with them.

But this one? This one had chosen *my* bathtub as a safe space to give birth in.

'Is there a reason why you're crying in your bathroom?'

I looked up to see Keres leaning in the doorway. I wasn't even ashamed that he saw my tears. Instead, I held up a cub and showed it to him. 'She chose my bathtub,' I sniffed. 'She feels safe here.'

Keres pushed away from the doorpost and joined me. 'I received a bit of a strange prayer – some fierce *matska* worrying about a scary ghost in her bathroom.'

'Did I send that to you?'

'Must've been the deal.' Keres grinned at me. 'So you're crying because you found them? Nothing bad happened?'

I looked up at him and smiled sheepishly. 'No, nothing happened.' His relief sent a flutter through my stomach. He never made fun of my many emotions, which I was grateful for. I'd grown quite fond of him, really liked it whenever he visited me and I found myself missing him whenever he wasn't around. And the hugs he gave me . . . I could take root in those embraces.

Unsure of what to do with that fun realisation, I put a cub in his hands. 'Feel how soft it is.'

We spoiled them until the mother grew impatient and

stole her cubs back, curling around them. Keres draped a soft towel over them, providing some warmth as well as a hiding spot. I also left a gilded pear behind for them to nibble on. Some part of me recognised that they would like it.

'I think those kaboloses are the luckiest creatures in all the realms,' he said while closing the door behind us. 'You'd skin someone alive before they'd get into your bathroom.'

I smiled and brushed a strand of hair behind my ear that had got loose from my braid. 'Of course, they're *adorable* and they're so incredibly *soft,* and did you hear those little chirps they make? They melt my heart. I can't imagine anyone wanting to hurt them. And it seems I'm not the only one fond of gilded pears and—' I was rambling again, so I closed my mouth, looked down at my hands and played with one of my mother's rings.

When Keres' arms slid around me to hug me, I shivered underneath the touch. I nestled my head just underneath his throat, closed my eyes and enjoyed how right it felt to be held by him like this. Like my body had been made to melt into the dips and curves of his body.

His hand moved to the back of my head to caress my hair. My shadows settled down, curling around his ankles and slowly, I grew warm. I barely noticed that my wings drooped.

I wanted to stay with him. I wanted to cuddle up to him and fall asleep in his arms.

I was relieved that I'd come to a point where I felt comfortable again in someone's arms, to have the desire to be around them. To *wonder* about them. I'd feared for so long that I'd never heal enough for that.

'Do you need me to check beneath your bed for scary ghosts? You did pray for assistance.'

'Cocky bastard,' I muttered against his chest.

Keres laughed, then let go of our embrace and stepped back, shooting me a sly grin. 'Don't bite the bedbugs.'

His hand closed around my wrist as he firmly pulled me back, fingers digging into my fragile skin. I didn't dare look down, certain that I'd find more bruises there. I tried to pull free, afraid to look into his eyes — to see what I might find there.

'Let me go.' It was a mistake to put such force behind the words. Kallias never liked it when I showed him attitude. He shoved me hard against the wall, curling his fingers around my throat while his brown eyes burned into mine. More bruises started to align with his fingertips.

'I didn't ask you to marry me, Midór. I told you that you're to be my wife. It was no question.'

I swallowed hard. 'I've decided that I don't want to marry you.'

Kallias laughed. 'Please, you don't even know what you want. That fragile little mind of yours isn't capable of making such serious decisions. It's why you let me make them for you, remember? Besides, if I let you go, you'll simply return to me in a few days — begging me to take you back, since no one else could ever want this.' He gestured with his free hand to me, like that was explanation enough. 'Allow me to spare you the embarrassment of that.'

Closing my eyes, I fought hard against the tears.

'Don't cry.' His voice was like a whip across my face. His grip on me tightened and I winced. 'Don't you dare act like I'm the one hurting you when you stand here refusing my love for you. I give you everything and it's never enough.'

I hated how I trembled. How some part of me wanted to beg him for forgiveness, while some other part screamed that I needed to get out of this mess before he buried me alive. But he loved me despite my endless list of faults and I hated myself for continuously disappointing him. I could do nothing right, no matter how hard I tried. And still, he wanted to take me with him, to have me all to himself. I'd always been so scared of the hollow loneliness that accompanied me everywhere I went, but Kallias tolerated me despite my flaws.

He loved me.

Right?

While still keeping one hand around my throat, he raised his other to lazily tilt my chin up with his forefinger. 'Have you gone simple?' I flinched and quickly shook my head, though it was hard to do so. His face was mere inches away from mine and his breath smelled of the wine we'd been drinking. 'Then fucking answer me. You don't want me angry, do you?'

'I'm sorry,' I whispered while I tried to keep from crying.

'No, you're not.' He roughly pulled me away from the wall and threw me hard against the dining table, where I hit the back of my head against the mahogany. My vision blacked out for a moment and when I came to, Kallias stood scowling in front of me.

I wondered if Sorin treated his lovers like this, though I doubted it. He had a patience to rival the God of Healing and the only time I could remember Zale being somewhat stern was when I'd been eleven. He'd taken me on a little retreat to a family estate in Aurnea. We'd played in the woods and I'd been chasing those little white foxes because it seemed like they were leading me somewhere. I'd slipped and fallen down the hillside, badly cutting my thigh on a sharp branch of a bush.

I'd expected him to viciously scold me for ruining my dress and getting hurt but he'd only told me to be more careful and not to stray so far. He'd healed my wounds, dusted off my dress and then hugged me.

Their love had never made them do things that ended up hurting me. That made me bleed and bruise and cry and beg and flee while *they chased me – grabbing me before I could leave the room.*

Maybe this wasn't love.

'Am I truly not enough for you?' Kallias asked in a low tone. 'Do you like wounding me like this?'

If this was love . . . if this was true love, then I didn't want it.

This wasn't nourishing. It was starving me. It didn't shine a bright light on my soul like I read in those books I liked, it had broken whatever glow had adorned it before I'd met him. There was no honesty, only tricks that left me questioning my sanity. It didn't make me feel alive, it made me feel like I'd long withered in the dirt.

'Do you even know what you want yourself?'

All I knew was that I didn't want to hurt anymore.

'Please, Kal,' I whispered. My trembling hands lay uselessly next to me. 'I can't do this anymore.'

'Up.'

I flinched but tried to rise, though I didn't do so quickly enough for him. He grabbed a fistful of my hair and forced me back down so my knees impacted against the marble floor and bruised.

'Let me put it this way, Diana, and I pray to Anaïs that you're still somewhat capable of thinking. Either you do as I say without complaining or I will tell those nobles in Orthalla that I found you sacrificing some innocent girl to Elyon – to return to Lorcán. There are plenty of people around to witness that murder – how wicked you are. And there are plenty of victims I can use to convince them.'

I stared at the floor through my tears. I couldn't stop sobbing, terrified of the threat.

I shouldn't have gone with him to Medos. I should have never blushed when he'd smiled at me at the Summer Solstice festival. I should have never said yes when he'd asked me to dance. I should've never felt giddy when I'd overheard the servants gossiping about how the Rhosyn heir appeared to be in love.

I'd been so stupid . . . naïve. I'd let him ruin me.

'Stop crying, you pathetic overreacting bitch!' His blow sent me down hard on the floor.

Something broke in me.

Something awoke in me.

Kallias leaned forward to grab me again.

I wouldn't let him hurt me.

Never again.

All-consuming rage took over my muscles and, somehow, I managed to push him away.

The fury in his eyes told me he'd make me regret this.

'I suggest you remember your fucking place, Diana,' he spat while he attempted to grab me again.

But I wasn't made to be conquered.

A rage like I'd never experienced before overtook me. Pure, dark hatred exploded in me and clouded my mind. When I lifted my hands, I somehow held a dagger and brought it down, over and over. While I broke in so many sharp pieces that even the most intricate mosaic would be jealous of me.

Again and again, I struck.

'Diana! Stop!'

I couldn't stop, couldn't stop the rage nor the pain that demanded an outlet. I couldn't stop lashing out at the lifeless body underneath me, slipping deep into madness. I wanted Keres to come. I wanted him to tear Kallias apart. I liked the iron taste in my mouth, the blood that already started clotting on my nightgown. Something in me needed to taste that blood – liked it. Something monstrous.

I really was a beast.

Why wouldn't Keres come to punish me? I'd killed an Orthallian lord. I'd proven to them all that they were right to hate me. Why wouldn't Keres come?

I shivered, my teeth chattered uncontrollably. I could barely see anything through my tears.

I couldn't stop. Even though I was exhausted and my headache felt like a thunderstorm. My chest could tear open any moment now, to let that broken and battered heart of mine fall on the cold floor so it could fully shatter.

I lifted my dagger again, but this time, someone's warm hand gently curled around my freezing skin.

And the scent of springtime filled my nostrils.

I fought with the blankets, unable to stop crying, convinced that the vision had been real. His blood coated my hands again and the bitter taste of his blood haunted my tongue. I even smelled that horrible cologne, which made my throat close up and sent my stomach into a riot. More visions swept over me, not only of Kallias, and I felt my tether to the real world slowly slip from between my fingers.

Someone pulled the blankets away, wrapping me up in a warm embrace while making soothing noises and that cologne made room for the spring meadow I'd come to love.

'You're safe, Diana, it was a dream.' Hearing his voice was enough to pull me back into reality, though I still trembled and cried. Keres brushed my hair back, laying us down so I could nestle against him. 'You're okay, it was a dream.'

I nodded feverishly, grateful when he covered me with blankets again, since I was still shivering.

A strange sort of warmth filled me, the kind that felt like sunlight washing over my soul. It caressed over those scars on my heart until the ache was gone. Keres had asked Aestor for a small blessing.

Once again, I was overcome with how different he was. His hands on my body didn't feel like a threat. His presence in the room didn't make me wary, didn't make me hunch in an effort not to affront him. And when Antheia had told him that she didn't want that bond, he'd let her go – because he'd sensed that she'd needed that moment alone. He hadn't ridiculed nor hurt her. He'd caught her falls and tended her wounds and then he'd kissed the ache away.

I'd seen and felt the love between my parents, Maeve and Cas, and even Vanora and Eos. But being around Keres and experiencing such gentleness for myself made me understand what love truly was.

When I'd finally stopped crying, I glanced up at him with puffy eyes. 'How did you know I was having a nightmare?' I croaked.

Worry had drawn his brows together. 'You prayed to me, over and over – in your dream, I think.'

'I'm sorry for waking you,' I whispered. I felt so stupid.

Keres brushed my hair back. 'There's no need to be, I don't mind.' I nodded slowly and laid my head back down on his chest, growing calmer and calmer with every steady beat of his heart. 'You okay?'

I nodded. Keres shifted to lie down next to me and slowly pulled me closer to tuck my back and wings against his chest. His arms banded around me to hold me securely in place. 'Warm enough?'

Aloïs had mentioned before that pups were very sensitive and didn't know the difference between pain and coldness. Lorcán had locked me up in a cold dungeon, where he'd hurt me over and over again. Which now meant that every time I was cold, my body thought I was in danger.

'I'm okay,' I whispered. 'You don't . . . you don't have to do this, you know. I'll be fine.'

Keres' hand gently brushed over my stomach. 'Being looked after by others doesn't make you a burden, Diana.

It makes you human. Besides, I know you can't fall asleep when you're cold like this.'

I wasn't sure what to say, so I kept quiet. His fingers continued tracing my stomach and the gentle gesture helped me grow calmer. My eyelids started to become heavier again and I felt my body slowly start to grow warmer. 'Thank you,' I whispered.

I let my wings relax against him and focused on the sound of his steady breathing and heartbeat, on how his fingers continued to caress my stomach. How the soft fabric of his shirt brushed against the membrane of my wings any time he inhaled. How the warmth of his body sunk into my skin to warm me up. All while a foreign sort of inner peace nestled inside of me.

The only thing I'd ever wanted was to feel safe.

And by the gods, I did.

Antheia liked the wary looks she received from the flustered gods as she walked into the meeting, and the way her father's gaze darkened. With a venomous sweet smile adorning her dark red lips, she met that stare. Both the train of her midnight blue dress and her loyal darkness followed in her wake.

Her back still ached and as she met Eiran's eyes, the scars throbbed as if her body remembered exactly who had pushed her past her limits. The violent wounds had finally closed months ago but she'd needed time to heal, to be able to get out of the bed in Aestor's palace. She hadn't even been able to walk. Physically, the wounds had closed but the thick scars on her soul still lingered.

She'd lost count of how many times he'd shattered her flesh and being – her very essence. Eiran had sent her tumbling straight into the darkness and that darkness had welcomed her with open arms, had caressed and soothed her through the agony. Like a father should have.

He'd been so desperate to make her appear unhinged and now she would show him that she was all of that and much, much worse. If her father so dearly wished for her to be a monster and continued convincing the other deities of her supposed wickedness, Antheia would gladly remind them all who could swallow the stars and drown them in darkness.

She circled the rounded table at which all those dainty gods sat. Every major god and goddess – except for her. They held their breath, quieting their raging heartbeat because of what they saw in her midnight eyes. How her darkness had gathered around her to guard her tender back. These gods had all ridiculed her and laughed at her because her divine power had taken its sweet time to manifest itself. But it was fully at her disposal now.

'Antheia,' Eiran said with a neutral face, comfortably seated in his chair like he couldn't care less about the uncomfortable gods surrounding them. 'I don't remember inviting you to this meeting.'

'You didn't,' she purred. 'I invited myself.'

Next to him, Zhella glared at her, at the wing-like darkness at her back. 'You look like those beasts of Hell.'

Antheia smiled, though it didn't reach her eyes. 'Do not mistake me for a circes, sister. Those know mercy.'

Zhella scoffed. 'Are you threatening me?'

She passed Melian, who stiffened in her presence – as she should. Antheia liked that she was afraid of her. Melian made a lot of noise and commotion for someone so incapable of self-defence. Yet jealousy was a slippery disease and it appeared that no salt in Melian's oceans could fend off the sickness. She'd seen it for herself when Anaïs had tricked Antheia, and instead of helping her, Melian had attempted to drown her as revenge for the attention her fiancé had given to the young goddess.

But all the loud thunder and storms and flickering lightning in the skies had watered down to nothing when Zhella had found them. When Zhella had defended her and torn Melian's back wide open with cursed wounds for touching her little sister.

And here they were now. Eye to eye and contempt to contempt.

Antheia's lips pulled into a cruel smirk. 'If you need someone to clearly inform you they're threatening you, perhaps you're not fit to be our King's Right Hand.'

'Antheia, behave.' Eiran hissed at her.

Once, those two words would've been enough to make her kneel. He'd ruined her reputation. He'd ruined her back.

He'd ruined her soul with that last Divine Punishment.

Antheia's voice was barely a whisper, 'I don't think I will.'

'Must you continue these wicked ways, Antheia?' Anaïs spat her way, and her body froze in place. Of course he would dare open his mouth; he thought his supposed wisdom and opinions were so important that they always needed to be shared. 'You have done enough already to those poor mortals.' She had done no such thing, but they were all happy enough to believe it. 'You seem to live and breathe to disrespect our King. If you keep stepping out of line, we will have to intervene, and judging from the limp in your step, that last Punishment did not leave you well.'

Anaïs had played with her and tricked her and then the God of Wisdom had gone ahead and convinced them all that she was a simple and naïve little fool. She would show them all that his wisdom was as fraudulent as his promises. And the hands he'd put on her body . . . she would break every single bone in them. Or maybe she'd leave the physical torture to Keres. She wouldn't want him to miss out on the chance of taking revenge for his dyad and she knew from experience how thorough he was.

Antheia stopped behind the dark-skinned god, resting her dainty hands on his broad shoulders. On the gold divine armour they all wore. Such a stark contrast to the simple silk she was currently wearing. As was Anaïs' skin against her pale skin. Once, it'd carried colour but it hadn't since Keres had hoisted her out of the Caerelian Ocean. After Eiran had dumped her nearly lifeless body in it.

The god stiffened underneath her touch and perfume. The night flowers that encompassed him. 'Answer me this simple riddle, little God of Wisdom,' she crooned. Anaïs' dark eyes shot to his King, whose gaze was glued on his youngest. 'What creature walks on four legs in the morning, two legs in the afternoon, and three in the evening?'

The god scoffed as if insulted by the simplicity of the riddle. 'A mortal.'

Antheia massaged his shoulders, bringing her lips closer to brush them over the shell of his ear. Like he had done then to warm her up to his advances. 'And what creature will beg for mercy in the morning, absolution in the afternoon and death in the evening?'

Anaïs opened and closed his mouth, then swallowed hard. 'I do not know.'

The goddess sweetly planted a kiss on his cheek. 'You – if you cross me.'

She straightened again and smiled sweetly at Eiran – innocence itself. Her hands still held the broad god securely in front of her with a strength Anaïs hadn't expected. 'Look at me, Father. I've become the daughter you always wished me to be.'

While I wrapped bandages around my knuckles to prepare for physical training with Aiden, my mind was a little preoccupied with the visions I'd been having all night and how Keres had stayed with me. I'd liked it. The warmth, the sensation in my wings. His fingers trailing over my stomach. I'd been exhausted then, but ever since waking up, my mind had started wandering in a direction that it hadn't in years.

'I'm ready to fight if you're done drooling over Keres.'

I scowled at Aiden. 'I was *not* drooling over Keres.'

'Sure, *love,*' Aiden purred. 'Your wings were drooping. I have a pretty good idea of the kind of thoughts you were having.'

I opened and closed my mouth several times, viciously blushing.

'You're adorable when you're shy.'

'I'm not shy,' I muttered. 'And *you* are only trying to distract me.'

'Is it working?'

I jumped him, wrapped my arm around his neck and threw him down hard onto the training mats, and like I'd done so many months ago, I sat down on his abdomen and planted my knees tightly to his chest. 'No, you failed.'

The cocky bastard intertwined his hands behind his head and grinned up at me. 'Explain to me how I failed.'

I blinked, hands still planted on his chest. 'Because I have you pinned to the ground?'

'Again: Explain to me how I failed.'

'Because I have you . . . you're . . . underneath me?'

'I don't mind having a witch on top of me.' Aiden winked at me and my cheeks exploded with colour again.

'How about *you* stop drooling and actually spar with me?'

Aiden snorted and started to scramble up again. 'That old trick usually works on the other *matska*,' he complained. 'Though I should've known it wouldn't work on you; with you drooling over Keres.'

I rolled my eyes. 'You're insufferable. I don't drool. *You* drool when you see tomatoes, perhaps you should fuck a bush of them.'

Aiden snorted. 'And you're a smartass.'

I smiled at him with a hint of mischief. 'You should've got used to that by now.'

'Are you this insufferable when you meet with the Lords and Ladies?' Aiden started our training. 'Or do you behave well then?'

I scrunched my nose at him while blocking his attack. 'Oh, they adore me. Danny even likes Aedlynn.'

'Speaking of Aedlynn, where's your second shadow?'

I snickered. 'Clacaster for the week, she's visiting Sorin.'

Aiden swung his sword for my side but I blocked it with my daggers and pushed the blade away from my body. 'I like her,' he said as he swung his sword for my other side, where I blocked him with a shadow. This time, I glided through the shadows to appear behind him and swung my dagger for his shoulder blade. His own *varkradas* shot up to meet the steel and stop the blow.

Aiden glanced back at me. 'Aedlynn respects you and isn't afraid to protect you, so it soothes me to know that your second shadow is as devoted to you as I am.'

As devoted to you as I am. The sincerity behind the claim left me breathless. 'You truly meant that pledge?' I swallowed. 'I thought you were just trying to make me feel better.'

Aiden turned around and shook his head. 'I meant every word of it; your sword, shield, servant. Whatever you need or want.'

My mouth opened several times while I tried to find words. Aiden sensed my gratitude, which made another one of those beautiful smiles bloom on his lips. 'I'd be honoured to stand by your side, to be your guard the same way Eos is for Aloïs. I would guard you with my life.'

I stared at him, caught off guard by the proposal and truly honoured that he wanted to do that for me. Someone offering to be my *Corusiar* wasn't anything to take for granted. Aiden would truly give his life to protect mine and he would haunt anyone who'd ever dare strike against me. He'd sacrifice his wings to protect mine, though the thought of him getting injured like that made me nauseous.

His gaze on mine was intense, and in his eyes, I saw nothing but certainty. He'd long made up his mind about this.

'You'd be my third shadow?' I joked in an attempt to appear a little less like an emotional mess.

Aiden smiled. 'Fourth, since Keres also follows you around everywhere you go, but Aedlynn could use the support, don't you think? You're quite the handful.' I rolled my eyes at him. 'That poor girl is already so overworked that she fled back to Clacaster for a week.'

'Ass.'

'Careful.' He wagged a finger. 'I could go to Keres and tell him you're not interested in him.'

'For fuck's sake, Aiden!'

'Just try to deny it.' He grinned. 'We can all see your shadows calm down when you're around him, can all see you blushing and feel how that heart of yours skips a beat when he laughs.' He flicked a finger against the membrane of my wing to tease me, which sent a shiver down my spine like he'd thrown a pebble in a lake. 'And last week, when he came over for dinner, you were staring at him and I could sense those naughty thoughts of yours. You wanted him to touch your wings.' Aiden gave me a sweet smile. 'The most vulnerable part of you.'

My cheeks heated horribly, and once again, I wanted to melt into the floor. '*Fuck*, you heard that?'

Aiden chuckled softly and patted my cheek. 'It's fine, I've heard far worse from my brothers and their mates and you do *not* want to know what it was like to be around Aloïs and Eva when they met. I don't—'

I cringed. 'You're right, I don't want to know.'

He snorted. 'Fine. Anyway, so what's going on with you and Keres?'

'Nothing.'

'Doesn't look like nothing.' I couldn't quite place the smile he gave me, like there was a stray ache hiding behind it.

'I won't deny that I like looking at him,' I muttered while I rubbed my upper arm. 'He's like a pretty painting. But I already have a lot on my plate right now.' I glanced at him. 'Besides, I highly doubt Keres is interested in me like that.'

Aiden nodded while he considered it. 'Understandable, though I disagree with the last part.'

I stared at him, completely taken aback. 'What? Really?'

Feigning innocence, Aiden smiled at me. 'I thought you were too busy?'

'Prick.'

'I love you too, witch.'

I couldn't help but smile. Aiden focused his attention on the loose bandage around his wrist. 'It's like you made him come alive again. He leaves those chambers in Aerelia more often. He's here more often. I haven't smelled a solera on him in a while; he doesn't appear to let them do whatever they want anymore because he's lonely and lost. I still feel the ache that losing Antheia left behind but he's *happy* again.'

By the Mother, I *needed* him to be safe and sound and happy.

'I still can't believe those Priestesses convinced me to fear him.'

'Well, Keres *has* done horrible things. Especially after Kaltain was killed.'

I glanced at him. 'I ehm . . . What exactly happened to Kaltain? I haven't dared ask him yet.'

Aiden drew in a deep breath. 'Eiran killed that boy when he was barely nineteen years old, claiming he'd grown too unstable, which basically means Eiran felt threatened by his power. He made them watch – to punish Antheia.' His throat bobbed. My heart dropped down into my stomach.

'Antheia turned the entire Caerelian Ocean bloodred as an omen of death for the mortals. They started murdering them in retaliation and Antheia left his palace in ruins. Their fight is what created the Wastelands, what reduced the country of Avalon to nothing but ruins.'

'Has no one ever tried to release Keres from his oath?'

His voice softened. 'Only Eiran can break it and he doesn't plan on letting his control go. It hasn't happened since Antheia's death but Eiran often took control over Keres to make him compliant or force him to do things. We knew what was happening then because we felt his panic right before all walls were thrown up and Eiran blocked us out.'

I stared at him in shock. '*What?*'

'Yeah . . . It's bad . . . It hasn't happened in a very long time though.'

Gods, I wanted to stomp over to Aerelia and tear Eiran apart for what he'd done.

'Don't,' Aiden warned me.

I groaned and threw my hands up in frustration. 'You're telling me that Eiran does that despicable shit and then expect me to be calm?'

'No, I just expect you not to rush over to whoop his ass. Eiran would crush you.' I wanted to protest, but Aiden shut me up, 'Antheia couldn't kill him. Yael barely survived him. You truly think you could stop him – on your own?'

I growled softly and crossed my arms. 'Perhaps I should seduce Eiran and cut his throat when I've lured him into his bed. And then put that damn crown on Aestor's head.'

Aiden's lips quirked up. 'I can definitely see why Keres is so fond of our devious little nymph.'

Chapter 21

Diana

Another full moon came around and I found myself prancing around Eiran's beautiful gardens in Aerelia once again. Today's festivities weren't dedicated to anyone or anything in particular. Apparently, Eiran often had celebrations organised – probably because he was bored out of his mind in his grand castle without wars to fight and little schemes to layout.

Asra had planted me in a dark green gown, with a plunging neckline that fell half over my shoulders. She'd also painted my lips and had given me a half updo, so the tresses cascaded down my shoulders. She'd decorated the knotted hair with silver thorns and roses.

Keres had been *flustered* when he'd seen me.

I made my way over to the table, covered with fresh fruit, cheeses and other dishes. While I walked, my eyes fell on the dais underneath a tent, where two figures sat on two marble thrones. My legs forgot how to move and my heart thundered in my chest, echoing through my bones.

He had short raven black hair, adorned with a golden crown of branches and thorns. Eiran appeared to be in his late twenties but he was obviously so much older than that. Though he had a gripping beauty that made me stare, it didn't have the same effect on me as Keres' had. I'd wanted to admire Keres, pull out a chair and gather my supplies to paint him. If anything, I wanted to stay as far away from Eiran as possible. Maybe admire him from afar.

The sun goddess' skin was perfectly tanned, exposed by the golden silk dress she wore that left little to the imagination. Zhella's long blonde hair – broken up with tufts of pastel coloured tresses, cascaded over her chest and a simple minimalistic golden crown rested on her head. I noted that unlike Antheia's, Zhella's ears were rounded.

I'd just gotten over my stupor when my heart skipped a beat. Because Eiran was looking at me.

I stared back, unsure of what I was supposed to do. I probably should've bowed or kneeled, but I was left paralysed under his scrutiny. Nothing came from him, not even his presence settled into my *varkradas*. It'd been overwhelming to feel all the rest of them but Eiran . . . My *varkradas* were blind to him.

The corner of his mouth quirked up and the King inclined his head – to *me*. My heart leapt out of my chest while I quickly dipped my head and then hastily made for the table.

Perhaps he'd decided to be civil because of Sorin and Zale. I had no doubt that they'd already informed Eiran of their worthy candidate. But then again, most were convinced that even being a Princess wouldn't be enough to warrant his respect.

Or maybe I had imagined things. That was probably it, yeah. This was probably one of those embarrassing instances where I believed someone was waving at me but was actually waving at someone behind me.

I let go of a shuddering breath to exhale the tension in my chest and stiff wings and took the crystal pitcher with nectar to refill Keres' wineglass.

'I'd hoped to see that Keres' bitch had some more manners compared to those beasts of Hell since you were raised a mortal.' My grip on the wineglass tightened when a sickly sweet and familiar voice came from my left. I looked up to come eye to eye with Khalyna. 'But you don't even know how to properly pay respect to our King.'

Our King. Like Eiran ruled over me.

I raised a brow and finished filling the glass. 'Go play somewhere else, Khalyna.'

She took a step closer to me while her eyes trailed over my wings and her lips curled into a vicious smile. 'I just wanted to know if the rumours are true that your *sort* purr like a kitten when you're getting fucked.'

I raised my other brow as well. I wasn't even insulted by her words, just amused. She appeared more than desperate to disrespect me, which gave me the idea that she *wanted* me to lash out. 'Have a nice evening.' I smiled sweetly at her and made to turn around. 'I do hope you find someone to make it more interesting since you're so desperate for attention.'

I turned my back to her and took a step.

'You know, I've been wondering something,' she purred. 'Do you beg for Keres' attention as desperately as you did for that mortal boy's?'

I stilled. I knew Khalyna could find someone's greatest fears and use those against them, to make them cower and beg on a battlefield, but I hadn't expected her to use those powers here. I decided to ignore her and took another step. And Khalyna decided to add more oil to her fire. 'That boy had the right mind to try and hit the beast out of you. Pity he didn't succeed.'

I snapped around. 'What did you just say?'

Khalyna's smug grin grew, contorting her face. She crossed her arms and leaned forward a little, perfectly mimicking his Orthallian accent, *'Have you gone simple?'*

Once, I would've felt like a small fawn but Khalyna was no predator. Only a bully.

Kallias hadn't only broken down the house that my body and soul had been, he'd destroyed the entire foundation until even the spiders, mice and ghouls found the ruins too dangerous to reside in. Yet it was restored now, the walls had been painted in bright colours by my friends and a serene light shone through the windows from deep within. Every little crack had been filled with love and the garden in my soul had been in full bloom for months now.

I'd been afraid of Kallias for so long. But I'd grown past it.

I'd grown stronger.

My lips curled into a sweet, cold smile that could've rivalled Antheia's as I subtly squared my shoulders. 'By all means, Goddess, search my mind for what I did to that boy. What I did to his father and his lackeys when they crossed me.'

Khalyna clicked her tongue and came to stand right in front of me, not at all pleased with my attitude, but that wasn't my problem. She'd decided to test the waters and it wasn't my fault that the fish enjoyed biting. 'Let me make something very clear, *pet*,' she spat. 'We do not invite blackbones into our realm and we do not accept them, so I suggest you tone down and show respect, or I'll add those pretty little wings of yours to my collecti—'

Khalyna didn't get to finish her threat, because rage whispered in my ear and it didn't like the idea of losing my wings.

My *varkradas* gripped her limbs and threw her hard into the white-clothed table. The wood groaned and broke on impact. I slipped out of her own shadow and I shoved my Erobian dagger in her abdomen.

Khalyna's scream echoed over the cosy garden party, overshadowing the small fact that the music had stopped. 'You fucking bitch! How dare you?!' she seethed while she scrambled up, heaving and clutching her bleeding wound. 'I'm going to cut up those wings. I'll teach you a little lesson in respect.'

The viciousness in her eyes should've made me take a step back. Instead, I growled with such rage that Khalyna paled. The ground shook for miles around.

All around deities surrounded us – while still keeping a safe distance. Murmuring about the audacity I had for daring to touch a goddess. How my sort really didn't know how to behave, that we truly were uncivilised and mad.

Wicked creatures. Blackbones. Ellowyn's mistakes.

Keres appeared to my right, his left hand clenching and unclenching. Ready to pounce. 'What. Did. *You.* Do?' he hissed at her.

'Your whore jumped me because I told it to show our King respect!' Khalyna yelled, gesticulating at me. 'Look at it! It's even got its fangs out! Why would you allow a beast to set foot on our sacred ground?!'

I was going to bury her without the proper rites.

Keres opened his mouth but Khalyna continued, 'Don't you dare turn a blind eye to this! She's insulted and disrespected plenty of minor gods already and you only watched – allowed her to do those things. And now she insulted our King! You're his Left Hand, fucking act like it!'

'I let her insult those gods because it was entertaining to watch,' Keres said coolly.

More deities started whispering, agreeing with the things Khalyna brought up.

'You brought a blackbone into our realm!'

I had to admit that I was caught off guard by the term. It appeared that the gods had hurt and thus seen the inside of my kin enough times to know that we indeed had black bones. Keres' eyes darkened. His left hand flicked ever so slightly but Khalyna screamed out from the pain – a Punishment for the insult. She might've hated me and what I was but she *loathed* Keres, and seeing him so keen on standing up for me . . . there was a wicked triumph that intertwined with her sneer. She *knew* Keres cared. Perhaps she'd only done this to confirm her suspicion.

'Is this how it's going to be, Left Hand? Will you once again allow your nymphs to wreak havoc, only to blame *me* when they die?'

I stepped in front of Keres before he could react, before he could open his mouth or lash out at her. Though I certainly didn't do it to protect Khalyna. She could see that in my eyes. 'Threaten the vesperae again and I will add another scar to your face.' I'd never heard my voice sound like this before. There was a regal edge to it, a hint of arrogance. Thunder at midnight, and the lightning would strike when one least expected it.

Khalyna sneered at me. 'Who do you think you are to threaten *me*? I am the Third God, *child*. Goddess of War, Madness and Bloodshed. Remember your place before I break your fickle little mind with your worst nightmares.'

Narrowing my eyes, I let my wings take on their full span, casting a shadow over the goddess. Power crackled in the air like savage lightning. 'And I am Diana Márzenas, Princess of Hell and Emissary for my King, the Lady of Shadows and Lady of Daemons. Heir to the Chosen King and heir to the Queen of Nymphs.'

With every word I spoke, the presence of my power suffocated them more. Yet their vile opinions didn't quiet down.

Blackbone. Whore. Beast.

I decided I'd make their insults mine. 'I am The Blackbone Witch. The *Výssar* born from Darkness and Light,' I purred and showed them my coldest grin, revealing my sharp fangs. 'And I have long killed my nightmares.'

Some deities actually backed away.

'The vesperae don't only serve Keres. They serve my father and thus me, so I suggest you refrain from harming them, little goddess, as I am rather fond of them and do not react well to threats.' I stepped closer, letting my smile become viciously sweet. A serpent sharpening its fangs before lashing out.

Khalyna subconsciously took a step back.

'I suggest you remember *your* place when your shadows serve me as well. Both the shadows that hide underneath your thickest armour and the one that follows you around day and night are more than happy to execute my every command. Think of me then, when the darkness catches up to you.'

Khalyna opened and closed her mouth. Whatever she saw in my face and the dark power I wove with my threat, was enough to shut her up.

Eiran's ancient presence snaked up on me as he stopped next to me, his hands neatly folded behind his back while he scowled at Khalyna, who was still bleeding. 'Why did you think it necessary to insult my guest?' His low clear voice flowed right through me and rattled my bones, gripping me in a way I'd never experienced before.

'She didn't pay you proper respect, Your Highness. She refused to bow.' Perhaps I'd been playing Keres' pet but it was painfully obvious that Khalyna was Eiran's utterly devoted lapdog. The goddess was desperate for him, craved his approval and attention.

He didn't appear impressed with her reasoning. 'She did incline her head to me.'

'She should've knelt or bowed! If we turn a blind eye to this sort of disrespect, those beasts will soon rise up again!'

Eiran met my gaze. His eyes weren't just dark, they were pure black. I couldn't read his expression, couldn't tell whether I was in trouble or safe. 'Is that so? Were you planning on usurping me before or after dessert, Lady Márzenas?'

I blinked. That sounded an awful lot like sarcasm. 'I guess that depends on what the dessert is,' I muttered in a daze.

The corner of his mouth crept up. 'Understandable.'

Keres grew calmer.

'My King, you cannot possibly allow a blackbone to mingle with us. You cannot allow Lord Keres to lower himself enough to take *her* as his courtesan.'

Eiran sighed, bored, and sauntered closer. 'That's quite enough foul language, Khalyna. Your concern has been heard loud and clear.' He glanced at Keres, who'd been ready to lash out at her again. 'Stand down, *aediore*.'

Keres complied and took a step back from her.

Khalyna scrambled up, still clutching her bleeding wound and quickly inclined her head to Eiran. But he paid her no attention as his eyes were back on me. 'My apologies for this behaviour, Lady Márzenas. Try to enjoy the rest of the evening and know that your vesperae will remain unharmed. I will see to it myself.' With that, he started to walk away.

What the Hell?

The crowd started to break apart and most decided to return their attention to the festivities, gossiping and chatting about what had just happened. Even the music started again. I met Keres' gaze while he silently asked if I was okay and nodded once. He was as confused by Eiran's reaction as I was.

Khalyna glared at me. She seethed with fury knowing that Eiran had backed me up and not her. His lapdog wasn't happy with it. 'That mortal boy should've killed you when he had the chance – to spare us all from *this*,' she gestured at me.

Like it was explanation enough.

One of those scars on my heart cracked wide open.

Before Keres could decide to get between us or to help me murder a goddess, I'd flung myself at her. If Khalyna wanted to dance, I'd leave her breathless.

Pinning her to the ground with my *varkradas*, I cut her face with *Aecéso* and then shoved it between her ribs on the left side of her chest. Khalyna grabbed a knife that'd been strapped to her thigh – which reeked of moonsbane. Before she could swing the vile weapon my way, I'd disarmed her and dragged her onto her knees by her loose hair. I channelled my roaring fury and lashed out at her back with shadows. I tightened my *varkradas* around her limbs to keep her on her knees while I gave her a whipping that left the grass stained with *ichor*.

For those sweet vesperae she'd maimed and killed. For hurting Aedlynn. For insulting me.

Panting, I relaxed my shadows again. Tears stained Khalyna's bloodied face. Her hatred for me was overwhelming – palpable.

I looked up to see Eiran standing some metres away. Just watching us. I couldn't read his expression, so I wasn't sure if I was in trouble or not, but there wasn't a drop of fear in my body as I curtsied for him; I held that dark gaze, an overexaggerated bow dripping with attitude. Ruse be damned, I'd never let anyone make me feel small again.

Keres shot a silent prayer to the Æther for mercy. Dreading the moment my parents would murder him for getting me killed by bringing me here tonight.

Zielle and Lycrius were ready to jump in between and I had the faint impression it was a good thing Aestor wasn't attending the festivities. He would've lost that endless patience of his.

Eiran's dark gaze lowered to Khalyna. 'Insult her again and I will punish you myself. I will not allow you to disrespect nor harm my Left Hand's servant. Nor will I allow you to jeopardise the already fickle peace that exists between the gods and daemons by insulting their Princess.'

Her face fell but she bowed her head. 'Forgive me, Your Highness.'

Eiran nodded once. 'Go to the healers.' Then he met my gaze, studying me for what felt like aeons before he finally spoke, 'I look forward to formally meeting you, Lady Márzenas.'

The King turned and sauntered back to the dais, to his throne.

Khalyna scrambled up from the grass. There was nothing

but animosity in those piercing eyes when they met mine. Her divine power crackled around her balled fists, which trembled from fury.

'You hold onto that dagger like it's a lifeline,' she said with a low voice. 'But know that when the time comes that you desperately wish to win, any weapon you touch or use will fail you.'

The coldness of her curse sank deep into my bones. Into the marrow.

Her smile sent shivers down my spine. 'Think of me then; when you lose everything.'

Chapter 22

Diana

My mom grinned down at me with her arms crossed, standing near the edge of the pond that she'd just thrown me into. Aiden and Eva had taken it upon themselves to keep the physical combat up to date. Keres helped me train my archery skills because I'd fallen in love with a pretty longbow I'd found in the weapon's room some months ago.

Aedlynn just generally liked to kick my ass – or Aiden and Vanora's. The fact that she could unleash herself on us without having to worry about actually hurting anyone was enough to convince her to just jump us from time to time. I sensed the same restlessness in her that I'd carried with me for years, the yearning to just . . . let go. The difference was that I hadn't known what it was and Aedlynn knew damn well it was her power calling to her, and that if she gave in, she'd find herself at Eiran's mercy.

I wiped the drenched hair from my face. My clothes were soaking wet.

'Looks like the moss was a little too slippery,' she mused.

'No, there was just this very talkative witch who swung me into the water.'

Eva laughed and extended a hand to hoist me out, which I gladly took. 'You seem a little distracted, something on your mind?'

'Didn't sleep very well, kept having visions.'

'Again?'

I nodded. 'I had more visions about Aedlynn when she was in Aysel with Lorcán.'

Eva considered it while she stared at the kabolos-duck in the pond. 'It's strange, what you two have. You're extremely protective and you can read each other perfectly, even when the others can't read any of her emotions because of those thick walls of hers. Almost like you're dyads.'

I nodded absent-mindedly, playing with a loose seam on the wrist of my sleeve. 'I wouldn't say *extremely*. I'm protect- ive of all of them.'

Eva rose an amused brow and crossed her arms. 'Aedlynn stabbed a lord last week – four times – because he called you Lorcán's whore.' She had indeed, when we'd gone to visit Zale in Orthalla.

I shrugged. 'Four's her lucky number and frankly, I wanted to stab him for calling her an Aspian whore.'

She laughed at that. 'See? That's what I mean. You're normally pretty collected. You're still careful to guard your reputation in Aeria – with the potentiality of becoming High Lady of Egoron.'

'But I didn't stab him.'

She shrugged lightly. 'I'm not one to judge. I ripped Morgane's heart out through her chest when she tried to kill Aloïs.' Eva wrinkled her nose and I recognised myself in the expression, which made me smile.

'Why do you have a thing for hearts?'

'I was taught that the hearts of the dead were weighed in our Afterworld. To measure how good they'd been. I figured that if I tore them out, they'd have no case to make.'

'Thinking about the different aspects of the afterlife and

339

the Fates gives me a headache,' I muttered. 'How can they guess that at some random point I'll decide to end someone's *Výsa*? How can they decide from my birth what path I'll follow? Do they sit down with tea while they decide I'll live to the ripe age of two-hundred-and-ninety before some mortal decides to make bat soup out of me?'

Eva threw her head back and laughed.

I grinned sheepishly at her. 'I'm just saying, it doesn't make sense.'

'I'm not quite sure how they do it but they do, and thinking about it gives everyone a headache, including Eiran. But if anything were to happen to them . . . Eiran doesn't viciously protect them for nothing.' She sighed deeply. 'Apparently, Antheia already managed to destroy one of them when Nikos killed her. I don't think anyone has any idea what a universe without them would look like. Yael believed the chaos that would ensue would rattle Elyon's cage enough to set him free.'

She kicked against a fallen twig of an oak tree. 'I guess we'll have to officially introduce you to Eiran soon. He already mentioned it to your father when he went to warn him to keep Khalyna in line.'

'You don't seem too happy about that.'

'No, not when he still has those *lovely* decorations in his hallway,' she muttered. My brows drew together in confusion. 'Eiran once invited Aloïs to a celestial meeting, only to show him that the hallways are decorated with spoils of hunt: colchian and circerian wings, fangs and siren tails.'

I shivered. 'Maybe we should've done something similar to send a message.'

'Aloïs did. He showed them mortals drained by aepokrae and the shell of a solera, the life sucked out of it by a colchian.

Eiran declared war on Hell then and there, claimed that attacking one of his daughter's nymphs was a personal strike against him and demanded retribution. But the bastard was just looking for another opportunity to wage war.'

I clenched my fists. 'Did we lose many?'

'No. Sirens come out of the Aenean Sea and return to it with the ebb and tide of the moon. Colchians dance underneath the stars, their wings radiate with moonshine. All of their rituals involve the moon. Circederae worship the night and carry it with them wherever they go. Now name one goddess who would wreak havoc when she found out Eiran turned against the very people who still worshipped her and her Mother.'

'Antheia,' I breathed.

She nodded. 'According to ancient myths, Eiran created mortals. Ellowyn created the daemons. And their joint power created most nymphs. Our guess is that Eiran has always been jealous of Ellowyn and the life she made. His creatures were fragile and broke easily. Daemons are sturdy, a true counterpart to the gods. Antheia adored her mother and treated her creatures with respect and honour. When Ellowyn died, Eiran and Zhella turned against them, but Antheia and Keres were close friends with your father long before he became King.'

'So when Eiran declared war on us . . .'

'Antheia declared war on him in return. She blacked out the moon, removed her stars and suffocated Zhella's daylight to create eternal darkness for the mortals. I've never seen Antheia and Eiran fight, even during their many arguments and discussions during the last War, but Aloïs showed me visions of their battles through our bond.' She shuddered. 'They didn't fight to teach a lesson. They fought to kill, to maim and tear the other apart. There was no honour in the way they struck, no semblance of family.'

'I still don't get what caused them to despise each other so deeply.' I nudged the tip of my boot into the mud. 'They were *family*.'

'No one really knows why.' Eva took my hand and brushed her thumb along the back of my hand. Like she wanted to assure me that would never happen to our little family. 'But the Néhairas are no gods. Maybe that's why we don't understand their reasonings and decisions.'

I blinked. '*What?*'

Eva snorted. 'Didn't those Priestesses teach you about that?'

'No.'

'Eiran and Ellowyn aren't gods. Neither are Zhella and Antheia. No one really understands *what* exactly they are. Their power is beyond our comprehension. They were made of the very fabric of this universe, created amidst the Chaos. But no other stories are known, only what Eiran recounted to us. How they banished Elyon to Séthoseros.'

'The gods were born from their power, which means that Eiran possesses Aestor's healing abilities, Keres' affinity for curses and Khalyna's skill for waging war. He owns every single one of them. If Keres places a curse on someone it can only be undone by Keres or Eiran, but if Eiran curses someone, it can only be undone by him,' she explained. 'It also means that if a god or goddess places a blessing on anyone, it's fully within Eiran's power and right to remove said blessing or keep it. So when Antheia tried to remove hers from Lorcán, Eiran punished her hubris by keeping it.'

'Diana? Eva?' Both of us looked up at Aiden, who'd just appeared in the garden. His face was alight with excitement. 'Maeve is in labour, Aloïs went to fetch Aestor.'

Aiden held my hand in his as he hauled me along. His excitement to meet his cousins sent a grin to my lips. He hadn't even seen those pups but already knew he would die to protect them. They all would.

Maeve held two teeny tiny circes against her chest, sobbing while Aestor held another one and Cas rocked the fourth pup. They'd been trying for so long and here they finally were, holding their little family. The sound I made when I saw the little ones wasn't entirely human and the immediate sense that I would throw myself into Erebus if it meant I could save them was overwhelming.

'By the Mother.' Eva sank onto Maeve's bed, gently caressing the soft black hair that sprouted from a little head. Vanora threw her arms around Maeve and showered her damp hair with kisses.

Eos stood with Cas, impatiently gesturing that he wanted to hold his cousin. And for the first time ever, my father flaunted his title in their face as he playfully pushed Eos aside. 'Kings go first, Eos. Get in line.'

I smiled at the scene in front of me.

Aestor walked over to Keres and me. 'You'd think something special happened here, huh?'

My grin quickly faded when Aestor put a little bundle in my arms. The one I held had auburn hair like Maeve and the *wings* . . . Mother above they were so small and cute that I felt like crying. It purred in my arms while I petted it. The small shadow that clung to its little feet warmed my heart even more.

Aestor moved through the room to check up on the other three pups.

Keres slipped an arm around me and used his free hand to stroke the pup's little head. A flutter passed through my chest at his touch; the way his forearm caressed my wing ever so slightly. 'Adorable, huh?'

'I want fifty of them,' I whispered back as I sniffed.

Keres snorted. 'Until their wings grow cartilage and they start flying. It's hard to watch fifty flying pups at once.'

'Party-pooper.'

Cas walked over to us with another auburn-haired pup. He gestured his head at the one I was holding. 'That's Nysa, this is Eris.' Then he nodded his head towards Maeve. 'Left one is Enyo and the right one is Zaina.'

Vanora yelped. We turned to look at her as she shot us a sheepish smile and held up her bleeding finger. 'They're teething already.'

Aiden laughed at her. 'How many times will you stick your finger near their mouth before you learn not to do that?'

She shot him an undignified look. 'As *godmother*, I—'

Aiden held up his hands. 'Godmother? You'd accidentally give them wine instead of milk.'

'You'd just shower them with tomatoes or put a knife in their tiny hands before they even learn how to crawl!'

Cas sighed and rolled his eyes at both circes, then gave a pleading look to Eos, who only snickered louder. Maeve grinned at Eva, and both exchanged a look like they were having an inside joke.

Finally, Cas couldn't take Vanora and Aiden's bickering anymore. 'Will you two – *shut it?*' he snapped. They both stared at him in wide-eyed and stunned silence. 'Finally.'

Maeve pointed at three of the pups while naming their godparents.

Cas pointed at Nysa in my arms. 'Diana and Keres.'

Conversation and banter started again, laughter filled the room as Vanora and Aiden continued making fun of one another, and Eos joined in their banter as well. I stared at them, then at the bundle in my arms. The golden eyes that smiled up at me, the little wings that were wrapped around the pup's body in a blanket of softest fleece to keep her warm and comfortable.

Tears blurred my vision as I looked back up at Maeve and Cas – utterly happy with their family.

I sank down onto a chair, hugging the little babe while I rocked it with Keres sitting on the armrest, gently caressing Nysa's hair with one hand and the back of my neck with the other.

I made a silent vow, that I'd protect them like they were my own children. The rumbling thunder was faint but enough to officialise my first ever vow on the Netha.

I plopped down on my mattress, feeling fulfilled and cosily warm, and stared up at Keres, who leaned against my paint-splattered desk with his hands in his pockets. 'You're tired,' he noted.

'Training an entire day with mom will do that to you. She spent the day teaching me some more things Yael taught her. And becoming godmother was quite emotional as well.'

Keres smiled. 'You were radiating when you held that pup. As much as you did when you found that kabolos in your tub.' My cheeks pinked and my heart skipped a beat at the warm smile he gave me.

I wondered if he'd stay again if I asked him. Gods, I ached to ask him.

Keres pushed himself away from the desk. 'Have you seen it since?'

'Ehm . . .' I pursed my lips. He'd laugh at me, I was sure of it. Aedlynn had laughed as well. Even Asra had, though she'd brought more mandarins.

Keres rose a brow at me, his lips curling. 'Well?'

'Let's just say . . . ehm . . . I've been taking showers instead of baths.'

Keres stared at me, then at the door to the bathroom. 'It's still . . .'

'Uh-huh.' I played with my rings. 'I just . . . I can't just toss them outside, it's been raining on and off for weeks and you know how fragile they are and they seem content in there and they don't make as much of a mess as you'd expect, they're quite tidy – though they do like playing with the toilet paper, so I give them a roll every day. They like cuddling up to me when I go to bed and they've grown very fond of mandarins and—' And I was rambling again.

Keres held my gaze, his smile growing and growing. But he didn't laugh at me. 'Never change, Diana. You carry a light inside of you that I haven't seen around in a long time, and you blind those around you with it.'

'I thought you . . . that you would laugh,' I said in a bit of a daze.

Keres shook his head and walked over to me. 'Why would I laugh at someone who respects life so deeply? Kaboloses are the most vulnerable daemons out there, but others wouldn't have cared about the weather, they would've complained and thrown them out the moment they'd found the mother. But you?' He chuckled. 'You cut them fruit and give them something to play with. You've been treated horribly and here you are, still kind and soft.'

I stared up at him. Maybe with burning eyes. 'That's very sweet of you.'

'I have my moments.' He smiled and wiped a stray tear away with his thumb. I instinctively leaned into that touch; the warmth of his hand that cupped my cheek. I wanted to feel his body pressed against mine. I wanted to taste his lips again, to feel their softness and the pressure of his passion. I wanted to feel his fingers drag over the membrane of my wings.

I wondered what it would be like to be with him, to be loved by him.

To make *him* feel safe and loved.

But Keres had spent so many evenings talking to me about Antheia and Kaltain. He'd fought in every Divine War, had defied Eiran himself to protect them. Maybe I had a crush on Keres but I doubted he shared it. I knew he cared about me, that he was fond of me, and I deeply valued his friendship. And as much as it ached, I decided to be content with just his friendship and to relish in the simple fact that I wasn't terrified to care about someone anymore. That I wanted to kiss someone and be intimate with them. To have them touch the most delicate part of me beside my heart. Because two years ago – even months ago, I'd never thought it possible.

But I still wanted to make him feel loved, so I smiled at him and planted a kiss on his cheek. 'You say such sweet things to me but you shine as well. For all your titles, your kindness rivals that of Aestor.'

Keres stared at me, almost bewildered. I took his hand in mine and gently squeezed it, thinking about how his friendship was one of the reasons I'd come this far. The many evenings I'd talked to him, where he'd helped me make sense of what I did and didn't feel. Anaïs could take lessons from Keres in my humble opinion. 'What you did for Aedlynn and me . . . Maybe you don't do that for mortals, but mortals have never done anything for you either. You deserve the world, Keres. You truly do.'

'Are you trying to make me cry?' He gave me a small smile. 'Because I will if you keep going.'

I wrapped my arms around his waist to hug him. 'If you need toilet paper for those tears, you'll have to fight Canelle for it.'

'Canelle?'

'My kabolos; the one who had her cubs in my tub. It's Clastrian for cinnamon.'

He grinned at me. 'You named her after cinnamon?'

'What? I like cinnamon. I might not be the best at names.' I shrugged. 'But I have other talents.'

'Like making a scary god emotional?'

'Oh no, that's just a regular Tuesday.'

Keres laughed and folded his arms around me to hug me back. 'Thank you for the kind words, they mean the world to me.'

I nodded, my face still resting in the hollow of his shoulder. 'Thank you for not smiting me when I summoned you. You're actually quite tolerable when you don't wear that mask.'

'And you're actually quite fun to be around when you're not fighting death, not as cranky. Unless I beat you at a game,' he whistled. 'Then you scare even *me*.'

Laughing, I pulled away from him. 'You're spitting nonsense again. I'm *always* fun to be around.'

He clicked his tongue. 'When did you become this cocky?'

I chuckled and walked over to my desk to grab the almost empty jar with Maeve's special moisturizer for my wings. Many canvases and painting supplies were stored next to it and on top of it. I'd always painted Orthallian landscapes, but since I'd come home, I'd painted portraits of all sorts of creatures. I'd also painted one of my favourite spot in Hell – Erisor. It was a strange place, a meadow of black grass mere miles away from Erebus. There was a small lake there, filled with pitch-black water. The only colour there came from the snow-white wildflowers that decorated the banks, which were always beautifully illuminated by the silver moon to make them appear ethereal. I'd spent many hours there bathing in the lukewarm water, enjoying the sound of the wind moving through the poplar trees, and wondering about the strange pull I felt to Erebus. My father figured it was because my daemonic side had fully woken up, responding to the darkness of which we'd been born.

I wasn't so sure.

'It's insane how well your wings have healed,' Keres said behind me. 'Even the scars have faded a little.'

I beamed at him. 'They have. Cas and Aiden don't even have to fly slower anymore to accommodate me and I've become rather good at it.'

His features softened. 'Of course you are. You were made for the sky, love. You were made to touch the clouds and flirt with the sun, to dance with the stars and kiss the moon.'

'Perhaps they should make you God of Poetry,' I quipped, though his comment made me smile.

Keres nodded his head to the jar in my hands. 'Need help with that?'

My cheeks burnt so horribly that I had to tear my gaze away. Normally, I did it myself or asked Aedlynn, but gods, I wanted nothing more than to feel *his* hands on my wings. Yet I worried what it would do to me. How I would react – if I'd embarrass myself. They were wholly sensitive, even a light breeze filled them with a sensation I couldn't quite put to words. Like something touched my very soul.

And the thought of Keres touching them . . .

'I . . . ehm . . . sometimes make strange noises when my wings are being touched,' I admitted. 'It's a bit embarrassing.'

His lip quirked. 'I know, I've been around circederae for a while. I don't mind it,' he said. 'I know wings and shadows are hypersensitive.' Pure amusement blazed in his eyes. 'Even Aloïs isn't immune to it, though I've seen him publicly lose control only once – during the War, when he sent his shadows to spy on Eva when they were still enemies. To this day, it's still a mystery what she did to the poor man.'

I gave him a crooked smile. 'I promise I'll behave.'

Keres snorted. 'Honestly, there's nothing that could ever make me think less of you, Diana. Certainly not something that is such a big part of *what* you are.'

I smiled softly and went to sit cross-legged on my bed. 'Same goes for you, you know.'

Keres joined me to sit cross-legged behind me, closing me in. The lovely herbal scent of the concoction filled the room as he started putting it on.

His touches were featherlight, his hands wonderfully warm. He didn't just rub it on, he massaged them and I enjoyed every careful yet deliberate movement of his fingers. How he kneaded the bone and stroked it.

'Tell me if it's uncomfortable,' he said.

I hoped my voice sounded steadier than I felt. 'You're doing fine,' I whispered.

I silently thanked the Mother Keres couldn't sense my traitorous thoughts and vivid imagination.

His hand smoothed down the thick bone and lightning crashed down my thighs. I tried to keep quiet, to keep my breathing even, but as he slightly tightened his grip and dragged his fingers down, a soft gasp left my lips and pleasure bloomed deep in my core.

'Too much?'

I should've ordered him to stop to create some safe distance between us. To guard that boundary between us that protected our friendship. Instead, all I could bring out in a strangled voice was, 'Don't stop, please.'

And Keres, bless him, heeded my plea.

His fingers started kneading the base and my back arched, the nerves in my wings tingled and I couldn't help the quiet moan that slipped from between my lips as I clutched the bedsheets. I would've been embarrassed but Keres gave me no time to think. His marked hand slid over my back and shoulder and loosely curled around my throat to caress the side of it with his thumb; painting over memories and gifting me new ones. My heart thundered against his fingertips but not out of fear. I felt beyond safe and secure in his arms.

His other hand teased along the bony part of my right wing, tracing a featherlight finger along the skin there. My wing twitched. Pleasure coiled in my abdomen.

'Tell me when to stop,' Keres murmured against the shell of my ear, his voice sounding rougher than before. When I felt his hardness press against my rear, a soft whimper fell from my lips and I tightened my grip on my bedsheets. The idea of Keres being aroused because of *me* made it hard to sit still, to not turn around and crawl over him to undo the laces of his trousers. To not kiss him senseless.

I imagined what he might sound like moaning, causing the tension in my core to coil tighter.

'I don't want you to stop,' I breathed, my knuckles bone-white as I held on to the bedsheets the same way I was trying to hold on to my sensibility.

His thumb smoothed over the apple of my throat when I swallowed hard. 'You want more, love?'

I nodded as my eyes fluttered close. 'I'm just . . . I'm curious,' I whispered. 'I've not felt so intensely before.'

Pride hummed within his shadows, a male satisfaction that *he* was the one having this effect on me and that I trusted him enough to let go around him. The thick sensation made my shadows shiver.

'Then let me indulge you.' He leaned forward, his lips trailing kisses from beneath my ear to my collarbone. My stomach fluttered. Lightning coated my nerves, running from my fingers to my toes.

Keres firmly kneaded my wing again, and this time, I couldn't stifle my moans. 'That's it, love,' he murmured against my skin. 'Let me take care of you. Let me hear you enjoy yourself.'

The hand around my throat left, instead venturing beneath my shirt to lazily smooth his fingers over my stomach while he kept kissing and sucking my neck.

I wanted it lower – so much lower. I needed to feel him. I wanted to show him how aroused he'd gotten me, how sensitive I'd become between my thighs because of his attentions. How he'd already ruined me for others even without fully claiming me.

Keres' fingers played along the top of my training leggings, ready to trail exactly to where I needed him. His lips moved to my ear again. 'This okay?'

Some sense started creeping back into my mind. 'Is it?' I managed to bring out. 'I don't want to ruin us.'

'We're just having some fun. See it as me raising your standards a bit for future lovers.'

I laughed softly. 'Another lesson?' I liked the idea of experimenting with him. No expectations or obligations, just some fun. I'd not done that before, certainly not within such a safe space, and something about it felt freeing. Healing. Thrilling.

He kissed my neck again. 'Something like that, yes.'

His teeth softly grazed my skin and something in me grew bolder as I curled my hand around his to guide it lower, beneath the waistband. 'Maybe I'll raise yours instead,' I said breathlessly.

I felt his lips curl into a smirk against my skin. 'There she is.' A shiver dripped down my spine.

Keres cupped my sex and I moaned in strained anticipation. His fingers slipped into my panties, pushing my folds apart and running through the wetness to coat me with my arousal from my entrance to my clit. 'You're so wet for me, *matska*,' he purred against my skin and I nearly came solely because of the way he called me *matska*. 'You should feel it for yourself.'

Oh gods.

He withdrew his hand and instead, guided my hand mine until he helped me strum my fingers over the swollen nub at the apex of my thighs. 'Feel that?' he murmured. 'How drenched you are?'

'Yes,' I breathed.

While I circled that spot, two of Keres' fingers filled me and pumped, causing me to cry out in pleasure. He continued lazily kissing and sucking my neck. 'That's it, love. You're doing so well.'

'More,' I pleaded.

Keres curled his fingers against the sensitive walls of my core and picked up his pace. My moans grew more wanton and I rolled my hips while trying to keep up with his movements. 'Look at you,' he ground out. 'Moaning so prettily, chasing my fingers so eagerly while you're dripping down your thighs.'

By the fucking gods, that mouth of his.

His hand withdrew again, leaving my core feeling painfully empty, and gently pushed mine away to take over and slowly strum his thumb over that nub. My head tipped back and I let myself melt against his hard body.

'You're making me feel so good,' I murmured.

I'd never felt anything like this before. I'd never been so sensitive and responsive.

'Of course, love. You deserve nothing less.' Keres sucked my skin, grazed his teeth over a sensitive spot and I could've sworn stars sparked alive in my vision.

He took his time learning what I liked, what made my moans become louder and my breathing hitch. What made my wings twitch and my shadows shiver, leaving them writhing on the bedsheets.

His fingers pumped me while his thumb focused on that nub. His other hand dipped beneath my shirt to lazily knead my breast and teasingly pinch my peaked nipple.

There was no rush, no impatience like there had been with Kallias.

There was just him and me and endless time.

There was only safety and pleasure.

'*Oh,*' I moaned, rolling my hips to take him deeper.

Keres obliged and I cried out in pleasure. 'That's it, love, ride my fingers.' My shadows coiled and shivered. 'I'm not sure who's enjoying themselves more,' he purred against my ear. 'You or your adorable little shadows.'

'Both,' I breathed, overcome with the different sensations blooming within my body and soul.

Keres chuckled at the strained moan I let out. 'Tell me what you need, Diana. I'm not stopping until your shadows are melting off the bedsheets and I have your come coating my fingers.'

'Mother save me,' I muttered to myself with blushing cheeks.

'Given how sweetly you're moaning and how wet you are, I don't think you want to be saved.' Keres changed his pace, the spot he was focusing on, and I whimpered as another wave of intense pleasure crashed over me. 'Here?' he murmured. 'You need my fingers here?'

'*Yes.*'

He kept up that pace – that angle, working me until I couldn't stop moaning and squirming against him. My fingers dug into his knee as I held onto him and my pleasure grew tighter and tighter.

And as that tidal wave of pure release finally fell over me, I cried out in ecstatic bliss before falling back against him. He held me securely against his body while my breathing eased and my thoughts cleared up a bit.

I tried hard not to think about what we'd just done.

Luckily, Keres didn't seem too fazed. He slipped away from behind me to sit next to me and winked. 'That'll be two waning gibbuses.'

I snorted, the hum of pleasure slowly growing into sleepiness. 'You and your fucking deals.'

The smile he gave me tugged at my heartstrings. 'I'm only this desperate for deals when they involve you, love.'

My cheeks heated. I couldn't tear my gaze away from that beautiful green I'd secretly painted so many times in my sketchbooks, or thought of late at night whenever I couldn't sleep because of visions. He was a work of art and all I could do was admire him from afar and paint him to keep the memory of moments like these in the deepest folds of my soul. Sharing pleasure with him and having some fun was one thing. Hoping he felt more for me . . . that was a different matter altogether.

I still prayed to the gods I respected, but I wanted to fall to my knees for Keres for an entirely different reason – an entirely different way of worshipping him.

Keres held my gaze, leaning in. Which was somehow too close and not close enough. His eyes rested on the curve of my upper lip, until they lifted back up with a shade in them that would've made the gods talk about us again. That would've made those solerae pray for my downfall.

Mother above, grant me the patience and prudishness of an Orthallian Priestess.

'You okay?'

I nodded, my cheeks turning a subtle rose. 'Very.'

His lip quirked and his eyes shone with male pride, making another flutter pass through my stomach. 'I'll let you rest. It's been quite a day for you.'

I nodded again, still holding his gaze. Neither of us moving. Neither of us acknowledging what we'd just done.

After what felt like ages, Keres broke our stare and

moved. He cupped the back of my head with one hand and kissed my brows. 'Sleep well, Diana.'

Slow, lazy footsteps echoed through the small hallway of Maeve's infirmary. The darkness was lit up by a single weak torch near the end of it, where two circes slept soundly surrounded by their newborn pups.

It reeked of her, that matska *that had escaped him to survive. It reeked of the weak sons who'd betrayed him and turned against him. Of that so-called King and that divine whore he called his mate. That god who'd cursed him to meet his end at the hands of a* matska.

There was another female scent, not entirely daemonic but also not divine. He didn't know what she was but there was power in the scent and he didn't like that. But he would find the bitch. If anything, he could tame her to carry his children. It would give him powerful heirs. Ones that wouldn't become failures like those other three had. Ones that could help him overthrow that pathetic excuse of a King, who only knew how to please the gods.

He sniffed again, noticing that the unknown female was Aloïs' spawn.

Half nymph. Oh, how easily tamed those were.

His lips curled into a malicious sneer. It was time for a little family reunion.

Chapter 23

Diana

I woke in a cold sweat from the horrible vision I'd had, panting as I remembered where I was and then quickly jumped out of the bed, slipping into clothes while I sounded the alarm through my *varkradas*, sending them to my father. To Aiden and the other circes.

I slipped through the shadows, right to the hospital.

Maeve's hospital was on fire, a true inferno that lit up the glimmering night sky with an orange glow and specks of still-burning ashes. I shot a prayer to Aestor. We'd need him; for my family and the circes who lived around the hospital. I decided to focus on my family and the pups I'd sworn to protect.

Inside, I followed the scent of burning flesh, dodging smouldering beams that fell from the ceiling. Wood fell down in front of me, and thick dark grey smoke sprouted from it and blocked my view even more. I coughed and pulled my collar up to cover my mouth and nose. My lungs begged me to flee from the fire, as did my wings. They didn't like the heat that pressed on them like a threat.

I dodged another beam but tripped over something and fell down.

Not something – *someone.*

Cas lay on his stomach, *inkor* gushing out of deep claw wounds on his side. One wing was badly burned, the other buried underneath a beam that had fallen on his back. I wrapped my shadows tightly around his chest and abdomen to close off the wounds, to stop the bleeding for now.

The moment they impacted on his blood, visions shot through my mind of what had happened. How Bastian had invited himself into their room. How he'd called Cas a weakling for lowering himself like Eos had, claiming that he'd stayed with a failure of a *matska* who hadn't even been able to give him pups until now. That maybe he should tear those weak pups apart and teach Maeve the same lesson as Vanora.

Bile crept up my throat and ice-cold rage settled in my bones.

My shadows hoisted the beam off and I wrapped my arms under his armpits to haul him up. I pulled him into the darkness and sat him down on the cobblestones, back against the wall. I didn't realise how badly I was coughing until Aestor's hand was on my back to relieve me. 'Aloïs is hunting him down. Eva and Vanora are on the other side of the building – searching.'

'Aiden?'

'With Eos, don't know what they're doing.'

'I'm going back in.'

'Be careful.'

I tried to find Maeve, to sense her through my *varkradas* and to make contact with her own but they were blocked. *Moonsbane.* He really meant what he'd said – to mirror Vanora's suffering.

There was something of those pups that cowered from the

swaying flames. Something only either my father or I could recover; their little shadows. Eris' shadows cowered in the room where Maeve had given birth, hiding underneath the bed that I now realised was covered in black blood and not all of it was Maeve's. I whimpered at the sight and quickly tied the little shadows to mine. My *varkradas* immediately latched onto them as if to soothe and calm the tiny shadows.

Zaina's shadows haunted the room. They weren't pure black like the others. They were fading, greying. Because she was dying somewhere. I tethered it to my own shadows, kept moving until I'd collected all of them. Their shadows were desperate – terrified while they sluggishly searched around for their circes.

The walls groaned, fighting hard to hold the weight of the roof but the building grew more delicate with every passing minute.

Someone slipped into the room.

I found myself eye to eye with a *mattas* who had the same bronze skin as the Alásdair brothers but whose smile was too sadistic, whose eyes were filled with more malice than even Keres carried with him on a bad day. Bastian clicked his tongue. 'There you are, *phádron*. I've been looking for *you*.'

I slammed him into the wall, listened to that voice that demanded I set my rage loose while I bared my fangs and snarled. But I sensed the limit, as if there was still a leash on my power. Something still held me back from fully digging into it.

'Behave, *matska*.' A command, like he'd thrown at his sons when they'd fought for Vanora. Like he'd thrown at plenty of *matska* to get his way with them. My fangs retracted but I fought hard to keep him in place. It was a good thing I also carried my mother's blood or I would've immediately fallen to my knees.

'Where are they?' I hissed through gritted teeth, eyes ablaze with fury.

Bastian's eyes trailed over my face and body, drinking me in like he was deciding what he wanted to do with me. He appeared to have plenty of ideas. 'I understand you were raised by mortals, but that's no reason to defy your Lord.'

Another pull on my instinct and he had *me* pushed against the wall. His lips brushed over my neck while his *varkradas* kept me securely in place. He teased his fangs over my throat, eager to claim me for himself. To taste my blood and stake his claim on me, to make me *his*. 'Such a beauty you are, sweet thing.'

I bared my fangs and growled like I'd done with Khalyna.

'*Behave*,' he snapped. I hated myself but I couldn't fight his control, no matter how hard I called upon my mother's power. My fangs retracted again, and though I wanted to rip him apart, my body slacked against the wall as I relaxed in his grip. Involuntarily, I moved my head so he had easy access to my neck.

'There's a good girl,' he whispered against my thundering heartbeat.

I hated that his praise made that instinct in me purr in contentment.

His lips brushed over mine while his compulsion kept me tightly under control. His power securely intertwined with my daemonic instinct and I found myself unable to do anything. 'I have plans for you, *phádron*.' He kissed me, slow and deep, nicking his tongue on one of my fangs so I could taste his blood.

Circes, blood tasted sultry and smooth, like a fine wine,

and I couldn't help but enjoy the taste. I couldn't stop myself from kissing him back to gather more blood on my tongue, softly moaning. Bastian kissed me deeply, cutting his tongue again to give me another taste. Even though it wasn't yet enough blood, I was honoured that he wanted me, that he had taken the first step in this ritual.

To create a mating bond.

'You carry a power with you I haven't smelled before.' One hand curled in my hair to make me look up at him with heavy-lidded eyes. Lost between the thorns of his compulsion. '*You will carry my seed, little Princess. I will make you mine – my mate and* matska.'

His compulsion hit me so hard that I relaxed even more in his grip. My knees buckled but he kept me well in place. 'Such an honour, My Lord,' I whispered before he kissed me again.

'Hmmm, indeed.' He kissed my neck, his hand now roving over my rear to cup it. 'When I'm done with you, *matska*, every little slit and crevice of yours will reek of *me* instead of that god you whore yourself out to.'

Keres.

Slowly, I blinked. Some sense crept back into my hazy mind when I thought of my god. My head felt like an Orthallian Priestess was burning her entire supply of incense in there, with thick grey and sultry smoke. But thinking of Keres somehow helped me find myself in that thick mist.

I seethed in my skin, unable to do a thing. For the first time in months, I was terrified. I'd heard enough stories about him and what he did to *matska*. What he'd done to Vanora. I didn't want to mate him. I didn't want his hands on my body. I didn't want his blood in my mouth and his lips on mine.

His fingers stroked the base of my wings. 'My mating gift to you is the permission to keep your wings, though I will not have you use them. I'll clip them if you do.'

I hated him. By the gods, I *hated* him.

Bastian pulled back to sneer at me. 'I'll show that fake king how his pretty heir moans and begs for me. How desperate she is to belong to a real *mattas*.'

I stared at him in horror. The foul things he said and promised left me nauseas. 'You sick *fucking* bastard,' I spat at him.

Something malicious gleamed in his eyes. 'Or maybe I'll have you all to myself while they're too busy to worry about *you*.' He kissed me again, pressing his hips against mine while he pinned my wrists next to my head with his *varkradas*. 'By the time I'm done with you, you'll be well-filled and happily reduced to nothing but my meek mate. And in mere months, you'll radiate while holding our offspring instead of those weakling bastards.' I whimpered, tightly shutting my eyes while I searched every last part of me to find anything I could use to fight that compulsion. 'Shhh, *matska*. Be a good girl and I'll even have you enjoy yourself. I can please well if I want to – if you do as I say.'

Even despite the groaning and creaking of the building, his hand slipped down to my pants, playing with the buttons while he kissed my neck. His fangs were so dangerously close to my blood. To start that damn ritual. My *varkradas* wanted to kill him but they lay uselessly curled beneath his own shadows. Subdued as well. The only thing they could do was shelter the pups' shadows.

I just attempted to growl at him, when Bastian was ripped away from me and speared against another wall. Pinned in place with furious shadows – belonging to someone equally angry.

Aiden heaved as he pulled his Erobian sword free from Bastian's chest, his face contorted in primal fury. When Bastian's grip on me fell away, I sank down the wall, panting and shivering while I was momentarily overcome with what would've happened if Aiden hadn't shown up.

'Stand down,' Bastian snapped at Aiden. But there was no compulsion behind the words. The Lord blinked when he realised it as well.

Aiden's lip quirked up while he twirled his sword with a cocky flourish. 'What's wrong, dear papa? Moonsbane got your tongue?'

Bastian's eyes slipped to me, to where I sat on my knees and watched them. Then he glared at Aiden. 'I'll tear the bitch's wings off if you defy me. I'll kill her.'

Something cold passed over my friend's features. His head turned to look at me and some of that warmth returned to his eyes. 'You okay, witch?'

'Yes . . .'

Aiden slowly turned to him. The look in his eyes made *me* flinch despite the tattoo he carried on his right arm, the one we shared, that marked him as my *Corusiar*. 'Remember your curse,' he said with a low voice. 'I wouldn't insult a *matska*, especially her.'

It was enough to silence Bastian.

I only now became aware of the scent of Aiden's blood. My gaze fell to the wound on his left side and I shot up to go to him and wrapped my shadows around his waist to stop the bleeding, sewing his skin back together. I didn't dare meet his eyes but I felt his gratitude – and his worry about Cas, Maeve and their children. His fury because he knew exactly what Bastian had wanted to do to me.

I'd just worked up the courage to meet his gaze, one filled with concern since I'd drawn my walls up thick and high, when Bastian growled so loudly that the building shook. He didn't approve of Aiden caring about me. Of another son lowering himself for some *matska*.

Bastian managed to escape Aiden's bindings and slammed me against the wall, piercing me with a *Damast* dagger right above my hip bone. I grunted from the pain, and Bastian pulled his dagger out and made to stab me somewhere else.

Blind fury shot through me, tearing at that leash on my power.

I flicked my hand and crashed my palm into his chest – along with crackling silvery *æther* that circled my lower arm and wrist. The impact sent him backwards and right through the wall.

The roof gave out but I'd already slipped away into the darkness while pulling Bastian with me. I let go of him in the cold night air for all gathered circes to see him. Aiden followed right behind me.

With the moonsbane slowly clearing from his blood, Bastian made to slip through the shadows but I blocked them, stopped him and nailed him against the wall of the hospital with my *varkradas*. And I threw one of Aiden's moonsbane-laced daggers at Bastian, aiming it at his chest. It hit the mark, scarcely missing his heart.

Aiden snarled at Bastian, 'Where are they?'

The bastard's lips quirked up, despite the pain from his wounds. 'You know me, pup – ever the generous Lord. I decided it would be selfish to have her all to myself, so I delivered her to some friends.'

Play with him, Vena. I know you like that, and he more than deserves it, don't you agree? I had never heard that sensual male voice before. The scent of fresh air and a rainy forest crept into my nostrils, and I faintly tasted pomegranate seeds on my tongue.

I cocked my head while I stared at Bastian, overwhelmed with the sense that the circes swayed towards one side of the world, while the rest of the world swayed to the other. The colours in my vision brightened, deepened. And something ancient and dark whispered to me, in a language I had never heard before.

'Which *friends?*' Aiden hissed at him, balling the fabric of Bastian's shirt.

In a daze, I stepped closer and gently pushed Aiden aside while I held Bastian's gaze. My voice sounded thick and seductive, melodious and pretty. Even I wanted to keep listening to it. '*Where is she?*' This wasn't something a circes should be able to do. This was a power that belonged to the colchians and aepokrae, though much, much stronger. But it overtook me, made me lean in so my breath caressed his lips. '*Tell me where Maeve is.*'

His eyes glazed over while he breathed, 'Persephian.'

'*Good boy.*' I smiled sweetly. '*Where in Persephian?*'

Aiden stared at me in bewilderment, desperately fighting my compulsion himself. My father had appeared as well, ready to tear the answer out of the Lord until he'd seen me use a skill that belonged to a different species. Now, he only came closer to watch and observe what else I could do.

I tilted my head and Bastian followed the movement, mimicking it. I tilted my head to the other side and he mimicked me yet again. Bastian's lips curled into a dreamy smile at the sight of me, the beautiful female who prettily smiled and slowly batted her lashes at him.

Aiden and Aloïs' confusion rose at the sight of me, of the power I held. I was a thing of desire and daydreams, hiding a nightmare. I liked this, the control that I had over the *mattas*. I would make him pay – for everything.

'Just over the border,' Bastian sighed. 'Near the entrance to Persephian.'

I stroked a lazy finger over his clean-shaven cheek and kept smiling while I ordered Aiden, 'Take Eos and go.' Not a request but a true command worthy of my title. Behind my back, Aiden nodded and left. '*Tell me, little mattas,*' I purred at Bastian while I rested a hand on his chest. '*Where are the pups?*'

'Divine shit,' my father breathed while he started putting two and two together. The moonlight that now subtly encased my wings, the way I could use skills that belonged to different species. This was why Lorcán had spent a year studying me. Somehow, I carried power from all daemonic species within me.

My *výssar* power was showing.

'One is in the mortal realm, one is in Erebus, one is with the *matska* and one is inside the basement of the hospital.'

Through my *varkradas*, I sent that information to Aiden and warned him to look for a pup when they found Maeve. My mother and Vanora already dived back into the ruins of the hospital to search there. I tilted my head while I let my eyes trail over his features. '*Where in Aeria is the pup?*'

'Near the Gates. Aurnea.'

'I'll go to Erebus,' Aloïs said, now standing to my right.

'I want to go as well,' I mused, smirking at the dazed *mattas* in front of me. I could remove my shadows and he'd fall to my feet to kiss them. He would beg for me. I liked that. I shot Aloïs a sly grin, my hand still resting on Bastian's chest. 'Do you reckon I could seduce Erebus?'

He raised a brow at me. 'I don't think you can seduce a place. I know you want to try but we have pups to find.'

Disappointment pitted in my stomach at the thought of letting Bastian go. There was power I could take from him to make my own and I liked this control. I liked that Bastian stared at me like I was the sun in his life and the stars that shone at night. I was this poor prey's beginning and ending and he didn't even realise it. But my father was right. Playing with Bastian would be for later.

I kept him nailed to the wall and separated those shadows from my own to hold him in place for Aestor to babysit. Aestor pulled at the shadows around my abdomen to see the wounds there and used his magic to stitch my flesh together without forming scars.

'I'll go to Erebus,' Aloïs said next to me. 'Go to Aurnea, Diana. You know that place like the back of your hand.'

I nodded. 'Say hi to Erebus for me.'

Aloïs blinked, confused about why I would want to greet a place. 'Why?'

I shrugged. 'To be friendly.'

He glanced at Aestor, who shrugged as well. 'Maybe the colchian part is getting to her brain? They do enjoy seducing and mischief. Or it's the smoke inhalation.'

I flicked his nose. 'Tittle-tattle god.'

Aloïs allowed himself a small smile. 'Go to Orthalla, Diana.'

He slipped into darkness and left me alone with Aestor. 'Careful with those powers, Diana. They're pouring out but don't let them take over. We don't know if there's a limit or cost to them.' He tapped my nose, his eyes creased at the corners while he smiled, which tugged at something deep inside of me. 'This tittle-tattle god would like to know you'll be safe.'

I planted a quick kiss on his cheek and smiled widely, careful not to let my colchian magic slip out, but it still made my eyes sparkle and light up. 'Thank you for your concern.'

With that, I slipped into the darkness.

Holding Enyo close to my chest, with his shadows restored, I travelled back to see Bastian still high on my magic and stuck to the wall, though I yelped when I saw Maeve, when I saw her matted auburn hair and awfully pale face. Her back rested against Aiden's chest while Aestor healed her bleeding throat, which had been clawed at. Her throat and arms were covered with bite marks. While she fought to stay awake and breathe, her eyes fluttered open and close. Her heartbeat was fast and the fragile sound of it echoed through my bones. Even Aestor couldn't keep up with the blood loss, with the many wounds. With the overdose of *aepokran* venom.

With her torn-off wings.

My heart broke.

Eos tried to close wounds with his shadows but she was losing most of her blood through the wounds on her back; where her wings had been. Her eyes fluttered open, faintly lighting up when she saw the pup in my arms. I sat down on my knees with them, held Enyo close to her so she could touch him while Aestor worked as fast as he could. I tied my own shadows around her chest. Aiden's *varkradas* were tightly pressed against her back to diminish the blood loss, but it was no use.

'Eris and Zaina are safe.' Eos brushed her hair. The

moment I'd learned they were safe, I'd sent their shadows back to their rightful keeper to finally start their bonding. 'They're okay. Aloïs is looking for Nysa. Cas is still unconscious but he's safe – he'll be okay.'

She nodded once. Her breathing was laboured and with each second, more colour drained out of her cheeks and lips, where blood bubbled. Death's presence started to surround her and I whimpered. I didn't like that presence, couldn't stand it. It wasn't her time. It couldn't be. She had a family, pups and a mate who needed her. *We* needed her. I looked at Aestor, desperate to find some hope there but all I saw was defeat.

The Second God, the God of Healing.

Defeat.

Maeve's eyes fluttered shut again, still fighting, and a part of me knew that right now, she scolded Dýs with the same viciousness that she showed Aiden whenever he took too many tomatoes from her dishes. Eos and Aiden fought hard to compose themselves. They'd been here before with Vanora and I couldn't stand feeling their hurt. I couldn't stand seeing Maeve like this, horribly wounded and yet the only thing on her mind was her family. If her pups were safe and sound. That Cas would survive. That they would still have a father.

I couldn't exactly explain what came over me. It was the same sensation as I'd felt before when I'd used compulsion, as if the universe itself were whispering to me, grabbing my attention. It whispered again – a somehow familiar feeling male voice, breathy and soft.

A name this time.

'Don't stop,' I whispered to Aestor as I let go of Enyo and rose.

'Where are you going?' Eos sniffed. His hand was so tightly wrapped around Maeve's that his knuckles were bone white.

'Clacaster,' I said quietly, still staring at Maeve while tears washed over my cheeks.

Aiden frowned at me. Tears stained that beautiful bronze face of his as well. I ached to see him like this. I wanted to wrap him up and hold him and tell him everything would be alright. 'Why?'

I couldn't explain it. I couldn't explain it because I didn't understand it myself. 'I'll come back.'

Aedlynn and I walked out of my shadows and stood in front of Maeve while Aedlynn fought off the nausea that always came with shadowtravelling for mortals and gods. My father still hadn't returned, which gnawed at my already fried nerves. She knelt before Maeve and brushed her cheeks with a gentle hand. Her lips parted into a smile. Somehow, she could sense what I'd sensed. The absolute scolding Maeve was giving the God of Death. 'Poor Dýs.'

Aedlynn turned to me. 'I can save her but we'll need to go to Ascredia.'

'You think the water will heal her?' Aestor asked. He was as confused as I was with this whole ordeal. I had no idea why that whispering voice had sent me to her. Though Maeve had been teaching her, Aedlynn was no magical healer.

She smiled sheepishly. 'No, that won't do a thing. It's just that I've been taking a shit ton of moonsbane for two years and cannot use my power here. Ascredia has pure moonlight, it will enable me to see her *Výsa*.'

'What exactly are you?' Aestor asked, caught off guard by the word *Výsa*.

She shrugged. 'Aedlynn.'

Maeve's blood was no longer black. It was dark red. Her heartbeat was fading.

Soaking wet from her dive into the cold water of Ascredia's pond, Aedlynn returned to us. 'Fuck, this feels good.' She sat down cross-legged in front of Maeve. Lifting her right hand, she twirled her fingers as if she were gathering threads. Aestor paled and his eyes grew wide.

He backed away.

The *Second God* backed away from my sister like she was a bomb that could go off at any moment.

I could imagine Aedlynn playing with silvery threads in her right hand; threads that showcased Maeve's life. Every achievement, threshold, failure and relationship.

Power gathered around Aedlynn, as ancient as this universe and as powerful as the old gods.

Maeve's heartbeat steadied.

As I glanced at Aestor, who stared at Aedlynn in bewilderment, I wondered if he was thinking the same thing; that maybe Eiran had good reason to be wary of hybrids. And maybe . . . I thought back to what my mother had said about Antheia allegedly killing one of the Fates when she'd died, and how mere months later, Aedlynn had been born.

I wondered if there was a connection there.

'What the fu—' Aiden gasped when he stared at Maeve's back, as he was pushed back by wings sprouting there. So long as they were still bleeding from the fresh wounds, she could reverse their damage by altering their reality.

Maeve's eyes fluttered open. Colour returned to her face. The gashes on her arms faded.

Eos' sob echoed through the cavern as he looked down at the pup in his arms, at the healthy wings that peeked out of the makeshift blanket. Eos and Aiden flung themselves at Maeve, overcome with emotion.

'Three of the children are safe and sound,' Aedlynn said. 'The fourth one is still surrounded by all-obscuring Darkness that I cannot penetrate.' Casually, as if she'd just announced she would take a small hike through the woods.

I grabbed Aedlynn by her shoulders and pulled her into the tightest hug I'd ever given anyone. 'Thank you. Thank you. Thank you,' I repeated the words, over and over until they lost their meaning.

She patted my back. 'You should be careful, *Nychter*. That Darkness surrounds you as well.'

I nodded, whatever that might mean. I buried my face against her shoulder and tightened my grip around her waist. 'You mentioned moonsbane, are you okay?'

'Pounding headache and the worst hangover ever, but I'll manage. Willow extract works wonders. I am, however, going to down two vials when things have calmed down and maybe finish a bottle of nectar.' She'd mentioned before that she took moonsbane but I thought she'd stopped taking it when she'd come to live in Anthens. Moonsbane was no joke. It could make someone horribly ill. Taking too much was lethal. Luckily, it wasn't as addictive as *morphilium* but it was still strong stuff.

'But you'll be okay?'

Aedlynn nodded, rested her chin on my shoulder and brushed my back. 'I'm just glad I could use it to help.' She'd used the power she'd just shown us so many times to kill but she'd also used it to officiate her bond with Kaelena and today she'd used it to save and heal. That was who she wanted to be, not the monster Lorcán tried to make of her.

I thought back to that night in the throne room, where she'd sat on the throne in the glowing daylight like a fyre-bird rising from its ashes. How I'd felt her heal these past months. If Lorcán ever had the gall to come for her, if he showed up with his pretty words to lure her back or to hurt or kill her, I wouldn't hold back. I would let no one hold me back.

If anyone dared touch my sister, I'd show them just how much of a monster I could be. I could be just as cruel and I was just as spiteful as Antheia underneath my seemingly endless patience.

Aedlynn met Aestor's gaze. He didn't seem as scared as before but he studied her with an interest that told me this wouldn't be the last time he'd speak of this. He nodded once, inclined his head almost as if he were showing her his respect. Aedlynn blushed and inclined her own head as well. 'My Lord.'

'My Lady.'

Her eyes widened in surprise and she quickly looked back up at him. Aestor simply smiled and winked before returning his attention to the chirping pup in Maeve's arms to make sure they were okay.

Aedlynn shot me a small grin and shrugged her shoulders. The fact that Aestor had seen her power unnerved her but she trusted him.

A well-familiar honey-lemon scent entered my nose and I looked up to see Aloïs. We were all ready to celebrate that this nightmare was finally over. But my father carried no pup.

His gilded eyes were on me. 'You can say hi to Erebus yourself.'

They fell silent, utterly silent as they looked from Aloïs to me.

'Oh?' was all I managed to bring out.

'I cannot enter, but it will let *you* in.'

Chapter 24

Diana

There were several things in life that terrified the shit out of me. Like spiders; whether big or small. Aedlynn or Keres had to catch them and put them outside, as I couldn't even look at them without feeling physically ill due to my intense fear. Almost similar to how I'd felt while being suppressed.

But given my father's stories about the place, entering Erebus was highest on that list.

Nothing but palpable, thick blackness spread out as I gazed up, to my left and right. The whispers that came from it were familiar and yet a stranger's voice. They reminded me of the whispers that surrounded *Aecéso*. The ones that often pulled at me when I was in Erisor. The voices were muffled, as if I heard them while being submerged in water. Not yet clear enough to be understood, though I instinctively knew it was the Darkness speaking to me.

'Just follow the path,' my father said with that soft voice of his. 'Stick to it until it ends.'

'And then what?' I looked up at him.

His features darkened. 'I don't know.'

'Sounds fun,' I muttered while I stared back at the black walls with my arms crossed.

He sighed deeply and I felt the strain of this night on him. Once again, someone had attacked his family. 'Be careful in there, Diana. Erebus tests you in ways that can leave your spirit broken and bleeding out into its Darkness,' he said. 'It's not interested in deals like Keres is or power like Eiran is. Its sole focus is breaking and killing – and taking back what it once gave Ellowyn. Keep a close eye on your shadows – and don't rely on them too much. When it comes to it, they'll always listen to their first and true master.' Aloïs crossed his arms. 'Out here, you're a force to be reckoned with. In there, you are as vulnerable as a newborn. Keep your wits about you.'

I nodded and took his hand in mine, carefully separating Nysa's shadows from mine and laying them in the palm of his hand. 'Look after them for me, will you? I'm not taking her shadows into such a violent place.'

Gingerly, he added the small tendrils to his *varkradas*, which immediately latched onto the tendrils to keep them safe and sound. 'I'll guard them with my life, pup.'

I drew in a deep, shuddering breath. 'In the odd case that I don't return, promise me that you'll look after Aedlynn.' At first, he wanted to protest that I'd come back but he saw the grave look on my face. He knew how deeply I cared about Aedlynn, how I considered her to be my sister. They'd grown incredibly fond of her as well. So instead, he just nodded.

I wrapped my arms around his waist and hugged him, burying my dirty face against his chest. 'And look after Mom.'

'Always.' He kissed the top of my head and ruffled my hair.

The whispers grew louder with every step I took, though I couldn't make out the words. My heart thundered in my chest. My hands trembled. This was definitely very high up on my list, but poor Nysa had been thrown into the Darkness and waited for me in there, scared and alone and that was enough of a slap in the face to pull me back from my rising panic.

Black sand crunched underneath my bloodied boots whenever I took another step until I neared the ending of the path. Goosebumps danced on my skin and every so often, a shiver crept down my neck like something was breathing down on it. Which was very soothing and calming.

I hadn't even fully entered Erebus yet but my connection with the others had already fallen away.

Finally, I stopped a few feet in front of the black wall. Should I just . . . take another step and walk right in? I settled on resting the palm of my hand against that Darkness. I'd expected it to feel cold but it felt rather warm and the peculiar wet-yet-soft sensation of that Darkness immediately sunk right into my bone marrow. It wanted to pull me in.

I felt like I stood in the middle of the ocean, peering down without knowing just how many ancient creatures lived deep beneath the surface. But these were creatures of nightmares and there were no gods here, there never had been. Yet there was a pup in there and there was no way that I'd let any of those creatures get to my godchild.

The Darkness wrapped around my arm and crept up to my shoulders as it tried to pull me in. My shadows stirred and wished to answer that ancient call but I forbade them. They might've been made of its harvested Darkness but they were mine, so I kept them tethered while I calmed my breathing.

It grew curious as it felt me calm down, tightening its

grip around my hand and arm that still rested against the black wall. '*Tell me who you are.*' An echo of voices breathed in my head in a language older than this universe, though it was no Aelerian. I had no idea what it was but I understood it perfectly.

'I am Diana Márzenas.'

'*Your name is inked in the endless marrow of your bones and cannot be erased. Speak it true.*'

'Faelyn Márzenas.' And for good measure, I added, 'Who are *you*?'

It grew quiet, as if I'd caught it by surprise with the question. '*I am the dark soil underneath mortal feet that houses the roots of Life, the space woven between the stars they have long forsaken, the Darkness that encompasses the moon so that it can show its light. I am the beginning of your gods and the extension of Chaos. I am the membrane in your wings, the Darkness in your bones and the power in your blood.*'

Overcome with curiosity, I pushed my hand in deeper. It felt wet – like I put my hand through a waterfall. It remained silent as I tested the Darkness, though the soft whispers still surrounded me. They changed until there was only a single male voice; ancient and powerful. And so eerily familiar. The voice reverberated through my body and echoed deep in my soul, as if there was a connection between us somewhere. '*I have waited aeons for my Acolyte, Faelyn Márzenas. Now, you must enter my realm.*'

I stared at the darkness in stunned silence. I'd always been taught that . . . that Erebus was only a place. The others believed so as well. 'Why . . .' I scraped my throat. 'Why ask for me?'

'*I wished to see you for myself now that their hold is weakened by the full moon and the presence of the Nólnyr. You have carried my Darkness in your every breath and beat of your delicate heart from the moment you were conceived but She has a claim on you as well and I will not let my blessing fall into scheming hands.'*

'Excuse me, but *what?*'

'*Truths told in deceitful light craft the grandest shadows. Know that hidden within a realm of mortal ending, the truth shall be set free by the merging of the living and the dead.*' I swallowed hard, heavily confused by whatever the fuck he meant. But I did understand that he wanted to test me. The tendril that encircled my arm hauled me forward until I nearly stumbled over my feet. '*This cursed and barren land will try to devour you as it does with all living things. It is in its nature, even if it does not wish to cause harm.*'

The thick Darkness in front of me took on the shape of a person, wrapped in nothing but shadows that evaporated like they did with my father and me. The eyes were a golden honey, with no pupils.

I was torn between running right back down that path and kneeling for this . . . this *being.* There were rumours that Erebus had existed since the dawn of this world, long before the gods were born. That it had already existed when Eiran and Ellowyn had made our universe. But no one had known Erebus to be a deity.

'*Come out of your hiding and sing for me, blackbird. Sing me a song of retribution and hope, for it has been too long since I have seen that light.*'

I was growing more and more confused by the minute. Erebus probably had a nice view of a very bewildered *matska* staring at him with an open mouth and her hand still held out. I was still processing and deciphering the things he'd dropped on me when that Darkness swallowed me whole.

I saw nothing while I tried to move around the pitch black. I waited for my senses to adjust to the dark but they didn't. My ears rang with the eerie silence that gathered around me, my eyes watered while they strained and desperately fought to focus on *anything*.

The silence became deafening while I stumbled around. But I much preferred the silence to the rustling of the sand when *things* started moving around me. I had no idea what they were, if they were big or small. I only knew that I really wanted to get the Hell out of here.

I moved around, shadows blinded as they clung to me. My hands patted the air in front of me, one firmly holding one of my *Damast* daggers. I'd decided that I wouldn't walk around Erebus holding a dagger dipped in its own Darkness. Khalyna's lovely curse still echoed in the back of my mind, which didn't help me calm down in the slightest.

He had Nysa, I reminded myself. Getting her out was all that mattered.

Bastian crept back into my mind and I found that strange disappointment bubbling up again. I wanted to play with him, and when I grew bored, I'd tear him apart and claim his title for myself.

Maybe if I truly carried colchian magic, I could've drained him.

I stopped dead in my tracks while a cruel grin spread on my lips. I could use that power on those lords in Orthalla. Gods, I'd love to watch the life leave their glazed-over eyes. Or Lorcán's. I would make them kneel – all of them. They would crawl over each other like ants for my attention. Beg and plead for me. They'd offer their finest riches and pray to me like they did to the gods and it wouldn't matter.

I could be merciful, I truly could be – if I *wanted* to.

My magic poured out, making my eyes radiate with moonlight. My beauty was a true rival to that of Zielle and Zhella. A pity that there was no one around to admire me, I was a nightmare gilded with grace and beauty. They would be drawn to me like a moth to a flame, and by the time they would realise that I was a predator, it would be too late to escape.

Like Bastian . . . I wanted to taste his blood again – to feast. I wanted to taste those Orthallian lords on my tongue like Zale's richest wines. Or maybe . . . maybe I didn't want a circes or mortal. Instinctively, I knew that gods tasted far better. My mouth watered at the thought; the sweet and rich taste of still warm *ichor* as it dripped down my throat. Nymphs tasted similar but not nearly as rich, and most of those damned greenery nymphs tasted of grass. Solerae came closest, maybe I could find one of those. It would certainly send another message to Eiran that he should think twice before coming for my people.

I wondered what Aedlynn would taste like, if I could decipher what she was by simply tasting her blood. I blinked, then gagged at the thought I'd just had, the thoughts that had made themselves master of me for the last . . . half hour? Hour? Time moved in a strange manner here. Sometimes it felt like it moved backwards.

I wanted to laugh at myself. *No one here to admire me? How vain could I be?*

Something heavy slithered over my feet and brushed my ankles. I screamed and stumbled back, tripping and falling down as I heaved in a panic. Whatever it was continued to circle me and from the sound of the crushing sand, it wasn't anything small.

Pride was the only thing that stopped me from whimpering.

That thing lashed out and sunk its teeth in my side. I screamed out from the painful venom as it burned my skin. It lashed out at the back of my head and knocked me forwards. I sank my dagger into its body and yelped again in disgust when I felt something slick and smooth, wet and scaled.

By the *fucking* Mother.

It lashed out again and sunk its thick and sharp teeth deep in to my upper arm. The sulphurous scent that came out of its mouth made me gag. I blindly stabbed at it and tried to scramble up but was overcome with vertigo. The venom made my heart pump three times as fast. My lungs were working overtime. Cold sweat trailed down my neck and forehead while I heaved and fought to stay upright. It slammed into my back, making me fall face forward as it pierced my lower back with its tail.

'Son of a bitch!' I weakly cursed.

I used my shadows to cut its tail clean off, then bound them around my abdomen to stop the bleeding and to stitch the flesh shut. I tried to rise up but my body swayed to the right under the weight of the poison. That thing continued to circle me but it didn't strike.

Like it was waiting for something.

My laboured breathing hitched when the voices sounded in my mind, latching onto me and bleeding into reality. The snake glided over my calves as I sat on my knees, hands on the ground, and heaved while I tried to separate reality from visions.

Night shall always make room for Day, and the Dawn shall always find her. I wasn't certain if my mind was trying to calm me by reminding me of the prayer I always used to soothe myself when I was younger, yet the sweet female voice recounting it was unfamiliar.

Sobs, heart-breaking sobs suddenly echoed around me. '*I did not mean to hurt her, Father, I swear it on the Netha. It was an accident and then she slipped and*—' Antheia.

'*And you will slip into a mortal grave if you hurt someone again,*' Eiran hissed. '*If you kill another, even if it is an accident. I cannot allow you to roam the realms when you are this unstable.*'

Groaning, I tried to focus on how that snake was wrapping itself around my chest. I had no energy to stop it, to pat the sand to find my lost dagger. It tightened its grip and started to compress my chest. I wheezed and fought to draw in air but I couldn't get loose and the visions didn't stop.

Antheia sat on her knees with her head deeply bowed. Blood stained the marble floor underneath her and the mortal bodies piling up on the floor left goosebumps on my skin. Dark veins tainted her fingers and her desperate sobs told me she had lost control over her power once again. Yet Eiran didn't scold her when he found her. He only calmed and held her until the young goddess succumbed to her exhaustion.

'*Green-eyed the storm will be that will begin to extinguish the Serpent's reign. Claimed from birth by Darkness, their deadly might will be his bane,*' a pretty woman with mesmerizing violet eyes crooned at someone I couldn't see. Her haunting pale face and luscious raven hair were accentuated by two black gazelle-like horns. '*Did my Laoise not warn you of that, my sweet? Your precious aelysiar he may be but his lineage will have no duty other than destroying you. You will lose. In the end, you will always lose — to me or all else.*'

The vision warped and I saw Antheia and Keres, sitting shoulder to shoulder on a bed in Aestor's manor while holding a newborn. The goddess' damp hair stuck to her face as she smiled down at the little boy, brushing a gentle finger over the dark fuzz of hair in motherly affection. Kaltain's tiny hand was tightly clamped around Keres' finger as he admired the boy's pale green eyes. Even mere hours after his birth, his divine power was already showing. Black ink stained his fingertips and spread out over his hands like ivy and when, hours later, Kaltain cried, every vase filled with the brightest of flowers withered and died.

'*Spirit and Hope won't leave bare her scars, for Love surrounds her like effervescent Stars,*' that same sweet voice whispered like a caress in my mind, sparking alive my fighting instinct some more. I fought for air and clawed at the scaled hide of the snake.

'*He loves me!*' Antheia hissed at her sister.

'*He fucked you a handful of times.*' Zhella sneered. '*That is not love.*'

It was – it had to be. Because his kisses tasted of pomegranates and an ancient instinct in her recognised the connection between love and the sacred fruit. The reason why they were linked rested on the tip of her tongue yet she couldn't find it.

I gasped for air and struck the creature with a sharp tendril of my shadows, cutting it in half. The pressure released from my chest and I swayed to the other side while I heaved and drew in air. The venom burned me from the inside, like it boiled my organs, but I still tried to crawl.

My knee slipped through the gore and blood.

'*Darkness shall not frighten her, but guide her safely through the Night.*'

I let my head fall back against the sand and allowed my-self a second to gather my thoughts. To catch my breath, to wrap my shadows around my wounds. Then I attempted to stand back up for maybe the hundredth time now. This time, I managed. Once again, I trained my sewing skills. Aestor could properly heal my wounds and remove the scars later if I made it out. *When*, I reminded myself, not *if*.

I smelled nothing but the sulphur that was still stuck in my nose. Maybe one of those fuckers had spat on me. Go figure why that worried me more than the venom that still dizzied me.

I stumbled around without getting attacked for what felt like either ten minutes, half an hour or a day. Time really fucked with my mind here.

I continued looking for Nysa, clutching my broken ribs.

His smooth voice sounded behind me, 'Look at you, *Midór*.' He scoffed. 'Some flesh on those bones really does it for you.'

I whipped around, tightening the grip on my dagger. Despite there being no light, I somehow saw him so clearly. Still wearing those dark trousers, his chique linen shirt from that fateful night. His well-polished shoes. I wasn't sure what I was feeling; there were a lot of emotions whirl-ing around in my head and chest. Mostly hatred and anger. I wanted to drown him in my wrath, especially as I saw those brown eyes of his roving over my body like he was imagining what I'd look like beneath the fighting leathers. As if he still had some sort of claim on me.

Kallias smoothly chuckled while he sauntered over. 'Always so theatrical. You should really learn how to take a compliment, you know.'

Months ago, I would've backed away. I would have fled. I would have cried.

Part of me wondered if I was hallucinating.

Part of me wished that I wasn't.

My grip on the dagger tightened. 'Oh, I've learned.'

One dark brow rose in silent question. Mocking me. 'What poor bastard complimented you? Some blind lord you lured into your bed because you were lonely again?' he purred. 'Or perhaps some lord who took you from behind because he couldn't stand to see your *pretty* face? Humour me, *Midór*, and be convincing. I remember how they talked about the corpse Zale was trying to keep alive.'

As I remembered how I'd been chronically sick for most of my life until Lorcán's suppression fell away, and how Kallias' presence in my life had made my illness spiral, I showed him a sickly sweet smile that didn't reach my eyes. And I stepped closer. 'Given how many there are, I ought to keep a list, yet the only list I ever made in my life was one that depicted your every sin against me and how I should have punished you for them.'

He laughed. Not at all threatened.

But I didn't need him threatened. I wanted him frightened.

I cocked my head, plastering the sweetest smile on my face that I could muster. 'Did you have fun, my love? With Keres?' His cocky grin fell. I'd struck a nerve. I closed the distance between us and touched his clean-shaven chin. 'I always wondered something about that night. Might you enlighten me?'

Given the height difference, he looked down at me. Like he'd always done. His natural arrogance tipped the corner of his mouth up. 'A favour for a favour? Is that what you're asking?'

I studied him. *Closely* studied him. His olive skin was marbled with faint scars. Kallias had been a *demiagi* when he'd been alive, a powerful one, but his magic appeared to be struggling with the glamour this ghost of his was using to keep up his pristine appearance.

I grinned when I realised this was not a hallucination. It was him – what had been left of his spirit anyway. 'Struggling a bit with your magic, I see.' Kallias sneered, moved and something old and yet so achingly youthful in me flinched in reply. Yet when he grabbed my throat, I only stared at him with more hatred darkening my eyes.

You are not helpless, my father had drilled into me. And he was right.

'Let me go,' I said with menace.

His grip tightened. 'You're so damn adorable, Diana. Bossing me around while you still flinch.' When the burning sensation in his hands caught him off guard, Kallias flinched and let go of me, then backed away a few steps. 'Fucking bitch!' he snapped. 'You'll regret that.'

'How did it feel, Kal?' I crooned while I started circling him like a predator. 'When I held you down? When I stabbed you? Over and over? While you begged me to stop and I didn't?'

He rubbed his hands together to heal the burned skin, glaring me down with that same fucking expression he'd given me every single time I'd stepped a toe out of line, and I loathed the part of me that shrunk down in fear. 'All I saw was a pathetic little bitch begging the gods to help her.' He sneered. 'What? Was I supposed to be intimidated by your crying?'

I roared and Kallias fought to remain standing upright.

'And there she goes again, fucking overreacting as always.'

388

Kallias chuckled. 'You want to pretend to be big and strong now, Diana?' His eyes burned with more malice than I'd ever seen in a person. 'That you can finally defend yourself? That you're no longer that fragile and naïve fool begging the gods to wipe her ass whenever she was sick again?'

'Shut your fucking mouth.' I seethed in my skin.

'Why don't you make me, *Midór*?' Kallias purred with a sickening grin. 'If you're so scary now, it shouldn't be a problem for you to silence me, right? Or are you still all talk and no action?'

Anger bubbled in my veins and hatred clouded my judgement. If my grip grew any tighter, the handle of my dagger might shatter.

He looked me up and down again with that vile and curious interest. Then his grin became cold, almost as if he'd found something else to throw my way. 'I see that nothing has changed, really. The moment I have you underneath me again, you'll call out my name like you always did,' he purred. 'The same way you're moaning that god's name now while you touch yourself because he could never want *this* – no one sensible anyway. Nothing has changed, Diana, has it? You're still as pathetic and desperate and lonely as always.'

A dam in me broke wide open and I felt how my hatred poured out of me, like darkness had been suffocating my soul for years now, only now breaking free.

And it stopped when I noted the relieved look that flashed in his eyes.

He was baiting me.

A strange, strangled noise came from me. Those scars. His fickle glamour. He wanted freedom. He wanted me to lash out and kill him and relieve him from the eternal

Punishment Keres had cursed his spirit with. For some reason, he'd fallen into Erebus' dark clutches, where he was continuously being torn apart by its creatures before healing enough to do it all over again.

A favour for a favour.

He wanted *mercy*.

'Oh, you poor thing.' My voice was a whisper. 'You're hurting, aren't you?'

I watched him struggle to decide what mask to put on. Intimidate me? Or play with my feelings?

He seemed to settle on the latter. 'Yes.' His throat bobbed. 'Please, Diana. It has been years. You're not cruel by nature. Stop hurting me. Show me mercy. Let me go and move on.'

Stop hurting me. Show me mercy.

I wasn't aware of how my breathing had grown laboured because of my anger.

Show me mercy.

If this was some twisted test where he expected me to show Kallias mercy when he'd made me forget that word even existed, I'd tear Erebus apart.

'Why don't you beg for it, Kal?' My voice was quiet, yet it didn't quiver. 'And make it convincing, *Midór*, because I still remember the boy who broke my bones and hit the light out of me.'

Kallias opened and closed his mouth.

'Go on, dear. *Beg.*'

His throat bobbed. Whether it was out of fear or to swallow his pride was beyond me, and I frankly did not care. 'Diana, please.'

I closed my eyes while I drank in those words. 'Again.'

'Please, Diana,' he whispered.

A wicked smile cracked open on my lips and I started to

circle him once more. 'You can do better than that. Perhaps you should grovel some more.'

I watched him take a deep breath. And then I watched how he sunk down on one knee. 'Please.'

I laughed. 'Such a spoiled brat you are. Did no one ever teach you how to properly grovel? My ex-fiancé trained me plenty. I even had bruises and cuts to prove it. And sometimes when I didn't grovel enough, he'd break a bone and claim I'd been clumsy again.'

'Diana. Let it go,' he snapped.

'Maybe I should return the favour,' I mused, completing another tour around him.

'*Diana.*' His hard gaze bore into mine but I saw the crack in his mask. The fear hiding away in those brown eyes. 'Stop being ridiculous and grow up. You're alive. I can't say the same given that you fucking *killed* me that night over *nothing*. Now, for once in your life, be sensible and give me the mercy of properly dying.'

If this was a test to see if I'd bestow mercy on him, I decided I would gladly fail. That dark beast that slept within me ruffled its feathers again. Kallias was right; I was not cruel by nature. But I remembered the sick young girl crying her eyes out until she was dehydrated. The girl who'd been sicker in that one year than in the entirety of her life combined. The broken girl who'd begged Sorin not to hurt her when she'd spoken up against him. The miserable girl who'd wanted to die because the pain had become unbearable. The young and hopeless girl who'd isolated herself because what if others would hurt her the same way?

I was not cruel by nature.

But I was fucking vengeful and my wrath knew no limit.

'You taught me how to lick mercy off of the sharp edge

of a knife. It's only fair I teach you the same thing.'

'You're fucked in the head,' he muttered before making to scramble up again. Yet before he could, I'd tied him down and stopped behind him to give him the same treatment I had given Khalyna. I formed my *varkradas* like a whip. And I struck. Over and over again, and this time I relished in seeing the blood run free. I relished in the cuts and lashes that appeared on his back and shoulders. How his pride kept him from crying out in pain. I wondered for how long, as I had plenty of ideas of what to do with him.

Like I'd warned him; I'd made a list.

'Don't be shy, Kal.' I grabbed his throat and let my talons dig into his neck to draw blood while I sneered down at him. 'Make some noise. Make some music. You know I like your screaming. It proves you're processing – learning.'

He still sat on his knees. Blood bubbled out of his mouth and he heaved, 'Fucking . . . psycho . . . bitch.'

I giggled and cut his cheek with my other fingers. 'Gods, you have no idea.' Pulling my talons free, I bent forward to lick the bleeding gashes I'd created, relishing in the iron taste of his blood. 'Yet you should remember whose fault this all is. If you'd just been *good*, Kal, none of this would've been necessary. It's only a lesson.'

I sunk my fangs deep into his neck and drank while he writhed in the grip of my *varkradas*. Yet every time he came close to death, Keres' curse made sure he healed all over again so I could continue to play with him.

I took my time.

I lost track of time.

I lost track of how many times Kallias should've died by now. How many bones I'd snapped. How many cuts

I'd made. Yet even death by a thousand cuts wasn't being merciful to him right now.

I wasn't sure how much time had passed when I sat in the bloodied sand, catching my breath while I watched Kallias bleed out again. Some sense had been slowly creeping into my mind and part of me was disgusted with myself. Seeing him like this was strange. It turned him human instead of the monster I'd been fleeing from in my nightmares. He had begged. He had grovelled.

He'd apologised.

Those words hadn't even sunken into me until now.

When he stood, he still towered high above me. But down on the ground he was as fragile as I'd always been. And hovering above him, I'd been as cruel as he'd always been.

I swallowed.

I didn't want to be like him.

I wanted to be better.

And yes, I had enjoyed hurting him back. But that would never change what had happened. It wouldn't erase the things he had done to me or how miserable I'd still been after his death. It wouldn't change that until I'd returned home, I'd still been broken.

Exhaustion washed over me, numbing me while I kept staring at him. His chest rose slowly and his breathing was still shallow, his eyes were closed. Exhausted as well.

'Kal?' My voice sounded broken. Like I'd been the one screaming.

Slowly, his eyes fluttered open, though he didn't look my way.

'Why?' was all I managed to bring out.

'Favour for a favour?' he croaked.

'Fine,' I whispered as I pulled my knees closer to hug them to my chest.

'Lorcán worked with my father. They agreed that the Rhosyns should rule Orthalla once Lorcán came back for a second war.' He coughed up more blood. 'They wanted me to soften you up so he could sweep in like a knight in shining armour to save you from your abusive betrothed – to use you.'

I closed my eyes, barely noticing the silent tears that streamed down my face. Lorcán . . . Again, it had been *Lorcán* who'd orchestrated my torture. And Kallias had been just another pawn in his twisted games. I wasn't sure which answer I wanted to hear but I still asked him, 'Did you ever regret it?'

'Sometimes,' he admitted with a hoarse voice. 'I liked the power I had over you; power I didn't have elsewhere. I liked how afraid you were of me. No one else was. My father didn't take me seriously until I started showing my magic. But one look at you and you were doing everything in your power to keep me satisfied.' He laughed humourlessly, then coughed again.

I stared down at the black sand. The dried blood. 'How did you know how to push my buttons so well? It's like you read my mind.'

Kallias snorted. 'I did, Diana. *Demiagi*, remember? I'm a mindwalker. It's why they thought I'd be perfect for the job.'

I nodded to myself, still hugging my knees. Knowing that I'd unwittingly allowed a mindwalker to roam around my head frightened me. For a whole year, he'd broken into my mind and stolen glances at my most intimate of thoughts, insecurities and worries. My nightmares and paralysing fears. And he'd used them all against me as weapons to shatter my spirit, break my heart and to double-cross my mind until I questioned my sanity. And I knew from my magic lessons that they could do far, *far* worse.

I made a mental note to ask my mother to teach me how to guard my mind when I returned.

'For what it's worth, I'm glad Lorcán didn't get you. I'd say I'm sorry but it doesn't change anything, does it?'

'No, it doesn't,' I whispered as I rested my chin on my knees.

Silence stretched between us while Kallias healed again. While my thoughts ran wild, and yet, my mind remained strangely empty. I felt hollow. Carved out. That anger and hatred I'd felt for him had become such a big part of me and now it kept crumbling down.

Zielle had never sent him my way, nor had the Fates. *Lorcán* had. It had been another attempt at goading me into a certain direction, another attempt to control me. And I hadn't been stupid or naïve as I'd accused myself, he'd used his magic to manipulate me like some twisted mastermind. Yet he'd been nothing but another pawn in Lorcán's game.

Another victim.

'Diana?' Exhaustion laced his voice. 'About that favour . . .'

'I still have a Divine Punishment to hand out to you.'

I watched him nod, how his shoulders sagged in weary disappointment. 'Fair enough.'

I wanted to be better than this – than Lorcán. Kallias had ruined me and it had taken me years to heal, to come to this point, but he'd had his Punishment. From Keres. From me. Maybe in another life, one where he wasn't surrounded by corruption, he would've been different. Maybe he would've been a better man. But he'd never had the chance to prove that.

On instinct, I flicked my right hand in his direction, severing his tie to Erebus.

Kallias tiredly lifted his head, slowly blinking at me in disbelief.

'Goodbye, Kallias,' I whispered while more tears streamed down my face. 'Promise me that you'll be better.'

His throat bobbed. He opened and closed his mouth, then swallowed hard again. I could scarcely keep up with the emotions rolling over his features in rapid waves. Gratitude, shame, fear and something delicate like hope. 'On the Netha.'

Beneath the rumbling thunder, I muttered a prayer into the Darkness. And I let him pass on.

I wanted a nap. Maybe two. But I moved on as I searched for Nysa, swaying on my legs and wobbling knees while the venom coursed through my body, as well as Erebus' own Darkness that kept sinking into my skin like it was claiming me. The latter latched onto my every nerve, onto my *varkradas*.

'*Have you gone mad?!*' Sorin yelled. '*You would declare war on them? On the gods?!*'

I groaned and sagged to my knees, clasped my hands and dagger over my ears as the loud voices of their argument bellowed in my mind.

'*I'll show them a true King when I take the throne,*' Lorcán spat.

Aestor's hazel eyes flashed in my mind. A golden crown on his hair that I hadn't seen before. And a beautiful woman stood by his side, with kind amber eyes and whose appearance reminded me of a nymph. Her long brown hair floated on a breeze while she stood atop a hill. *Ellowyn*.

But there was another deity, clad in black with sun-kissed skin and golden eyes and hair as black as night. His handsome features would have appeared cold had there not been a sweet smile on his face as he looked over at Ellowyn taking in this world they had all created together.

One of black sand and endless green.

'*Never be so kind you forget your power.*' Ellowyn kissed young Antheia's forehead and ran a hand through her snow-covered hair. The little goddess beamed at her mother. '*But never wield such power, you forget to be kind.*'

Two energies swaying in the endless abyss, their fight reminiscent of an endless dance. Ebb and flow. Push and pull. A forgotten song that had become a haunting melody, an echo stretching over time and distance.

The voices ebbed away and I let out a shuddering breath, glad that it was over. Gods, I needed a drink and a nap. I heaved as the vision subsided, laying on my back. I guess I looked up at the sky – if there even was one. I missed the stars from home, the soft light they provided.

Closing my eyes, I tried to calm my breathing but my stomach disagreed, and for the first time in months, over-whelming nausea made me hurl my guts out. I just hoped that I wasn't walking in circles or I'd slip on my own puke.

'*Make me your martyr, Dusan, it won't stop me from haunting you.*' Yael.

I tried to keep moving, to ignore these visions as best as I could but they were unforgiving and took over, making me lose my fragile grip on reality again.

Aeneas, dragged before a white-haired woman in tattered

clothing. His throat was slit in front of her by Dusan, as punishment for their deeds against the High Coven. They tried to burn her but the flames didn't touch her once. Neither Zhella nor Antheia would allow anyone to harm the *Aurealis* they both favoured.

Blue eyes filled with primordial power and cold determination, with no regard for her own safety or anyone else's – and an altar under the full moon. And Eiran, who stared at Yael in disbelief while she bargained for her lover's life with the Æther. Her arched ears and the colchian markings that were tattooed on her lower arms, were enough proof of her true nature. Golden specks danced in her eyes – a sign of ancient power.

Mother above, I hated this.

'*You are pure sunlight after the barest winter of my life,*' I heard Keres lovingly whisper to someone.

Dark brown eyes with golden specks flashed through my mind, the scent of a beach and fresh linen drying in the sun. The gentle hug of a pine forest surrounded me. I was cold, so godsdamned cold and numb to my bones. But his warmth made me feel alive again.

There was hope in his light. A promise. A new beginning and a chance to be better.

'*Mind the carpet, sweetheart. It's Clastrian, do you have any idea how expensive those are?*'

I stopped dead in my tracks at the unfamiliar, playful voice.

'*Truth for a truth, Diana?*' I told him all – everything wicked I'd ever done.

He ran, but never away. Always towards.

Serpents, antlers, chains and dove. All of it, the price for love.

And then I heard Antheia again, humming and singing

while she haunted the gods and mortals.

I groaned and slapped my cheeks to get rid of the visions while I lay on my side in the silent Darkness, slowly realising how utterly lonely I felt. I missed my friends. My family. I missed Keres' soft smile, his teasings and how even just one look from him could make me feel safe and sound. Utterly secure in his warm embrace. To soothe my melancholy, I allowed myself a moment to indulge in memories of his pretty eyes, his calloused hands roving over my body to explore it and his soft lips kissing my neck as if he were worshipping at an altar.

Then, I picked myself up again to continue my search for Nysa.

The male who appeared in my mind's eye was both beautiful and terrifying. The latter because of how mundane he appeared – as far as deities went. I'd expected scaled hide or a hideous face, a sulphuric scent or monstrous features to prove to me *who* it was I was looking at. But he was breathtaking.

A scent curled into my nose; a rainy forest mixed with wild berries.

Elyon.

His almond-shaped eyes were as dark as a Winter Solstice night. Strong dark brows and a neat stubble framed his square chin, making him look handsome. His short dark hair was longer in the front, which more than suited him. The tan of his skin was a work of art, as were the black markings creeping up his neck on both sides – like fern. A black serpent crawled around his right arm, its head on the back of his hand. Perfectly showcased by the rolled up sleeves of his simple black shirt. And through the open

buttons on the top of his shirt, I noted a marking of a pair
of antlers decorating his collarbones.

His presence pressed into every fibre of my being, sank
straight into my bones and quickened my breathing. He
was a Serpent wearing human skin and yet I couldn't stop
admiring him.

He stared at me, slowly circling me. '*Vena*.' His sensual
voice thundered through my bones. 'Here you finally are.'
A sly grin crept on his lips. 'But where, oh where, is your
pretty bow? Where is that wondrous hunting instinct?'

I tried to snap out of my daze but this day or week or
whatever had been a non-stop tidal wave of confusing
things. Every single thing I'd heard had been more confusing than the last.

Elyon's steps were silent as the night and lighter than a
shadow. He gazed right into my soul. 'Such fickle stability
resides within you. One little breeze and that house of cards
shall fall.' I shivered under his scrutiny. 'Ellowyn has truly
outdone herself trying to protect you from your nature,
but those mortals will try to take everything from you and
leave you with nothing but the evergreen scars on your
back. They will make that noble boy look like a saint.'

I couldn't stand the sense of dread that filled me, like my
entire being knew him to be right.

'You shouldn't trust them, not even when they appear to
worship you. Their loyalty is fickle, their love is nothing
but deceit, and their true nature should disgust you as much
as you fear me.' His gaze softened ever so slightly. As if it
pained him that I was wary of him. 'The moment Fate
realises she cannot use you and turns against you, Diana,
you will understand. Though I shall protect you from her
– like I always have.'

What?

The Serpent took another step towards me but my hand shot out to stop him. 'You're just trying to scare me – deceive me,' I whispered. 'Mortals may have their flaws but they're not wicked. But you . . .' I swallowed hard. 'You're nothing but a villain, a lying and scheming villain.'

Elyon made a *tsk*-sound. 'I am indeed a villain.' He took my chin between his thumb and forefinger. The gentleness behind the gesture shouldn't have been possible for a creature like him. 'But I will be the villain *for* you, Diana, never *to* you.'

'Stop lying,' I hissed while I slapped his hand away. Blind fury shot through me. Lorcán had already attempted to trick me and I wouldn't let a deity known for manipulation get to me.

Elyon regarded me for what felt like ages while I stood nailed to the sand and couldn't tear my gaze away from his. 'Know that I am here; always. Call to me and I shall come for you.' He inclined his head as if he was paying respect to *me*.

I blinked and I was once again alone.

More hallucinations entered my mind, monsters from my mythology books and nightmares. Two-headed, three-headed, no heads. Sharp teeth and fangs, wyverns flying over a burning city as the tower of a light-stone castle cascaded down onto the neighbouring village.

Shadowfire burning a path through ancient history.

They crawled out of my nightmares and straight into my reality as I fell to my knees. By now, my sight had adjusted to the Darkness, so I could see my surroundings to a certain degree; the ruins around me. Those things had me surrounded again and one pierced the skin of my left shoulder with its three rows of sharp teeth. I screamed and tried to fight the daze of the poison but could scarcely move. Lifting my arm to shield my upper body was already an effort that made me want to vomit. Another one bit my right calf, tore at the flesh. Its tail knocked the breath out of me as it slammed against my chest and sent me down on my back with my wings splayed out underneath me.

In the back of my mind, I wondered why those things attacked me but steered clear of my wings.

I dug my dagger into one creature, then another as I seethed with fury. Another one stabbed me above my hip bone and I whipped around to cut its head clean off its body. There was still nothing but Darkness, but I saw them in my mind so clearly. They were hideous, snake-like creatures. Their black scales were slimy and wet and coated with poison that left my skin highly irritated.

Another monster struck me, sent me crashing into the carcass of another beast. Covered in gore once again, I heaved as I tried to rise. The venom and lingering Darkness in my veins split my vision, doubled it. My knees wobbled as if I'd drunk way too much nectar with Keres and Aiden. My hands trembled so badly that I had to concentrate all my focus on even holding that dagger.

It lunged for me, mouth wide open, but I was too slow and exhausted to react properly. I cried out when it sunk its teeth into the tender flesh of my left side and tore at the skin, at the muscles, until it had ripped me open completely and feasted.

I wouldn't survive this.

I was no healer, but having several gaping and bleeding wounds, and a big fucking monster that was feasting on my flesh didn't exactly scream *'tis but a scratch*. The venom didn't help either. My heart seemed to be beating right against the walls of my chest, desperate to flee and save itself. There was an iron taste in my mouth as blood made its way up my throat. I wheezed and it became harder and harder to breathe.

With a groan, I dug my dagger into the head of the beast at my side. I was getting sick and tired of being used as a pincushion by these things, could feel my anger bubbling up.

That's it. Show me that wicked fury, Faelyn. Let it tether you.

And I was done with these *stupid* visions and hallucinations.

I was attacked again. At the last moment, I managed to roll away but that meant that the sharp tail scratched my wing. I cried out from the intense pain that shot straight to my soul, though there wasn't even a wound left behind on the membrane. And with it, my anger fully exploded.

No one touched my wings.

The scream that came from me was deafening in the eerie silence that followed. The power that escaped with it was a shockwave that sent the sand scattering and the beasts trembling.

There you are. Come out of your shadows and sing for me.

Most beasts whimpered but one tried to strike against me – tried to sink its teeth into the membrane of my wing. I threw my head back and roared, bellowing with seething fury. Power reverberated through the sand, sank into it and made the floor tremble – quake, for miles around.

It spilt out of me, my magic – that last barrier gone.

My wings spread far and wide to their entire span as I rose and snarled at the beasts that still surrounded me. I tipped my head back and roared again, causing another ripple to move through the sand. But that wasn't the only thing that happened. My fury and the sheer might that radiated off of me fought against the Darkness, and for one long moment, I pushed it aside to watch those beasts as they were lit with sunlight for the first and last time in their existence.

I controlled the Darkness.

I controlled *Erebus'* Darkness on pure instinct and curled the smoke around their bodies and throat and tightened it until the thin threads sliced them open and the creatures crumbled into ashes and dust.

One had the gall to try and sneak up on me from behind, once again attempting to touch my wings. I cut it open from the inside until it stopped writhing. Until all of them lay dead and maimed on the sand.

And finally, Erebus himself appeared in my line of vision.

I gave him my sweetest smile, circling him with grace, like I wasn't supposed to be dead. My death was quickly approaching but sheer spite kept it at bay for a few more minutes. Though I faintly felt him. That god had walked beside me for many years now.

'*Look at you,*' he purred. '*You did more than well. I outdid myself with you.*' I couldn't judge his facial expressions, as he had none. But his voice dripped with reverence while he regarded me. '*My Acolyte,*' he said with a soft voice. '*Finally.*'

I tilted my head and slowly approached him, batting my eyelashes. My smile was loveliness itself, radiant like a thousand suns. Suns he hadn't seen for aeons, I knew that somehow. I planted my hand against the shadowy chest and leaned forward like I'd done with Bastian. '*I wish to see you fully,*' I said with a sultry voice as I brushed my lips along the smoke of his jawline, speaking his strange ancient language with ease. '*Stop hiding from me.*'

'*You will give me my retribution.*'

I curled against him, chest-to-chest and sighed as I trailed his throat with a lazy finger. '*I will give you all of that and so much more, if you give me what I desire most – to see you.*'

That damn husky laughter filled the air again.

'*It must have been so long since you have been touched by a living thing.*' I trailed my finger along the jawline. '*Allow me to do so, My Lord.*'

'*You will not see me for a long time, little one, and you will not pierce my heart as you so deeply desire.*'

I growled and pulled away, staring at him with disdain as the corner of my mouth lifted up to reveal a fang. But my power ran out, my body started to shut down from exhaustion and blood loss.

'*Your godchild is not here. I sent her back the moment you entered my realm.*'

'Why?' I whispered.

'*I do not forsake our creatures. No matter how their control grows, I will not turn my back on you.*' I tucked my wings in to try to stay upright. '*I have kept you here long enough and it will be mere minutes before the umbra's venom stills your heart. You have done well, Faelyn.*' He twirled his right hand and something warm splashed against my back. '*Their control comes and goes like the tide of the ocean. When you return, be prepared for the worst.*'

I nodded, still mad at him. Still confused. Also bleeding and dying.

'They never . . .' I panted. 'Never wounded my wings.'

'*I wished to test you and see what you are for myself. Not to ruin you – never to ruin you.*'

I nodded again, though I understood nothing. My heartbeat was slowing down.

Erebus made a strange gesture with his right hand and my every sense imploded as I staggered forward and fell through a veil of Darkness.

Chapter 25

Diana

The pretty chandeliers above me were a personal attack on my eyes. My head didn't agree with the lighting either, nor with the venom. I tightly shut my eyes to keep that brightness out. I hadn't felt this awful since Ascredia.

Voices called my name and hands latched onto me as I was eased on my back but none of them fully penetrated into my exhausted and fried mind. I'd hit a limit and then gone over it. My blood had gone dark red and my *varkradas* were taking a well-deserved nap.

Someone brushed my cheek, words were spoken, but they were a strange language, as I'd grown used to Erebus' ancient speech. The throbbing pain in my lower side made me groan and when someone laid their gentle hands on the wound, I cried out and fell back with a *thud*.

Someone laid my head on their lap and brushed their fingers through my hair. The pain dulled, enough so my groans and whimpers could ebb away. 'Thank the Æther you're safe.' The violent relief I heard in his voice nearly made me weep. I tried hard to but couldn't open my eyes.

'I'm going to slap Erebus into a fucking coma.' I sobbed when her voice came through and weakly lifted my hand to find hers. She took and squeezed it. 'It's okay, *Nychter.*'

I groaned when more pain throbbed in my side. It

immediately eased again and I knew Aestor was here, that he was healing me. 'Nysa?' My voice was hoarse, my mouth and throat parched. My tongue felt like sandpaper.

'Safe – they're all safe.' Keres. 'Not a scar left.' My eyes fluttered weakly open to see him hovering above me, those wonderful green eyes that carried a forest inside of them. Keres smiled at me, hiding his concern. 'If you wanted the entirety of Hell worried about you, you could've just said so.'

'Silly me,' I croaked. Talking took too much energy. I let my head fall back onto his warm lap, and fought the vertigo and nausea because of the effort it'd taken to speak. Aedlynn sat on her knees to my right while she helped Aestor heal me. She wasn't as strong as him, but it was enough to clot the blood.

'Aloïs and Eva are still in Erisor, with Aiden. They've been there ever since you left,' he said. 'We tried to let them know you're here but also sent someone to them to make sure it reaches them. There were three massive ripples of energy that tore through everyone's *varkradas*. They've been acting strange ever since, don't properly communicate, don't let messages come through. Even æriating is difficult.'

'How long . . .' I breathed.

'Three weeks.'

'What the fuck?' I whispered. 'It felt like a . . . like a week.'

'Do you have any idea what happened?' Keres continued brushing my hair. I only realised now that he'd cleaned the blood and gore up. Most importantly, that stinky spit was gone.

I scraped my throat. 'I did that.' Both gods looked at me in bewilderment. 'I just . . . lashed out at those monsters.'

I glanced down at my abdomen but the gaping wounds had disappeared and the only scar that remained was on my left side, where that overgrown noodle had decided to feast. 'And I kept having visions . . . tricks or hallucinations and he—' I groaned when I tried to sit more upright. My muscles refused and I only sagged more against Keres' chest. 'He tried hard to get me angry, succeeded at it and then I . . . I did that. I even parted the Darkness.'

Aestor's smooth hands stopped moving on my outer thigh, where he'd been stitching up another gaping wound. His hazel eyes shot to mine. He seemed just as bewildered and wary by that as he'd been of Aedlynn when she'd summoned Maeve's *Výsa*. 'He? Who is *he?*'

'Erebus,' I said.

Aestor blinked.

'It's not just a place, Erebus is a deity.' I opened my mouth to tell them more but found my memory growing hazy. 'He . . . ehm . . .' I frowned.

Keres looked at me with wide eyes. 'You . . . *parted* . . . Erebus?'

I nodded again, grateful that Aestor was still gilding my nerves to soothe the headache – because it was a bitch that didn't like it when I moved my head. The only thing that helped my headache was the warm caramel scent that drawled from both gods and teased my fangs. Normally, I would've minded my fangs. It felt a bit like I'd just tied a napkin around my throat and had my fork and knife ready while I stared at them, you know? But now? I didn't mind the daemonic urge. I felt pretty good, kept teasing my tongue against the back of the sharp canines while I wondered if Keres would mind it very much if I sank them in his neck.

'Okay . . . That's . . . interesting.' Keres exchanged a glance with Aestor, processing what I'd told them. 'We'll tell Aloïs when he gets here.'

I snuggled closer against his chest and looked up at him with sparkling eyes. The colchian magic woke up a little while I smiled sweetly. *'You smell nice, you know that?'*

Aedlynn snorted. Keres' cheeks pinked because for the smallest moment, he'd fallen for the fragile magic. His eyes had been glued on mine, pupils dilated because my smile had intoxicated him like a drug. He averted his eyes to Aestor, who gave him a shit-eating grin.

I trailed a finger over the fabric of his shirt, over his strong biceps. *'I could draw you, you know.'*

Keres closed his eyes. 'Æther curse me,' he muttered.

Aedlynn doubled over, shoulders shaking. Aestor's eyes creased while he looked from Aedlynn to Keres to me, wholly amused by Keres' blushing cheeks and my very obvious and transparent attempt at seducing him. 'Something you need, Diana?' Aestor asked.

I sheepishly smiled, which let my fangs poke out in all their daemonic glory. Keres took my chin and tipped it upwards so my eyes were on him. I admired the many green shades, remembering how Aloïs had taught me how to feed, hiding in a luscious forest near a village in Egoron. I'd liked the effect my venom had; the deep sighs, the full relaxation, how she'd draped herself against me. Circes venom erased pain and memories, and my venom seemed amped up with that effect, working more like a drug than simple sedation.

Keres snapped two fingers in front of my face, wearing a wicked grin. I realised I was just smiling at him in a dreamy haze. I blinked and shook my head. 'I asked if Aedlynn is right.'

She rolled her eyes. 'I'm always right.'

'Judging by the fangs and how her eyes are a little too focused on your carotid, I'd say she is,' Aestor said. Strangely, I felt no shame that it was this obvious.

My eyes slipped back to Keres' neck. Keres focused on me, on the curious look on my face, the longing in my eyes as I watched how each beat of his heart echoed through his carotid. 'Diana?'

I tore my eyes away, back up to his. 'Uh-huh?'

He smiled. 'How about we heal your back and then you and I will retreat somewhere a little more private?' He brushed my hair behind my ear. 'And then you can have your taste of *ichor.*'

My pulse quickened as my pupils dilated. My mouth watered at the thought. That old familiar restlessness settled in my bones. I swallowed, then averted my gaze and muttered, 'I'm sorry.'

Keres gently tipped my chin back up. 'You were gravely wounded, it's perfectly natural.'

'But you don't have to—'

'It's fine, the others drank from me plenty of times during the War.'

Aedlynn pointed up a finger like a wise sage. 'And now he can add fruitpouch to his resume.'

'Don't you have anywhere to be? To spit your nonsense elsewhere, little one?'

'Not until five.'

I laughed at the deadpan answer and serious look on her face. Aestor returned his focus to my wounds and eased my torn-up shirt upwards to reveal my back. 'Æther curse me,' he muttered. Partly because of the many wounds. Mostly because of the painting Erebus had left behind. Keres cursed when he saw the marking that adorned my entire back. And through my *varkradas*, I could view it as well.

Erebus had painted a masterpiece. On the nape of my neck, a solar flare was painted in dark ink. Right underneath it, he'd painted a vertical trail of moon phases, starting with a waning crescent moon. A fyrebird with intricately paint-ed feathers had its wings spread out, carrying a branch of wildflowers in its beak; lupines, daisies, forget-me-nots and other pretty flowers. The feathers of its long tail connected with a star flare beneath it.

While I still tried to process that *Erebus* of all deities had blessed me, Aestor healed the wounds.

Keres rose a brow at me. He was shocked and very much in awe. 'What did you do to poor Erebus?'

My lip quirked up. 'I may have tried to seduce him.'

'Oh, did you?' He sounded amused.

I giggled, still feeling the effects of the venom and the colchian side of me that was disappointed I'd failed in wrapping him around my finger. My pride didn't like that.

'Your dyad has a pretty voice but her singing and hum-ming nearly drove me insane.'

'What?' Keres frowned, completely bewildered with the comment.

I smiled up at him. 'I heard Antheia. I may have tripped on that venom.'

He blinked. 'What . . . What did she say?' There was something so tender about him, about the way his voice softened. The need to hear her words, even if they were spoken in another voice.

'She sang of that time he used his whip on her to see how many lashes a deity could take before breaking. I saw her with Ellowyn when she was younger.'

Aestor rubbed his back, sent some of that soothing power he had into my friend's aching heart. Though I felt pain from Aestor as well, who'd been close friends with Ellowyn and dearly missed her as well as Antheia, who'd become like a daughter to him.

Keres shot him a grateful look. 'I'm okay.'

Aedlynn didn't take her eyes off of Keres, her voice was gentle like I'd never heard before. 'If you'd stayed with her, they would've found another way to kill her.'

Keres glanced up, pain flashing in his eyes. In his very soul. Aedlynn took his hand in hers and squeezed it. She knew Keres blamed himself for the death of his dyad. They had that in common. 'If there is anyone to blame, it is the Fates for deciding against her and it was Nikos who gave into their whisperings, who saw a vulnerable goddess and exploited her. Nikos went mad before he died.' Aedlynn's lips quirked up into that chaotic grin of hers. 'And you will forever have your revenge with that curse on his family name. Every new generation will be haunted by what he did.'

Unease slipped into my shadows and it came from Aestor, who carried his own worries with him. Ones he hadn't shared with anyone yet but I saw the flashes of memories. Of tan skin, deep brown eyes and free-flowing black curls. Bare toes digging into the white sand while she showed him their many beaches, ones she'd shown me herself whenever I'd visited Veshos. How she told him stories about her parents, how Nikos would sneak her off to the farmer's fields to nibble on stolen strawberries under the bright sun, how Helia and Meira would pretend to spar with twigs and broken branches from the grand willow trees in their garden, surrounded by the lushest and most colourful gardens I had ever seen.

I stared at Aestor in shock as I realised who his dyad was: Meira De Mesogna.

Mother above, the Fates really hated my friends, huh?

Aestor had gone back to his smiling self, yet I wondered if he was scared. If he was angry with the curse. If he'd dare ask Keres to lift it. Keres couldn't, even if he wanted to – and for Aestor he would. The curse was a Divine Punishment. It couldn't be revoked until the sentence had been fully served.

I couldn't stop anxiously tapping my fingers on my knees, eyes darting back and forth between Aedlynn and the two gods. Maybe Aestor would let me taste his *ichor* as well. Shaking my head, I snapped out of my thoughts, only to realise that once again, Keres had asked me something.

I blinked at him. 'Huh?'

His lip quirked up to reveal that dimple. 'Still thirsty?'

'Yes,' I breathed.

He scrambled up, straightened his shirt and cleaned the blood smears I'd left behind by leaning against him. Then he extended his hand to help me up. Standing upright re-awakened the venom in my veins, which made me stumble forward, though Keres easily caught me. He slipped an arm around my lower back to guide me along. 'We'll be in the living room,' Keres said to Aestor over his shoulder.

'Enjoy your fruitpouch!' Aedlynn called over.

I tried very hard not to stare at Keres as he went to sit on the couch – at his neck or the veins that rolled along his forearms and the back of his hands. Instead, I looked around the room with exaggerated interest, like I was seeing the black-and-gold wallpaper for the first time. Keres started to unbutton the cuffs of his sleeve and it took every ounce of dignity I had not to jump him and impatiently sink my teeth into the fabric.

'Diana, look at me.' His voice was gentle, tender even. I kept focusing on the burning hearth. 'The first time I offered Aloïs my blood to heal, he lost full control and Aestor had to intervene. Maeve had to be dragged away by Aloïs and Vanora or she would've drank me dry.'

I stared at him in horror. 'Then why are we *alone?*'

Keres lazily stretched and rested his legs on the coffee table. 'Because you're sleeping upright. Even with those wicked powers, I could easily take you right now.'

I scoffed. 'Cocky bastard.'

He smirked. 'I'm still a god, love. I can handle an overgrown leech.'

'As if.'

'A tired little *matska?*' He chuckled. 'I'll tuck you in after I've knocked you out.'

Irritation flashed through me. I knew he was teasing me to distract me but his confidence poured out of every crevice and made me want to prove to him just how easily I could take him. I might not have been able to trick Erebus but Keres was no all-powerful deity and he'd fallen for it before. So I conjured up a smile that carried the warmth of the hearth in the room, that made me radiate with loveliness. Conjuring up that power was as easy as breathing. The grey in my eyes became a molten silver. My overthinking stopped as I just . . . *became.* The instincts, the power.

I moved like the vesperae did, graceful like liquid.

Keres' eyes didn't leave mine. His lips slightly parted while he took me in. I swung one leg over his and perched on his lap, facing him as I stroked his jawline. Power coursed through my veins and gilded my nerves. If this was exertion, why could I still channel my power? Why did it feel as easy as breathing and blinking? Why did unleashing it feel so *right?*

I tipped his chin up and let my gaze trail from his eyes to his lips while I lazily brushed a thumb over his bottom lip to pull it down. I leaned in and my warm breath caressed his lips, made them tingle with desire. Keres' hands rested on my hipbones while he stared up at me, his eyes filled with lust. I liked that shade in them, it suited him. His breathing deepened and slowed, his heartbeat was steady but quicker than before. Utterly intoxicated.

I brushed my soft lips from the crook of his neck to right underneath his ear, earning a soft gasp. Keres' head tilted back and to the side as I did. My fangs were aching to pierce his skin, my tongue yearned for the taste of his *ichor.* Keres' hand smoothed over my throat to cup the back of my head and he intertwined his fingers with my hair. With his mouth so close to my ear, his own breathing tickled my heated skin.

He tenderly kissed me there and my soul grew quiet.

'This okay?' he whispered.

I nodded slowly and Keres traced a slow path over my neck with his lips. I may have moaned softly, overcome with a primal need for his touch – to be wrapped up in his tender passion again. Lightning shot down my nerves and heat gathered between my thighs.

His grip on my hair tightened, and his breathing came in low and uneven pants as his lips arrived back to my ear. 'Feast, Diana,' he murmured. 'Show me what that venom of yours does.'

Underneath all that magic, he knew damn well what I was doing, and for one horrible moment, I feared I was no better than Eiran – toying with Keres like this. But Keres liked it when I channelled my power and didn't hold back. And with or without colchian magic, he thought I was wickedly attractive. A part of Keres wanted to ravage me right now.

His lips brushed underneath my ear to kiss me there. They curled into a smirk against my skin when he heard the soft needy noise I'd made. 'The things I'd do to you, *matska*, to make those adorable little moans of yours loud enough to rattle the walls.' His own voice was a perfect drug, thick and dripping like honey.

I stilled, softly panting. His hard length pushing against me, so close to my drenched core, was the sweetest torture.

Gods . . . Gods I wanted him. I needed him. I wanted to experience what he promised.

But maybe not right now. Not while we were both high on my compulsion.

So instead, I slowly kissed his neck and then sunk my fangs in his flesh, cupping the back of his head to gently hold him in place. His *ichor* tasted like everything good in this world. Dewy honey and caramel. Warm and bright. My body started to relax, all tension started to leave my muscles as I leaned more into him.

Keres' head tilted back to rest against the couch. My venom hit him hard – harder than any of Aestor's soothing had ever done. His breathing deepened, his heartbeat slowed so much that for a moment I worried that I'd gone overboard. But he was very much alive. Alive and pain-free as his body loosened. The injuries he'd received during the War after Antheia's death no longer bothered him. The ones he'd refused to let Aestor heal.

All of it dissipated.

I drank while teasing his skin with my tongue in a way that made him wonder what I might do between his legs, making another soft moan bubble up in my chest as the imagery clouded my mind.

'Fuck,' he breathed when he heard me moan again. His fingers dug into the skin of my waist and rear, absent-mindedly guiding my hips to rock against his hardness. 'You like the taste of me, love?'

My grip on his hair tightened and the only response I could give him was pressing myself tighter against him, sucking his skin harder to draw more blood into my mouth. But it was answer enough.

His hand smoothed over my rear, over the curve of it to firmly grab me there, and all I could think about was what we'd done last time. How he'd made me feel things I'd never felt before.

How he'd been slowly teaching me that language of tender hands and soft smiles.

Keres groaned, his hands firmly holding my hips in place to keep me from rolling them. 'I'm trying to be a gentleman here, Diana, since you're exhausted and still healing, but if you keep doing *that*,' he said with a low voice while squeezing my rear for emphasis. 'I'm not so sure how long I can continue behaving myself.'

I pulled my fangs out of his skin, caressed my tongue over the two bleeding puncture wounds to heal them and then licked up the column of his throat – a dare.

One of his hands wove through my hair to intertwine with the tresses and he made me look up at him. 'You're still wounded, love,' he warned me, his voice thick with the strain on his self-control.

But I didn't care. I didn't care that it might hurt, that I was still bleeding.

I'd missed him – so much.

I started kissing his neck the same way I'd so often done in Aerelia, except now, there was no one to put on a show for. I simply wanted to make him feel good, to thank him for taking care of me and selflessly gifting me some of his blood to help me heal. My hands roved over his chest, travelling lower and lower until I fought with the buttons of his trousers.

'*Diana,*' he breathed in a warning as I playfully nipped at his neck.

'Let me,' I murmured against his jawline. 'Let me thank you.'

'You don't need to repay me, love.'

'That's not what this is,' I said softly, before kissing his lips. 'You've been taking care of me since the moment I prayed to you. Let me take care of you for once.'

His hand smoothed over my back. Over my hair. 'You're injured.'

'I'm fine,' I promised. 'Let me be good to you, *please.*'

'You're always good to me,' he argued softly. His hand cupped the back of my head as I bent forward to slowly kiss him again. Lazily. Like we had all the time in the world.

Last time, we'd convinced ourselves we were simply having some fun. I tried to convince myself of that again now. That this was nothing more, that these flutters in my stomach meant nothing. That the way my shadows caressed his legs in affection was simple friendship.

I attempted to undo the buttons of his trousers again, but his hand curled around my wrist to stop me and guide my hand to rest against my thigh, his fingers weaving with mine. His other hand tucked my loose hair behind my ear so lovingly that I could've melted in his arms. He pulled me closer, kissed my lips once and then guided me down on the couch so he could climb over me and settle between my legs.

Keres' head dipped to kiss my exposed collarbone. The sensitive spot beneath my ear. My cheek and jawline. My nose. Until he found my lips again.

'You scared me to near death, you know that?' he whispered against them. 'I was worried sick.'

'I'm sorry,' I whispered back.

His hand tenderly caressed my throat. The other was still intertwined with mine, resting above my head on the pillow. 'Don't leave me like that again, Diana, *please*. I can't lose you.'

Something burned in my eyes and all I could manage was a simple nod at the soft plea.

Just some fun, I reminded myself. And yet this thing between us felt like a shy seedling slowly learning how to bloom and grow. Like a small bird finally daring to learn how to fly. Like lightning finally decided to demand its due attention during a storm.

My arms banded around his waist and I pressed my cheek against his shoulder, allowing Keres to turn us so I lay on top of him, my arms still around him while I felt his magic brush over any little cut and bruise Aestor had overlooked. All while he softly caressed my hair and back.

I'd expected to feel more awake, to gain strength and energy from the *ichor* – to heal. Instead, I grew more and more drowsy. My eyelids were becoming too heavy to keep my eyes open. My mind had gone completely empty, like my thoughts had decided to go to bed as well.

My body leaned more against Keres until he slipped both arms around me to hold me in place. My vision kept going out of focus and I realised just how tired I was, how my body only now seemed to catch up to what I'd been through. That I'd been gone for a month. Without food or sleep. The strange things . . . *someone* . . . had said to me. I vaguely remembered seeing pretty dark eyes.

I relished in the sensation of Keres' warm body against mine. Of being held so tenderly by him. He made me feel safe and protected and normal and – by the Mother, I'd *missed* him. So I just lay there while he held me and brushed my hair.

'Don't forget to tuck me in,' I whispered.

His chest swayed as he chuckled. 'Feeling better?'

I nodded, felt how sleep was tugging at my torn-up sleeves like a small child begging for attention. I was already drifting off when the warmth of my softest blanket sunk onto me as Keres made good on his promise.

Chapter 26

Diana

The fact that I hadn't seen Zale in a while, even before I'd ventured into Erebus, gnawed at me. Zale had raised me, had held my hair while I'd desecrated the porcelain toilets, had forced me to drink hot chicken broths to keep me from dehydrating. He'd told me stories and held me through nightmares. He'd played with me, had let me put ribbons in his hair to make him look pretty like a princess and then told me I was the prettiest of them all, and that had meant everything to five-year-old me. It still did.

So when he stuck his head inside to see if I was still sleeping, I slipped in and out of a shadow and flung myself around his neck. 'Gods, I've missed you.' I sniffed and tightened my grip on him.

Zale pressed me closer, weaving his fingers through my hair and planted a kiss on the top of my head. 'I'm sorry for being so absent, *Vaelip*. Orthalla has been incredibly busy and Egoron had some issues.'

'It's okay.'

'Gods, you had me worried,' he whispered, tightening his grip even more. 'Are you okay?'

It'd been a week since I'd returned, since I'd found my daemonic instinct wide awake and a new sort of power surging through my veins. My nightly visions had grown more vivid and intense and often even slipped into my daydreams, where I saw flashes of black sand beaches, tall waterfalls reaching for the heavens over luscious rainforests. The venom still lingered and even simply washing myself was enough to make me pass out afterwards. My nightmares hadn't ebbed away either, so Aedlynn still spent the nights cuddled up to me to calm me down whenever I woke up in a panic.

'Sure, things have been . . . interesting. But I'm fine.'

'How was your month of vacation?'

I snickered. 'Wasn't much sun and the host was a bit creepy.'

Zale laughed but underneath that, I felt how worried he'd been and how he'd missed me these past months. He hadn't wanted to mention it since I'd been settling down here so nicely.

I pulled him onto the bed and made myself comfortable on his lap, resting my head on his shoulder while I told him about my time in Erebus, like I used to do when I was little. Only then, our conversations had been about my lessons from the Priestesses or school and not about little Lord Darkness Incarnate.

When I'd spilt it all, I leaned my head on his shoulder. 'I'm sorry for not visiting as often as I'd promised.'

'It's okay, I understand.' Zale kissed my hair. 'You've flourished – grown happy. You smile almost continuously, you're not as timid anymore. You're surrounded by people who love you and would do anything for you. They had to hold Aedlynn back or she would've broken into Erebus to get to you. Keres was ready to tear Erebus apart.' He sighed and I nearly felt the lump forming in his throat. 'I've watched you heal these past months, even the scars

Kallias left behind.' I blinked the tears from my eyes when I remembered the run-in in Erebus. I had let him go, yes, but what he'd done to me would always remain a part of my past. Nothing could erase that, though the scars had indeed healed thanks to my family. They no longer ached or threatened to break open.

Not sure what to say, I only nodded.

'And I couldn't be prouder of the person you've become through it all, Diana.'

Fuck.

Zale chuckled and gently rocked me back and forth while I broke down.

When I managed to compose myself again, I told him about my friends and the things we'd done. How I loved flying, that my wings had finally grown thicker. That Canelle's cubs had gone out to venture into Anthens but that she'd stayed because she liked me. Aedlynn had given her a cute nickname as well because I was terrible at thinking of decent names. Apparently, little Nelle had laid small pieces of mandarin on my pillow every night that I'd been gone. Now that I was back and spent my time resting, she followed me everywhere, and as Zale and I talked, Nelle lay curled on my feet.

Zale listened to my rambling with a sweet smile, draped a blanket over my lap and brushed my back with his knuckles. His scent of clean linen surrounded me, made me feel nostalgic and safe. My eyelids grew heavier, my sentences less and less coherent while I started to doze off again. I tried to fight the tiredness. I wanted to stay awake longer to talk to him but my body ignored me and ordered my eyes to shut as it relaxed fully against Zale.

I wandered through a pretty meadow, admiring the softly glowing wildflowers. A black sky spread out above the bluish grass, decorated with the full moon and adorned with stars and aurora. My silk silvery dress trailed behind me like the veil of a wedding dress. It contrasted my pitch-black shadows that loyally followed in my wake. The silver circlet I'd been gifted by my parents as a sign of my Márzenas lineage rested on my arched ears and intertwined with tendrils of shadows. Power crackled in the air surrounding me and reverberated through all living things around me. The roots and saplings, the Darkness of the fertile soil. It all called to me in return.

'I see you're settling into your new power, aediore.*'*

I turned my head to look at where the familiar voice drawled from.

Her sleek raven hair fell to her waist, the simple silver circlet glowed with moonshine and her midnight eyes curiously studied me. The simple long-sleeved dress of pitch-black gently swayed in the night air, clinging to her like night, and the neckline revealed thin strands of gold scars on her chest.

Her lips curled into a sweet smile.

The contrast to the painting of her that once decorated the ceiling in Clacaster's throne room before I'd altered it was breathtaking.

'Antheia?' I whispered. 'How?'

'You were blessed with a curious and wandering mind, one that loves exploring. You're a nyghtrá – a nightwalker.'

'Nightwalker?'

Antheia nodded and approached me, taking me in with quiet pride while my shadows excitedly curled around her calves to greet her. 'Nightwalkers are those blessed with visions of past and future and everything in between during the night hours or when they sleep.' She brushed a strand of blonde hair behind my ear. I stared at her in awe and wondered how our myths had ever been able to reduce her to nothing but a goddess of hatred. She radiated serenity. A peaceful winter day personified.

'Where are we? What is this place?' I could almost feel how the sand in the hourglass fell down and down. Antheia felt it too – how something ancient stirred as if to silence her. To claw through this vision until it disappeared.

I clasped her hands in mine. 'Why am I seeing you? Are you alive?'

'This is Vāela, a realm my mother made aeons ago. Once solely a physical creation, Vāela evolved and has become what some might know as the Inbetween; the Gate of Wyrd. It can house a night-walker between visions. It can house a spirit so long as it cannot move on. Anything that lives in-between before deciding on a path to take.'

I needed a moment to process all this but I knew I had no time. 'Then why . . . why are you here? What are you?'

'A spirit.'

'You've not . . . moved on?'

Something like cold amusement shone in her eyes, a hint of that goddess who enjoyed her trickeries and schemes. 'In a way, I have. But I came here to guard you until you safely find your way back to your body. You're most vulnerable when you aimlessly wander, especially to desolate and forgotten places like Vāela or Séthoseros. They lure you in with their haunting song and won't let you go until you've lost your sanity.' She squeezed my hand. 'You should be careful of that.'

'So you've made yourself a Guardian?' I asked curiously.

I still couldn't quite grasp that I was talking to Antheia.

Her lips tipped up into a sly smile that told me there were plenty of secrets hiding behind those closed lips. 'I've done a lot of things to spite the Fates.' Something feral blazed in her eyes; the promise of a reckoning. 'I do not like being shackled, nor being told what to do. So yes, Diana. I've made myself something – made myself an independent piece on their little game board.' She tucked another strand of hair behind my arched ear. 'And I suggest you do the same, aediore. *If you don't, the Fates will soon bleed you out until they can rip your heart out and use you as another puppet in their twisted games.'*

'I'm not sure why the Fates would be interested in me.'

Her eyes twinkled with amusement. 'Indeed, why would they be interested in Darkness Incarnate?'

I stared at her wide-eyed, at a loss for words as I remembered the things my father had told me about Erebus months ago – about Elyon and the duality of the place. Of the power.

If Eiran found out that I wasn't just a výssar *but that Erebus had chosen me . . .*

Antheia nodded when she noted the panicked look on my face. 'The Fates will watch you, Diana. They all will; some more malevolent than others. Keep your wits about you while you dance with the serpents.' Her lips pursed a moment as she studied something in my face. 'And when you're in doubt – when you don't know what choice to make, stay with Aedlynn. Let her be your guiding light.'

I nodded, highly overwhelmed by the information she'd dumped on me. Something told me that Antheia was trying hard to warn me of something – someone, but couldn't outright tell me.

'I need you to carry over a message from me to Aedlynn as well,' Antheia said, holding my eyes captive with her own. 'Lena wasn't only a nymph. Her výssar *blood made her more – the Goddess of Spring, like I am of Winter. And the quintessential thing about Spring is that it is a season of rebirth.'*

I stared at her as the words sunk in.

The meaning of them.

Rebirth.

She nodded. 'Tell Aedlynn.'

'Yes,' I whispered. 'Yes, of course.'

She touched my cheek in affection. 'Thank you.'

I looked down at the hand that I still tightly clasped in mine. It felt wrong to receive her gratitude knowing the things I'd been doing with Keres – her dyad. Guilt opened a pit in my stomach and I didn't dare look her in her eyes.

Antheia's hand cupped my cheek to make me look up at her. 'I'm glad that he's happy again, that he found hope in you. Someone who will fight for him the same way I have always fought for him.'

I smiled at her, feeling the guilt ebb away a little. 'I promise I always will – on the Netha.'

Faint thunder rolled through the skies at the second vow I'd made on the river. 'I don't doubt that, even without that vow. I know what it feels like to be loved by him, how healing for the soul it is. After everything you've been through, you deserve that fresh start.' She gave me a brave smile.

I swallowed hard, unsure of what to say to that. I didn't need shadows to know that she ached, it shone within her midnight eyes. And I couldn't blame her for that. They'd been dyads. She'd been his heart and soul and pulse.

And I was just . . . me.

Antheia's expression softened when she felt my struggle. 'There is something so beautiful about having a dyad. All the stories and myths are true. You know them better than you know yourself and they become so ingrained in your very being that you don't know who you'd be without them.' Her throat bobbed. 'And that is absolutely wonderful – until that other half is taken away. That wound in your soul never closes. You learn how to live around the pain but it takes months – years. His heart was torn apart, his soul was ripped in half and his pulse had to learn how to beat without its twin echoing in his chest. I can only imagine how terrifying it is to experience that and then slowly learn to love someone again. But *he is doing that with you, and I am glad to know he's living again.'*

Tears burned in my eyes as I remembered how he'd held me after Erebus. How he'd begged me not to do that again. I stifled a sob, wiping away the tears from my cheeks. 'Thank you,' I whispered.

She smiled sweetly, though that ache in her eyes didn't leave. 'Will you tell him something for me?'

'Of course.'

'Tell him that I am sorry for what I said to him then, that I meant none of the things I said.' She swallowed hard. 'I don't blame him, and I will not have him spend the rest of his existence blaming and punishing himself. I don't want him to be sorry, I want him to be happy.'

My vision started to darken around the edges and dissolve and I felt how somewhere, my body was waking up.

'You were tested in Erebus, Diana,' she hastily told me. 'But you will be tested again by Eiran in ways you cannot possibly fathom. Erebus' trials are child's play compared to what Eiran is capable of. Be prepared for him.'

I nodded once. 'I will.'

'And when you wear his crown, Diana,' she took my chin to make me look at her and slyly grinned, 'aim for his throne as well.'

I couldn't help but grin. Even as a spirit, she was still scheming to overthrow him.

Antheia smiled one last time, tainted with deep sadness. Grief for the loved ones who lived, whom she couldn't reach. 'Tell Keres I love him, tell your parents as well. Tell Aestor I'm happy he found his dyad and that she is everything he deserves after all these years. Tell my vesperae that I love them.'

'I will,' I said, and I thought of the visions I'd had in Erebus. Of the little boy she'd held with nothing but pure love twinkling in her eyes. 'Have you . . . Have you found Kaltain?'

Gods, I hoped she had.

*Antheia's gaze twinkled with something mischievous. 'I have.'
She brushed my tears away and hugged me. 'Think of me when you
look at my stars,* aediore, *and when you do, remember that they will
work hard to drive you into the ground but you are as relentless as the
tide of the ocean and as inevitable as mortal death. Do not yield and
do not kneel, Diana. No matter what fate throws your way.'*

*There was a knowing look in her eyes, proving to me that she
indeed knew something – something she couldn't share with me.*

*Antheia kissed my forehead. Her words settled into me, charging
me with energy and power. The energy I'd lost after Erebus' trials,
now refilled. There was so much I wanted to say, so many things
I wanted to ask and I knew Antheia hadn't been able to tell me
everything she'd ached to tell me.*

But the vision tore apart.

Slipping out of the shadows in Keres' living room, still
wearing my silvery vespera-woven nightgown and a warm
vest, I looked around to see that the hearth wasn't burning.

As I walked barefoot over the cold and dark marble
floor, my eyes fell on the moonstones scattered throughout the room and I thought of the vision of Antheia. How
my mother had received a moonstone ring from her, how
Keres still wore his necklace and the amulet Aedlynn still
wore. Antheia reminded me a bit of a crow collecting shiny
things, and I wondered why those moonstones had been so
precious to her.

I moved on to his bedroom, where I perched next to him
on the bed and gently shook his shoulders to wake him up.
'Keres?' No reaction, even when I shook more firmly.

Some apex predator he was, softly snoring and wholly
unaware of my presence.

Finally, Keres opened his eyes, looking at me in a sleepy

430

haze. When he realised who I was, he shot upright in bed, fighting with his blankets. 'You okay?'

'Yeah,' I breathed, forcing myself not to look at his nicely sculpted chest. But *damn*.

Keres rubbed a hand over his face, then glanced at the clock. 'Not that you're not welcome, but why grace me with your presence in the middle of the night?'

I took a deep breath. 'I ehm . . . I need to talk to you.'

He nodded, blinking the sleep from his eyes while I sat down cross-legged on his duvet to face him. Keres handed me a blanket – the softest one he had, which I highly appreciated and gratefully draped over my lap. I looked at him, wondering how to tell him. 'I thought my dreams stemmed from the shadows I sensed but it turns out I'm a nightwalker.'

'Oh?' Keres processed that. 'How do you know – about them? They're extremely rare.'

'Antheia told me.' He blinked. His lips parted. I took another deep breath. 'I had a vision. She said I was in Vāela.'

All sleepiness washed away when he realised I'd truly seen her. 'Tell me everything.'

So I did.

'She asked me to tell you something.'

Sadness flashed in his eyes, pain knocked on my shadows. 'Yes?'

Gods, I felt for him. The quiet hope, the throbbing chasm that still lingered in his very soul after all these years. He had hurt so intensely after she'd been killed, had gone through such deep agony that Zielle had had to dim their bond so he could even just *breathe*. And that had only taken the edge away.

Exactly like Antheia had described to me.

I'd been wanting to talk to him about our kisses after I'd returned from Erebus and how deeply I cared about him, but I hadn't found the courage yet and now . . . seeing his grief for Antheia made the quiet hope that'd been blossoming in my chest shrink down. He had every right to miss her, to still love her and to grieve her. It just made me wonder if I could ever be enough for him.

I decided to push down those overwhelming feelings, as I felt beyond selfish worrying about my crush on him while Keres was hurting. My voice quivered while I repeated her words, 'She wanted me to tell you that she's sorry for what she said to you, that she meant none of it, and that she's sorry she hurt you.' Tears rolled over his cheeks. 'She doesn't blame you, and she doesn't want you to spend your existence blaming and punishing yourself.' My voice broke. 'She asked me to tell you that she loves you, and she said she's found Kaltain.'

The noise he made was one between a sob and a whimper, and a sound of pure heartache. I couldn't stand the hurting he felt, to see him so vulnerable and fragile. To see his shoulders heaving as he cried. My shadows nestled against him to soothe him.

I pulled him close, wrapped him up in my arms and held him through his sobs, shielding him from the world with my wings. I caressed his back and hair, desperately wishing I had Aestor's healing power, his soothing skills to help him. His sobs tore at me until tears ran over my own cheeks.

'She seemed absolutely lovely,' I whispered to him.

'She didn't . . . didn't deserve it . . . none of it.' I nodded, resting my lips on his soft hair. 'I miss them so . . . so *gods-damned* much. Every fucking day.'

I sobbed and held him closer. I'd always been taught how

rare and coveted dyad bonds were. People prayed daily for a dyad but with Antheia's comment and seeing and feeling how Aedlynn and Keres ached to lose theirs . . . Perhaps such a bond was a curse as well as a blessing.

I didn't know how to take away this insane hurt he felt, and how could I, when not even Aestor could fully take away that pain?

Keres' head rested on my chest while we lay down and I held him. 'It just feels like I'm stuck in some frozen land and every time that I realise I miss her – that I miss Kaltain, I get pummelled into ice shards.' He took a shuddering breath. 'It's got better throughout the years but . . .'

'But?'

'It's childish.'

'Try me.'

He hesitated a moment. 'Aloïs thought he lost his dyad and then got her back. They grieved you for years and then you showed up – alive and well. Aestor found his dyad and gets to love her. Cas and Eos mated the loves of their lives and Cas and Maeve have finally started their own little family. They nearly lost their children but they survived – free of any scars or memories.'

'And you only get to watch,' I whispered, brushing a hand through his hair. 'Knowing damn well what you lost and that you won't get them back.'

'Yeah.'

'That's not childish, Keres. That's human.'

'Thank you,' he said quietly. 'For coming to tell me.'

'Of course.' I glanced down at his honey waves. 'I still had to thank you for the blood anyway – and apologise for the compulsion.'

'Yeah, I had to explain to Aloïs why his daughter had

draped herself over my body before he decided to chop my head off.'

'He's not *that* protective.'

'Sshh, love. I'm trying to be dramatic.'

'Aren't you always?' He laughed softly and I much preferred the sound to the sobs from before. 'I am sorry about the compulsion, by the way.'

'Don't be. I liked it.'

'I liked it too. Not ehm . . . seducing you, you know. Using my magic, I liked it.'

Keres shifted so he sat upright to face me. 'I could tell. I liked seeing you like that – so free.'

I smiled. 'You always like it when I show off my power.'

'Can't argue with that,' he shrugged. 'You were already suppressed your entire life, Diana – against your will,' he said. 'Don't willingly supress yourself now.'

I nodded again. 'It's just . . . What the others might think—'

'Who gives a fuck what Orthalla thinks? Fuck them. As for the others, there's no need to be a saint around them, they're not without sins themselves.'

'I know . . . It's just . . . I've spent so long . . . I'm so used to . . . to just doing everything in my power to convince those nobles I was no beast or monster that it's hard to let go of that.'

'You're so used to bending forward to kiss their ass that you've forgotten you can straighten your spine. You have every right to defend yourself and those you love. You have every right to be proud of your titles, to use your power, to bask in the fact that you are the first person ever to receive a blessing from Erebus, even if we don't fully know what that means yet.'

'I do.'

'Damn right you do. Let them scatter before you.'

My lips curled into a little smirk. 'I came here to give you a message and it turned into some inspirational breakthrough. How'd we get here?'

He shrugged. 'Consider it a thank you for the message.'

'In case I do see her again, is there anything you want me to tell her?'

His gaze travelled from my face to the wall behind me. 'Tell her that I've long forgiven her for what she said, and that, overall, I am happy. It just still aches in my soul where she used to be.' I nodded and absent-mindedly brushed my thumb over his knee. His lips quirked into a sweet smile when he glanced back at me. 'And tell her that I still have every single moonstone that she ever gifted me – there were a lot.'

I returned that smile. 'I will.'

'And that I've harboured every single smile she showed me, every single aurora she ever made for me . . . that I've harboured them all deep in my soul. Where no one can steal them, not even Eiran.' Something liquid travelled over my cheeks and there was a very annoying lump in my throat. Keres raised a brow at me. 'Why are *you* crying, love?'

What he said sounded like poetry. Pretty, romantic and utterly sweet and enchanting. A testament of just how much he loved her. And I wanted someone to say such lovely things to me.

No, I wanted *Keres* to say such things to me.

'Who would've thought you were so romantic?' I said in an effort to appear fine.

The corner of his lip quirked up. 'I have my moments.' He tapped my knee when he remembered something. 'I do hope you told Aedlynn you didn't sleepwalk to Erebus again?'

I blinked and stared at him, caught off guard. 'I did what?'

Keres studied me. 'After you fed, you fell asleep. Eva stayed with you to watch over you, but she dozed off and when she woke up in the middle of the night, you were gone. Just gone. Nowhere to be found in the castle.' It felt like someone had replaced my blood with ice. He frowned, surprised that no one had mentioned it.

'And then?'

'We split up to look for you. Aedlynn found you, soundly sleeping at the end of that path that leads into Erebus. Like you'd wanted to go back in.'

I swallowed hard but my mouth had gone dry like old parchment paper. 'I don't . . . I don't remember that. They haven't mentioned it.'

He nodded once. 'Do you still get nightmares?'

I fumbled with the blanket. My heart still skipped beats from the lingering venom and the scar on my flank ached at times. And those nightmares weren't pretty at all. I glanced at him and muttered, 'Sometimes.'

'About?'

My eyes fell back to the blanket on my lap. 'Those monsters, and sometimes I dream that I'm being tortured or starved, and sometimes . . . I wake from a nightmare with no orientation at all and I forget where and even *who* I am for a moment, and . . . it's stupid but . . . losing Aedlynn.'

The look on his face softened. I fought off the overwhelming emotions, the fear and worry of losing her, but tears still filled my eyes. Keres touched my cheek to wipe a tear away that had managed to escape and I bit my tongue at the stray flutter that passed through me. 'I swear you two share *something* of some sort. Aedlynn was beyond herself when you didn't return, kept slipping into Aspian. The first day was doable but then . . . Even Sorin couldn't calm her. Eos had to drag her back from Erisor, we had to guard *her* or she would've tried to find a way to destroy Erebus and with her power . . . she might've pulled it off and cast us all into Chaos.'

I wiped the tears away and rested my head on his shoulder. 'She did?'

'Yeah.' He brushed a hand over my upper back. 'She lashed out at *me* several times when we pulled her back, with an anger that indeed reminded me of Khalyna. Might've feared for my life then.'

I tried to imagine Aedlynn scaring Keres, of her overcome with emotions at losing me. 'You really were scared of her?'

'Don't tell her that, it'll go straight to that pretty head of hers.'

I smirked. 'She's managed to terrify Aestor and now you as well?'

'Can you blame us?' He shook his head while he laughed. 'Life's been pretty tame since the War and then you show up with the power of all daemons combined. Erebus' new Chosen. Aedlynn shows up, a halfgod who has a thing for pretty ribbons and reeks of Chaos. Pardon us for being a little overwhelmed as to what this all means.'

I grinned at him. 'And what does it mean, God of Malice?'

'War is coming.' Keres showed me a wicked grin. 'And I fear not even the Fates know what will come to unfold.'

'I've been hearing a lot about the Fates lately,' I said. 'But all I was taught by the Priestesses is that they oversee the grand scheme of things, but that it's the gods who shape the world around us into what it is.'

'We do, yes. But the Fates are also an entity on their own,' he explained. 'Zielle didn't send Kallias your way, they did. Whether it was with malevolent intentions or with the knowledge that because of it, you would end up summoning me and eventually return home, that is to be guessed.'

Pursing my lips, I stared at him while my anger woke up. 'Next time they fuck me over, I will tear them apart and feed them to our hell hounds.' The gleam in his eyes intensified. 'And once the realms are cast into Chaos, it won't be them laughing at *that* divine comedy.'

Keres looked me up and down, the corner of his mouth quirking up into a cocky grin.

I leaned back and let my own lips curl into a smirk. 'What?'

'You say such *wonderfully* sinful things to me, love,' he drawled. 'And I adore listening to it.'

I snorted. 'You just like it when I show you my violent side.'

His lip moved up further to reveal one dimple. 'Perhaps. I do know that I look forward to watching you slaughter Bastian. That title is still dangling between you two. I want you to finish him off.'

'Of course you do,' I drawled as I leaned forward more.

'You devoted yourself to me with a vow of revenge, love,' he purred. 'It's only natural I encourage you to extend your wrath to that bastard and not solely focus on Lorcán.'

'Oh, I plan to.' I showed him a wicked grin. 'No one touches my family without losing a limb or two. I'll give him a Divine Punishment of my own.'

'He seemed surprisingly immune to my whip.'

'I doubt he has a soul to punish.' I grinned. 'So I'll hurt what he does have; pride and a horrible ego. I'll make them all watch how he gets beaten by a pretty *matska*. I will make him beg for death, but why would I listen to the pleas of a man who never listened to those of others?'

Keres gave me a look that made my stomach flutter, but after seeing Antheia and comforting him, it felt wrong to even think about how I'd kissed him. So I started to rise from the bed.

'Is the slumber party over?'

I snorted softly. 'I'll let you commence your beauty sleep, you need it.'

Another sweet smile crept on his lips. 'There she is.'

'Will you be alright?'

The look on his face softened. 'Yeah.'

I smiled at him. 'Goodnight, Keres.'

'Night, love.'

Chapter 27

Diana

'I'm a nightwalker,' I said with a smile on my face while we were having breakfast.

Aloïs stared at me, his cup of coffee still resting against his lip. Eva stopped chewing her bread. Aedlynn had paled, still holding her large mug of coffee with both hands to enjoy its warmth.

'How do you know?' Aloïs asked me.

'I had a vision of Antheia. She said I was.' I recounted the vision to them, told them of the things she'd said to me. The things she wanted me to tell them.

Aedlynn stared at me after I'd told her about Lena, opening and closing her mouth. A vulnerable expression crept over her face and I felt her ache: the fear that this was some trick. That this was too good to be true. 'Did she . . . did she tell you how?'

I shook my head. 'She was rather vague in everything she told me. She only said that Spring meant rebirth.'

'It makes sense,' Aloïs said quietly, rubbing a hand over his stubble. 'Spring. Rebirth.' He looked at Aedlynn. 'And a dyad with some sort of power related to the Fates.'

Her eyes widened and, slowly, some hope crept into her heart. 'You think . . . I could . . .'

'Yael brought her husband back from the dead,' Eva said. 'She never told anyone how, though rumour has it that she used alchemy or a deal with Elyon, but it *is* possible.'

'You'd have to be careful, though,' Aloïs warned Aedlynn. 'There is the Rule of Equivalent Exchange in magic – in everything, really. If you wish to bring back Lena, you will need something of equal value to gift Death in return.'

Aedlynn nodded, slowly growing hopeful that there might be a chance. Yet she also grew restless, as this meant that Lena was out there somewhere, and we had no idea where or what was currently happening to her. She hadn't been in the Inbetween and Antheia hadn't made it sound like she'd passed on, so where exactly was she?

'I'll find something,' she said breathlessly. 'Anything. I just . . . I'd have to find a way into the Afterworld, if she's even there. I just have to find her.'

Aloïs rested his hand on Aedlynn's across the table. 'You're not doing this alone.'

'But—'

'You've become like a daughter to us, Aedlynn. If your dyad is out there, we are bringing her home. You're not doing it alone.'

Her eyes reddened. 'Thank you,' she said softly. She looked over at me, blinking back tears. *'Thank you.'*

I smiled at her, leaning over the table to take her other hand in mine and squeezed it.

'Did you tell Keres that you saw Antheia?' Eva asked me.

I nodded. 'I visited him when I woke up during the night.' My lips pursed as I remembered something. I looked back at them, a flicker of annoyance passing over my features. 'Were you going to tell me I walked to Erebus or were you going to hide that?'

Aedlynn snickered. 'When should we have told you? When you were snoring as loudly as a wyvern?'

I grinned.

'We were going to tell you when you'd regained your energy,' Eva said.

'Well, I have.'

'You sleepwalked to Erebus,' my father said helpfully.

I raised an amused brow and refilled my cup with coffee. 'Oh, really? That's the first I've heard of it.'

He chuckled softly, though his brows were slightly drawn together, his lips a tight line when he was done laughing. He tried to hide it but he was worried about what this all meant for me. 'Aedlynn found you sleeping at the end of the path,' he explained. 'We couldn't wake you. Aestor checked you over but found nothing strange, said that your body was just too exhausted. I tried to communicate with your *varkradas* to find out what had happened but they slept as well. So we wanted to ask you what happened when you woke up, but when you did, you had no clue anything had happened.'

Aedlynn tapped my arm, munching on an apple. 'Did you lose your daggers in there?'

The question took me by surprise. 'Which one?'

'*Aecéso* and the one Zale gifted you.'

My eyes went wide while I instinctively patted my thighs. 'I did.' I glanced at my father, overcome with shame that I'd lost the dagger he'd gifted me. And Zale's dagger . . . that'd been a Losaño heirloom.

Aedlynn nodded and simply left the table. I looked after her in confusion, as did Eva and Aloïs.

'It's fine, sweetheart,' Eva said. 'We'll get you a new one.'

'Yeah, but . . .'

'Truly, Diana, I wouldn't give a shit if you'd lost your crown in there,' Aloïs said. 'I only care that *you're* back.'

I nodded and looked down at my plate. Even though it

was a gilded pear, my appetite had left me.

Aedlynn walked back in with her usual fluid grace. She carried a piece of dark green fabric that enveloped something, which she laid down next to my plate and opened to reveal my daggers. I stared at them in shock. At the pitch-black one, at the one Zale had given me when I'd turned eighteen. It was a light, *Damast* steel, the waves some shades darker to create a beautiful contrast. The hilt was crafted from green opal, with the Losaño crest carved into it and painted with gold; a cursive L with a luscious branch of wisteria encircling it.

Knowing that I hadn't lost this precious gift kicked the weight off my shoulders that had gathered there. I looked back up at Aedlynn, about to thank her for bringing them back.

'I think he called to you to give them back,' she said. 'They were laying right next to you.'

'Really?' Aloïs now stood next to her, studying the daggers himself. Black sand fell from them, a reminder that they'd indeed bathed in the Darkness there.

'No, I'm making that up.'

Aloïs ruffled her hair and let his hand rest on her shoulder. 'Why didn't you tell us?'

I felt the cosy warmth in her chest at the affection he showed her. Aedlynn shrugged. 'In case they fell out of her shadows. I thought that maybe she'd sneezed again.'

I rolled my eyes, though a little smile still crept on my lips. Sometimes when I sneezed, my wings spread out behind me. 'You think I'll shoot daggers out of my shadows when I sneeze?'

'You're the one with curious new powers, *Nychter*. I sharpened and polished them for you while you rested.'

Aedlynn proceeded to steal my pear. 'The *Damast* one was dull, you're welcome.'

I smiled at her. 'Thanks.'

Eva leaned back in her chair. 'So . . . a circes who carries the full spectrum of daemonic power with her, who's a nightwalker and was blessed by Erebus.' She glanced at Aedlynn. 'And a halfgod who can manipulate reality and thus Fate.'

'I can also lick my elbow.' Aedlynn offered up another talent, which made Aloïs and I laugh.

Eva gave her a sweet smile, then looked at Aloïs. 'Still no idea what Erebus blessed her with?'

Aloïs crossed his arms and nodded once, meeting my gaze. 'I think he claimed you.'

'Darkness Incarnate,' I said softly.

He nodded again. 'The blessing feels like an outlet but also an ancient sort of claim. So yes, I do think Erebus chose you to channel his Darkness.'

'When you mentioned it before, you spoke of Elyon. It sounded . . . bad, to say the least.'

'Yes, but you didn't *spawn* there. You're our child. Eva gave birth to you and there is plenty of nymph blood in your system.' His lips pursed for a moment. 'It was deliberate. He waited for you, specifically. He tested you beforehand, as if to make sure this wouldn't fall in the wrong hands. Maybe that is what happened with Elyon; his blessing fell into the wrong hands. We know too little about them to understand what this all means.'

I opened my mouth to say something but Aloïs shot up from the table with an alarmed look on his face. 'Aedlynn.' His gilded gaze shot to the double doors. 'Go to Clacaster.'

'What? Why?'

Aloïs' gaze darkened. 'Eiran is coming for a visit.'

I became awfully aware of his ancient presence, like it was taking root in my bones. Forceful like life itself and potent beyond imagination – as old as the making of this universe. His presence gnawed at me, clawed at my *varkradas*. When I turned my head to the left side of the room, I met those dark eyes. He appeared casual enough in his thick black coat, embroidered with black vines and thorns.

Years of lessons from the Priestesses kicked in as I rose from my chair and elegantly bowed. Though neither my mother nor my father moved to show him respect. 'It is an honour to officially meet you, Lord Eiran.'

'The honour is mine, Lady Márzenas. Please, rise.' His voice didn't just reach my ears, it reached me deep in my soul. I looked up to see a warm smile that showed off his perfectly white teeth.

'Thank you.' I inclined my head while I rose, wings rustling behind me as I did.

Eiran sauntered over until he stood close enough that I could reach out a hand and touch him. Not that I wanted to do that. I feared he'd melt my hand right off, maybe even by accident with all that compressed power swirling inside of him. So I neatly folded them behind my lower back.

'Lord Eiran.' My father gave him a curt nod, his arms folded.

'Lord Márzenas.' Eiran looked at my mother and nodded his head to her as well. 'Lady Márzenas.'

Eva gave him a cold look. 'Lord.'

I stared at him in utter awe. This was a god I'd worshipped for twenty-four years. Now that there was no

Khalyna around to snarl at, or wounded pride, I couldn't help but admire him and be in awe of the sheer might that he radiated.

'Forgive me for inviting myself over so abruptly,' he said. 'But my schedule for the rest of the week is rather busy and I wished to meet you properly – without deities around to offend you.'

I nodded in a slight daze.

Eiran returned his attention to Eva. 'She really is your spitting image.'

'In more ways than one, Divine King.' Amusement came from my father at the subtle warning my mother had just given Eiran, who simply smiled. He probably still remembered Ascredia.

I decided to be polite. 'Would you like some wine, Lord Eiran?'

His dark gaze returned to me. My mother hadn't joked when she'd said Eiran had thick walls. Nothing came from him, nothing at all. It made me feel blind, since I'd become so used to reading others. Though I doubted a twenty-five-year-old daemon could start to understand the depths of him, the layers and layers of who and what he was – and why. Maybe no one could. Maybe only Ellowyn had been able to.

His lips parted in a half-smile. 'I would, thank you.'

I poured some red wine into a glass and Eiran sat down. He accepted the glass from me and sipped from it, then elegantly set it back down at the table. 'Orthallian?'

My gaze flickered back up to him in surprise. 'Yes.'

He nodded with approval. 'Lord Losaño gifts me Orthallian wine from time to time. Those bottles never remain full for very long.'

I smiled at him. 'Zale does have a special talent for pick-ing a good wine.'

Eiran returned the smile and my nerves slowly settled down. 'He also seems to have a special talent for finding competent High Ladies.'

Heat gathered on my cheeks. 'He told you?'

'Many years ago. Both thought you a fitting candidate,' he said. 'But why should I choose *you*? Why not someone else? My gods believe you are nothing but a little toy for my Left Hand. They will question why I made you High Lady.'

Evenly and confidently, I held his gaze. 'You know why.' Something flashed in his eyes, maybe a hint of surprise. 'I ventured into pure Darkness and returned with its blessing. I survived in Erebus on spite alone, and it was in awe of me.' I subtly squared my shoulders and crossed my legs, regality itself as I sat on my chair as if I sat on a throne.

Eiran nodded once. 'What about my Left Hand and your deal?'

My lip quirked up. 'I wish to destroy Lorcán Andulet with any means necessary. Pretending to swoon for your Left Hand to stroke his ego to make sure he'll help me achieve that goal is easy enough and Keres seems pleased enough with my services to keep to his end of the bargain.' Aloïs' silent curse echoed through my *varkradas*. He was impressed with the quick thinking. 'The true question is why *you* think I would be a good High Lady.'

Eiran kept his eyes on me like he was trying to view into my soul. 'You'll take my tests.'

I nodded once. 'Thank you but you didn't answer my question.'

His lip quirked up. 'I'd like to speak to her alone.' Eva opened her mouth to protest but Eiran held up a hand.

'She's capable of deciding for herself whether she dares be alone in a room with me, isn't she, *Evalynn?*'

It was both a stab and a challenge, a reminder of how she'd repeatedly been shut up and handled in Odalis by people who believed they knew better for her; her mother, Lorcán, Tarniq, and so many more. People who'd made decisions *for* her and about her. I couldn't help but respect Eiran's masterful stab. The open challenge in that one sentence, in the way he used her old name as a reminder. 'I do.'

Eva's nostrils subtly flared before she shoved her chair back. 'Touch her and I'll see if you still have a heart left in that chest of yours.'

Eiran simply smiled at her. 'Noted. Your daughter will be fine.'

Aloïs rose slowly, letting me know through my *varkradas* that they'd wait in the living room.

'I hope so for you, Eiran. You don't have a very good record of caring for daughters,' she said before she swung the double doors open.

Oh, shit.

Aloïs looked back at Eiran before leaving as well. 'You heard my dyad.'

I carefully studied him, as I couldn't decipher whether my mother's comment had angered or insulted him. I was trying to gauge his thoughts, but Eiran seemed to decide to share them on his own accord. 'I do understand her anger,' he said to me. 'I haven't always shown your people the respect they deserve. Though I wish for peace.'

'Your hallway decoration doesn't help.'

'They are spoils of war and hunt. Removing them would be the greater insult.'

I raised a brow at him. 'You want to regain favour with

my people? Return them to our rulers so they can give them the proper burial rites. Apologise, it would suit you well.'

Those black eyes didn't leave mine, didn't back away from my piercing gaze. 'I will return all but the colchian wings. I don't need Lady Dáneiris' forgiveness after her own despicable stunts.' Danny once seduced him, using compulsion, during a war to distract him. I couldn't blame Eiran for being angry about that, it didn't reek of consent.

'Then you will return those to my father as well,' I said firmly. 'I don't care that you have personal business with her. Her people deserve their kin's remains back.'

'I will not—'

'You wish for peace? I suggest you start working for it.'

He nodded once. 'Very well.' His lip curled upwards. 'I will let them know that their Princess ordered the remains to be returned.'

'I'm not ordering you to do this to receive credit.' I crossed my legs the other way. 'I'm simply disgusted that you have held on to them for so long.'

'And I do not wish for my High Lady to be disgusted with me.'

'I'm not your High Lady yet.'

If I didn't know any better, I'd dare say Eiran liked me. There was a glint in his eyes, though not malicious nor angry, and the more firmly I stood my ground, the more that lip of his curled up into a smile. 'Will you take the tests?'

I regarded him in silence, tried to decipher what I saw in his eyes, what I felt in his too-quiet shadows. What I heard in his voice, the meaning between his woven words. To see if there were thorns to watch out for. And I thought back to

Antheia's warning. 'Tell me the truth as to why you want me.'

Eiran leaned back in his chair, now really smiling. 'For the reason I mentioned before. I wish for peace and you,' he gestured at me, 'will do wonderfully. You do not bite your tongue and you stand up for your people. I have no doubt you will do the same for the people of Egoron.'

'And how will I know that my tongue will not start to aggravate you?'

I sensed the barest trace of approval. 'Contrary to what you might have been told, I do not smite those whose opinion differs from mine. If I did, I wouldn't have a Right Hand nor a Left Hand. Keres is my advisor as much as Zhella is, though it is Keres who stops me when he believes I go too far.'

And it was Eiran who punished him for it, though I bit my tongue to keep silent. If I truly was nothing to Keres, he would've never told me about it. And if Keres was nothing but a means to an end for me, I wouldn't care.

'Know that when you speak your opinion to me, it will be listened to. As long as it is said with respect, I will listen.'

I nodded slowly. 'Okay . . . Then I will take your tests.'

'Good.' He leaned forward again, resting his arms on the table. 'I will let you know when your trials are to take place.'

'Very well.'

Eiran extended his hand over the table, which I took in mine to shake. Surprisingly, his hand was comfortably warm. His gaze lingered on our hands, though I had no idea what passed through his mind. Then those black eyes met mine again. 'I'll make sure the remains are returned.'

I nodded once and then the King of Gods was gone.

Chapter 28

Diana

The stone hallway seemed to stretch for miles as I followed behind Aiden in Anthen's prison quarters. The evening air cooled down more and more every day, signalling that summer had officially passed and autumn was arriving. Eiran's visit still burned in my mind and the embers of our conversation were still smouldering. I'd liked challenging him, sticking my toes in the murky water to see if the fish would bite.

But most of all, I'd liked the power and control I'd felt. I was proud of myself that Eiran had agreed to return the remains, though part of me knew he hadn't agreed out of the goodness of his ancient heart. Just like Erebus, that deity was interested in what I could do. And just like Erebus, the King of Gods would play a game of thorns with me. I looked forward to bringing my own cards to the table, my own dice to roll. And I'd decided that I was ready. For becoming High Lady – and for taking what rightfully belonged to me.

I was ready for Lorcán. For Bastian.

I felt him long before I saw him. The gnawing loathing he felt for me, the viciousness with which he spat at Vanora in an attempt to intimidate her. The lashes he'd received from her in return still bled and throbbed. The vile words he swung at Eos for his betrayal.

I sensed Bastian's agony – because of the Stygian iron they'd bound him with. Aestor had put it on, without hesitation or moral conflict. I smelled the fear he tried to hide as he felt his title slipping away through his bound fists.

Aiden stopped in front of his father. Every single limb of Bastian's was bound with a Stygian cuff, leashed to a wall to keep him in place. The chain was dipped in moonsbane to nullify any of his compulsion. The circes weakly lifted his head to look up at his son. His eyes were sunken, the skin underneath it had darkened from the pain and lack of sleep. 'Aiden,' he croaked.

Pain crashed through Aiden's chest.

Cas had never favoured Bastian, since he'd abandoned their mother after exploiting her. But young Aiden had wanted his father's approval, a relationship with him. He'd loved training and sparring with his father, the special attention he'd received and the praise. Until Bastian's behaviour started to spiral, until *matska* started to disappear only to be found weeks later with their wings torn off, their bodies drained of blood and desecrated. With his father's scent on them. Aiden had grieved him while he was still alive. But everything he had done – Vanora, Maeve, Cas and their pups . . . It was beyond unforgivable.

'Bastian,' Aiden said coolly. 'Still hanging in there, I see?'

Vanora snorted, which sent a flare of hatred through Bastian.

I stepped into the light as well. More hatred crept into those golden eyes while he looked me up and down with disdain. He opened his mouth to start talking but I held up a hand and kept it up. My eyes became molten silver and the circes meekly closed his mouth. 'My people would see you slaughtered like an animal since you have never treated anyone with dignity or respect. They would see you meet your demise hidden in the half-dark of a dungeon. They would show you no mercy, no dignity. The only dignity I will grant you is to die with a weapon in your hands.'

A low growl came from him.

I smiled at him, though it didn't reach the tundra in my eyes. 'We will move you to the Ylva in an hour.' A plain in Erisor, where nothing but grass grew for miles around. 'Where we will fight until one of us survives to claim the title that's been swaying between us for weeks now.'

'I will rip apart your wings until you scream for mercy,' he snarled at me. 'And when I'm done with them, I'll show that bastard king how meekly his little bitch heir serves me. I'll make you *my* whore instead of that god's you reek of.' His eyes narrowed.

The only reason Vanora didn't tear his windpipe out with her talons was because I'd silently ordered them all to stand down. Even though Aiden wanted nothing more than to tear him apart for the blatant disrespect, and *what* he threatened me with, he remained silent. Eos' clenched fists trembled.

My lip quirked up. 'Such a confined little mind, you have,' I purred while I curled my fingers around the cold bars of his cell. 'It is always tear apart, rip off wings and dominate. I have so many more creative ideas of what I will do to you.'

Bastian saw something in my frigid gaze that made him hesitate to press on with his threats. That made his throat bob.

'Tell me, Bastian.' My voice became quiet and sweetly venomous as I rested my temple against the bar. 'To whom or what will you pray to save you when you are all alone on that battlefield?' He'd long forsaken and disrespected all gods, all deities who might find some interest in helping him.

He remained silent.

'Do tell me, I am curious.'

For the first time in their life, Eos and Aiden saw their father looking wary.

Finally, Bastian found the courage to answer. 'The Darkness from which I was born – Erebus.'

I showed him my sweetest smile. 'When you do, tell him I said hi.'

Bastian glanced at Aiden to my right, uncertain about what I meant. Aiden lifted his chin and held that gaze, a proud glint in his eyes as he presented me, 'You stand in the presence of our Princess, the Lady of Daemons, the Lady of Shadows and the Lady of Eres. Favoured and Blessed by Erebus.'

Eres – Darkness. My shadows hadn't just strengthened, they'd expanded to include pure Darkness.

Bastian fought hard to keep his eyes from widening. Eos was wickedly grinning as he studied his father's reaction. Though they indeed looked similar, Eos was endlessly well-groomed and held himself with dignity and grace, and I couldn't at all picture him as he'd once been – another vile predator.

I let go of the bars and stepped back. 'Should you find someone who wants to mark you for luck, they're welcome to do so.' If there was enough time before a battle, we marked each other with black, white, gold and silver paint for luck. The black was to grant enough *inkor* to survive blood loss, the white stood for hope, gold for glory and silver for the moonlight that watched over us.

But Eos looked at him with nothing but quiet disdain. Aiden already said he would paint me. And there was no way Cas would help Bastian. He knew he was on his own, and judging by the quiet shade of panic in his eyes, he seemed to realise that the sand in his hourglass was running out.

The atmosphere in the room was thick, like everyone was tiptoeing around a slumbering wyvern. Unfortunately for Aedlynn, there was no actual wyvern in my room. A breeze passed and my eyes shifted to the mirror, which reflected the two daemons that'd appeared. I stepped back from Aiden, turned around and bowed my head in respect for Faolán and Dáneiris.

Danny's long sleek hair and brows were snow white. Her simple white dress exquisitely showed off her sculpted pale body. Her multicoloured and delicate wings were pretty and translucent with shades of green, pink, black and purple. The beauty carved into her high cheekbones, almond brown eyes and curves was enough to make even the most pious person yearn for her to even just smile at them.

Faolán on the other hand, had dark brown skin and even darker eyes. A ring broke up the black of his pupils, the colour of Zale's finest red wine. His black hair was cut utterly short at the sides, the rest of his long tresses were gathered in small braids. Perhaps he wasn't a colchian but he was just as gorgeous. His full lips were parted into a kind smile while both of them returned my show of respect.

'Scylla asked me to wish you luck. She wanted to come but it is a full moon.' Danny's voice sounded lilted and beautiful.

I smiled. 'Thank you.'

Faolán waltzed over, regarding me intently. 'A certain king visited me mere hours ago, brought to me the remains of my kin. Kin who have been missing from Persephian for centuries.' He stopped in front of me. 'Kin that our Princess ordered to be respected.'

My cheeks heated under his intense gaze. 'It was only right.'

He nodded once. 'Thank you.'

I was about to tell him that he didn't have to thank me but Dáneiris interrupted me before I could, taking both of my hands in hers. My godmother sweetly smiled at me. 'We have never liked the Lord of Circederae, though you might wonder why, as he is so wickedly charming and sweet-hearted.'

I raised an amused brow. 'Indeed.'

'The only thing Bastian has ever done is murder innocents. He's one of the many reasons the mortals fear aepokrae and vampyrs and all the other daemons,' Faolán said. 'I do not think he has ever done anything for his people and only the Mother might know how he ever received his title. We have never trusted him, never extended a hand to him. We always worked directly with Aloïs or Eva.'

I nodded. 'He has caused pain for your people, as well as mine. He would have slaughtered four pups, and threw my friend to vampyrs to be devoured.'

Dáneiris ran her pale fingers along the black and white stripes Aiden had painted. 'Know that when you win, we will accept you and that your people will accept the *matska* who ventured into the treacherous Darkness of Erebus, risking her life to retrieve an innocent child.'

My smile grew wide at her kind words.

She started tracing my shoulders. Marking me with

colchian paintings. Thin pale blue and green vines that crept around my upper arms like ivy. Faolán stepped forward when his mate was done and tore his thumb over one of his canines, then smeared his black blood over my chest, right over my heart, and then over my forehead. *Blood of my blood, bone of my bone.*

'Show us why it blessed you, Lady. And make sure we do not forget it.'

Daemons of all Greater species had gathered. There'd been no change in Lords and Ladies since Aloïs became King of Hell and divided the regions. This was history and they were here to watch it unfold.

Next to me, Aiden's warm hand wrapped around my wrist to halt me. I glanced over my shoulder to see a proud look on his face as he saw me like this. Marked, and not only by circes.

To him, this was the start of a new era.

I smiled at him. 'Quit drooling, I might slip.'

Aiden grinned. 'Good luck, witch.'

Aedlynn's gaze met mine. 'Be careful. Do not hold back. Show no mercy.' She wrapped her arms around my waist and hugged me, resting her head on my shoulder. 'You better survive. I still want to find my wyvern together.'

Aiden snorted. 'You know, not because she loves you or anything. Just to find her wyvern.'

Aedlynn pulled away and flicked his nose, hiding her worry – the quiet panic because she couldn't for the life of her imagine losing me. It would break her.

Whatever this bond was between us, it was strong.

I squeezed her hand before glancing over at where Aloïs now stood with Bastian, who glared at me with such hatred that I would've believed he'd become God of Hatred. I decided to answer his animosity with a radiant smile while I slowly walked over.

My *varkradas* loyally followed in my wake, already spreading out to defend me. My wings were thicker and stronger than ever, casting a shadow over Bastian as the moonlight illuminated us.

Eos opened the cuffs one by one until they were all removed.

And Bastian stepped forward to meet me.

Diana's prayer

The following text is a tapestry of recovered material, woven together and translated by Diana Losaño to the Common Tongue, under the tutelage of High Priestess Iolanthe Echores for her fifth year dissertation.

As different versions of the same prayer-like text and fragments were discovered around the world, from different sources and in several languages (such as Ancient Orthallian, Clastrian, Vehonian and Aspian), with the oldest scraps dating back to ancient Avalon before its fall, it is unclear which version of this ancient text is the original and finds itself closest to the will of the gods.

Some scholars believe the origins of the text date back to the Dawn of the Worlds, as many versions refer to the Serpent, Mother and Allfather, as well as their children. Some argue that the sibylline nature of its content and Lady Zhella's fondness for exploring the Æther, are proof that she must have been the goddess who created the original version to honour her mother. Others suspect that perhaps, once upon a time before the Serpent's uprising and rebellion, something akin to an Oracle must have guided the Divine King and relayed these words to him.

However, one thing every scholar and scribe agrees on is that this text was never truly finished.

Night shall always make room for Day
And the Dawn shall always find her

Like the Sun, she rises with fire in her bones
And the flame in her heart is a weapon she hones
Like the Moon, she illuminates the darkest of skies
As no scheme gets past her clairvoyant eyes
Spirit and Hope won't leave bare her scars
For Love surrounds her like effervescent Stars

When Night at last falls, the Huntress' aim shall strike true
And the Serpent's Chaos will be hers to undo

Darkness shall not frighten her, but guide her safely through the Night
Light shall guard her heart and soul, and keep that fire burning bright

The Serpent crawls throughout the realms as he hunts for a new pawn
Yet The Mother shall protect her until the next rise of Dawn

Acknowledgements

I still can't fully wrap my head around everything that's been happening regarding A Curse of Crows and I still have a hard time believing that this is real life. If this isn't real, please do *not* pinch me. I'm enjoying it immensely.

Writing A Curse of Crows was an exploration of myself, and writing certain scenes left me feeling absolutely raw. It felt a little like I'd gone through my own personal Divine Comedy by meeting all these characters and exploring my own morals and values through them, and, looking back, the fact that the first draft was called 'Exile' (in which Diana had a *very* different storyline) even before I'd read the Divine Comedy seems to be more than an ironic coincidence. There is so much of me in these pages, so many things I've processed through writing. I'm not the same person now as I was before I started writing this book, and I'm thankful for it. Back then, my mental health wasn't great, but writing Diana's story as well as switching jobs when I did, really helped me find myself – and *like* myself. I'm in a much better place now than I was before, and so much of that is thanks to these silly characters and their endless shenanigans, as well as the friends I made along the way.

When I finished writing A Curse of Crows in 2022, I

planned on self-publishing because I thought no Belgian publisher would release an English written novel. Then fate intervened through a bizarre ISBN mix-up and I met Sandra Vets, who believed in my potential and wanted to take a risk and release it. Next thing I knew, A Curse of Crows was traditionally published in Belgium in October 2022 by Hamley Books. That already felt like a fever dream, but then Melissa Hartman – Hamley's wonderful foreign rights agent – worked her magic and sent the manuscript around until it landed on Gollancz's doorstep. And then Áine Feeney, now my editor, stepped in with so much love and excitement for this story that it rivalled only my mom's and closest friend's.

A lot has happened between then and now, so I want to take a moment to scrape my throat and shout my gratitude for some incredible people off the rooftops.

I'm still eternally thankful to my ARC readers in 2022; for their enthusiasm and feedback. They were the push I needed to fully believe this book was worth (self-) publishing and that it wasn't just a massive file of chaotic soup.

I want to thank Lotte and Anneleen, my lovely friends and bètareaders. The saying '*I promise not to tell anyone – except for my mom*' also applies to these two. They're the first people I send ideas to and the people I turn to for an honest opinion. I love ping-ponging my ideas with you, that you let me ramble on and on until I find the details or edge I need. And I love how protective you are of this story and of me. I appreciate you guys so so so so much!

Nîne, who worked for my Belgian publisher but became a very close friend after that first coffee date to discuss socials. Thank you for always being there, for being so excited for me, for letting me come steal your dog. Love gossiping with you and Daan over homemade mojitos!

A big shoutout to my Swedish fish: Wendy Heiss, a fellow author I befriended through the 'Gram. Thank you for shaking me whenever ye olde Imposter Syndrome kicks in and for fainting along with me whenever news hits me like a brick on steroids.

I want to thank my colleagues at my day job for their excitement and investment as well, and how ready they are to switch shifts so I can go to book events. In nursing, they often say that the older nurses eat their young. At my first workplace they definitely did, but I'm lucky enough to now work in a team where 'so bite back' is normalised.

I want to thank the wonderful team at Gollancz too; all their effort and love for this book. The lovely export team for pushing this story overseas, the rights and marketing team. At the moment of writing this acknowledgement, I haven't met you in person yet, but you're making a childhood dream come true so . . . THANK YOU!!

I want to thank my parents, because the close relationship Diana has with hers was heavily inspired by the one I have with mine. You have always done everything you could for me, went as far as you could for me (and then some) and been a safe space at times where my world was anything but that. Words can't describe how much you mean to me.

And lastly, in a day and age where AI and its threat on real artists is more prominently present than ever, I want to take another moment to thank the artists I've been working with:

- Franziska Stern, for designing this beautiful cover as well as the 2022 version

- Nemaiza and Mellendraw, for creating beautiful character art
- Hillary Bardin, for creating the perfect 'throne' character pieces, my couples and incredibly cool character art
- Alice Maria Power, for drawing Antheia exactly how I envisioned her
- Brina Williamson, for creating the world maps
- Elithien, for designing more beautiful character art.

ABOUT GOLLANCZ

Gollancz is the oldest SF publishing imprint in the world. Since being founded in 1927 Gollancz has continued to publish a focused selection of bestselling and award-winning authors. The front-list includes **Ben Aaronovitch**, **Joe Abercrombie**, **Charlaine Harris**, **Joanne Harris**, **Joe Hill**, **Alastair Reynolds**, **Patrick Rothfuss**, **Nalini Singh** and **Brandon Sanderson**.

As one of the largest Science Fiction and Fantasy imprints in the UK it is no surprise we have one of the most extensive backlists in the world. Find high-quality SF on Gateway written by such authors as **Philip K. Dick**, **Ursula Le Guin**, **Connie Willis**, **Sir Arthur C. Clarke**, **Pat Cadigan**, **Michael Moorcock** and **George R.R. Martin**.

We also have a strand of publishing in translation, which includes French, Polish and Russian authors. Gollancz is home to more award-winning authors than any other imprint, with names including **Aliette de Bodard**, **M. John Harrison**, **Paul McAuley**, **Sarah Pinborough**, **Pierre Pevel**, **Justina Robson** and many more.

The SF Gateway
More than 3,000 classic, rare and previously out-of-print SF novels at your fingertips.
www.sfgateway.com

The Gollancz Blog
Bringing you news from our worlds to yours. Stories, interviews, articles and exclusive extracts just for you!
www.gollancz.co.uk

GOLLANCZ
LONDON